The Argentia Dasani Adventures

The Shadow Gate Trilogy
Lady Dasani's Debt
The Gathering
The Dragonfire Destiny

The Reaches of Vengeance Duology
The Crown of the Revenant King
The Guildmaster's Gauntlet

The Tokens of Power Trilogy
Mouradian
Sylyth
The Aefryt's Lamp

The Aefryt's Lamp

An Argentia Dasani Adventure

C. JUSTIN ROMANO

THE AEFRYT'S LAMP
AN ARGENTIA DASANI ADVENTURE

iUniverse books may be ordered through booksellers or by contacting:

iUniverse
1663 Liberty Drive
Bloomington, IN 47403
www.iuniverse.com
844-349-9409

ISBN: 978-1-6632-3443-8 (sc)
ISBN: 978-1-6632-3444-5 (e)

Library of Congress Control Number: 2022900384

Print information available on the last page.

iUniverse rev. date: 02/07/2022

For Sam and Daniel,
this (mostly) Mirkholmes tale…

Acknowledgements

Thanks are as ever in order: to the superb iUniverse team that supported this book; to Zach Turner, the djinn in the lamp whenever I need to conjure up some cover art; and to my family and friends and fans of Argentia (and Mirk) for your patience with a writer who finds too few hours in the night to be a prompter scribe for these adventures.

CJR

Prologue

Every city has a bad tavern.

Dangerous places, they draw through their doors only those who belong there: cutthroats, thieves, hard men who would stick a knife between their mother's ribs if the price were right. All others instinctively shun them.

In Duralyn of the Crown, the bad tavern was called the Boar's Belch.

Squeezed between a warehouse and a gnomish usurer's, it hid behind blackened windows and a door that was the green-gray of dungeon mold. Once there had been a handsome wooden sign hanging over that door. Now only the rusted chain fastenings remained.

Within, the drink flowed long and cheap. Patrons competed with roaches for whatever passed for food on whatever passed for plates. The furniture was rat-gnawed and filthy. The air was full of smoke and anger.

At the back of the Boar's Belch was a private room. A nothing space stinking of old urine and stale vomit, its walls and floor stained with liquor, wine, blood.

Nonetheless, it was useful.

Tonight, while a summer storm thundered over the Crown City, it played host to the Harvester's Gryphons. The seven mercenaries were cramped and sweating around a rickety table littered with empty glasses and empty bottles of rotgut whiskey. Their shouting carried through the thin, warped wood of the locked door. If anyone in the crowded bar heard, they paid no mind.

The Gryphons were not the first men to gather in that room to plot a murder.

For eight months, the Gryphons had been hunting the treacherous woman who had butchered Vartan Raventyr. Though they were very good at their trade and had many contacts across Teranor, neither skill nor coin nor threats availed them in their search.

It was as if the woman had vanished from the world.

Then, two months ago, she reappeared in Harrowgate at the very inn where she had left Vartan's severed head floating in a tub full of blood. The Gryphons' web had passed the news quickly. The mercenaries chased the woman to Duralyn only to discover that she was lodging in the one place that provided her unquestionable sanctuary.

"What do you plan to do, attack Castle Aventar?" Bogden Gash demanded. Like all the Gryphons, Bogden had been a soldier before he sold his sword. He retained the blunt demeanor of a man used to giving orders.

"Nah, nah. She'll come out eventually," said Lucianos Lazanios. "When she does...." He drew a line with his finger across his throat, smiling as he did so. Lucianos was fond of boasting that no one knew Vengeance like a Cyprytalyr, for She had been born on his island.

"So-fine, but what to do until she comes?" asked Cree, the slim Nhapian who acted as the Gryphons' scout and archer.

"We wait," Temrun Raventyr said.

"Not so very profitable," Cree said. "We are sellswords but we are not selling our swords these many—"

Leaning across the table, Temrun poked a stumpy finger into Cree's chest. "Keep talking and I'll rip your throat out." Temrun was not an overly tall man, but he was cut from a block of granite. His round head had a bristle of pale hair, his face a squashed pugnacity accentuated by a flat nose over thin lips. Small gray eyes glinted with piggish meanness and something else: something dangerously not sane. "This isn't about coin. It's about Vartan. About our oath. A blade-oath *you* swore." He poked Cree again, harder this time.

"Temrun!" Delk Raventyr grabbed his older brother's shoulder, pulling him back. "Calm down! Cree didn't mean anything. It's just that we all thought we'd have her already."

"Truth. Who could know she would go to the castle," Wojek rumbled. At six-foot-eight, the Norden barbarian was easily the most physically imposing of the Gryphons and he had an even better chance than Delk of calming Temrun. Wojek was the only one in the room Temrun was not absolutely certain he could kill.

"We'll get her," Delk continued. "We know where she is. Like Lucianos said, it's just a matter of time."

Temrun glared at him. "I should've killed her out on the Heaths. I never trusted that bitch. Not from the beginning. I knew she was no good."

That was not how Troyen Kressid remembered it. The graybeard of the Gryphons, he was likely the only one of the mercenaries who could honestly say that he had been immune to the spell the woman had cast on them during the fortnight they spent raiding goblin warrens together. Not that he had not found her beautiful, only that he was under no illusions he might wake up one morning with her beside him in his bedroll.

And they had all trusted her. That was part of what made this whole disaster so difficult to comprehend. Either the woman was a consummate actress, or there was something seriously amiss.

That was a possibility Troyen had spent months wondering about. He had only dared broach the subject with Delk, who was the youngest of them but in many ways the most reasonable. While Delk had not disagreed, he had been quite clear about one thing: not to mention such doubts in front of Temrun. Ever.

So the question had nagged, but it had not seemed so important as long as the woman remained beyond their grasp. All that had changed now. If Troyen was going to say something, this was the time. The worst Temrun could do was kill him, and Troyen had faced death so many times that it no longer held any terror for him. He glanced at Delk. The young man's face was unreadable. He was on his own. "I still can't believe she did it."

Temrun turned slowly to Troyen. "*What* did you say?"

"I just think we should be certain—"

"I'm certain!" Temrun said. "She cut off Vartan's head and then she ran."

"Yes, but *why?* She didn't rob him—"

Before anyone could react, Temrun yanked Troyen out of his seat, slammed him to the ground, and jammed a huge, serrated knife beneath his chin. "Traitor talk. You know what happens to traitors." Blood began to trickle down Troyen's neck as Temrun put pressure on the blade. "I'll cut your throat. I'll kill—"

"Stop this!" Wojek wrapped arms like oaken logs around Temrun and hauled him off of Troyen.

Temrun struggled, thrashing and snarling, but he could not fight free. "All right," he said. "All right!"

Wojek released him. Temrun stomped to the door and then turned and pointed his knife first at Troyen and then at each of the others in the room. His eyes were full of furious madness. His voice was an awful whisper.

"She dies. That's what we swore. You want out, get out. But you're an oath-breaker. After I've avenged Vartan, I'll hunt you down and kill you too." He slashed the blade across his palm. Held his bleeding hand up for them to witness. "Blade-oath. You quit, you run, you die. Any of you."

Silence held the private room at the back of the Boar's Belch. Temrun laughed into it: a trollish chuckle. "Tell you what," he said to Troyen, who had picked himself up off the floor and was holding a dirty napkin to the bloody nick on his throat. "You're so damn curious why she did it, you can ask her after I gut her. You'll have time. She's gonna die real slow."

Troyen did not say anything. No one said anything. But no one left.

It was not Temrun's wild threat that held them. It was their oath. They had been men of honor once and they retained a twisted vestige of that virtue.

Temrun extended the dagger to Delk. "In blood," he said. "Again."

So the Harvester's Gryphons passed the knife. One by one they drew red lines across their palms, reaffirming a vow first sworn eight months earlier beside the fresh grave of Vartan Raventyr.

A vow not to rest until they had found and killed Argentia Dasani.

PART I

The Lure of the Lamp

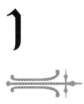

1

Mirkholmes the meerkat came out of the shadows in the chamber of the Archamagus.

Ralak the Red might be the most powerful wizard in all Teranor, but that had never stopped Mirk from plundering his spell books. After all, he had done it to the former Archamagus as well, and Relsthab the Red had been much more likely than his younger brother to make good on his threat to turn Mirk into a worm if he ever caught him.

Tonight, however, it was not spells that Mirk sought in the high tower chamber.

Amber eyes glowing, he wove his way past stacks of books many times his own height and hopped up onto the desk, which was cluttered with scrolls and artifacts. He glanced around, his fine whiskers twitching. His fuzzy face scrunched in disappointment. *Mirk does not see shiny stone....*

The stone was a fragment of a rare, star-shaped diamond that Ralak had recovered from the ruins of the mad wizard Mouradian's tower on Elsmywr. The shard had lost its soul-reaving enchantment, but even a piece of a thing so powerfully charged with the aether could be dangerous in the wrong hands. The Archamagus had brought it back to Castle Aventar for safekeeping.

Mirk did not know any of this history. He simply loved gemstones. In the meerkat's view, Ralak already had many more gems than he needed; surely he would never miss this one shard.

Where is shiny stone?

It had been here earlier in the day, when Mirk had accompanied the Crown to Ralak's chamber. Mirk wanted to steal it there and then, right out from under the nose of the Archamagus, but the Crown had made him promise to behave if she allowed him to join her in the wizard's rooms.

The meerkat was under no such restrictions now. The Crown was sleeping in her chambers and would never even know Mirk had been gone.

But where is shiny stone? The meerkat stalked across the desk, checking behind a crystal oculyr, lifting up a sheaf of parchment. Nothing. The diamond was not anywhere on the desk.

A clock in the shape of a dragon hung on the wall, its tail ticking off the seconds. Mirk could not afford to linger here. There were magical eyes and ears in this place. The spell he had cast to conceal himself from their detection would not last long.

He rubbed his paws together, the sense of danger vying with the desire to have the gem. Pride was at issue as well; since discovering the secret way into the Archamagus' chamber, he had never left without a prize.

"Mirk will find stone," he muttered, looking around. The circular walls were dominated by shelves full of dusty books, statues, glassware, ceramic jars, lead boxes, velvet pouches, random stacks of coins, and other devices too arcane for the meerkat to identify what they even were, never mind what they might be for.

Mirk's gaze roved upward from shelf to shelf. He saw plenty of other gems, but not the one he—

Shiny stone!

Mirk hopped off the desk and scampered across the floor, climbing delicately up a twisting stack of books and bounding onto the shelf that held the star-diamond shard. As he landed, his tail clipped something precariously close to the edge.

The clatter of the lamp striking the stone floor echoed terrifyingly through the chamber. After an instant of startled paralysis, Mirk thrust his paws out. They glowed with pale blue light as he levitated the lamp back up to the shelf almost as swiftly as it had fallen. He had just set it back in place when he felt a surge in the aether that made his hackles stand as if he had been lightning-struck.

Screeching, Mirk leaped off the shelf onto the stack of books, which promptly toppled beneath him. Springing clear, he raced beneath a table and was gone a split second before the entire room blazed with light.

"Who dares?!" Ralak the Red materialized out of the aether. He was wearing a rumpled blue dressing gown and his black hair was sleep-mussed, but his hawkish eyes were alert and angry and the silver Staff of Dimrythain glimmered balefully in his hands. The air simmered with the intensity of a storm cloud.

After a moment, Ralak relaxed. The incandescence of ready magic dispersed. Whoever had been in the chamber—an overly intrepid meerkat, perhaps—was gone, if they had been there at all.

A quick survey confirmed the warding magic on the door and window remained intact and the piece of Mouradian's diamond that had so plainly fascinated Mirkholmes that afternoon was where Ralak had left it. The pile of books on the floor was certainly *not* as he had left it, but he might have shifted the stability of the stack when he placed the volume of Quafk's *Ars Metamorfoses* he had been reading atop it before retiring.

"Very like," he murmured, gesturing at the mess of books, which fluttered into the air and settled in a perfectly aligned tower. *I should clear this place up....* He knew he would not. The chamber appeared chaotic, but Ralak knew precisely where every spell component and scroll was to be found. There was no need to organize it, and he rather preferred the clutter. This was how he had inherited the chamber from his brother, and how his brother had inherited it from his predecessor, Isulac of Orn. Perversely, it seemed to Ralak that part of the duty of the Archamagus was to increase the holdings—and thereby the disarray—of the chamber for those who came behind.

With a nod and a final glance around him, Ralak tapped his staff on the floor and vanished in a flash of aether.

Darkness returned to the tower chamber, but it did not hold.

A glow sparked up from the spout of a certain tarnished lamp, growing until it filled the room with a rutilant light.

The thing imprisoned in the lamp was awake again.

And hungry.

2

Argentia Dasani tracked the leather ball through the air, swung the stick hard, and missed. *Damn it!*

"That's two!" Croftian v'Ap crowed. "One more and it's *over!*"

"Red!" the dwarf Griegvard Gynt bellowed from the bench where he sat with the rest of Argentia's team. "I ain't fer losin t' these bloody horse lovers!"

Me either.... Argentia blew a strand of her fiery hair out of her face and dug her bare feet into the sand of the Academy practice yard. This sunny summer morning, the first in the week since she had arrived in Duralyn that the skies did not promise rain, the yard had been converted for an impromptu game of stickball. The men training to be Guardians were playing those hoping to join the ranks of the Unicorn Cavalry. The Guardian side had been a couple men short, so they had corralled Argentia and Griegvard when the two passed by walking Argentia's Nordic sled dog, Shadow.

Everyone was happy to see good weather again. There were a couple dozen people in audience, including several of the Academy instructors and Lord Paladin Grefaulk, commander of the Crowndom's knights. The game was in its final stages. The Guardians were down a point. Argentia was down to her last swing.

She was a tall, slender woman, beautiful by any measure, with a carved aristocracy about her high cheeks and slim nose that was softened by her full lips. Her eyes were cobalt blue, like the ice of the Sea of Sleet at dawn. Thick hair, red as a cardinal's plumage, dangled down her back in a long ponytail. She was wearing a black halter tightly knotted beneath her high breasts (she was on the 'skins' team but there were limits…). The bare plane of her stomach was flat and firm. A small diamond twinkled in her navel. Black linen pants, hemmed above her calves, molded her long legs as the wind gusted across the yard.

Squeezing the dragon's tooth token hanging below her throat for luck, she flexed her leanly muscled arms, swinging the stick over the shield in the sand. "Come on, then."

Croftian was a good hurler. His first throw to Argentia had curved suddenly away from the shield and she had missed it. His second had curved in at her hands; expecting the ball to move away again, she had missed that one, too.

If she missed this one, the game was over. The question was, would he throw inside again, or outside?

Argentia surveyed the yard, where nine cavalrymen waited to grab a ball in play and throw her out before she could run to the first of the four shields at the corners of the stickball diamond. She had hit safely in her previous attempts, but that was before she faced Croftian.

Argentia blocked out the noise of the Guardians chanting and stomping, focusing solely on Croftian as he cocked his arm, twisted, uncoiled.

The ball hummed in, breaking over the plate, diving hard away.

In a blur of motion, Argentia swiveled her hips, dipped her hands, swung—

Crack!

The ball jumped off the stick, bounding up the middle of the diamond and into the hands of a knight who had raced over from his position guarding the second shield.

Argentia was flying toward the first shield as the fielder pivoted and threw. The ball came in high. The knight guarding the first shield leaped to snare it.

Argentia dove, sliding headfirst beneath him, her outstretched hand touching the shield an instant before the knight swatted her rear.

"Haven!" barked Lar Garu, a paladin charged with ruling the game. The Unicorns protested, but Lar waved it off, repeating his emphatic gesture that Argentia had beaten the throw.

Grinning, Argentia pumped her fist and popped to her feet.

"Nice slide," said the knight guarding first shield. His name was Kion. He was young and handsome, with a wave of dark hair, a clean-shaven face with just a hint of arrogance in the set of his jaw, and a powerful build.

"Nice tag," Argentia riposted. "Next time try using the hand with the ball?"

"What, this?" Kion's brown eyes sparkled cockily as he tossed the ball back to Croftian. "I was supposed to tag you with the ball? Really?" All innocence.

"Cute," Argentia said.

He shrugged. Flashed white teeth at her. "Can't blame me for trying."

"I'm old enough to be your mother." Not quite true: at thirty-two, she doubted she was even a decade older than the knight. *Well, maybe just that....* He was young, but attractive. *Definitely attractive....*

"Nope. Older sister at most. Besides, you should be looking for younger men."

Argentia arched a brow. "Oh really? Why's that?"

"Stamina."

She laughed, enjoying the banter.

"If yer done yappin, might be we kin get on wit winnin this game?" Griegvard shouted.

"Whenever you're ready," Argentia called back.

"Hate to tell you, I might have something to say about that," Croftian said.

"Don't matter," Griegvard grunted. The dwarf was five-feet tall and built like an oak stump. His bare chest and broad shoulders were thick with muscle and mostly hairless, but his mouth was lost in a forest of blonde beard and moustache, and his yellow hair stuck out in every direction from his head. Wild brows overshadowed his keen gray eyes and dagger nose.

He had never even heard of stickball before this morning, but he proved a natural, pulverizing two balls out of the yard and nearly taking a knight's head off with a third line-drive shot. Now he picked up the stick in his stony hands and thumped it on the shield. "Want me t' tell ye yer mistake now or later?" he taunted Croftian.

Croftian shook his head. Scuffed sand. Squeezed the ball tightly. "Let's go!" one of his mates yelled. Nodding, Croftian wiped an arm across his forehead, set himself, and fired the ball in as hard as he could.

"Oops," Griegvard snorted—

—and crushed the pitch, launching the ball high and far into the air. He stood for a moment, watching as it soared clear of the wall surrounding the training yard. Then, flipping the stick disdainfully to the ground, he started walking toward the first shield.

Argentia clapped her hands in celebration. "Bye," she said to Kion, grinning as she trotted around the diamond to score the tying point. Griegvard came behind her, stomping the winning point on the shield with his hairy foot. Argentia touched fists with him, and then the two were mobbed by their Guardian teammates.

As the celebration died down, Argentia wandered over to a bench where she had left her sandals. Now that the rush of competition and victory was over, she realized she was hot, sandy, and itchy. *Need a shower....* Shadow greeted her with a deep bark. She ruffed the big dog's silver-black head, took a long drink from a water jug on the bench, then tilted her face to the sky and dumped the contents over her head. *Ahhh—much better....*

"I'm fer thinkin t' tell King Durn about this game," Griegvard said. He had recovered the stick and slapped it across his palm. "Needs a new name, though. Bashball...somethin like that."

"In Argo they call it 'haven,'" Argentia said. "Good game," she added as Croftian joined them.

Croftian shook his head. "Do you *ever* lose?" A few winters past, he had helped Argentia prepare for a particularly dangerous hunt by practice-battling a pair of spotted lions. He knew how fiercely competitive she was.

Argentia shook her head. "Nope."

"Speaking of which, what was my mistake?" Croftian asked Griegvard.

"Ye threw it where I could hit it," the dwarf said.

"Oh, that makes me feel a lot better."

"You throw well," Argentia said. "That second ball really tied me up."

"Who's getting tied up?" Kion said, walking over. He had stripped his shirt. His body was as impressive as Argentia had imagined, but his brashness was wearing thin. "You're all wet," he said, eyeing her openly.

"Brilliant observation," she said, shifting to create more space between them.

"Maybe we can head somewhere more private and I can help you dry off?"

"No, but thanks for asking." The frost in her eyes should have been clear warning, but in case Kion was as dense as he seemed to be, Argentia picked up her sandals and walked away.

Why does this always happen to me? Her flirtatious nature was constantly getting her into trouble. She liked men. Liked to ride with them, hunt with them, talk with them, eat, drink, and dance with them. She liked sex, too—with the right person, in the right circumstances— but invariably she would find the one man in a company of ten or twenty or a hundred who misconstrued her playfulness for serious interest.

It's like I'm cursed, she thought, not for the first time. She stared up into the sky as if seeking an answer to the riddle of her terrible Fortune with men.

"Who's th' jackass?" Griegvard asked Croftian, gesturing with the stick as Kion followed Argentia.

"Kion Steppentor," Croftian said. "First marks in his class at anything involving weapons, but he'll never rank above a lieutenant no matter how much clout his father thinks he has. He's a little—"

"—stupid," Griegvard completed. "Aye. Don't take an Ancient's wisdom t' see that. He don't back off, yer gonna see stupid get what stupid's deservin."

Kion caught up with Argentia. "What's the hurry? Stick around. Relax," he said, placing his strong hands on her shoulders.

"Let go," Argentia said.

"Why?" He kneaded her muscles, his thumbs working the base of her neck.

She closed her eyes. Sighed. "Don't make me do this."

"Do what?" His hands kept massaging.

"This." Hooking her foot behind his ankle, Argentia snapped her head back, butting Kion in the face.

Kion staggered and tripped over Argentia's cleverly positioned foot. Arms pinwheeling wildly, he crashed on his back. He tried to sit up, one hand clutching his bleeding nose, but Argentia pinned him with a bare foot on his chest. "Gagh—broke my nose," he groaned.

"Next time a lady tells you she's not interested, believe her," she said. "It's a lot less painful."

Kion moaned something unintelligible. Shaking her head, Argentia walked back to where the others were waiting. "Sorry about that," she said to Croftian.

"He had it coming." Croftian looked disgustedly at Kion, who had finally managed to sit up. "You sure you don't want a faculty post teaching combat?"

Argentia laughed. "Not a chance in—"

A lightning flash seared the air above the bench.

What— Blinded for an instant, Argentia dropped to the sand and rolled hard, hoping to put distance between her and an attacker. Cries of surprise and Shadow's deep barking filled the yard.

Argentia snapped to her knees, her spotty vision clearing. Griegvard was hunched over, a hand before his face.

A disembodied eye floated above them. It was as big as a muskmelon, with a dark brown iris and a cornea bloodshot with pulsating vessels. A fibrous tendril of nerves trailed it like twine from a kite.

"Bloody Hell!" Griegvard shouted, jerking upright and raising the stick. Like all his kind, the dwarf was unfailingly suspicious of any magic that did not involve forging weapons or armor.

"Put down that splinter, fool!" The voice that emanated from the eye's black pupil belonged to Ralak the Red. It struck the dwarf like an aethereal hammer, hard enough to knock him back a pace and shake the stick from his grasp.

The eye swiveled until its gaze came to rest on Argentia. "I have need of your services. Immediately," the Archamagus said.

The eye vanished.

3

Castle Aventar's dungeon was fittingly miserable.

It was a dimly lit vault of mostly empty stone-and-iron cells. The air was chill and dank. Argentia found it particularly disturbing after the morning's bright sunshine.

She had left Griegvard at the Academy. The dwarf was too volatile to bring into contact with Ralak. "I'm keepin this stick," Griegvard said. "Next time I see that bloody spell-tosser I'm shovin it right up his skinny—"

"Enough already! Go walk it off," Argentia interrupted before Griegvard could launch into a full-blown tirade. "I'm sure he didn't mean anything by it. He just wanted to get our attention."

In truth, Ralak's whole curt message—especially his use of his magic on Griegvard—had Argentia on edge. It was not like the Archamagus to be anything but civil and controlled. *I've got a bad feeling about this,* she thought as she and Shadow hurried back through Duralyn's concentric rings to the castle in the center of the city.

She crossed the drawbridge, crossed the interior courtyard, and climbed the steps to the great bronze double doors of Aventar. "What happened?" she asked the two Guardians stationed there.

"Prisoner escaped," one of the knights answered.

"Which one?" Only criminals whose offenses were against the

Crown or threatened the whole of Teranor were incarcerated below the castle. Argentia had put several of the current residents there herself. To a man, they had been locked away from the world for good reasons.

"Don't know," the knight answered. His partner shook his head. "Me either. But the Archamagus is expecting you in the dungeons."

The knights opened the castle doors. Argentia headed below. She did not speculate on who might have escaped. The list only went from bad to worse.

A Sentinel in black and gold armor stood beside the dungeon door. He nodded at Argentia as she went by. The knight was part of the Crown's personal guard. His presence told Argentia that it was not only Ralak awaiting her in the dungeons. *Must be really bad*, she thought.

The winding stairwell, lit by evenly spaced lightstones, corkscrewed almost as deeply into the earth as the castle's towers rose above it. Argentia took the steps two and sometimes three at a time. She hurried past the torture chamber, whose windowless iron door did not mute the thrashing and grunting of something being wracked by one machine or another.

The Crown, Mirkholmes, Ralak, and Seb Karal, commander of the castle's defenses, were gathered in an empty cell. Ralak had his back to the door as he spoke to the Crown. His voice was harsh with tension: "... above all we must find *it*—and swiftly."

"Can't you wizards ever keep track of your toys?" Argentia said.

Ralak turned and glowered at Argentia. Only months ago, she had been burned nearly to death by dragonfire. Though she had survived, the ravages of a dragon's breath knew no remedy from the hands of apothecaries, magi, or even Aeton's clerics. The prospect of living out her winters like some grotesque, charred goblin had almost broken Argentia's spirit. Lost in misery, she had wandered far from herself, but in the end, the flame of her will had burned bright enough to light her way to Frostwood and the elf city of Rime, where a deeper magic had awakened to her need and restored her.

Unfortunately—at least in Ralak's view on this particular morning—it had also restored her impertinent tongue. "I am in no mood for your sass," he snapped. "And when I say I need you immediately, I mean *immediately*."

"Do I look like I stopped for a bath?" Argentia retorted, brushing her hands across her thighs, where her pants were still dusty with sand. "If you wanted me here any faster, you should have conjured me an aethergate."

"Please!" Solsta Ly'Ancoeur said. The Crown of Teranor was petite and trim, with ivory skin and fine, small features. She was young in winters but she could command a room to silence with a glance. Now her dark eyes looked reproachfully out at Ralak from beneath the white blaze in her chocolate tresses. "I'm sure Argentia came as swiftly as she could."

Ralak slowly nodded. "I suppose. But the situation here is much more grave than any of you understand. If Erkani—"

"*Erkani* escaped? You've got to be kidding me," Argentia said.

"I wish I were," Ralak replied.

"Where's Tandun?" Argentia asked. The dungeonmaster was noticeably absent.

"That is a very good question," Ralak said.

"He was seen leaving the castle early this morning," Seb said.

"Prior to the discovery of Erkani's escape," Ralak added. "Believe me, that toad is involved in some way."

"We will come to the bottom of that mystery later," Solsta said. There was longstanding enmity between the wizard and the jailer. The Crown was not about to let it distract them from the matter at hand. "Regardless, this Erkani escaped his cell and found his way to Ralak's tower."

Argentia frowned. "Let me guess. He got the lamp."

"How did you know that?" the Archamagus asked, arching a dark brow.

"I was the one who caught him the first time he stole it. It was the last job I did for your brother."

"What is this lamp?" Solsta asked.

"That is what I have been trying to tell you, Majesty," Ralak said. "The lamp is no ordinary lamp. It is a prison for an extremely dangerous entity."

Mirk blinked, his ears flattening, but no one noticed.

"It better not be another demon," Argentia said. "I'm so sick of fighting demons."

"Not a demon," Ralak said. "Something worse."

"*Worse* than a demon?" the Crown said.

"Yes, Majesty," Ralak replied. "It is called an aefryt."

Seb Karal rubbed his bald head. "In Tradespeak, please."

Argentia smiled. Wizards were forever assuming that everyone knew as much arcana as they did. Ralak was better about it than most, but that left a lot of room for improvement. *I swear he's becoming more like his brother every day....* Relsthab had been the absolute worst when it came to guarding information and talking in obscurities.

"An aefryt is a fire spirit," Ralak clarified. "There are many types. From what I could find in Relsthab's notes on the lamp, he believed this one to be a salamander."

"Is that good or bad for us?" Argentia asked.

"Very bad. A salamander's appetite for destruction is insatiable. If such is its whim, a salamander will burn until there is nothing left to burn."

Solsta began to pace. "And this salamander, it resides in the lamp?"

"It is *imprisoned* in the lamp, Majesty," Ralak said. "And it would like nothing more than to be free."

"How can it be freed?" Argentia asked.

"It must gather enough strength to break the binding enchantments of the lamp. Then it must find a host to inhabit. It has no shape of its own in our world."

"But it's not powerless, even in the lamp, is it?" Argentia asked, reflecting on her hunt for the thief. "Relsthab gave me a lead box to hold the lamp—for my own protection, he said. When I captured Erkani, all he did was whine for the lamp like some seed addict who couldn't smoke."

"Aptly put," Ralak said. "A salamander preys upon desires, making men believe it will grant them their most secret wishes in exchange for its freedom. The victim becomes enthralled with the visions he sees when holding the lamp. His entire purpose becomes to make those fantasies reality by releasing the salamander. So consuming is this focus that he neglects to even eat or sleep. Thus, when the salamander gains enough power to escape the lamp, it will find a host too weak to prevent its habitation."

"Could the salamander have helped Erkani to escape?" Seb asked.

"Unlikely," Ralak said. "A salamander has no physical power in our world until it is freed from the lamp—and believe me, had that thing escaped already, we would know it. As for what powers it can exert through the magic of its mind, they are great, as I said, but the salamander must be awake to use those powers. I know for a fact that the one in that lamp has been asleep since Relsthab took it back into his possession."

Mirk hesitantly raised a tiny paw and then swiftly lowered it. Once again no one noticed.

Argentia, who had been lingering in the doorway, entered the cell. She caught a whiff of old sweat and infinite exhalations: the rank perfume of a single body that had occupied too small a space for too long a time. *I'd go mad if I was stuck in here*, she thought, shaking off a memory of her own imprisonment in a crystal cell by the wizard Mouradian: an ordeal it had taken all her considerable will to survive. To the huntress, who valued her freedom above all things, a barred door was the worst horror she could imagine.

She glanced around. In one corner there was an iron bedframe with an indented mattress and a single blanket. An uneaten plate of gruel that looked like a glop of plaster sat on the floor beside the bed. An unemptied chamber pot squatted in the other corner. The wall had marks scratched into it: a single word written over and over again. Argentia traced a finger over the letters. BAZU. It meant nothing to her. She guessed the scratches had been made with the spoon stuck in the gruel. She could not imagine what kind of frantic energy it had taken to etch stone with such a tool. "What do we know about Erkani's escape?" she asked.

"Not much. We don't know how he got out of his cell, but however he did, it happened sometime during the night," Seb said.

"I discovered the lamp was missing this morning," Ralak added. "Knowing it had been in Erkani's possession before, I immediately descended and found his cell open and empty. What I have not yet found is Tandun."

"The Guardians at the door reported letting him out just after dawn. He hasn't returned," Seb said. "I alerted Duralyn's Watch. They're looking for him and for Erkani. I have to agree with Ralak that this is all pretty suspicious. Tandun rarely leaves the dungeons, let alone the castle, yet there are reports of him going out three times this week."

"You searched the castle for Erkani?" Argentia said.

Seb nodded. "With men and magic both. Erkani's long gone."

In Argentia's experience, people did not simply vanish, especially not out of dungeons like the one in Aventar. The castle was a second home to her; she knew how well it was protected. "Well he didn't get out by magic, right?"

"Indeed," Ralak confirmed. Aetherwalking was impossible in the castle for all save the bearer of the staff of Dimrythain, whose magic had conjured Aventar's shield wards. "I can assure you Erkani did not leave this castle by any aethereal art."

"Who has the keys to these cells?"

"There are two key rings. Tandun keeps one. The other hangs by the dungeon door," Seb said. "That set's accounted for."

"Someone could have used them and put them back," Argentia said.

"True."

"So Erkani may or may not have had some kind of help getting out of his cell, but what about getting into your tower—how the hell did he do that?" Argentia asked Ralak.

"Another fine question. He needed a powerful runestone to disarm my glyphs."

"Who could provide such a thing?" Solsta asked.

"Sadly, Majesty, I can think of a half-dozen magi in Duralyn alone who could create sufficient stones."

Argentia frowned. "I thought Aventar was supposed to be the safest place in all Teranor."

"It is," Ralak said. "But the castle's defenses are concentrated on repelling external threats. The magic within these halls is by no means weak, but comparatively speaking it is more vulnerable than the exterior wards."

"Huh." Argentia put her hand to her chin, her index finger crooked over her lips: a habit when she was deep in thought.

"I need not mention that fact is hardly common knowledge," Ralak added.

"But anyone who *did* know could have brought a runestone from the city, is that what you're saying?" Seb said.

"Precisely. I have interrogated the knights on duty last night and this morning. None of them know anything and none of them could have concealed a lie from me."

"What about Tandun?" Seb said.

"What could Tandun gain by freeing a prisoner?" Solsta asked.

Ralak's eyes flashed with ill-concealed anger. "Perhaps if we knew where he was, we could ask him."

"So let's go ask him," Argentia said.

5

They found Tandun in the torture chamber.

The dungeonmaster was strapped to a dusty rack, his mouth gagged with a horse's bit and a wad of filthy cloth. Solsta gasped when she saw him. Even Ralak's eyes widened in surprise.

"Aeton's bolts!" Seb hurried forward to release Tandun, who had begun to thrash furiously the moment the door opened.

"How did you know?" Ralak asked, looking curiously at Argentia.

"I heard noises in here on my way to meet you, but I was rushing and I didn't even stop to think that this place probably hasn't been used since before Solsta's father was Crown."

"But the Guardians said Tandun left," Solsta said.

"That wasn't Tandun, Majesty," Argentia answered. "That was Erkani."

There was a moment of silence and then Ralak said, "Transmogrification?"

Argentia nodded. "Why not? If Erkani had someone get him out of the cell and bring him a runestone to beat the glyphs in the tower, why not a transmogrification potion, too? Then he really could just walk out the door." *And imitating Tandun was a great choice. He's pretty much despised, so no one would approach him to talk....*

Free of his restraints, Tandun leaped to his feet, shoving Seb aside

18

with one hand as he tore the binding from his mouth with the other. "Bastard traitor thief!" he roared, starting forward so ferociously that Solsta took a step back and Argentia dipped a hand for a katana that was not at her hip.

Ralak thrust the glimmering Staff of Dimrythain toward the dungeonmaster. "*Stop!*"

Tandun froze, his face contorted as he strained against the magical paralysis. He was a short, muscular Nhapian dressed all in studded black leather. His skin was covered with scars whose origins were as much a mystery as his age—he might have been forty or sixty, it was impossible to tell. His head was shaped like a potato, with a spatulate nose, thick black moustache, and small, round ears. His black hair was braided and reached almost to the floor; it was capped with a heavy steel ball. His eyes were narrowed to almost reptilian slits.

"Release him, Ralak," Solsta said.

"As you wish, Majesty." The aetherlight faded from the silver staff.

Tandun shook his head like a dog and glared about, as if taking measure of his rescuers. His serpent's gaze lingered longest on Ralak. "Erkani escape?" he said.

"Yes. Now tell me what happened," Ralak's shadow fell over Tandun. The dungeonmaster fixed a sullen gaze on the floor. His report was brief. He had awakened to noises in the dungeon. Found Erkani out of his cell. Confronted him, but was overpowered. "Hit head. Woke here."

"You didn't see anyone with him?" Seb asked.

"No."

"Incompetent fool," Ralak snarled. "Had you sounded the alarm rather than trying to apprehend Erkani yourself, all this might have been averted!"

"Filthy liar! You will not blame Tandun!" He lunged for Ralak but the wizard got his staff between them. There was a pulse of light. Tandun flew back, smashing into the rack and falling to the floor.

"Ralak! Enough!" Solsta cried. "Both of you stop it! We will not tolerate this behavior! You will put aside your differences and work to catch this thief. Do we make ourselves clear?" If her rare use of the royal pluralism was not evidence enough of her ire, Solsta stamped her boot on the stones, hands on her narrow waist, eyes blazing.

"Yes, Majesty," Ralak said. Tandun, on his knees, smoke curling from his leather vest, nodded.

"I will hold you to your word." Shaking her head like a mother frustrated by her children, Solsta turned to Argentia. "Can you help? She could have just commanded the hunt, but such a loose wielding of her influence was not the Crown's way, especially among her friends.

Argentia flashed her insouciant grin. "I thought you might ask that."

"What you do?" Tandun asked, rising and staring suspiciously at Argentia.

"I caught Erkani before. I'll catch him again."

"I go too. No one escape Tandun's dungeon."

"No," Argentia said. "This is a job. It isn't personal." Except, in a strange way, it almost was. Three years ago Argentia had put Erkani into his cell. Now he was out. It felt like unfinished business. "I work alone."

"As you will," Solsta said, settling the matter before any argument could ensue.

Tandun clenched his fists. "You kill?" he said to Argentia.

"I will do what I must," Argentia replied.

Tandun sneered in satisfaction, having read whatever he wanted to read in Argentia's steady cobalt gaze. With another hateful glare at Ralak, he withdrew from the cell.

"He's a pleasant one," Argentia said.

"Vile troglodyte," Ralak said.

"Archamagus...." Solsta's voice hit a warning note.

"I am sorry, Majesty. Truly. But I simply cannot suffer that barbaric ass."

Solsta sighed. "Your brother felt much the same. Tandun can be difficult. Aeton knows I certainly would not want to dine with him."

"Or meet him in a dark alley," Seb muttered.

Solsta allowed herself a small smile. "We are all agreed he is a less than...savory associate," she said, making an effort at diplomacy because she needed to enforce this point to Ralak. "But he served my father and he serves me."

"Was he telling the truth about last night?" Argentia asked. Tandun's account was plausible—he clearly had not tied himself to the rack—but something did not sit well with Argentia. "Erkani's no fighter. I have trouble believing he could overpower Tandun without help."

"I cannot say," Ralak replied. "I saw no lie in his thoughts, but his mind is mostly closed to me. There is much anger, much hatred. Beyond that little is clear. Nhapians are notoriously difficult to read, and Tandun is more difficult than most. There is too much history of strife between him and myself and my brother."

"Yeah, what exactly is the story there?" Argentia asked.

"Let us say that Relsthab and I did not see eye to eye with Tandun on many matters, including the definition of the duties of a serving girl in Aventar."

Solsta's eyes widened. "I've never heard that," she said.

"You were but a child, Majesty. The matter was kept quiet. My brother's punishment of Tandun—sanctioned by your father—was quite severe. It seemed to serve. He has been as manageable as such a brute can become, but the basilopard changes no spots, as the saying goes. I do not trust him. Which, unfortunately, may make me suspect him without cause."

"If he is guilty, it will be discovered in time," Solsta said. It was hard not to imagine Tandun was guilty of something—he was one of the crudest, cruelest people the Crown had ever met—but she tried to rule with an open mind until she had proof with which to condemn. Here there was none and Ralak's usually valuable opinion was tainted. "For now, let's concentrate on finding Erkani and this lamp before it can work any mischief."

"Leave that to me," Argentia said.

6

"Honey, it's *so* good to see you," Amethyst Pyth cooed, embracing Argentia.

The Guildmistress of the Golden Serpents was a short, voluptuous woman with a mane of brassy curls. She looked like a succubus conjured from some wizard's fantasy, but Argentia knew that beneath the make-up and jewels and expensive clothing was a street-tough and savvy mind. Amethyst had not become the leader of one of the most powerful thieves guilds in Teranor on looks alone.

"Sit, sit." Amethyst gestured to a plush sofa. They were in her mansion on the outskirts of Duralyn: a den of luxury furnished with mostly stolen treasures. "Can I get you anything?"

"No, thanks."

Amethyst signaled to a servant anyway, then turned her jade eyes back to Argentia, giving the huntress a long once-over. "You look stunning," she said.

Argentia, who had left the dungeon, gotten cleaned up, met briefly with Seb Karal, and headed for Pyth's, was wearing another pair of the linen pants she'd found favorable this season and one of her traditional halters, this one the deep green of midsummer grass. She was not sure if the comment was just Amethyst's penchant for hyperbole or a veiled reference to her recovery from the dragonfire, though Amethyst had not seen Argentia before the elf magic in her token had restored her. "Thanks. You're not looking too bad yourself. I thought once you got married you were going to just let yourself go."

"Honey, I'm not married yet. But can I tell you, planning a wedding is more work than running a guild. Just the guest list...."

"Too many people?"

"Too few."

"You've got to be kidding. You know everyone!"

"But most of them I've robbed and the rest are afraid they'll *be* robbed at the banquet."

This set both women laughing. When they finally composed themselves, Amethyst took a sip of the pear juice the servant had brought. "Now, what's the problem?" She tapped an oculyr on a table beside the couch. "Seb told me you were on your way, so I take it this isn't a social call. Something about that prisoner who escaped last night?"

"Exactly." Amethyst's network of thieves had helped Argentia several times in the past. "Seb's working with the Watch, but I need information from the streets. Anyone stealing rubies."

This was how Argentia had caught Erkani the first time: tracking his trail of stolen rubies. It was some type of compulsion with him and Argentia was willing to bet it had something to do with the lamp. If that were true, Erkani would begin doing it again.

And I'll have him....

"Just in Duralyn?" Amethyst asked after Argentia explained her reasoning.

"For the next couple days. If we don't catch him by then, we'll start in some other cities. But I don't think we'll have to. He can't have gotten far yet."

7

Argentia was wrong.

At that moment, Erkani was leagues away from Duralyn, in the port of Harrowgate on the Sea of Val.

The thief had taken a room at The Barnacles, a cheap wharfside hostel, paying with coin he had stolen in his escape from the Crown City. He did not intend to stay long, but he needed a place to pass the night; he had arrived too late to make passage on an outbound ship.

The room had a mirror. In it Al'Atin Erkani took his first look at himself in more than three years.

His weaselish face was bearded, his oily black hair hung past his scrawny shoulders. His skin had exchanged much of its natural tan for the sallowness of one who lived a sunless life. His pants and shirt were threadbare and faded. He had always been thin, but what was left of him was almost emaciated. His eyes, dark and squinty, were so used to the dim of the dungeon that he could barely stand the light of day. Outside in Duralyn, his eyes had been tearing so badly that he had been forced to steal a hat from a vagrant sleeping the morning away in an alley. A cloak with a hood would have been better, but it was summer and that would have drawn attention to him.

He looked a wreck, but that did not matter. At last, after three hopeless years, he was free.

Free and reunited with his lamp.

He could still recall with perfect clarity the moment a week earlier, when the lamp's voice had called him out of sleep. He had not heard it since the red-haired bitch had captured him and stolen it from him, but he knew it as surely as he knew his own.

FREE US! FEED US!

He sat bolt upright in his hard bed, beads of cold sweat erupting on his torso and brow as he stared into the dark of his cell. He must be dreaming—gods knew he had longed so to hear that precious voice again, with its promise of dreams fulfilled, power untold: Al'Atin Erkani, lord of all the thieves of Acrevast.

"Bazu?" he whispered, trembling, not daring to believe.

Yessssss....

And he knew he was not dreaming. "Oh, Master."

Free us. Feed us....

Erkani was shaking now. "I will! I will, Master!" he cried.

As the echo of his voice died into silence, there were mutters and shouts to "Shut up!" from the other prisoners he had awakened, then the clanging of a door and the heavy tread of the dungeonmaster and the growing light of his lantern.

"Silent!" Tandun said, and the dungeon fell quiet except for Erkani's whimpering iteration. Tandun's squat shape appeared at the bars of Erkani's cell. Erkani was crouched at the corner of his bed, his arms wrapped around his knees, rocking back and forth like one entranced, repeating a word that had no meaning to the dungeonmaster.

Tandun banged on the bars. "You! Silent! What problem?"

Erkani's eyes snapped open, glinting ferally. They seemed to look right through Tandun. "Nothing," he said. "I had...a dream."

"Make too much noise. Now I be nightmare," Tandun unfastened the door and strode into the cell.

"No!" Erkani tried to shrink away as the dungeonmaster caught the braid of his hair in one hand, spun it expertly, and sent the steel ball capping its end whirling into Erkani's mouth like a fist. Blood and teeth spattered the wall.

Erkani crumpled onto his bed, moaning. Tandun whirled his braid again and again, raining expert blows onto the thief's limbs and torso. Had the Crown or Ralak ever descended to Tandun's subterranean kingdom to inquire, Erkani could have told them that while the torture chamber itself may have lain idle for many a year, the practice of torment was alive and well in the dungeons of Aventar.

"Now silent. Sa-so!" Tandun struck a final blow, spat upon the inert thief, and left the cell, locking the door behind him. Erkani lay upon his bunk. He was not unconscious, nor had he lost consciousness during the beating. There was power in him once again, but now was not the time to use it, even if his hatred of Tandun was almost as great as his hatred of the red-haired bitch who had deposited him in the Nhapian monster's care. He had waited this long. He could wait a little longer.

Wiping the hot spittle off his face, Erkani drew his thin blanket over his scrawny frame and listened to the voice of the lamp tell him how to escape the dungeon.

8

The plan worked to perfection.

Even now Erkani reveled in the music of the hinges as the cell door opened in the dark of the night, the feeling of supreme satisfaction as hated Tandun's jaw smashed under the impact of his fist; a fist full of power that was not wholly his own, and more than a match for the dungeonmaster. He would have gladly killed him, but the transmogrification potion was waiting just as Bazu had promised it would be, and its magic worked only to imitate the living. So instead of death, Tandun was bound to the rack. Disguised as the dungeonmaster (in this, at least, Argentia had guessed aright), Erkani used the glyph-disarming stone, broke into the tower of the Archamagus, regained the lamp, and passed the unsuspecting guards on his way out of the castle and into the dawn.

Then followed a nervous time of lurking. Duralyn was not yet awake. The seven rings of the Crown City were largely empty save for Watchmen on their patrols. Erkani hid himself in an alley, sucking down a second potion to recover his own form, clutching the lamp close and breathing freedom for the first time in three long years.

The enormity of what he had accomplished had not yet taken hold. The lamp would not let him rest for long enough for such musings. The creature within was weak. Its needs soon drove Erkani out of hiding.

By now the sun was up and the streets were swarmed with early shoppers. Erkani, the lamp stuffed into his shirt, warm and pulsing like a second heart against his skin, moved among them like a shadow. His hand was trembling so badly when he picked the first purse that he thought he had botched the job for sure. But the fat woman merely grunted as he bumped her, shunting him aside and continuing on her way, all unaware of what had happened until she reached to her ample waist to pay for her sack of muffins.

The second purse went smoother. The third smoother still. Erkani knew he would be pressing his luck to try a fourth. He fled the vicinity of his last mark and put the coin to use. The information he bought was good. Late in the afternoon, he found the place and offered the lamp to the man there in exchange for the man's services. The man performed his task admirably, but the bargain was one Erkani had never intended to keep. They struggled and Erkani had choked the man (to death) unconscious.

Leaving the body, he entered Harrowgate. Gazed upon the tall ships in the sunset. He could have easily fled Duralyn on foot or stolen a horse, but he had learned from his mistakes three years ago. There were powerful forces in that city. They had captured him once, and although this was a different Archamagus and the red-haired bitch was dead—he had seen her body when it was brought through the dungeon to be prepared for burial—he had no doubt they would try to capture him again. He would not make it so easy for them this time, and he had done well to place as much distance between him and the Crown City as possible.

Still, as he stood before the mirror in his wretched little room at The Barnacle, he knew he should book his passage away from this cursed land. He would, just as soon as he looked at his beloved lamp one more time.

He checked the door. It was locked, but the wood looked flimsy. He took a chair from the small table. Jammed it under the handle. Not much extra resistance, but the room was on the first floor and it might buy him the seconds he would need to escape out the window.

He checked the closet. No one was hiding there.

He checked under the bed. No one there either.

He pulled the dirty curtains closed. Gave the room a last glance to make sure no one had snuck in while he was not looking.

Satisfied that he was alone and shielded from spying eyes, Erkani drew forth the lamp from within his shirt.

The keening began immediately, throbbing in his mind: *Feed us! We starve!*

"But I've nothing—"

WE STARVE! FEED US!

Erkani could not resist.

Went out to steal rubies.

9

Argentia sighed.

She was wrapped in a towel and lying on low chaise, her head leaning back into a raised sink of warm suds while one of Aventar's serving girls massaged scented soaps into her hair.

"Bliss, isn't it?" Solsta said from the adjacent sink.

"Well it beats streams and lakes. I haven't relaxed like this since Frostwood."

"What was it like there?" Solsta had never been to the fabled elf wood or its mystical city of Rime, which was thought a ruin until Argentia had returned to report otherwise. Even more than that, Solsta was curious to know what had happened to Argentia there.

After Argentia's burning by dragonfire, Solsta had seen only her hand—a thing withered and blackened as a dead tree—but that was enough for her to imagine what lay beneath the hood and cloak and wraps that Argentia had shrouded herself with in the depths of her despair. Whatever her friend had suffered, it had been as horrible as her recovery had been miraculous, yet since her return to Duralyn Argentia had spoken of neither.

"Rime is beautiful," Argentia said after a lengthy pause. "Beautiful and at peace. The elves of Falcontyr's Forest rebuilt it. There's magic there. So much magic...."

"Was it this magic that...healed you?"

Argentia reached to her throat, closing her fist over the dragon's tooth token: her gift and last remembrance of her husband, Carfax of Frostwood. It was the magic in the token that had saved her, perhaps in conjunction with the magic of the elf wood, but more, she knew, in conjunction with whatever strength lay within her.

"Yes," she said quietly. The maids had finished their massage and wash and had withdrawn. Argentia was alone with Solsta in the steamy chamber. She had rescued the Crown from a vampyr when Solsta was still only the heiress to her father's throne. That adventure had brought her into the company not only of Carfax but Artelo Sterling and many others she held among her closest friends. It had also set her on the deadly chase for the Wheels of Avis-fe and the race to stop the demon horde from coming to destroy Acrevast. Though she had suffered much pain and loss, still she believed that much more good had come of the fellowships forged in that quest. Not the least of them was Solsta, who was like a younger sister to Argentia.

She might have spoken then of what had happened to her: of rejecting Artelo in his need after a demoness kidnapped his daughter. Of wandering Harrowgate in burned despair until, at last, she found her way back to herself, summoning the courage to face what had happened and move forward.

Of journeying to Frostwood, meaning only to catch Artelo there and help him rescue Aura. Of the miracle in Rime where, as she took up the task of forging a new blade to fight the demoness, the magic of the elves wrought what no human magus, apothecary, or cleric could manage, restoring her body from the ruin of the dragonfire.

But these things were still too private and painful for Argentia to find words for, even to Solsta, so she held them mute in her heart and let her simple answer stand.

Silence and steam for a time.

Then: "Does Artelo blame me for Brittyn?" Solsta asked. The knight and the Crown had been lovers once, in fairer days before the tragedy of duty tore them apart. Both had wedded others and both had lost their spouses to violence—Kelvin Eleborne to an assassin's dagger meant for Solsta, Brittyn Sterling to the claws of the child-stealing demoness.

Argentia thought about it. The Crown had mustered Argentia's friends to the rescue after learning of her imprisonment by the mad wizard Mouradian, but it was Ralak, not Solsta, who had drawn Artelo in. While Artelo was abroad fighting Mouradian's monstrosities, Pandaros Krite, an apprentice magus boarding at Artelo's farm, had unleashed a succubus from the Fel Pits, leading to his death, Brittyn's death, Aura's abduction, and the perilous hunt that followed.

"No and yes," Argentia decided. "He blamed me, and you, and Ralak, but most of all he blamed himself. He knows no one forced him to come after me, just like no one forced him to let Pandaros stay there—and if there's fault to be laid at all, it belongs at that fool's feet."

"But why did he say he never wanted to see any of us again?" Ralak had been the recipient of Artelo's parting message and had conveyed it to Solsta, who of course understood it was directed chiefly at her. "If he knows it wasn't our fault...."

"Knowing isn't the same as accepting. Give him time."

"It was never the right time for us," Solsta said, showing for a moment the heart of a twenty-one year old she usually kept carefully hidden.

"Keep hope," Argentia replied. She did not add that for her there was no such hope. Her love was bound to a ghost and for her there would only ever be liaisons like Vartan Raventyr, who could touch her body but never stir the depths of her heart.

She had made her peace with that; it could not hurt her anymore. So she just closed her eyes again and let herself drift in the good heat and steam of the bath...

...until the footfalls coming fast down the corridor brought her alert moments before the knocking on the door.

"Come," Solsta called after she had adjusted her towel around her petite body. Argentia sat up and rolled her head from side to side; for once, the crick in her neck was gone.

The door opened, but only partially. "Sorry to disturb you, Majesty," Seb Karal said without entering. "Amethyst says we've got something."

"Erkani?" Argentia asked.

"Maybe. There's a missing wizard. His servant says a man came to see his master yesterday morning to purchase an aetherwalk. The wizard hasn't been seen since. Servant's not talking to the Watch because selling aetherwalks isn't legal, but he's talking to other servants. That's how someone in Amethyst's network heard."

"What's this got to do with Erkani?"

"The servant remembers because the man didn't have any money. He offered a lamp in payment."

"That's him." Argentia said.

"But where did he go?" Solsta asked. "If he aetherwalked..."

"He could be anywhere," Seb completed.

Argentia sat up. "Only one way to find out."

10

A quick change of clothes and Argentia was on her way, accompanied by Griegvard Gynt—who had learned that if he hung around Argentia long enough some mayhem usually ensued—a pair of Watchmen, and Spero Zart, the head of Duralyn's Watch Wizards.

Duralyn was a city of concentric circles, separated by walls and centered on Castle Aventar. Three great avenues ran like the spokes of a wheel through the central ring to the outer wall, subdividing each ring into six wards. The Trade Ring, where the preponderance of the city's shops, restaurants, and inns were located, was sandwiched between the ring just outside the castle grounds, where the mansions of the nobility stood upon the manicured lawns of tree-lined streets, and the ring of common residences, outermost in the city, home to the general citizenry of Duralyn.

As they moved through the Trade Ring, Argentia thought she spotted a familiar face in the crowd. Just a flicker and then she got jostled by someone rushing the other way and Griegvard was grumbling about the "all th' damn people on all th' damn streets all th' damn time." Argentia laughed, thinking how very different the chaos of the city was from the organized efficiency of Griegvard's holt, rubbed her shoulder absently, and walked on.

The wizard, Xeres Elektros, lived in a ward just outside of the Trade

Ring. His servant, a gnome named Banbu Tamm, blanched when he saw the Watchmen, but admitted them to the house. It was a small home, expensively furnished. Griegvard recognized a credenza in the entrance hall as the work of Knoffer Stonedust. He elbowed Argentia in the hip, pointed at the piece.

Argentia nodded. She had two Stonedust end tables in her manor in Argo; she knew how much they cost. There was no law against selling magic and many wizards made a tidy living enchanting items for the non-magical public, but certain spells were viewed as too dangerous to be made available. Aetherwalking was among these, and for good reason. But there were always people willing to pay for the service, regardless of the risk, and there were always wizards ready supply the spell at an exorbitant price.

Banbu Tamm, clearly aware that he was about to be interrogated, managed to fumble through the niceties of offering drinks and seats before Argentia cut to the questions. The two Watchmen and Zart were just window-dressing. This was her show.

"Where did the man with the lamp want to go?"

"Many apologies, but Banbu does not know."

"You are Electros' servant, aren't you?"

"Banbu has the pride of that place, yes," the gnome replied.

"And you expect us to believe that he didn't tell you where he was going or how long he was going to be away?"

Banbu's eyes widened. "Yes. Yes, that is so. Master often went here, there, few days, many days, without telling."

"You do understand that the man who came here was a criminal, and that helping him was a crime, just the same as selling aetherwalks is a crime? Your master is going to spend a long time in a cell, but that doesn't mean you have to take the fall with him."

"The fall?"

"Th' dungeons," Griegvard interjected. He stood with his brawny arms folded across his barrel chest, glowering down at the beardless gnome. "That's where ye'll be goin if yer lyin or holdin back information we're needin."

Banbu blanched. "No, no. No dungeons!"

35

"Then start talkin," Griegvard said.

Banbu talked. The problem was, the gnome knew little that they had not already heard from Amethyst's report. They did learn that Erkani had resumed his own form, for the description Banbu gave in no way resembled Tandun. Assuming he had no additional transmogrification potions, Argentia would know her quarry on sight. That was one point in their favor.

When it was clear there was nothing more to gain from interrogating the gnome, they left, with Spero Zart making the only official contribution to the conversation on behalf of the Watch by telling Banbu he would like to have a word with his master whenever Elektros did return.

Back at Castle Aventar, Argentia went to see Ralak in his tower to talk about walking the aether. She had done it more times than she cared to remember, but she did not have a clear understanding of the rules governing the magical travel.

"It depends upon the power of the magus," Ralak said. "One strong with the aether might transport himself across the Sea of Val—if he had intimate knowledge of where he was coming out. As the distance increases, so too must the perfection of the image of the place. For example, if I wished to teleport to the throne hall, I need do little more than think of it, for the distance is negligible and the throne hall so familiar in my mind that it is like walking through a door."

The Archamagus went on to explain that in addition to distance and an accurate vision of the destination, the number of people being transported through the aether was another consideration. "Much easier to go alone. Opening the ways for more than one person is taxing. It considerably shortens the distance you can travel."

"So this Elektros...."

"I know the name," Ralak said. "Powerful and greedy. If Erkani offered the lamp, he would have leaped at the chance to gain such a token."

"Even if Erkani offered the lamp there's no way he would keep that bargain. Could he have overpowered a wizard like Elektros?"

Ralak spread his hands. "He apparently overpowered Tandun. A wizard is weak after an aetherwalk of significant distance. If Erkani acted swiftly, he might have escaped him with the lamp. But...." He paused, studying the mess of papers on his desk. "There is another possibility we must consider."

"What?" Argentia asked. *Whatever it is, I'm probably not going to like it....*

"The lamp may no longer be with Erkani."

11

The wind whipped a persistent drizzle over the roof of Castle Aventar's north tower.

Argentia moved back and forth across the circular space, her bare feet sure on the slick stones as she whirled her katana through the misty air in a rigorous practice dance. She was a natural with a blade, though she also had the benefit of training at the hands of Toskan Ini, a Milantyr swordmaster. For years after parting ways with him she had hardly practiced at all, relying on her skill and speed to see her through her battles. But after Togril Vloth's cat-woman twins had nearly killed her, she had made it a point to practice every day.

Today, practice was not the only reason she was on the roof in the rain. She did her some of her best thinking with a weapon in her hands—and she had a lot to think about.

Ralak's suspicion was that it was Elektros who had overpowered Erkani, taking the lamp himself and becoming thrall to the salamander.

Argentia had objected. "I thought you said the salamander wanted a weak host. Why take a wizard over Erkani?"

"It may not have had any choice," Ralak said. "Nor does it particularly care. Such creatures always prefer the path of least resistance, but to it, one human is almost as weak as the next. A person of great will might oppose it. Other than that, it would have its way regardless. If Elektros took the lamp, the salamander would simply have started to work on his mind. From what I know of him, he would have been easily susceptible to such cozening."

Argentia frowned, remembering when she had first captured Erkani and taken the lamp from him. Relsthab had given her a lead box to put the lamp in. She could still recall the strange and urgent voice that had whispered at her from the lamp. The voice of the salamander. She had resisted, but hers was one of those iron-cold wills Ralak had mentioned.

If Xeres Elektros heard the salamander's voice, would he have succumbed? Ralak believed so. Argentia did too. What she did not believe was that the wizard had taken the lamp from Erkani. She had seen Erkani with the lamp. Nothing short of death would separate him from it a second time.

So she set her mind to figuring out where Erkani had asked Elektros to teleport him. Even if Ralak was right and Elektros did have the lamp, they would have to know where he had taken it from Erkani to know where to begin looking for him—though tracking a wizard who could walk the aether from place to place made matters more complicated.

Argentia grinned a little at that. She had never hunted a wizard before. It would be a challenge all its own.

Still, dead or alive, Erkani was the key. Last time, he had taken a horse out of Duralyn. This time, he had used a wizard to make his escape. There was something significant there. *But what....*

Argentia danced in the rain with her katana. A half-hour later, when she pulled open the trapdoor leading down to her chambers, she was smiling.

Without pausing to dry off or pull her boots on, she went down the tower steps, dripped through the royal library, and chatted easily with the Sentinels outside the throne hall's golden doors while waiting for Solsta to finish her session with the Peerage. When the great doors finally opened, the emerging nobles and their pages cast suspect glances on the beautiful, barefoot woman whose red hair glittered with rain and whose damp halter and pants clung fetchingly to her body. Most of them knew who she was and that the blood in her veins pulsed with a birthright as noble as any of theirs, but still they did not deign to acknowledge her. That was fine with Argentia. Bandying niceties with hypocrites had never been her long suit.

When the parade of Peers was finished, Argentia ducked inside the hall and caught Solsta, Seb, and Mirkholmes at the foot of the flight of steps that mounted to the throne of Aventar. "There are hundreds of servants in the castle," Solsta said, running a hand through the white blaze in her dark brown tresses. "Do you expect me to believe that not one of them remembered to leave towels in your rooms?" She said it with a tone.

"Bad session with the peacocks?" Argentia countered. Nothing could put Solsta out of her spirits faster than hours of listening to the Peerage make petty complaints about her policies.

Mirk tugged on Argentia's sodden pant leg. "Mistress said Lord Persh should be struck mute so he would not waste air with talking," he peeped.

"Mirk!" Solsta exclaimed. Seb coughed into his hand and the meerkat wisely ducked behind Argentia, who was looking at Solsta with both her brows arched.

"What?" Solsta demanded.

"Did you really?" Argentia asked, chuckling.

Solsta blushed a little. "Well...not so loudly that anyone heard me."

"Mirk heard," the meerkat said.

"Clearly. I'll remember that next time," Solsta said, shaking her head and laughing. When she looked back to Argentia, the mood had lifted off her like a cloud. "I guess it hasn't stopped raining?"

"What makes you say that?"

Solsta swatted Argentia's arm. "Enough out of you. What do you want?"

"We need to alert the Watches in the major ports," Argentia said. "Erkani's trying to get as far away from Ralak as fast as possible. Last time he tried to hide in Byrtnoth and got caught. He thinks distance means safety. It doesn't."

12

Still raining.

The incessant pattering on the tower roof and window woke Argentia. She blinked blearily. The quality of light was all wrong. Gray and gloomy, which befitted yet another rainy day, but too dim. *Early....* Groaning she raised her head and squinted at the clock. *Way too early....* She did not mind chasing the dawn up if she had something to do, but under normal circumstances, she preferred to sleep until at least ten bells.

Stretching languidly, she settled back into the comforting warmth of her bed, letting her head sink into the soft pillow. She drowsed until a roll of thunder stirred her again. Normally she loved stormy mornings—waking and just laying there, listening to the wind gust and the rain play and letting laziness have its way with her—but this morning the rain made her restless.

It's Erkani, she realized. Three days had passed since word had been sent to the ports. There was no sign of the thief. He was out there somewhere, still free, and it was her responsibility to catch him. It nagged at her. She wondered if she had been too late in guessing his course, or if she had made an error in her judgment.

She was confident that Erkani had headed for one of Teranor's coasts, which reduced the direction of his flight to east or south. To the north was the Gelidian Spur and the ice reaches of Nord, and to the west the

Dragon Mountains, where man had yet to set a foothold for habitation. The question was whether she was right about the ports.

She thought she was, because she thought Erkani was going to try to get even farther away from Ralak than the shores of Teranor. But she did not know where. South to his homeland was logical, but he might anticipate their expecting that and head east to Nhapia or to any of the myriad islands in the Sea of Val.

If she could not determine his port of departure, she was going to have to face the fact that she probably would never find him. That galled her. To be helpless, to rely on others and Fortune to bring her to a place where she could act was the hardest thing in the world for her—yet she knew there was nothing she could do but wait....

She tossed and turned for a few more minutes before she gave up. *Never get back to sleep now....* She shoved the blankets aside and swung her long legs out of bed. Padded naked across the room, yawned, and looked out the window. The rain was steady: a nasty day unfolding. Maybe she would swing by Amethyst's guildhouse. That way she would be right on the spot if there were any news of the thief.

She started her morning ritual. Dropped down and did push-ups. Flipped onto her back and did sit-ups, clenching her abdominal muscles until they burned. She was very vain about her stomach; she thought it was her best feature and worked hard to keep it that way.

Her exercises complete, she pulled on a long silk robe and made *esp*. The elven drink was a delicacy almost unknown outside the elf-woods in Teranor. It was brewed from beans cultivated in those magical forests that had the power to awaken and amplify the senses. Carfax had introduced Argentia to it, and the elf prince D'Lyrian had gifted her a magical pouch that would replenish itself so long as one bean remained ever in the bag. It had quickly become one of her most prized possessions. While she liked tea well enough and caf—a more common cousin of the elven beverage—even better, there was nothing to compare to esp. *Especially on a miserable morning like this....*

She ground the fragrant beans in a mortar, dumped them in a well-used mesh sack, and brewed them in a kettle of boiling water. A few minutes later, she decanted the esp into her mug, breathing in the steam fragrant of pecans, and let the first gulp slid hot down her throat, hitting her stomach like a burst of liquor. She inhaled deeply, her eyesight sharpening. *Ahhh....*

Another pull and she headed for the bath chamber. It was much smaller and less luxurious than the bath in her manor in Argo—these had been Carfax's rooms originally and he had minimal use for creature comforts—but, as she'd quipped to Solsta the other day, it was better by far than streams and lakes.

She had just unbelted her robe and turned on the spigot when she heard the pounding on her door. *That figures...* "Hang on!" She hurried out, fastening her robe again as she went, and opened the door.

Seb was standing there, bent forward, out of breath.

"What's the matter?" Argentia asked. "Is Solsta—"

"No, no, she's fine. It's—"

"Amethyst?"

"No." Seb shook his head and held up his hand. Took a deep breath. Argentia could see the perspiration on his stubbled scalp and wondered how fast he had run. He had been wounded in the Battle of Hidden Vale and the cut from the demonic blade had left him nearly crippled. He had mostly recovered, but he would never ride or run or fight as he once had.

But he ran this morning... That told Argentia everything she needed to know about the urgency of whatever message the knight was bringing. "Seb, what is it?"

"They found the wizard," Seb said.

"Where?"

"Harrowgate. He's dead."

Argentia did not waste time asking for details. She would learn what she needed to know when she got there. Time was what mattered now. "Get the aethergate ready. Tell Solsta and Ralak I'm going. And wake Griegvard. Tell him to meet me at the monastery."

She closed the door on Seb, grabbed her mug as she passed the table, downed the rest of the esp in a swallow, and hurried to get ready. Seb's news was both heartening and troubling. It gave her a starting point and a hope that Erkani might not yet have escaped Teranor, but it also forced her to revise her opinion of the thief.

The Erkani she knew was not a killer. *At least, he didn't kill anyone last time....* In anger or to save the lamp, he might try violence—he had gone after her with a poker—but he was not a skilled fighter. If he had killed the wizard, it probably meant the lamp's hold on him was complete, which could only mean trouble for Argentia in trying to capture him.

What else is new? Everything the hard way....

13

Argentia wiped a stray strand of wet hair out of her eyes and considered going back for a cloak. But it was not really cold, she was already wet, and in a few minutes she would be leagues away from Duralyn. *Hope it's not raining in Harrowgate, too....*

She had done perhaps her fastest packing job ever, jamming everything she might need into her travel-worn pack, throwing on the first clothes she put her hands to, grabbing her katana, and heading for the door. Traveling without Shadow would be strange, but the dog had free run of the castle and she did not have time to look for him. It was not only the need to get closer to Erkani as quickly as possible that impelled her, but something deeper: the customary thrill of the chase rushing through her. She was never more alive than when she was hunting. This was what she loved. What she lived for.

Her thoughts were already far ahead, wondering on what she would find in Harrowgate. Was Erkani still there? Was he responsible for the wizard's death? Had the lamp—

"Wait for Mirk!"

Argentia spun around in surprise. "What are you doing here? Does Solsta know where you are?"

"Mistress knows." The meerkat was wearing his sword—a letter opener imitation of the demon-slaying blade Scourge—and his fine whiskers twitched as he regarded Argentia with his big amber eyes. "Mirk has not ever left without telling Mistress—except to go to cold place and see ice triangle," he added, seeing Argentia's look.

Argentia spread her hands. It was not that she was averse to taking Mirk with her—he was a good companion and more oft than not proved helpful, as he had when they journeyed to rescue her butler Ikabod from an ice pyramid in frozen Nord—but she did not understand why he wanted to come. "What's this all about?"

"Mirk is tired of rain and boring castle," the meerkat said.

Argentia could sympathize, but something about Mirk's presence did not ring right. *No time to worry about it now....* "All right. If you're coming, let's go. But if I find out you didn't tell Solsta about this...."

"Mirk told her!" The meerkat put such a note of indignation in his voice that Argentia had to laugh. Shaking her head, she started walking again, Mirk scampering beside her.

They crossed the rest of the stone courtyard between Aventar's moat and the wall girdling the Royal Ring. Passed over the patch of dry stone beneath the archway in the wall and out into the rain again. The dragon's-tooth token at Argentia's throat, perhaps catching the light from the lamps on the wall, gleamed sharply just as Mirk screeched in alarm and darted away as the seven shapes burst from the misty gloom on either side of the archway and circled Argentia in a ring of steel.

"GAH! Die, bitch!" One of the seven came hurtling at Argentia. He was a shade shorter than she was, solid looking, and had some combat skill. He held his knife-thrust until the last moment, so she could not knock his arm aside. But the blow was telegraphed and Argentia's instincts had her body moving even as her mind tried to catch up with the fact that she had been surrounded and attacked outside of Castle Aventar, of all places. In his haste, the knife-man had not allowed the others to close in tight enough. She had room to spin past the thrust at her stomach, lashing out with an elbow to the knife-man's cheek as he passed. Not much behind the blow, but it was enough to stun her assailant for the instant it took her to get Lightbringer free.

The katana, forged by her own hand of dwarven mithryl and elven magic, gleamed long and deadly in the twilight. There was no fear in her as she settled her feet and swept her head back and forth, surveying her enemies. "Back the hell—"

She recognized them.

The knowledge of who they were and what they wanted hit her like a hammer in the gut. Hard on the heels of this came another flash of memory and realization: *It was Bogden I saw in the crowd that morning Griegvard and I were going to Elektros' house....*

Argentia lowered her sword, raised her hand, palm out. "I didn't kill your brother!" she shouted as Temrun slashed at her again. She leaped aside and brought her sword up at Wojek: the biggest of them, but the slowest. He flinched reflexively, raising his axe to block. Argentia ducked and lunged past him. If she could break clear of the ring she could—

Cree caught her ponytail and yanked her off her feet. She hit the wet ground hard. Heard Temrun coming like a charging bull. Rolled aside. His stab missed her again. She scrambled to her feet on the slippery stones.

"Grab the bitch!" Temrun ordered. The ring pressed closer.

"Stop it!" Argentia shouted. "I won't fight you!" She kept turning in a circle within the circle, her sword up high; she had no intention of not defending herself. "I didn't kill Vartan!"

"Lies!" Temrun roared. His eyes bulged in his head. The muscles of his neck were steel cords. His face flushed with fury, veins throbbing. Argentia saw there would be no reasoning with him, but Delk and Troyen had glanced at each other and there had been uncertainty in that look. "Listen to me! I didn't—"

She caught Temrun glancing past her and spun hard, katana slashing easily through the thick rope Bogden held between his hands.

An instant too late, she realized her mistake.

Her back was to Temrun and his knife. Even with her uncanny speed she could not get around fast enough.

She tried, whirling away from Bogden's hideous grin, turning left to give herself a bit of extra space from Temrun's right-handed attack. Quick pain, hot and sharp, as the knife gashed her side. She slipped on the slick stones. Temrun kicked her, flipping her onto her back, and stomped down. Agony as her ribs broke under his heavy boot—

Temrun screamed, dropping the knife, his face on fire as Mirk leaped into the fray, blue aether darting from his glowing paws, sending Temrun howling back.

The Gryphons froze, too shocked to respond. On the ground, Argentia scrabbled for her sword, trying to get to her knees. *Hurt....*

She heard growling thunder and a roar and then the ring of Gryphons was blasted apart as Shadow launched himself at Bogden, driving the bald man down.

"Hang on, Red!" Griegvard was a step behind the surging dog. He smashed Delk and Troyen aside. His huge axe was still on his back; his rock-hard fists were weapons enough.

One punch put Cree on the ground. Wojek stepped forward. "Yer a big one, ain't ye?" Griegvard said. A twitch of his stubby legs sent him airborne. He clapped his hands viciously against the barbarian's ears. Wojek staggered and dropped to his knees. "That's better." The dwarf—now standing eye-to-eye with the Norden—smashed his forehead into Wojek's nose. Blood sprayed and the giant man crumpled like a hillside in an earthquake. "Who's friggin next!" Griegvard challenged, clashing his fists and glaring wildly.

"The Watch!" Delk shouted. "Go! Go!" He hauled Wojek to his feet and shoved the dazed barbarian ahead. "Everyone out!" As the Gryphons gathered themselves and raced away into the rainy gloom, Temrun lingered long enough to shout, "This isn't over, bitch!"

Then he, too, was gone.

"Bah!" Griegvard watched the Gryphons flee. "Seven on one and they're bloody runnin away." He shook his wild beard and turned to Argentia as the Watchmen rushed up. "What in Drim's name was that all— Hey, Red! Don't ye dare!"

Argentia slumped beside Shadow. The puddle beneath her was pink with running blood.

14

"You cannot go," Middlewyn said.

"I'm going," Argentia replied.

"You are not fit to walk forth from here, much less to walk the aether, child," the High Cleric said. He was an old man, white haired and white bearded. There was compassion in his gray eyes, but stern resolve also. "The strain might kill you. You *must* wait."

Argentia shook her head, pretending the movement did not hurt her ribs. *I can't believe it happened again....* Two had been broken. It was an injury she seemed doomed to incur: this was the fourth time. As usual there was nothing to do but wait for them to heal.

Fortunately for Argentia, that was all that remained of her injuries. Though she had no memory of Griegvard carrying her unconscious, bleeding form from the street into the Monastery of the Grey Tree, or the Light of Aeton flowing through Middlewyn's hands to close the deep gash in her side, she had been healed by clerics enough times to surmise what had happened.

She was not sure how long she had lain in the narrow bed before waking to see Griegvard sitting in a chair, Shadow at his feet, Mirk pacing back and forth on a table, but however long it had been (in truth, less than an hour) was too long. She started to shove the sheet aside and sit up when she realized she was not wearing a top and that her whole

49

body hurt. Sinking back onto the pillow, she looked at the dwarf. "Thank you," she said.

"Bah. No need t' thank me, Red. Ye got any idea what King Durn'd do t' me if I were lettin his favorite human lass die?"

"Mirk helped," the meerkat sniffed.

Argentia smiled. "Thank you, too," she said. Her memories of the rescue were vague. Everything was vague after Temrun's boot came crashing down. She peeked under the sheets and gingerly touched the bandages. Winced. "Bastard," she muttered. "How bad was it?"

"Weren't good. Who th' hell were those clowns, anyway?" the dwarf asked.

"Some old friends."

"Ye ain't got enough enemies, now yer friends're tryin t' kill ye?"

"We had a...misunderstanding."

"What kind o' misunderstandin?"

"They think I cut off their leader's head."

Griegvard stared at her. "Pretty damn big misunderstandin."

"Tell me about it."

A knock on the door preceded Middlewyn and another cleric. Argentia thanked them for healing her. Temrun's dagger had cut deep along her side; they had closed the wound but there would be a scar.

"Start of a brand new collection," she muttered. When the elf magic had healed her from the dragonfire, it had restored her flesh smooth and whole, without the innumerable blemishes from a decade and more of a warrior's life.

"Pardon?" Middlewyn said.

Argentia shook her head. "Nothing." Scars meant she was still alive; that was all that mattered. She asked if the aethergate was ready, prompting the argument with the High Cleric.

"I can't wait," she said. "Besides, the gate comes out in Coastlight Cathedral. Colla will be waiting for me. If I'm dying, she'll take care of me."

"Do not be presumptuous of Aeton's grace," the other cleric said. He was a swarthy man from the Sudenlands. "You have received a gift of healing. It is not to be taken lightly."

Argentia's temper flared. "The longer I wait, the more likely people will die at the hands of the man I'm hunting," she said wrapping the sheet around her and rising with a grimace. "How would that sit with Aeton, you think?"

"Forgive Garlatyn," Middlewyn said, raising a finger to stay the other cleric from speaking further. "He has a convert's zeal, even if it is sometimes misdirected."

"Whatever. Look, are you going to open the gate, or do I need to send for the Crown?"

"She is already here." Solsta swept in with Seb and Ralak behind her. She nodded to Middlewyn and squeezed Argentia's arm. She was wearing a sealskin cloak against the rain, a long skirt, and a silk blouse, but her face lacked its usual tasteful makeup, and her hair was drawn back in a ponytail, the white Mark of her rule a prominent streak above her forehead. "Seb woke me as soon as he heard. *What* happened? Are you all right?"

"Fine. It was some...enemies from before Mouradian kidnapped me. They wanted revenge."

"For what?"

"Something I didn't do." From the set of Argentia's lips, Solsta knew no more information would be forthcoming.

"Ye catch 'em?" Griegvard asked Seb.

"They escaped. The Watch is searching the city. We'll find them."

Argentia looked at Solsta. "I need to go. Erkani...."

"I know. Seb told me about the wizard. Are you *sure* you're up to this?" Argentia nodded.

"Majesty, I do not think it is prudent for her to walk the aether," Middlewyn said.

"If she is well enough to argue, she is well enough to use the gate," Solsta said. She knew Argentia was more hurt than she let on. She also knew there was nothing she could do, not with all her power, to stay her. "Griegvard will go with you?"

"Aye." The dwarf nodded to the Crown then looked at Argentia. "Where're we goin, anyway?"

"Harrowgate," Ralak said. "And you had best get moving."

Shadow sounded a deep bark and fixed Argentia with stormy eyes that were uncannily like Carfax's eyes, and the huntress could only stare back and wonder, her hand fast around her dragon's tooth. "I suppose that means you're coming, too," she said in mock exasperation.

There was a sneeze from the corner of the chamber. Everyone turned in surprise. "Mirk!" Solsta exclaimed. "Come out from there!"

Since he had heard Solsta's voice, the meerkat had been hiding behind a large potted plant. Now he came forth, ears flat, head down, muttering about "stupid smelly weeds."

"What are *you* doing here?" Solsta demanded.

"Mirk was going with Lady on adventure."

"Oh really? I thought we discussed this the last time. No more running off without telling me. Mirk—you promised!" Solsta turned and stared accusatorily at Argentia.

"Don't look at me." Argentia raised her hands to protest her innocence. "I didn't have anything to do with it. He swore he told you."

"Mirk *did* tell Mistress," the meerkat said. "Mistress said 'Lady is going after bad man with lamp,' and Mirk said 'Mirk wants to go, too,' and Mistress said 'I'm sure you do.'

"And?" Solsta said.

"Mistress did not say 'No.'"

"Mirk!" Solsta exclaimed. Seb burst out laughing and even Ralak turned away to hide his amusement.

"Let him come, Majesty," Argentia said.

Mirk blinked his big amber eyes at Solsta. "Oh, stop pouting," she said. "You can go. She drew the meerkat into her arms and kissed his fuzzy head. "But promise me you'll come back safe."

"Mirk promises." He wriggled in Solsta's embrace. "Mistress is squishing Mirk."

"Enough out of you! Go on!" Solsta released him. The meerkat jumped down and drew his little sword.

"Mirk is ready for adventure!"

"I hear ye," Griegvard said. "Let's bloody go."

Argentia pointed at the door. "If all of you would *get out* so I can get dressed, we'd already be gone."

15

Aetherwalk.

Because of the dangers inherent in teleportation, the Council of the Magi had banned wizards from taking others with them through the aether. As Ralak had explained to Argentia, the ban was routinely ignored, particularly if the interested party could afford to pay whatever price the wizard was charging for his services, as in the case of Erkani and Xeres Elektros. Even if it had been effective, the Council had recognized from the beginning that there might be instances where mass teleportation was required, so they banded their powers together and created fixed aethergates that were capable of transporting multiple people. The gates were for the most part located in the great wizarding towers of the major cities, but three were not.

The gate in the Monastery of the Grey Tree was secret to most of Teranor. It had been built as a last means of escape for the Crown should Aventar fall to siege. A tunnel connected the castle to the monastery. From there the Crown could get as far south as Argo or as far east as Harrowgate.

Argentia had never needed to flee the castle, but she had used the gate many times. Too many, in her opinion. Walking the aether was a matter of an instant—you stood in the circle of runes, the gate was activated, and you were gone in a silver flash, rematerializing at your destination before you could as much as blink—but it took a brutal toll on the body, leaving you feeling as if you had been torn apart and jammed back together again.

Which, essentially, was what happened.

For those not gifted to touch the aether as wizards were, the longer the teleport, the worse the debilitation. Argentia had aetherwalked enough that she hardly felt short trips, and she usually held up well over the long ones, but her weakened condition left her on her knees in the gate-chamber of Harrowgate's Coastlight Cathedral. Her head was spinning and she was marshaling every ounce of self-possession not to vomit.

"Mirk is dizzy...." The meerkat staggered past, wobbling like a drunken sailor. Shadow whined and even Griegvard was sitting on the stones, shaking his bearded head.

"Bloody teleportin's th' worst," he muttered. "Ye should let th' dwarves build iron rails from city t' city. Get ye there as fast," he grumbled, rising. "I felt better after a binge o' Stromness stout."

"Surely a testament to the dwarven constitution more than the rigors of walking the aether," said Colla. The High Cleric of Harrowgate was standing in the doorway. She was unattended and barefoot, dressed in blue and white robes. "Welcome," she said, smiling warmly as she came forward. She was a short girl with dark, curly hair. She had been a shepherdess prior to Aeton's call and retained much of the simplicity of her country upbringing, as well as a round-faced, doe-eyed beauty that people often mistook for innocent foolishness. But Argentia knew her to be far from innocent and farther still from foolish. Colla had stood against much evil in her twenty-eight years, particularly since rising to the third-highest seat in the clerical hierarchy. To her credit she had done so without ever losing her essentially joyous nature.

The High Cleric placed her hands on Argentia's shoulders. She closed her eyes, her lips moving in a silent prayer. Argentia felt a sweet coolness flow through her. The nausea vanished. She took a deep breath. The soreness in her ribs and side remained, but much of the pain had abated: enough that she thought she could get rid of the ridiculous bandages and possibly use her sword again. She did not know how things were going to end when she found Erkani, but she doubted the thief would come quietly. She had other weapons besides her sword, and Griegvard gave her an advantage in a fight that Erkani would be hard-pressed to match, lamp or no lamp, but she would have been happier if she were unhampered. *Can't do anything about it now....*

"Better?" Colla asked.

Argentia stretched carefully and smiled. "Much. Thanks. Good to see you again."

"You as well," Colla said. Argentia appreciated that the cleric left unspoken the fact that the last time she had seen her, the huntress had been scorched by dragonfire and looked more like a goblin than a woman. If she was surprised by Argentia's recovery from those supposedly permanent injuries, she gave no hint.

"Did Middlewyn—"

Colla nodded. "We know your needs and your haste. When you are ready, a Watchman is waiting below. He will take you to the wizard."

16

It was worse than Argentia had imagined.

They were at the morgue in Harrowgate's Watch garrison. The wizard's body was under a heavy sheet on a stone table. It had been found in a room above a shop called Intrigues and Enchantments, a sister store to Elektros' establishment in Duralyn. That the wizard kept shops and residences in both cities Argentia had learned from Vigo Starker, the Watch Captain assigned to the case. "Guess the illegal aetherwalking business was doing well for him," Starker said.

"Where was the aethergate?" Argentia asked.

"Room above the shop," Starker said. He was a tall, fit man with slick brown hair and a lupine cast to his features that made Argentia a trifle uneasy. "Runes painted on the floor and hidden with some invisibility magic."

It made sense. The pulse of aethereal power that would mark the gate opening would be effectively concealed by the presence of the magic items in the shop below.

"Who found the body?" Argentia asked.

"It was shoved under the bed. Maid bumped it with a broom. Been there the best part of four days, what we can tell." Starker pulled the sheet off the body. "Bet you never seen anything like that," he said. "Bet if they found this body in the wilds, they'd say sure it was an ogre or some giant-kin got him."

This is much worse than an ogre....

In life, Elektros had been a man in his middle fifties—or so Argentia judged from the quantity of gray in his long hair. She could not judge by his face because it was basically gone: pulverized beyond recognition by a club or a mace or some other rounded implement. Cause of death was a broken neck—she saw the livid fingermarks on the wizard's throat. The other wounds had been inflicted postmortem, in some sort of frenzy.

It was the power of the lamp they were seeing here, Argentia knew. "Were there signs of a struggle in the room?"

"None," Starker shook his head. "If the maid hadn't poked under the bed, he'd still be there." He pointed at the mangled corpse. "Think you can catch someone who did that? Think you can stop them?"

"I want to see the dockmaster," Argentia said, pointedly ignoring Starker's questions. "I want to know if Erkani's booked passage on any of the ships here."

"Don't need my permission," Starker said. "You're the Crown's Huntress, right? What I hear, you could just wave a Royal Sigul and it won't matter what I say."

Argentia frowned. While what Starker said was true, she tried never to pull rank on people she was working with. In fact, in the many tasks Solsta had set her on, Argentia could remember only one instance where she had used the Royal Sigul, and that had been a matter of life and death—not her own, either. "Look, let's not turn this into a spitting contest. We're all here for the same thing: to catch this maniac before he kills anyone else. If you've got a problem working with me, either tell me what it is, get somebody else to help me, or get over it."

Starker turned aside from the cold, steady light in Argentia's cobalt eyes.

"Glad that's settled," Argentia said. "Can we go to the dock now?"

"Whatever you say." Starker's tone was brusque and he marched away without another word. Argentia could not tell if her attempt to save him further embarrassment had helped or just made matters worse.

"What's his problem?" Griegvard asked as they trailed the Watchman up the steps and out of the morgue.

Argentia shrugged. She knew exactly what Starker's problem was:

she had encountered it enough times in her career as a bounty huntress. Men were either threatened by her prowess or they did not take her seriously. As her reputation grew, it became something of a challenge to them to prove she was not all the talk said she was.

She had heard and seen it so often that it rolled off her like water from an osprey, but that did not mean she was unmindful of it. She did not care what Vigo Starker thought of her, but if they were going to be hunting Erkani in Harrowgate things would go easier if they had the cooperation of the Watch.

"He keeps yappin, I'll have t' shut his mouth fer 'im."

"Let it go." Argentia stopped walking and looked at the dwarf. "And if anything needs to be done about it, I'll do it. Since when did you start protecting me?"

A sly grin appeared in the blonde forest of Griegvard's beard. "Since this mornin."

"I don't want to hear it," Argentia warned. "I had it all under control...."

Outside, Harrowgate was a gray city beneath a gray sky, wet from the Sea of Val and the rain that it seemed had become the norm for Teranor this summer. The streets were full of puddles. The air was damp. There were people out and the stores were busy but the city seemed quiet, subdued. Or maybe it was just Argentia's mood.

After Mouradian's island and the dragonfire, she had wandered the streets of Harrowgate for almost a month, burned and broken, before circumstances forced her to face herself and come to grips with what had at that time seemed an irrevocable harm. The city had seen her at her worst, at her weakest.

It had seen her stand by as three people were murdered.

She shook her head, dismissing the memory. She had balanced the scales with her ghosts in Harrowgate, avenging Vartan Raventyr's death on Mouradian's assassin and hunting down Merek Quicksilver, the thief whom, in her despair over her ruined body, she had failed to stop from killing a nobleman and his wife. She was square with the city, and knew it was not really Harrowgate that was raising these dark phantoms.

The attack in Duralyn and what it represented both in terms of her past coming back to haunt her and of future danger hung like a black drapery in the back of her mind, fluttered by a wind of failure. She could say what she wanted to Griegvard, but she knew she had very nearly been beaten. She would not concede that she would have been killed—certainly she had been in worse situations and survived—but that did not change the fact that she had been taken off her guard and trapped like a rabbit in a snare.

It left a bad taste in her mouth. *The Gryphons are good, but not that good....*

She pushed those thoughts aside as well. Turned her mind to the hunt at hand. The intimations of what she had seen at the morgue were deeply troubling. Erkani was a small, rat-like man, built for speed and stealth, not for brute force and certainly not for the inhuman savagery of Elektros' injuries. Of course, they did not know for certain the thief had killed the wizard, but the odds against it were so slim as to be negligible.

No, he killed him.... It just felt right to Argentia, and she had learned long ago to trust her instincts, even when they ran contrary to what she knew of her quarry. What she was not convinced of was whether the thief was in control of his actions, or if the aefryt was using him like a puppet.

Either way, Erkani was a danger best brought down quickly.

17

"No more," Erkani whispered. "Please...."

The thief was crouched behind a bushy Fantostian moonpetal, his back pressed to the wall beneath a picture window. The house to which this window belonged was a big brick affair at the end of a stately, hedge-lined brick path on a quiet, cobblestone street. Inside the house there were rubies. Erkani knew because the lamp could sense them. There was also a dog. He knew because he could hear it.

Feed us.... The voice from the lamp was unrelenting. Over the past four days, Erkani had robbed fourteen houses of their rubies. He was pressing his luck trying for a fifteenth. What he should be doing was boarding a ship and leaving this gods-forsaken country behind.

Feed!

The primitive part of Erkani's mind, where reptilian-eyed survival kept vigil from its cave, was growing more and more concerned about the increasing power of the lamp. But the clamor it raised in warning was the cry of a castaway echoing unheard on the empty sea.

Erkani was slave to the voice from the lamp and the dreams of glory it had once more fired in his heart.

He raised the runestone to the window. It had disarmed the wards on the Archamagus' door. It disarmed the ones on this glass as well. The window was not locked, which saved him having to break in. Erkani slipped inside the house, hiding behind the draperies, listening intently. *Where's the dog?* He could not hear it anymore. He peeked out. The room was a den of some sort, with book-lined shelves and a writing desk and a thick carpet. No sign of the dog. No sense of anyone else in the house, but since his escape he had barely slept or eaten and he was not sure he trusted his senses.

Erkani came out, moving quickly, the lamp extended before him, his knuckles white around the handle. He let it guide him down the hall—never mind the ragged, insomniac specter he glimpsed in a gilt mirror—and up the steps and into a woman's bedroom.

Almost all her jewelry was rubies: rings, necklaces, bracelets, and brooches. More here than his three previous takes combined. *What is she, obsessed with them?* An ironic titter escaped him as he plucked the items up and fed them to the lamp, which was throbbing with greedy heat. The spout expanded to swallow the larger stones, widening enough for Erkani to see the lurid glow within the ancient metal. One by one he dropped the rubies into the lamp. He heard none of them land.

The dog in the doorway started barking.

Erkani jerked around, fumbling rubies onto the rug. The dog was hardly worth the name: a dirty white ball of fuzz no bigger than a rabbit, shaking and snarling and yapping with comic ferocity.

The woman's voice from downstairs was not so funny.

"Berry! Stop that right now!"

More barking. "I said stop it! Are you *upstairs*? You're not supposed to be *upstairs*!"

Erkani's gaze wavered between the dog and the hallway beyond the door. The stairs were at the far end. They were wooden. He could hear the woman's sharp heels as she ascended.

The dog rushed forward, springing up and pawing at Erkani's thigh. "Shut up!" he hissed, kicking at the dog. It went tumbling back, scrabbled up, charged again.

There was a pulse of ruby light from the lamp. An aborted yelp. The dog was fire and ash.

"Berry?"

Erkani heard the woman hesitate on the steps. He stared at the smoldering remnants of the dog, his surprise and horror rapidly turning into a kind of giddy jubilation as he realized the power of the lamp.

"Berry?" A note of fear had replaced the annoyance in the woman's voice. She was coming again. It crossed Erkani's mind to simply stand his ground and incinerate her, but the little of him that was still sane realized that he had done nothing to make the fire come from the lamp. If it did not strike the woman down as it had her stupid dog, he would be seen. While he did not doubt he could escape, she would summon the Watch and have his description, making it next to impossible for him to get passage out of Harrowgate.

There was a better way.

Erkani slipped off to one side of the door, listening as the woman poked her head in various rooms, still calling for Berry. Closer, closer, her shadow across the threshold. He could smell her perfume; so cloyingly floral he almost preferred the stench of burnt dog. He waited for the screaming to start.

The woman did not disappoint. A couple of steps into the room, he heard her sniff and stop. She was well-dressed and average height, plump, with a coif of blonde hair. She saw some of her rubies on the floor and a stinking smear of charred fur.

Her screech-owl wail filled the air. She staggered forward, falling to her knees in her expensive red-and-gold skirt, making Erkani's task that much easier as he stepped from his hiding place and whacked her over the head with the lamp, dropping her in a senseless heap atop the remnants of her precious Berry.

The rage was not on Erkani as it had been when he throttled Xeres Elektros, so he did not use the lamp to bludgeon the woman after she fell. Pausing only to scoop up the fallen rubies and to pluck the ruby bracelet from her wrist, the thief fled the bedroom and left the house by the front door, hurrying down the hedged path until he reached the iron gate, which he pushed open onto the street. His heart was beating fast, but there were no cries from the house. He glanced around. Seeing no one coming in either direction, he stopped and quickly fed the rest of the rubies to the lamp. *Hiding the evidence...* He knew the lie for what it was, but he clung to it as he replaced the lamp in the satchel at his hip.

Surely he was in control. He, Al'Atin Erkani, master of the lamp and all its glorious promise and power.

Surely.

He started walking. A couple of turns brought him into the mercantile district of Harrowgate. He did not quite blend in, but neither did he stand out as anything other than a shabby, dirty, crazed-looking street dweller. People gave him the same berth they gave the homeless and beggars.

He skulked along, his feet leading him down toward the docks, his mind wrestling with the fact that he had robbed fifteen houses and had taken nary a coin to book his passage south.

He was inside the jeweler's before he fully realized he had stopped and opened the door.

The store was small, with a rectangular display case in the center of the floor and another one running along each wall. There was a closed door at the back with "Private" carved in a wooden relief above a small curtained window. Near it, the proprietor—a thin, swart, balding, bespectacled man in a green-striped apron—was busy showing another man a ring on a swath of black velvet.

FEED US! The voice of the lamp pierced Erkani's mind like a spike. He staggered against the glass case, rattling the contents. "You there! Please to have a care!" the proprietor said. Excusing himself from his customer, he came bustling forward, waving a hand at the ragtag man who looked as if he had dragged himself out of the sewers. "You should not be in here! There is nothing for you here."

"Oh, but there is." Erkani smiled a jackal smile that made the jeweler pause.

"What do you want?"

"Rubies," Erkani said. He reached into his satchel and drew forth the lamp, cradling it to his chest. It was hot and growing hotter, like a kettle about to burst to boil.

Doubt and disgust were plain on the jeweler's face. He shook his head. "No barter. Only coin."

"I can pay."

"Even so, you must wait," the jeweler said, edging away from Erkani.

The thief could predict what would happen next: under some pretext, the jeweler would disappear into that private room and from there summon the Watch. "As you see, I am already assisting another customer."

"What customer?"

A bolt of fire speared from the lamp, striking the unsuspecting patron and burning him instantly into bones and soot.

The jeweler staggered backwards. Would have fallen but he struck the counter and it held him upright. His mouth gaped. No sound emerged.

"Rubies," Erkani repeated. The lurid glow from the lamp painted his face demon-red.

"H-h-how m-many?" the jeweler squeaked.

Erkani smiled the jackal smile again. "All of them."

18

"You're a long way from home, Lady Dasani."

Harrowgate's dockmaster was an obese man named Scutt. Argentia knew him from Argo. He had grown a moustache and goatee since last she had seen him. *Gained some weight, too. Didn't think that was possible....* Argentia almost smirked, but the situation wasn't amusing, considering she was part of the reason Scutt no longer worked in Argo. From the hostile look on his fat face she doubted he was going to let bygones be bygones.

"The docks haven't been nearly as efficient since you left," she said, trying flattery.

"That so?" Scutt ran a hand through his thin, gray-brown hair, scratching at something on the back of his pumpkinesque head. "Got nobody to blame but yourself. Was you got me beat me half to death."

"You tried to bribe some people who were looking for me. They decided there was a cheaper way to get the information out of you. How's that my fault?"

Scutt's pale eyes narrowed. "Think it's funny, do you?"

Argentia blew a strand of hair out of her eyes. Through the window behind Scutt, she could see the ships in the harbor, their tall masts lifting like lances toward the low clouds. Erkani might be on one of them, ready and waiting to sail away from Teranor. *Or he's already gone...*

"Look, I'm really sorry about what happened in Argo. I'm here because I need your help. Captain Starker and I are looking for a murderer. We think he may be trying to use one of these ships to escape."

Scutt looked at Starker. "That true?"

"It's a possibility," the captain said grudgingly.

Scutt grunted. "What's it got to do with me?"

"We'd like to see the passenger manifests for the ships in harbor and the ones that just left," Argentia said.

"Nobody sees those without authorization from the Magistrates," Scutt said. "You have that?"

"I'm with him, aren't I?" Argentia gestured at Starker.

"He's not a Magistrate. No offense, Captain."

Starker nodded and smiled. "None taken."

Argentia set her hands to her hips. "Why didn't you tell me this *before* we hiked all the way over here?"

"You didn't ask, did you? Knew exactly what you were doing, didn't you? Besides, it doesn't matter. You can get around a writ from the Magistrates, can't you?"

Argentia understood what this was all about. Starker wanted to force her to use Solsta's Royal Sigul to get her way. It would validate his opinion that Argentia was nothing more than a woman hiding behind the throne's authority to gain her ends. *Screw that....*

"I guess we need to see the Magistrates," she said.

"I guess we do," Starker replied. It took all of Argentia's restraint not to punch him in the mouth. She reminded herself of what she had told Griegvard. Headed for the door.

Mirk, riding on Shadow's back, tugged on her hand. "Mirk is hungry," he complained.

"Aye," Griegvard said. "Could stand a bite meself. Been a busy mornin."

"Later," Argentia said through gritted teeth. She shoved the door open.

Chaotic shouts rang through the air. About a block up from the docks, smoke was pouring out of a storefront. People were clustered around, pointing and yelling, but it was the man running away from the fire that Argentia locked on like a lioness sighting a straggling gazelle.

She recognized him even though it had been three years and more since she had dragged him to the dungeons of Aventar. If she had any doubts, the lamp he was clutching as he ran toward the docks put them to rest.

Argentia's hand blurred to her hip, drawing a small, silver handbow from its holster. The bow had been Carfax's weapon. Made by the ranger at the forges of the cyclopes of the Skystone Mountains, it was full of the cunning and powerful magic of those one-eyed giants.

She steadied her aim with her other hand, her feet coming apart, knees dipping slightly to center her balance. It was a long shot across a wide street, with pedestrians crossing in and out of her line of sight, but for a moment Erkani was in an open space. *I can take him. End this now, before it gets worse....*

Her vision narrowed onto the thief's knee. She felt the red heat behind her eyes as she shut away everything except the shot.

"Hell are you doing?!" Starker grabbed Argentia's wrist.

The handbow discharged a silver blast into the stone at Argentia's feet.

"Are you completely crazy?" Starker shouted. "Give me that!"

"Get off me!" Argentia twisted free of Starker's grip. "It's Erkani, you idiot! The one we're looking for!"

She tried to get another shot lined up but it was too late. Across the square, Erkani's head jerked around at the sound of his name. "NO!" he screamed. Raised the red-glowing lamp with both hands.

A fireball blazed at Argentia.

She dove forward, tackling Starker down beneath her. The flamestrike seared over them. Argentia felt the incredible heat and heard the crackle of burning air as the fireball blew the door of the dockmaster's office into kindling.

"Drim be damned!" Griegvard, staggered by the explosion but still on his feet, swung his huge axe off his shoulders, meaning to charge Erkani. A squealing from the dockmaster's office made him turn. The office was on fire. Scutt was trapped behind his desk, wailing like a pig on its way to slaughter. "Bah!" the dwarf spat, ducking into the burning building. "C'mere, ye sack o' blubber."

Shadow bounded into the street, dodging amid the panicked crowd. Mirk clung to his back, his tiny teeth bared. More fire blazed from the lamp, exploding the street in front of Shadow, throwing people to the ground with the force of its blast, tumbling the big dog over and sending Mirk flying.

Argentia shoved off of Starker just as Erkani scrambled into the street and grabbed a little girl who was tugging desperately at her fallen mother's shoulder. The child screamed in terror. Jamming the lamp against her head, the thief turned toward Argentia. "Drop it or I'll kill her!"

Argentia knew she could take Erkani with a headshot, but she did not know what the lamp would do. *Ralak never said anything about this!* If it exploded when Erkani died, the girl was dead, too.

"Drop it!" Erkani screamed.

Argentia crouched, set the handbow on the ground, and then slowly stood up. "Let her go," she said.

Erkani cackled. "I don't think so." Moving sideways, keeping Argentia ever in sight, he dragged the screaming girl across the dock toward a ship with its gangplank lowered. "Everyone keep away! Just keep away from me!" he shouted at the sailors and workers who had rushed out to investigate the fire and the chaos on the street. Some of the sailors had weapons, but no one did anything. They had seen the power of the lamp.

Erkani was up the gangplank now. The girl was finally beginning to struggle, but Erkani struck a sharp blow to her head with the lamp and dragged her past the rail and out of sight behind the mainmast.

A Watch patrol raced into the square, weapons drawn. Starker ran to meet them. After a moment of shouting back and forth, the whole group headed for the ship.

"Wait!" Argentia scooped up her handbow and sprinted to intercept them. "You can't just storm the ship! What about the girl?"

"We know what we're doing," Starker said. "He's trapped on that ship. I'm not letting him get off it." He turned away from Argentia. "You men, cover positions. The rest of you, get ready to board."

"Listen to me!" Argentia grabbed Starker's jacket and wrenched him around. "You go charging up there and that girl dies!"

"Please!" The woman from the street came running up to them, bleeding from a cut high on her forehead. "Don't let him take my Anja!" she shouted. "Anja! Oh Aeton, please don't let him hurt her. Please don't—"

A howl from the ship cut her off. Argentia saw lurid light bloom like a great bonfire behind the mast. *Not good....*

"Aeton's bolts!" one of the Watchmen shouted. "Look out!"

The ship's mooring lines were ablaze. "What in the hell?" Starker shouted. An instant later, the gangplank went up like a log in a hearth. The ship lurched backwards in her berth. "What's happening?"

"You don't want to know!" Argentia shrugged her pack off and backed up. With a running start she thought she could jump the space between the dock and the ship.

Before she could try, a thing appeared at the rail.

It might once have been Al'Atin Erkani, but no more. The face was flattened and blunted. The nose was little more than nostril slits, the brow ridge wide and low over eyes like black fire, the lips broad. The flesh looked pebbled, reptilian, and it had the ruddy cast of rubies or blood. What remained of its hair was a few smoking clumps. Patches of its clothes were on fire, though it did not seem to notice.

It stood there, bent forward at the waist like a hunchback. One red-scaled hand held the lamp. The other had the little girl by the scruff of her dress. For a long moment it stared at the receding dock, as if assessing the Watchmen and their crossbows.

Then it hoisted the girl up and held her beyond the rail.

"She can't swim," the salamander said.

Dropped the girl overboard.

19

Argentia bolted forward.

She heard Anja's mother scream and the Watch crossbows firing and then the end of the dock was there. She sucked in a breath. Dove into the harbor. She had grown up by the sea and was an excellent swimmer. Even hampered by her injured ribs, she used her long legs to propel herself down through the shockingly cold water, orienting on the fast-sinking shape of the thrashing child.

Argentia kicked furiously, angling below Anja. Her lungs were starting to burn but she shut the pain out, twisting around and grabbing the now limp child. She kept kicking, holding fast to the child, rising toward the pale surface, up and up, shapes that looked like people plunging into the water, sinking past her. She breached with a great gasp, gulping in air, keeping Anja's head out of the water. The little girl was unconscious. Not breathing. Argentia covered Anja's mouth with her own, blowing air in. *Breathe*, she willed. *Come on, breathe....*

Anja shuddered and choked and vomited out grayish water, then started coughing and breathing raggedly. *Oh Bright Lady, thank you....* "It's okay, sweetheart," Argentia said, but Anja was still unconscious, and all Argentia could do now was hold her tight as she treaded water. She was too far below the level of the dock to see what was happening there, but she could hear a lot of screaming. Turning, she saw the ship with Erkani on it moving through the harbor. Its sails were aflame, but the fire did not appear to be burning the rest of the ship.

Magic. The lamp.... Argentia looked to the mouth of the harbor and her spirits leaped. Closing in to block Erkani's escape was a battle frigate.

The frigate, the Crown's sun-and-throne pennant snapping from its mainmast, turned broadside to the approaching schooner. "Desist and drop anchor!" a voice from the deck boomed through a hailing horn.

The schooner did not slow. Argentia thought it was going to ram the frigate: a suicidal maneuver. The schooner would never survive the impact with the warship, and even if it did, it would be too crippled to voyage on.

"Turn aside and drop anchor. This is your last warning!" The portals on the frigate's side opened and the cannons slid forward, ready to fire.

Argentia watched the flame-sailed schooner for a reaction. She saw the Erkani-thing scuttle to the prow, clamber all the way to the bowsprit, and stand up amid the lines. It spread its arms. Fire spewed from its mouth as from a dragon's maw.

Oh my God no....

The fireball ripped into the frigate. The middle of the ship simply disintegrated. The schooner plowed through the remains, out of the harbor to the open sea. Argentia did not turn her gaze from it, letting the burning sails etch their image on her memory as they carried Erkani and the lamp away....

"Hoy there! Hold on, we'll get you out." A skiff manned by a couple of sailors was coming toward Argentia. It was one of several small craft in the harbor now: some headed for Watchmen who had leaped in flames from the dock, others for the fast-sinking wreckage of the frigate; if Fortune was kind they might find a survivor or two.

The skiff pulled beside Argentia. "Give her here," the sailor said, drawing the child into the skiff. The huntress hauled herself on board and took Anja back into her arms, huddling there with her while the sailors turned toward the dock. No more than five minutes had passed since her dive into the harbor, but it had seemed much longer to her as she treaded water, helpless to do anything but watch Erkani escape.

"Brave thing you did," the sailor manning the tiller said.

"Thanks." She stroked Anja's blonde hair gently. The child was breathing more normally, but showed no signs of waking. "I just hope she's okay."

"We'll find her a cleric," the first sailor said. "Bound to be a few around by now. Never seen nothin like that in my life. What was it on that ship, some kind of wizard?"

"Something like that." Argentia didn't have the strength to explain. She was exhausted: physically and emotionally spent. She stared at the burning wreckage of the frigate. Felt a flare of anger. *If that jackass Starker hadn't grabbed my arm....*

She knew that was true, but it was also true that Starker had just been doing his job. He was a jackass, but he did not know what Erkani looked like. He had seen Argentia draw a weapon with no warning and aim it across a crowded street. Had she been in his position, she would have done the same thing.

She sighed and closed her eyes. Rubbed Anja's back gently, loving the wet, shivering, alive weight of the child against her. Some good had been salvaged from the disaster. She wondered if Griegvard, Mirk, and Shadow were all right. She had lost track of them early in the fight. "What's the situation on the dock?"

"Bad fire. Lots of Watchmen got burned. Bunch jumped in the water. Don't know what happened to the rest." The sailor shook his head. "Bound to be some were killed, I expect. Damn wizards and their magic. Not natural, I tell you."

"Jep, don't you start your preachin now," the other sailor said. "Let the lady rest. She don't want t' hear it."

"Maybe she does," Jep said sullenly.

"Well *I* don't want to hear it," the other sailor said. "Just shut up and bring us in."

Argentia, her eyes still closed, smiled a little and let the rhythm of the rocking skiff carry her to the dock.

20

"Anja! Oh Aeton, is she all right?" Anja's mother rushed over to meet Argentia as the huntress climbed up the ladder onto the dock.

Turning, Argentia took Anja from Jeb and handed her to her mother. "She needs a cleric— Colla!" She waved to the High Cleric, who was approaching with Griegvard stomping alongside.

"Enjoy yer swim?" the dwarf asked.

"Water's a little chilly," Argentia said, grinning despite the fact that she was dripping wet and freezing cold. She turned to tell Colla to help Anja, but the cleric had already assessed where she was most needed and was laying her hands on Anja's forehead and chest. Argentia saw golden light radiating from between Colla's fingers like sunbeams sifting through a forest.

Anja's eyes opened.

"Hello," Colla said.

"Oh bless you." Anja's mother hugged her daughter tightly. "Bless you both," she said. "You saved her life."

"Take her home now," Colla said. "This is no place for a child."

The dock was a disaster: wounded men being tended by clerics, patches of fire still burning on the stones from Erkani's fire-spitting retaliation against the Watch crossbows. The dockmaster's office had burned to the ground, but not with the dockmaster in it. Griegvard had

carved a path through flames and furnishings with his great axe and
hauled the squealing Scutt outside. The fat man, his clothing charred,
his shiny face blackened with smoke, was still sitting where Griegvard
had dumped him, occasionally lifting his round head to glance at the
smoldering heap that had been his office.

Reinforcements from the Watch garrison arrived too late for
anything but keeping order in the growing crowd and assisting with
the boats bearing bodies back from the water. Clerics summoned from
Coastlight set to work immediately, but there was little they could do for
too many of the injured.

"Seven Watchmen are dead. Many others are likely to die despite our
efforts," Colla said. "This is evil fire."

"Mirk is here." The meerkat looked none the worse for his tumble
off Shadow's back.

"Where were you hiding?" Argentia asked.

"Mirk was not hiding." The meerkat sniffed indignantly. Argentia
laughed, wincing at the pain in her side; the dive into the harbor had
not helped her ribs. "Mirk was trying to help dog. Mirk cannot make
dog get up."

"Shadow?" A surge of panic fired through Argentia's heart. "What
happened? Where is he?"

They found Shadow across from the dockmaster's office. Stone
shrapnel from the explosion where the lamp's fire hit the street had
flayed the Nordic dog. His stormy gray eyes were glazed with pain, and
blood matted his silver-black fur, but he managed to raise his head when
Argentia knelt beside him, and licked her weakly when she pressed her
face to his muzzle.

"Hang on, it'll be all right," Argentia whispered, though she felt a
great dread in her heart. Indomitable Shadow, who had rescued her
from certain death in icy Nord and followed her on her adventures ever
since, looked broken. *No. No you can't die....* The dog had been her closest
companion for the last three years, in some strange way almost filling
the void of Carfax.

I can't think about this.... She looked up at Colla. "Can you help him?
Please...."

"You're asking a cleric to waste her gifts on a *dog?*" Starker said from behind them. The Watch Captain was one of the few soldiers who had not been hurt in the attack. "I don't really think—"

Argentia snapped to her feet. "I don't give a damn *what* you think. If I were you, I'd walk away before you make me wish I'd let that fireball burn you up."

She turned back to Colla. Starker grabbed her shoulder. "You've got a lot to answer for here, and—"

Argentia clamped her hand over Starker's wrist and spun hard, twisting his arm as she turned, breaking his grip. "Don't touch me." She shoved him away. Starker stood there for a surprised moment, his face red as a pomegranate. Then he went for his sword.

Argentia's katana was out before Starker's steel was even a quarter clear of its leather. She slapped the flat of her blade across his hand, stopping his draw. "That would be your worst mistake today."

Starker, clutching his stinging hand, backed away. "Bitch. I don't care how many writs from the Crown you have. I'll—"

"Yer a real slow learner, ain't ye," Griegvard said, stepping forward.

Starker might have had enough bluster and ego to take on Argentia, but he wanted no part of the wild-looking dwarf. His threat unfinished, he stormed away. "Bah! Spineless little weasel," Griegvard muttered, disappointed.

"Forget it," Argentia said. "We don't have time to worry about him. Can you help Shadow?" she asked Colla. "And we need to use the aethergate."

"I will care for him," Colla said. "Go and stop this scourge before it brings more death."

"I'll do my best."

"Aeton's Light guide you."

Argentia bent and kissed Shadow between his eyes. She started to go, but turned back, kneeling beside the dog and reaching behind her neck for the clasp on the chain bearing her dragon's tooth token.

Shadow's head lifted. He loosed a deep growl, so forbidding in tone that it stopped Argentia before she could unfasten the chain. Only when she had lowered her hands did Shadow lower his head again. "Okay, okay," Argentia said. "But you'd better be alive when I get back."

"Where're we goin now?" Griegvard asked.

"Argo. We need a ship."

"Somethin wrong wit th' ships here?"

"You saw what Erkani did to that frigate. Even if we caught up with him, we can't take him on ship-to-ship. Not with that fire. We need to get ahead of him and be waiting when he arrives."

"Ye know where he's bound?"

"I've got a hunch."

21

"Welcome home, Lady Dasani," Ikabod said.

The butler was waiting outside the aethergate chamber in Argo's Wavegard Cathedral. He was closer to eighty winters than seventy, but his carriage was unstooped. The gray jacket and black pants of his livery were impeccably starched and neat on his tall, thin frame. His hair was still the color of iron, neatly trimmed and slicked to his lean head. A black patch covered the empty socket where Argentia's enemies had gouged one of his eyes out.

"Ikabod." Argentia embraced him fondly. The butler had served in her family since before she was born. He was all she had left now, as dear to her heart as a father. "How are you?"

"Well, Lady. The *Reef Reaver* is in harbor, ready to depart. Will you be coming to the house?"

"I think I'd better. I have a feeling this is going to be a long hunt."

"Very good, Lady." Ikabod inclined his head and gestured toward the door. "The carriage is waiting. Master Gynt, it is a pleasure to see you again."

Mirk tugged on Ikabod's pants. "Mirk is hungry. Cruel Lady promised to feed Mirk many hours ago."

"I heard that," Argentia called from the front of the procession.

Argo spanned the Dimrythil River on a great bridge of magically reinforced white marble. Most of the city was constructed of the same material, earning it the sobriquet The White City. It was Teranor's largest and wealthiest port, its inimitable market square and mercantile district dominating the convex streets of the bridge, while its residential areas sprawled on the hilly banks of the river.

Dasani manor, like most of the noble estates in Argo, was set well back from the city on a hilltop west of the river. A winding drive of white gravel lined with beautiful crimson pear trees led past manicured gardens to a turnabout encircling a three-tiered marble fountain decorated with the Dasani lion crest.

Beyond was the manor itself, with its columnar facade and great bay windows glittering in gray stone. Argentia was pleased to see the white wisteria was beginning to grow in on the walls. Her ancestral home had been destroyed in an explosion meant to end her as well. She had rebuilt the manor faithfully to the original architecture, but some of the finishing touches, like the wisteria and the gardens, were necessarily works in progress.

The great doors were flanked by lion statues and bore bronze lion-head knockers. Beyond them, much of the interior also had been reconstructed to mirror the home as Argentia remembered it from her childhood, with a few embellishments. Her favorite of these was her bath chamber, complete with a shower of her own design and a sunstone bench. She intended to make good use of that room tonight, but the one that was most important to her now was the study.

It was in the same spot where her father's study had been and had the same shelf-lined walls, though not so crammed with books; Argentia loved to read, but she had not had time to fill out a new library after the fire. It was also absent her father's collection of maps showing the shipping routes and tradeways that were the keys to the Dasani fortune. Those had been destroyed with the original manor and Argentia, who could not stand the clutter that came with so many maps anyway, took advantage of the circumstances to make an improvement. Instead of dozens of rolled parchments, she commissioned a single map to be engraved beneath glass on her desktop. It showed Teranor, the waters around it, and the known lands across those seas. All the trade routes were clearly marked, as well as the chief exports from various ports.

The map was the reason she had come home. She studied it until she found what she was looking for. With a little help from Ralak, she would learn if her hunch was right.

She raised the Archamagus by oculyr. "We had word of a frigate destroyed by fire in Harrowgate's harbor," Ralak said without preamble when the mists in the crystal ball cleared. "I take it things are not going well?"

"You might say that."

Ralak's only discernible reaction when Argentia told him what had transpired was a quick touch of his tongue to his lips and three brief nods. "How can I be of service?"

"Can you track the ship with your magic?"

"I already am. Heading due south."

Argentia looked at the map again and smiled. Her hunch was not confirmed yet, but it was clearly a possibility. "Can you warn all other ships to keep clear?"

'Of course."

"Good. I need you to tell me more about this lamp. Where did it come from? Who imprisoned the aefryt in it to begin with?"

"The aefryt, obviously, is a fire spirit. It was summoned by Balabia, a magus from the kingdom of Makhara, who bound it to the lamp."

"What can it do—besides light things on fire?" Argentia asked.

"Among other things, aefryts have an unerring sense of where precious gems—especially rubies—are buried. In addition to their fiduciary value, such stones are useful to spell-casters in harnessing the aether."

"So this Balabia summoned an aefryt to be his personal divining rod?"

"I do not know why he summoned it at all," Ralak said. "Greed? Power? I can only speculate on the reasons why one might do such a thing. I know only that my brother traced the origins of the lamp to Balabia of Makhara, from whom it was later stolen, sold, lost, found, and bandied through the centuries before finally coming into Relsthab's possession, from whence it was stolen by Erkani, recovered by you, and now stolen by Erkani again."

"Speaking of Erkani, when an aefryt takes possession of a host, does it alter the host's shape at all?"

"Yes," Ralak said. "Aefryts are notoriously prideful. Even the lowliest of them, where the salamander counts its rank, disdain any shape other than their true form. All they require from their host is the physical shell to reshape." He paused for a moment, and then added, "Why do you ask?"

"I don't think it's taken full possession of Erkani yet."

"Ye sure, Red? Looked pretty damn monstrous t' me. N'er seen a human could spit fire like some damn dragon," Griegvard said.

"Oh, it started to take him. But that body was still essentially human."

The dwarf shrugged his broad shoulders. "Don't see how it much matters. Gotta kill it anyway."

"It matters."

"Why?"

"The transformation was incomplete. That means the salamander's not free yet."

"Go on," Ralak said. His dark eyes were full of challenging curiosity.

"To get free it needs more rubies."

"Rubies?" Griegvard said.

"The last time I hunted Erkani down, he was stealing rubies everywhere he could find them. I didn't understand the reason for the compulsion but I think I do now—providing I'm right about one thing. Ralak, if magi can use gems to harness the aether, can a salamander use them that way too?"

"Yes. A salamander is an elemental creature, and elemental magic has an affinity for certain stones: sapphires for water, diamonds for air, emeralds for earth, and rubies for fire."

"There you go, then. The salamander is hoarding rubies, converting them into the aethereal energy it needs to break the hold of the lamp. Now, anybody want to guess what one of the chief exports of Makhara is?"

"Mirk will guess shiny red stones," the meerkat ventured.

"Prize to you. Makhara exports more rubies than all the other Sudenland kingdoms combined."

Ralak appraised Argentia silently for a moment. For some reason—call it a wizard's arrogance—he still was sometimes surprised that there was more to Argentia than a quick mouth and a quick blade. "Well reasoned, Lady Dasani," he said. "Sail for Makhara. I will keep you apprised of Erkani's progress. He is moving at speed, but you should be well ahead of him."

"Thanks, Ralak." Argentia waved her hand over the oculyr. The crystal ball went dark. "We'll leave in the morning," she said to Griegvard.

"Whyn't just leave now?"

"No ship can sail out of Argo Harbor after dark," Ikabod said. "The seawall is too hazardous."

"Well, *almost* no ship," Argentia said.

"Ye done it?" Griegvard asked.

"Under duress. I was on the run from the Watch. Another misunderstanding."

"Ye seem t' have a lot of those."

"Funny. Anyway, we're leaving in the morning because I want to, not because of the seawall. Trust me, after three weeks on a ship, you'll thank me for tonight."

22

Argentia gave Griegvard a tour of the manor while Ikabod prepared dinner. The dwarf was most impressed with the glass-walled training room at the back of the house: a rectangular chamber with bamboo mats on a hardwood floor. Wooden practice pylons—tree-like trunks with arms at various levels that swiveled on weighted bases—purchased through her friends in Argo's Watch were spaced about the floor. All of them were worn and battered. Tables and racks of weapons, all polished and honed, lined the wall opposite the glass. There was a row of suits of armor supported by steel poles. The breastplates and faceplates of the armor were full of charred holes. "For the handbow," Argentia explained. "Straw targets catch fire."

At the rear of the chamber was a separate bamboo mat, just wide enough for one person to stand or kneel on, set before a sculpture of speckled, silver-gray stone: two waist-high, twisting posts, carved like pillars of flame, spaced about three-feet apart on a smooth white marble slab. Argentia unfastened the belt holding her katana over her shoulder and reverently set the weapon to rest on its stand.

They headed out one of the glass doors onto a stone patio overlooking a rolling expanse of green lawn. Argentia went down the steps, kicked off her boots, and strolled barefoot out into the grass, enjoying the springy warmth beneath her feet and the evening sun on her face. Mirk chased brightly colored lepidoptera and Griegvard studied the walls of the house with a master mason's eye. "Good work. Not dwarf good, mind ye, but fer humans, they had some feel fer th' stone," he said when Argentia returned from her walk, which had taken her past her parents' gravestones to the edge of the wood behind the house.

"Thanks. It better be good. It cost a small fortune."

A bell rang. "Food?" Mirk asked, whiskers twitching hopefully.

"Yes," Argentia said.

"Mirk is starving!" The meerkat raced back into the house. Argentia and Griegvard followed, and they all enjoyed a hearty meal of blue crabs and rare emerald oysters from the cold waters off the coast of Cyprytal. Argentia matched the food with a dry white wine from the same isle. Afterwards they sat around drinking caf and eating fresh fruit and sweet cream on shortcakes, talking about everything but what lay ahead.

Ninth bell tolled in the city. The group broke up for the night. Argentia went to her chambers and took the black velvet swath off the small oculyr on her nightstand. "Colla," she said. The crystal swirled. A few moments later the High Cleric appeared.

"How's Shadow?" Argentia asked. The house felt strangely empty without the big dog. All day long, Argentia had not been able to clear her mind of the image of Shadow laying in the street, panting and bloody and unable to rise—though she did hear the echo of his growl when she had tried to give him her token and told herself he had some strength left if he could do that.

"Resting," Colla said. "He was badly hurt but with Aeton's grace, he will be well."

Thank God.... Argentia felt the frightful serpent that had coiled around her heart unwind. "I owe you, Colla."

"Nonsense. I raised many sheep before being called here, remember? I know what you're feeling."

"Thanks. Can you keep him for awhile?"

"As long as you need me to."

Argentia thanked Colla again, covered the oculyr, and headed for her bath, stripping as she walked. Last to go was the binding cloth about her torso. She had an ugly bruise beneath her left breast courtesy of Temrun's boot, but her ribs were not tragically painful. *Been worse...*

The bath chamber was a huge room of mottled pink and gray marble. The right-hand corner was the toilet, cordoned off by a short marble wall from a porcelain pedestal sink and a wrought-iron rack of fluffy towels and scented soaps and lotions. Along the left-hand wall was a wide marble bench beneath an array of sunstones. The center of the floor was a big sunken tub. Beyond it, the back of the chamber was a glass-partitioned shower: lion-head spouts were set on the three marble walls.

Argentia ran the tub and stepped into the shower, vigorously washing her long, thick hair and shaving carefully. When the tub was full and steaming, she dumped in a few handfuls of rose petals from a jar on the rack and sank in after them. It was going to be a long time before she saw another tub or shower. She intended to make the most of hers tonight.

She dozed for better than an hour, the water up to her neck, her head tilted back to rest against the rim of the tub. When she had soaked enough, she rose and climbed the steps out of the water, touched the control gem activating the row of sunstones in the ceiling, threw a towel from the rack onto the bench, and padded to the shower again, her wet hair heavy on her back.

She turned the sprays on cold, spread her hands against the glass wall, and let the streams hit her from left, right, and behind, until she was shivering. Invigorated, she stepped from the shower into the warm embrace of the heated towel, drying herself slowly while the steam cleared out.

Sitting at her vanity, she brushed her hair free of tangles, tied it off in a long, slick ponytail, and slipped into a blue silk robe with a dragonfly embroidered on the back. The design was the same as the tattoo given to her by Toskan: her first blademaster, her first lover, and her first relationship to end in blades and blood. Her mind flashed on the attack outside Aventar, reminding her that though the tattoo itself was gone now—burned away along with every other scar and imperfection by the dragonfire and the elf magic that had restored her—she had yet to break whatever cursed Fortune made her dalliances into disasters.

Shoving the thought aside, she went down for a cup of tea and sat in her study, checking the trade routes again. There were plenty of other places in the Sudenlands where rubies could be found, but none of them had the resonance of Makhara. It just felt right to her, and Argentia had long ago learned to trust that instinct when she was on the hunt.

Midnight was drawing nigh when she finally doused the light and went up the spiral staircase connecting the study to the sitting room annexing her bedchamber. She had a gift of being able to sleep hard and fast under almost any circumstances. She could remember only one completely sleepless night—when Carfax had died—and one period of months after the Battle of Hidden Vale when she was haunted by a nightmare of being burned to death by a dragon: a terror spawned from survivor guilt that had almost become eerily prophetic. Other than that, when her head hit the pillow, she just shut down.

Tonight was no exception. It did not matter that another hunt was beginning in just a few hours or that she was facing an enemy the likes of which she had never faced before. She just stripped off her robe, slipped naked under the cool silk sheets, closed her fist around the dragon's-tooth token at her throat, and slept.

23

The *Reef Reaver* was the envy of every ship owner, captain, and mate in every harbor where she dropped anchor. A black-hulled, black-sailed, three-mast schooner, she was sleek and fast and had sailed the most dangerous waters of Acrevast, first as a pirate ship and then as a pirate hunter.

"Mornin', Cap'n," Dorn Ironclaw said, nodding his bristly, gray-haired head as Argentia, Griegvard, Mirk, and Ikabod entered the Dasani berth at Argo's sea dock.

It was early. The mist was still on the water. The air held the fresh chill particular to seaside climes before the sun was much above the horizon. Argentia, dressed for the road in her customary black buckskins, boots, and a sleeveless white cotton halter, shivered as she waved to the First Mate. "Hey, Dorn. Good to see you."

Dorn was a big, brawny former captain in Harrowgate's Watch who brought the discipline of the barrack to the deck of the ship. The crew mostly hailed from the Sudenland kingdoms. They were wildly attired—at heart, they were still the pirates they always had been—but somewhere on their outlandish garb was sewn the insignia of the Crown, marking them as lawful servants of Solsta's realm. To a man they had been with the *Reaver* before Argentia came to own her; their respect for her was a thing she had earned battling storms and dangers beside them on the wide waters.

Argentia was a born sailor. Her father had taken her to sea many times when she was a child, and some of her fondest memories were cruising along Teranor's coast, all her intensity focused on her father's lessons of lines and sails, winds and currents. She loved the sea. Its vast expanses and unfathomable power made her feel small and humble and good to be a part of something so much greater than she could conceive.

She bid farewell to Ikabod. Followed Griegvard and Mirk up the gangplank. Made the rounds with the crew, shaking hands and chatting with the men. Griegvard leaned on the rail, his pack between his boots, pipe clenched and smoking between his teeth, and watched Argentia's easy way of assuming command. He had a dwarf's natural suspicion of humans; at a glance this crew looked like the worst sort of cutthroats and rogues, but he knew them from previous voyages to be true to a man.

"Come on," Argentia said, waving at him from near the mainmast. "I'll show you your cabin."

"Nah. Sleep in th' commons, like th' rest," Griegvard said.

Argentia shrugged. "Okay."

"Mirk will sleep in commons, too."

"Oh no you won't. You're staying with me," Argentia said. From the gleam in the meerkat's amber eyes, she could tell he had been envisioning a rich plunder of scrimshaw and doubloons from the crew. "Come on."

Mirk pouted but followed Argentia obediently to her cabin on the second deck. A few minutes later, the *Reaver* set her black sails and glided out of the harbor, heading south across the White Sea to hunt down Al'Atin Erkani and his lamp.

PART II

Sea of Fire

24

Doldrums.

The *Reef Reaver* rocked on the vast, still waters of the Sea of Schisimer. She was ten days out from Argo, just about half way through her journey to Makhara, and going nowhere. The wind had vanished, leaving the schooner's black sails drooping at Fortune's mercy.

The crew, all veterans of the doldrums, knew there was nothing to do but wait. They had ample supplies and busied themselves as idle seamen were wont, scrimshandering and contesting with daggers and harpoons and crossbows at various targets.

One day turned into two and then a third.

Argentia remained outwardly at ease, participating in the sports when the mood took her—she also practiced with her katana every day, the ache in her side growing less and less until it hardly inhibited her movements at all—sharing in the various duties of the ship, and doing what she could to keep morale high.

Privately, she was concerned that they were losing all the time they had gained. She had Ralak tracking Erkani's ship. It was still heading south, but they had been nearly out of reach of the oculyr's enchantment when the winds died; once they got moving again, it would only be a few days before all communication with the Archamagus ceased.

"We'll be in uncertain waters then," she muttered, smiling bitterly at her pun.

"What're ye babblin about?" Griegvard asked. They were in Argentia's cabin, playing chess. The dwarf was a canny player; in the dozen or so matches they had played, Argentia had yet to best him and she was no slouch at the game.

"Nothing. Just thinking out loud."

"Ye talked t' th' meerkat yet?"

"No. And don't tell me you believe he's responsible for this, too. He's caused enough trouble, but staying the winds is a bit out of Mirk's league."

Griegvard shrugged his broad shoulders. "Some o' yer crew're fer thinkin it's a mite coincidental. Keep talkin o' some fable where a sailor shot some big damn bird and brought misery on his ship."

Argentia moved a cleric diagonally down a row of white squares, taking one of Griegvard's knights. "Check," she said. "I didn't shoot Mirk." *I would have liked to, though....*

Argentia and Mirk had not spoken since the night before the *Reaver* entered the doldrums. She had called Mirk into her cabin after dinner. "Time for Mirk's prize?" the meerkat asked.

"What?"

"Mirk's prize for guessing red stones came from...Mak...from far away place on map."

"Oh. No, that's not what I wanted you for." Argentia put a pot of water over the small hearthstone in the corner of the well-appointed cabin and took her pouch of esp out of a teak cabinet.

"Mirk have esp?" He scampered up on an antique sea desk, perching on the small writing platform to supervise the grinding of the beans.

"Sure. If you answer a question."

"What question?"

"What are you doing here?"

The meerkat scrunched his fuzzy face. "Lady asked Mirk to come to cabin."

"I mean here on this ship. Why were you following me that morning in Duralyn?" Argentia posed the question merely to satisfy her curiosity.

She had all along suspected there was more to Mirk's sudden appearance than his simple tale to Solsta.

"Lady is going on adventure. Mirk wanted to come." He put on his most innocent face, but Argentia had seen it before. She did not like the fact that she was seeing it now.

"Stop. No games. Tell me the truth."

"That is—"

"Mirk." Argentia shook her head forbiddingly. The meerkat's posture slumped. He tilted his head, looking up at her with wet amber eyes.

"Mirk is sorry," he said.

Here it comes.... She wondered what mischief the meerkat had left behind him in the palace and if Solsta or Ralak, one or the other of whom was bound to have been involved in some way, had discovered it yet. "What are you sorry about?"

"Mirk did not mean to make lamp fall down."

"Lamp? What— Wait. *The* lamp? The one Erkani stole from Ralak's tower?"

"Evil lamp, yes. Mirk was trying to get shiny stone from same shelf and knocked lamp on floor."

Argentia swore. "And what happened? Mirk—*what* happened?"

Mirk rubbed his paws together nervously. "Mirk thinks monster in lamp woke up when lamp fell on floor."

Argentia was silent. She did not doubt that Mirk was telling the truth—the meerkat was a magical animal with a proven affinity for things of the aether—she just could not believe what she was hearing.

"Mirk is sorry," the meerkat repeated.

"No. Sorry's not good enough this time. People are *dead*, Mirk. Innocent people. They're dead because of the thing that you woke. Because you had to go sneaking around in Ralak's rooms."

"Mirk knows this!" His chirruping voice rose as high as it could in response to Argentia's berating and his whiskers trembled. "Mirk came to help catch lamp. Cruel Lady does not have to yell at Mirk and make him feel worse!"

The meerkat bounded off the desk and raced from the cabin. That was the last time they had spoken. *Let him stew*, Argentia thought. She knew Mirk had meant no harm to come from his mischance in the tower, but that was just the problem. Mirk was one of those impulsive creatures that never intended ill but frequently caused it through his thoughtlessness and then skated past, unaffected by the strife his actions inflicted on everyone else around him.

And I have to clean it up, as usual, Argentia groused. Mostly she took Mirk in stride, but every once in a while his behavior infuriated her. *He never learns. That's the worst part. He just goes and does whatever he wants like some selfish child....*

It was not fair of her to think that, she knew. Mirk was a good and loyal friend; if his ingenuity and subtle ways occasionally made for trouble, they more often than not proved useful. Argentia owed him her life at least twice and he had saved her companions several times as well. But that night in her cabin it was not in her to forgive him for his accident with the lamp and her bitterness held out against her conscience until Griegvard put the question to her over the chessboard.

The dwarf said no more about it after Argentia's deflection, but when the game was over (he beat her soundly again), she went to find the meerkat. She did not believe Mirk had anything to do with the *Reaver* sitting idle on the sea, but she did believe she owed him an apology.

25

Argentia found Mirk sulking in the crow's nest.

"Leave Mirk alone," the meerkat piped when he saw Argentia ascending the mast. "Mirk does not want to talk to cruel Lady." But he did not run away, though he was more than capable of scampering down the mast or using any of the lines or limp sails as highways.

Argentia levered herself up onto the top platform and climbed into the nest. "Aeton's bolts, it's hot up here." The sun in the blue sky seemed to be broiling directly above them. "Why don't you come down?"

"No," Mirk said peevishly.

"Look, I'm sorry about what I said, okay? I know what happened was an accident. I know you feel bad and I know you came to help make it right."

"Mirk told Lady all this already."

"What else do you want me to say?" Argentia spread her hands.

"Mirk does not want Lady to say *anything*—especially not to Mistress or Red Wizard. Mirk would be turned into worm for certain."

"*That's* what you want? My silence?"

Mirk nodded.

"You're unbelievable."

"Mirk knows this."

Argentia started laughing. "All right. Our secret. You have my word."

She extended two fingers and Mirk shook them in both paws. "Now can we go down?" she asked, shoving her hair off her damp forehead. "I'm gonna drown in my own sweat in a minute."

So Argentia and Mirk were reconciled. That night the wind rose and the *Reef Reaver* started on her course again. "Told ye t' talk t' th' meerkat," Griegvard said at breakfast the next morning.

"Horseshit," Argentia retorted, setting down her mug of caf. "Mirk, tell him you didn't have anything to do with the wind."

The meerkat licked his paws clean of duskberry jam. "Mirk most probably did not have almost anything to do with wind," he said loudly enough so the crew gathered in the galley could hear him.

"Mirkholmes!" Argentia exclaimed.

With a wink of his amber eye, Mirk scampered away. "He had nothing to do with the wind," she said to the crew.

"Aye, Cap'n," Dorn replied. But Mirk's ploy was wholly successful. For the rest of the voyage the crew treated him with talismanic deference that the meerkat parlayed into many pieces of scrimshaw, a few coins, extra food, and the occasional thimble of rum.

Unbelievable, Argentia thought.

26

They raced south, sailing hard, making up what time they could. Six days later, they angled their course across the mouth of Talon Bay, heading west toward Makhara. Argentia was reading in her cabin when there came a knock on the door. "Come in," she said.

The door opened. Dorn gave her a nod; it was the closest thing she would permit to a salute. "Cap'n? Sorry to disturb you, but I think you should see this," he said.

"What is it?"

"It's...better if you just come."

He's afraid... Argentia had never known her first mate to be afraid of anything. She marked her page in her book, swung her feet to the floor, and followed Dorn topside.

The ship without sails floated with the currents. Even if Argentia had not recognized its markings from Harrowgate, one look at the charred masts left no doubt that this was Erkani's ship.

Question is, where's Erkani? There was only one way to learn. Argentia refused to allow the *Reaver* to close within striking distance, fearing what might happen to her ship. She and Griegvard and Mirk took the lowering boat, the dwarf rowing with powerful strokes across the water between the two almost idle vessels.

As they approached, Argentia felt her nerves rising. There was something decidedly eerie about the skeletal, blasted ship. She remembered all the tales she had heard about haunted vessels with phantom crews and invisible sails rolling into ports amid cloaks of fog to ravage the city and vanish before the sun rose.

"Suren a ghost ship," Griegvard said as he drove them closer.

"What are you, reading my mind?" Argentia kept her eyes trained on the deck, watching for the slightest motion. She remembered all too well what had happened in Harrowgate when Erkani unleashed the fire of the lamp. They were vulnerable targets in the boat. She did not like the trapped feeling. *Hurry the hell up*, she thought, wiping at her lip with her thumb.

They came into the shadow of the *Wave Leaper*, closing until the ribbed hull rose like a wall, blocking out the sky. Griegvard turned the boat and bumped them gently against the ship's side. Argentia fastened a line. "Mirk," she said. "Go first. See if anything's up there. And be careful."

"Mirk will be careful." Checking his little sword, the meerkat jumped onto the *Wave Leaper's* side and scampered up a mooring line. When he reached the top he vanished for a moment, then reappeared and waved to Argentia.

Argentia started climbing. The side of the ship was slick beyond purchase, so she had to haul herself hand-over-hand, pinching the rope between her boots to help herself along. She felt like a caterpillar crawling up an endless blade of grass.

Mirk lingered by the rail for a bit, then vanished again. "Mirk!" Argentia hissed as loudly as she dared. She hung still, waiting for him to reappear. When several long seconds passed without a sign of the meerkat, she cursed under her breath and started climbing again. Griegvard was behind her now; she could feel the tension in the rope as the dwarf added his stony weight to the line.

Almost to the top, still with no sign of Mirk. Argentia caught the rail and chinned herself up until she could peek over the side. Seeing nothing in the immediate area, she took a deep breath and shoved upward, planting a foot on the deck and springing up and over the rail. Her katana was in her hand before her boots hit the ground. She swept a glance everywhere.

Empty decks.

"Mirk!" she whispered. *Where the hell did he go?*

She waited for Griegvard to clamber over the rail and free his axe from the sheath across his back. They started forward together. The ship's deck was deserted. Lines on the foredeck sails, which had not been touched by the strange fire that drove the ship from Harrowgate, swung in the breeze. How long that blaze had burned Argentia did not know, but she could smell the charred wood of the mast, which rose blackened but still intact toward the azure sky. It reminded her of the way her skin had looked after the dragonfire. She shuddered.

"Takes a lot o' heat t' do that," Griegvard said, following Argentia's gaze. The dwarf, like most of his race, was a master smith. "Concentrated fire. Burns so fast an' hot it fuses."

Just what I wanted to hear... Argentia was still not quite good with fire after her experience with the dragon in the wizard's tower. Cooking flames and torches and the like were fine, but monsters that used fire as a weapon... *Come on, Gen. Get it together...* She blew a stray strand of hair out of her eyes and put on a brave face. "So when we find him, don't get burned. That's what you're telling me?"

Griegvard's blonde beard parted in a huge smile. "Aye. Now let's go get 'im. If he's still here."

"He's here," Argentia said. When she was in Argo—which was not very often even after she had rebuilt her home—she sometimes liked to take one of her ships out alone to spend the night anchored beyond the seawall with a book and a bottle of wine. She enjoyed the solitude of knowing she had the whole ship to herself, with only the seeming endless ocean around her, the infinite stars above her: a sense of space so impossibly vast it became intimately private.

This ship's emptiness felt wrong to her. The same eeriness that had gathered around her as they rowed over had only grown once they set foot on the ship itself. There was something oppressive in it. Something dangerous. There might be no one on the deck, but there was someone on the ship. *I'm sure of it....*

"Mirk is here!"

They spun around to see the meerkat racing toward them. "Where did you go? I told you not to run off," Argentia whispered.

"Mirk did not run. Mirk walked very quickly."

Argentia shook her head in exasperation. "Where did you go?"

"Mirk went down." Mirk pointed to the hatchway and the steps descending into the hold.

"Did you see anything?"

As Argentia spoke, the dark of the hatchway flared like sunrise in the Fel Pits.

"Mirk thinks we should leave now," the meerkat said.

But it was too late.

27

Al'Atin Erkani was going insane.

Huddled in the hold of the *Wave Leaper*, gnawing at his already ragged fingernails, wracked with fever, he could do nothing except clutch his precious lamp to his emaciated chest. The picked carcasses of two rats, charred to their tiny bones, sat unnoticed beside him, drawing black flies whose incessant buzzing also went unnoticed.

Erkani had little recollection of almost anything that had transpired since his aetherwalk to Harrowgate. He remembered knocking out (murdering) the wizard and stealing rubies to fill (feed) the lamp, but how many homes he had robbed and whether he had encountered anyone he could not quite say. He thought there had been a dog in one house, and possibly a woman. He did remember setting fire to the jewelry shop and running into the street, and he recalled with perfect clarity that the redheaded bitch Argentia Dasani had somehow been there. Whether the corpse he had seen had been a deception or whether she was arisen from the grave like some avenging divae he did not know. But he knew she had come for him. Come to steal his lamp again and haul him back to rot once more in the cell beneath Castle Aventar.

Wrath at the unfairness of it all had risen in him when he saw her across the street. He would not be taken. He had used the lamp's power—it felt as if he had channeled his hatred and fury into the bolts of fire that came from the antique vessel—and he had fled, only to have his enemies pursue him and bay him and force him to take a child hostage in his retreat to the ship.

Huddled behind the mast, he had sunk to his knees and shoved the sniveling brat down. He was trapped. They would storm the ship and not even the power of the lamp would preserve him.

They will not—if you heed us! Bazu's voice impelled him.

"What can I do?" Erkani groaned.

Release us....

"How?"

Rub thrice the lamp. Do it and we will save you....

Erkani heard the shout to surrender from the Watch on the dock. Tittering madly, he rubbed the lamp three times. Its round sides grew burning hot. Alarmed, Erkani tried to thrust the lamp aside, but he could not move. Red smoke and light poured from the mouth of the lamp, engulfing him. He heard the child scream. Or perhaps it was his own scream.

And then....

Then he knew nothing until he had awakened as from a long sleep to find the child was gone, his enemies were gone, and the harbor was gone. He was alone on a ship with sails of flame, tracking across the open sea. He felt immeasurable relief, but at the same time a strange and disquieting sense of violation. Something had clearly happened to him and he could not remember what it was.

Light...heat...nothing.

Except, not quite nothing. There were fragments, like the broken glass of a dream: dropping the child (she can't swim) overboard; breathing fire that devastated a frigate, his body so full of elemental power it seemed to be fire itself.

And then...

Withdrawal. The power rushing out of him, the fire extinguished, leaving him crumpled and shaking on the deck, too weak to stand or crawl, passing in and out of consciousness for hours that turned into one day and another, burned by the sun over the ocean, chilled by the night wind.

Hunger woke him—but not his own hunger.

Feed us! Bazu's voice drummed at his mind until Erkani forced himself awake. It was an unknown time of an unknown day. The ship was still coursing through empty waters—wither bound, the thief had no idea—on sails of sheeted flame. He stared at these from his knees until disbelief released its hold on him. Then he staggered to his feet like a drunk waking in an alley. His eyes felt dehydrated. So did his face: like the skin was stretched too tightly over the bones. There were deserts less parched than his mouth; his tongue was swollen, his lips cracked and blistered with sores.

He was cruelly thirsty, but Bazu hungered and its need rampaged over Erkani's. He fed a few rubies from the bag he had taken from the jewelers into the lamp, dimly aware that the supply had to last him until they made landfall somewhere.

When Bazu had ceased mewling, Erkani crawled down the steps into the hold. It was dark and cool out of the sun. It was also virtually empty.

Erkani had commandeered a ship that had put to port that morning and was not scheduled out again for a week. All her cargo had been offloaded save for some stores of rum and salted pork. Erkani found those barrels, but he was too weak to open them. He would have starved, but a rat came to investigate him as he lay prostrate before the implacable oak containers. He snared the rodent with pickpocket speed, squeezing the hot, greasy, squirmy body until he felt things inside it squish and pop and the rat went limp.

He begged a little power from the lamp. Roasted the vermin with a finger of flame, searing the fur, scorching the flesh. He ate it all. It tasted like cinders.

Propped against the barrels, Erkani held the lamp and stroked its warm, curved side, slipping in and out of consciousness. His dreams were haunted by flashes of the monstrous things he had done since escaping Aventar. His waking hours were slave to hunger: both his and the lamp's. He managed to kill and cook another rat and there were still a few rubies left for Bazu, but by the time he was a fortnight out from Harrowgate (he had no knowledge of this interval—in the hold of the *Wave Leaper*, it was always night) the rats were too wise to come near him and the rubies had dwindled to two.

That worried Erkani more than the rats. His mind was not so fractured that he did not understand that something awful would happen if Bazu demanded food and there was nothing left to give it....

Three more days.

Hunger drove Erkani into unconsciousness. The flame sails went idle; the salamander could work its powers through Erkani while he was waking or sleeping, but this sleep was deep beyond Bazu's ken, extinguishing its flame like a snuff to a taper. Within its gilded prison, the elemental thing chafed in sulfurous fury, hungering for more of the stones that were the only way it could gather enough strength to be free.

It was farther from that goal now than it had been since it awakened, for it had been forced to come forth too soon to escape the thief's enemies. The salamander did not know the names or nature of these enemies, only that if they captured Erkani its own plans would also be thwarted. So it had taken possession of Erkani and secured their escape, but at great expenditure of its powers: too great for it to retain its hold on Erkani's body. As the thief collapsed, the salamander's essence was sucked inexorably back into the prison of the lamp. There it languished, so near to escaping, to loosing its fires across the mortal world, devouring all in its path...but now fearful its chosen host might fail it.

It waited, its frustration growing, until it sensed another presence.

Strange magic seized the lamp, threatening to break the connection between Bazu and the thief. The salamander sent its power into Erkani again: sent all the strength it had left. *Awaken! AWAKEN!*

Still unconscious, Erkani felt Bazu's cry in the deepest core of his being. As the lamp left his embrace, pain like a living tooth ripped from its socket galvanized him. His hands shot up toward the lamp, which was floating away from him toward a rat-like creature standing at the foot of the stairs, its tiny paws glowing bright with blue aether.

The thief and the meerkat were locked in a momentary tug-of-war of magic. The savage anger flooded Erkani again. He felt himself kindle with power like a furnace coming to life. He clenched his scrawny hands and the lamp flew back into his clutches.

The last thing Erkani remembered was seeing the meerkat flee up the hatchway. Then the bonfire force of the salamander surging through him burned away consciousness.

The hold filled with firelight and the hunched thing that was both Erkani and not Erkani strode toward the hatchway and sprang onto the deck.

28

Fire blazed from the upraised lamp.

Argentia dove to one side, Griegvard to the other, and Mirk flattened straight down. The fire missed all of them, setting the deck aflame where it struck.

Then it was the street in Harrowgate again: Griegvard charging, Argentia on a knee, triggering her handbow. The silver crescents streaked at the Erkani-thing, but more fire poured from the lamp, this time forming an ovular shield that the Erkani-thing swung in front of it. The aethereal crescents struck the flames and disintegrated into sparks.

Griegvard roared in. The fireshield blocked his axe. Before Griegvard could attack again, the Erkani-thing grabbed the dwarf's beard flung him across the deck.

"Griegvard!" Argentia shouted as the dwarf smashed through the rail and tumbled over the side.

The Erkani-thing leaped for her with terrible speed, the fireshield becoming a morning star whose ball flamed like the pitch load of a catapult. Argentia leaped aside. The ball seared past her, smashing a flaming hole in the deck. She ducked and spun away from two more devastating blows, the deck shattering where the ball struck. She couldn't get her katana around fast enough to counter; the speed and strength of the salamander using Erkani's body were impossible to match.

Mirk harried the Erkani-thing with bolts of magic. If it felt the stinging darts it gave no sign and did not slow its relentless advance.

Argentia retreated before it. The deck was burning and broken in a half-dozen places. The fiery holes gave her a desperate idea. She dodged sideways. Ran a circle around the Erkani-thing, long legs flying as the fire-star blasted down behind her, scorching at her bootheels, singing at her ponytail. She kept a step ahead until she completed the circuit, then veered and sprinted away.

Behind her, she heard a series of sharp cracks. Spun around in time to see the expression on the Erkani-thing's cracked, scaly face change from triumph to surprise—

—and it was gone, swallowed by a gaping hole as the flaming deck gave way beneath it.

"Mirk! Run!" Argentia shouted.

The meerkat was already ahead of her as she sheathed her katana and raced toward the broken rail where Griegvard had gone overboard. The dwarf, soaked and furious, was hauling himself back up the ship's side.

"No, no! Down, go down!" Argentia shouted. "In the boat!"

"What're ye—"

From the bowels of the ship, a howl of rage.

"Aye, mayhap yer right." Griegvard descended, Argentia and Mirk coming fast above him. They clambered into the boat. "Get us out of here!" Argentia said, slashing her dagger through the mooring line.

The Erkani-thing appeared at the rail.

Fire from the lamp slammed the boat. Argentia was flying, falling. Water closed over her. She choked on the ocean. Thrashed toward the surface. Broke through gasping and hacking, wiping at her eyes, disoriented but knowing the thing must be somewhere above her. *Where, wh— Ah, no....*

She sank fast, covering her head with her hands. Fire speared into the water, lancing past her, turning the ocean into a froth of scalding bubbles. She stayed under as long as she could—not very long since she had not fully recovered from choking—and swam closer to the shadowy shape of the *Leaper's* hull to minimize the angle from which Erkani could attack her.

She came up: just her head, blinking furious to clear her vision.

The Erkani-thing was leaning over the rail directly above her, grinning.

Oh shit!

BOOM! BOOM! BOOM!

Cannonfire from the *Reef Reaver* hammered the *Wave Leaper,* rocking the whole ship. The Erkani-thing staggered back from the rail, lurched forward again, roaring, and aimed the lamp at the *Reaver.*

"No!" Argentia shouted. This was why she had forbidden Dorn to engage the other ship. Helpless, she watched the fireball streak from the lamp.

But Dorn had the *Reaver's* sails trimmed tight for maximum maneuverability. He had turned the ship broadside to use the cannons, and immediately after firing had swung her to face the *Leaper.* The fireball still hit, but it was a glancing blast along the curve of the prow instead of a clean strike.

Dorn let the front cannons go, slamming the *Leaper* again. A return blast from the lamp found the foresail, punching a flaming hole through the black cloth and bringing fire to the foredeck. But the *Reaver's* crew was ready with buckets, dousing the flames before they could spread.

Aeton's bolts—is he mad? Argentia watched in growing horror as Dorn kept the *Reaver* moving, tacking boldly forward, coming full tilt, as if he meant to ram the *Leaper.* Two more fireballs struck the ship, but none with the apocalyptic force the salamander had displayed in Harrowgate.

The *Reaver's* front cannons spoke again, this time blasting the deck of the *Leaper,* sending the Erkani-thing sprawling. The lamp skittered from its grasp, rattling and tumbling across the deck. Howling, the Erkani-thing scrambled and pounced on it. When it did, the flamesails burst to life. The *Leaper* surged forward, its wake slamming Argentia, spinning her around, forcing her under.

When she came gasping to the surface again, the *Leaper* was plowing away at a speed not even the *Reaver* could match. Dorn did not try. He brought the black ship around. Argentia could see men battling several fires while others lowered boats to come after her as she bobbed like a cork in the chop.

Okay, all right.... She made herself relax. The battle was over. She caught a decent breath, and then: *Oh Aeton— Where's Griegvard? And Mirk?* The dwarf had been in his armor....

She swiveled around. Spotted Mirk clinging to a piece of driftwood. And there was Griegvard, hanging onto the shattered keel of their wrecked boat. *Thank God....*

Argentia turned to watch the *Leaper* until the fiery sails were lost in the distance. Slapped the choppy water in frustration.

Erkani had escaped her again.

The anger gathered in her, simmering through the whole ride back to the *Reaver*. She went straight for Dorn. "What's the point of my being captain if you don't listen to my orders?" She set her hands on her hips, glowering at the First Mate.

"All due respect, Cap'n, but what's the point of listening to your orders if they're going to get you killed?"

"I had it all under control. What would have happened if that thing had destroyed the *Reaver*?"

"That's the risk we take. No different than when we raid a pirate ship."

She arched a brow. "It's a little different."

He shook his head. "Nah. Catapult could do what that thing did. We've taken worse from pirates plenty of times. I don't see why you wouldn't let us pursue and finish the job."

"You didn't see what it did in Harrowgate. I did. That's why." But she was wondering: the attack on the *Reaver* had been nowhere near the cataclysm that had destroyed the Crown's frigate in Harrowgate. Had she misjudged the salamander? Were there limits to its power? Was she making a mistake now in not chasing it down?

"Well, you're the Cap'n," Dorn said, smirking.

"Wiseass." Argentia shook her head. "Thanks for disobeying."

Griegvard stomped up. He had lost his armor, forced to strip it off or sink after he had gone overboard, but even worse, half his beard was gone, burned away by the furnace grip of the Erkani-thing. What remained ran just halfway down his chest, ending in ragged, singed points. "Be another three-hunnerd years growin back," he grumbled. "Damned if I ain't fer takin e'ry hair out on that thing's friggin head."

"We'll catch him, don't worry," Argentia said.

"Yeah? Why ain't we chasin 'im, then?" They had turned their course south into Talon Bay, foregoing the pursuit.

"Alright, everybody listen to me," Argentia said, getting the attention of the crew. She was not going to explain herself twice. "We're not chasing the *Wave Leaper* for two reasons. One, I'm not sure how much power the thing we're hunting really has. It destroyed a frigate in Harrowgate and I'm not going to risk that we didn't get very lucky just now and catch it with its powers at ebb or something. And two, we just lost the element of surprise—so we're going to make a stop and get it back."

"Where?" Griegvard asked.

"Khan," Argentia said.

29

Three days later, the Floating City appeared on the horizon.

It was aptly named, for it was built on stone platforms where the delta of the Pythos River met Talon Bay. Canals cut the city into squares: dark water flowing around white adobe buildings. There were people everywhere, colorfully dressed in the wraps and scarves of the Sudenlands: a ceaseless tide of trade moving through the bazaar beyond the docks as the *Reaver* pulled into port.

Argentia wiped a forearm across her brow. *I swear it's even hotter than last time....* The air was like thousand dogs panting on her at once. The fact that she was crusty with dried seawater did little to improve her disposition. She had given herself a sponge bath in her cabin, after hanging a blanket across the portal and setting Griegvard to guard the door—the crew were still men, and pirates at that, and she was not in the habit of giving out free shows—but it had hardly helped at all.

To combat the humidity, she knotted her halter below her breasts, exposing her taut, bejeweled midriff and creating the illusion of more comfort. The first time she had come to Khan she had worn a chasubla—a kind of half-cloak common to the Sudenlands—both to hide her weapons, which women were forbidden to bear, and to cover her arms, which women (excepting those in the Sultan's harem) were forbidden to bare.

This time, she was stepping off her ship exactly as she was now: boots, buckskins, halter, katana, daggers, whip, and handbow. *And I don't give a damn what anyone thinks. It's too damn hot to curry cultural favor....*

But as she reached the top of the gangplank, she saw that her defiance would meet with no challenge from anyone in Khan.

Coming toward the ship, his long strides outstripping his retinue of black-uniformed guards, was a tall man somewhat shy of his fortieth winter. His skin was dark, which made his mane of white hair all the more striking. He wore white silk pants in gold boots, and a gold silk shirt, unbuttoned three down, clung to his broad shoulders and muscular chest. A white-and-gold turban crowned his head. He stopped short of the gangplank, waiting silently, brawny arms folded, staring at Argentia as she descended. Only when she dropped to a knee before him and bowed her head did his handsome face lose its stern facade. "What in de Hells're ye doin?" Skarangella Skarn asked.

"Hail, Sultan," Argentia said, peeking her eyes up, her lips twitching in a smirk.

"Get de hell up here." He pulled her easily to her feet, crushing her in a hug.

"Hi, Skarn." She returned the hug just as hard and laughed. "It's good to see you."

"Dat right?" He put her to an arm's length. "Den why'd it take ye de three years t' get back?"

She raised her hands in protest. "Hey, I've been a little busy."

He shook his head. "Three damn years, not one word. Nothin."

Argentia blew a strand of red hair out of her eyes. "Okay—I've been *a lot* busy."

Skarn laughed, flashing his golden teeth. "Dat's me girl. Sounds like ye got de tale t' tell."

Argentia smiled, thinking of the mad chases that had led her all over Acrevast in the time since she had parted company with Skarangella Skarn. "Oh, one or two...."

"De Lady, de Lady!" A child dressed in green and yellow burst from the ranks of the guards, his dreadlocks flopping wildly as he ran to Argentia. "De Lady came back!"

"I promised I would, didn't I?" Argentia caught Demby up and lifted him over her head until he squealed. Setting him down, she ruffed his hair fondly. "You've grown," she said, remembering the street urchin who had befriended her on her first trip here and ultimately followed her and Skarn into danger as they fought to save the sultanate. Now Demby was Skarn's jester, living in the luxury of Mebulkar Palace; Argentia could not have been happier for him.

One of the guards was coming forward, leading an old man in blue robes and a slim woman richly dressed in plum silks, her head wrapped and her face veiled from her eyes to her chin. Argentia knew all of them: the old man, Sanla the meja, was to Skarn what Ralak was to Solsta. The woman was his daughter, Skritlana, a meja of no little art herself.

"Lady Dasani," the guard said, nodding his head. He was taller than Skarn, wiry, with coal black skin. His name was Trokelo. He was Skarn's closest friend and the commander of his guards. "Well met."

"Well met, Trok—and don't call me Lady. You know better."

"Aye. Must've forgot. Been so long since I seen ye." He grinned slyly.

Argentia punched him in the shoulder. "Don't you start too."

Skarn laughed again and motioned to Skritlana, who came beside him. "Ye know de Sultana, of course," Skarn said.

"Still wearin dem boots," Skritlana said with a cluck of disapproval.

"You know it." Argentia grinned. Her boots were precious to her: after her dragon's-tooth token and her katana, they were her most prized possession. She looked at Skarn. "So you finally wised up and married her?"

"What's dat supposed to mean?" Skarn said.

"Come off it. She's been in love with you since forever. I knew that three years ago. How long did it take you to figure out?"

"Me father had to tell him," Skritlana said, rolling her eyes.

"Now dat's de lie and ye know it," Skarn protested.

From the ranks of the guards, a baby cried. Skarn and Skritlana both looked reflexively toward the sound.

Argentia's eyes narrowed. "What was that?" she asked.

"De royal baby," Demby said, clapping his hands.

Argentia looked at Skarn as a nursemaid came forward with an infant swaddled in gold satin. She handed the baby to Skritlana, who fussed with him until he stopped crying. "What?" Skarn asked innocently.

"You know what."

"Deh. You're not de only one been busy. Give me de boy." He took his son from Skritlana. "A male child," he said proudly.

"This is Seibu," Skritlana said, leaning on Skarn's arm.

Argentia cooed over the baby, who had his mother's tan skin and his father's big, dark eyes. Then she remembered something. "Skarn! The law...." On her last trip to Khan, she had learned that an appalling Sormorian law required the Sultana to kill herself after she gave birth to a son, her highest purpose having been thereby fulfilled.

"Skarangella did away wit dat foolishness," Skrit said. "Did away wit de royal harem, too."

Skarn shrugged. "What's de good of bein de Sultan if ye can't change de laws?"

"Oh, Skarn." Argentia leaned in and kissed his cheek. "Well done."

"Deh. I was afraid her father'd turn me into de camel or somethin if I didn't."

"Keep dat talk up and I'll do worse to ye myself," Skritlana said.

They all laughed. Argentia introduced Griegvard, who had been standing patiently at the foot of the gangplank during the reunion, and Mirk, who made quite a stir, especially with Demby.

"De pet talks!" he exclaimed gleefully when Mirk said hello.

"Mirk is not pet," the meerkat huffed. "Mirk is on adventure."

"Remarkable," Sanla murmured. The meja stooped beside the meerkat. His cheeks were dotted and scrolled with tattoos, and he had that ageless air common to wizards about him: he looked to have seen seventy winters, but might have seen seven hundred.

"Uh-oh. Better lock your tower, Sanla," Argentia teased. "Mirk's very fond of magic trinkets."

The *Reaver's* crew was disembarking, led by Dorn. Many of the men shouted Skarn's name. He waved and called back in return. The

Reaver had originally been Skarn's ship. When he first met Argentia, he had been the most feared pirate on the oceans of Acrevast. When they crossed paths again, he had switched sides in a bargain with Ralak and was rapidly making a name for himself as a privateer. Then Fortune called him home to Sormoria to claim the throne. Fearing that having the ship in port would be too tempting a reminder of his days on the open seas, he gifted the *Reaver* to Argentia as payment for her help defeating the Revenant King of Yth.

"So, what's de trouble dis time?" Skarn asked Argentia.

Argentia's mouth opened in a pretty O of mock astonishment. "What makes you think I'm in trouble?"

"So dis is just de social call, den?"

"Well...it's like this...."

30

Mebulkar was a sprawl of golden domes and spires, sapphire ponds and emerald palms.

The passage by gondola along the canals of Khan was still one of the most impressive spectacles Argentia had ever seen, almost rivaling the view of Argo from the White Sea. But death and betrayal had dogged her first visit to Skarn's city and a melancholy rose in her as those memories returned.

Skarn draped a strong arm around her as they passed through the glittering gates of the palace. "No ghosts in Mebulkar, Gen," he said.

"I know." She leaned her head on his shoulder for a moment. "Thanks."

They continued on through bright gardens and a hall of pools whose turquoise waters were accented by gilded lily pads, through the pillared throne hall and into a small audience chamber. Huge pillows and chaises surrounded a low, circular table. Food and wine were brought. They ate, talking of casual things. Argentia avoided telling her own tales and mostly pressed the former pirate for news of his rule.

"He is de born leader," Skritlana said, smiling proudly. "De people trust him."

Argentia knew firsthand how good a leader Skarn was, so she was hardly surprised. She was more curious about his perpetual restlessness.

Like her, he was an adventurer at heart, and he had been concerned that his responsibilities to the throne would make him miserable. But as she listened to his tales of bickering sheiks and selfish merchants trying to steer the throne into decisions that benefited their greed (tales she had heard cousins to many times from Solsta), she sensed that he was amused by politics and not unhappy with his lot.

She suspected that Skritlana and Seibu had a great deal to do with that. Wondered if her own Fortune with men would ever turn, leading her to a similar place in her own life. Part of her hoped so and part of her—the part that heard the call of the road and the whisper of the wild—doubted.

Eventually, the talk turned serious. Argentia and Griegvard narrated the tale of Erkani and his lamp. True to her word, Argentia omitted Mirk's accident in Ralak's tower.

"Can't ye ever chase down de normal people?" Skarn groaned. "It's always got to be dese damn demons and monsters all de time?"

"Erkani's just a thief."

"Deh, but dis lamp he stole wit de salamander sleepin in it, *dat's* not normal."

"Hey, it's a start...."

"Dis is known to me, dis lamp," Sanla said. "Ancient and dangerous."

"Tell us somethin we don't bloody know already," Griegvard said.

"Easy." Argentia said, though she could sympathize with the dwarf's impatience with wizards and their crypticisms. Carfax had practically made a philosophy out of not trusting wizards, and she smiled a little, remembering lounging with him in their bed, laughing uncontrollably as he mocked Relsthab or Ralak with uncanny imitations. "Can you help us?" she asked Sanla. "Find out how we beat it?"

"Perhaps dere is de way," Sanla said. "I must search de scrolls."

"How damn long's that gonna take?" Griegvard muttered.

Sanla looked at him, eyes glimmering. "For a dwarf dat has seen de sun rise on de three hundred and forty three summers, ye are de shameful stranger to patience."

"Bloody thing burned half me damn beard off!" Griegvard snapped. "How much bloody patience do ye expect me t' have?"

117

"Enough so dat when ye meet it again, de way to de victory is known and de rest of ye does not follow de beard," Sanla said, folding his hands into his robes.

Argentia and Skarn exchanged glances. Griegvard caught them. "Bah! Might be he's got a point..."

31

Later that night, the chamber was empty save for Argentia and Skarn. Skritlana had retired, sensing her husband and the huntress had things to speak of that did not involve her. Sanla had gone to his scrolls. Demby and Mirk, two kindred spirits—the urchin had survived by his quick wits and quick hands on the streets of Khan after his parents had died of a plague—had gone to explore the palace. Griegvard had trudged off to his chamber with a bottle of rum.

"How'd ye meet de dwarf?" Skarn asked.

"I actually met him when I went to Stromness for aid against the demons, but I didn't really get to know him until after I left here. Remember I was having that trouble with Vloth and the cat-women?" Skarn nodded. "Well, when I got home from here, Ikabod had been kidnapped. I chased him all the way to Nord. Griegvard and some Norden tribesmen and some Watchmen from Argo helped me rescue him...." Her voice trailed off a little, memories gathering.

"What happened, Gen?" Skarn asked gently.

She was silent for a moment. "It was after we rescued Ikabod," she began. The tale of her capture by Mouradian, who tore her spirit from her body and imprisoned it in a diamond while he used her shape to make an army of simulcra—a tale that ended with her burned by dragonfire— was not one she had found the courage to tell until now. Skarn had always been easy for her to talk to. She trusted him with that trust that is only possible between people who have risked their lives together many times. More than that, Skarn was just a good listener. He never judged without consideration and his indefatigable optimism was impossible to resist.

"I'm guessin dat's not all de tale," he said when she paused. "'Cause if dis is what bein burned by de dragonfire does, I'm goan tell more women t' go find dem lizards. Ye never looked better—and ye know dat's sayin a lot."

"Flatterer." But she was touched. There had never been anything but flirtation between Argentia and Skarn, yet she found his compliment mattered to her more than most. *I chose the wrong brother,* she thought ruefully. *Story of my life....*

For a moment it was on the tip of her tongue to tell him that she had made a mistake when she had briefly involved herself with Calif—a dalliance that had ended as badly as the rest of her affairs when Calif turned traitor and she was forced to kill him to save Skarn—but it had never really been a case of choosing one brother over the other and she did not want to bring up bad memories. Besides, Skarn was clearly happy and in love with Skritlana, and she with him. *And I wouldn't ever want to be a queen—especially not of any place this hot!*

"Deh, ye know it's true. But tell me de rest. What happened? Ye were burned, and den...." Skarn poured more rum for them and motioned for Argentia to continue.

"Dark days," she said. And they had been: the darkest of her life. Worse even than the abyss that had swallowed her after Carfax had died in her arms. "I was hopeless. They told me there was nothing that could be done. No magic known to wizards, no clerical power, no apothecary's potion. Nothing. I was going to look like a goblin for the rest of my life." Bitterness came through, even in remembering.

"So what happened?"

"I ran. Hid on the streets for weeks. Got drunk every night. Rotgut whiskey. And then...someone died. Two people, actually. A nobleman and his wife, caught in a street robbery. I could have saved them. I didn't. I was too busy feeling sorry for myself to care what happened to anyone else."

That had been the bottom. The pit that she would either rise from or be buried in.

She rose.

"After...I kept hearing them shouting for me to help them. The echos...I tried to drink them away too. But I got sick. I've never been sicker in my life."

"It'll do dat," Skarn said. "Nasty stuff."

"Yeah... I guess it's called rotgut for a reason."

"Wasn't talkin bout de drink. Was talkin bout de guilt."

"Oh." All at once Argentia realized what her heart had known all along: that Skarn understood exactly what she was talking about, where she was coming from, and that now, as always, he would not turn from her.

"You're right," she said. "I couldn't stand what I'd become anymore. Not on the outside. On the inside. Who was I? The ruin I saw in every mirror? A monster that fled her friends and left people to die in the gutter? I couldn't accept that. I had to at least try to face what had happened to me and move on. So I did. I got back to Duralyn and then to Frostwood and that's where I...got better."

"Ye keep sayin, but ye still don tell me *how*. What happened?"

Argentia held up the dragon's-tooth token. "Magic."

"But ye said dey told ye...."

"They were wrong. This was elf magic. Deep magic. I don't know... but it worked."

Skarn nodded. He had seen the magic of that token at work before, in a desperate hour in a crypt beneath the Wastes of Yth, when his life and Argentia's life and the fate of Sormoria were in the balance. More, he knew how dear the token was to Argentia; hadn't she almost died to retrieve it after that battle, racing back into the crypt as the whole place was collapsing, willing to lose her life to recover the token? If any magic could have restored her from the ravages of dragonfire, it would have been that.

Argentia blinked, coming back from her reverie. "And look," she said, retrieving her katana and tossing it to Skarn. He caught the scabbard easily, studied the hilt, with the lion's head pommel and the ashwood grips wrapped with red leather. Reverently, he drew the blade partially free, observing the custom among bladesmen that a weapon was only fully unsheathed to draw blood. The sword gleamed with the mellow paleness of true silver. "Mithryl?" he asked.

"From Griegvard's holt. Forged in Frostwood."

"By de elves?"

She shook her head. "By me. Well, the blade. D'Lyrian—he's an elf prince—made the pommel and the grips and the scabbard."

Skarn arched a brow. "Consortin wit de elf princes now?"

Argentia blushed. "Oh shut it. He's just a friend."

"Deh. Whatever ye say, den." He handed the sword back to her. "Gen, dis is perfect. All de smiths of Sormoria couldn't equal it. Where'd ye learn de craft?"

"I don't know. I mean, I had some lessons—just the basics—when I was learning the sword. I never thought I'd ever have to use them. But my katana was lost on Mouradian's isle and I needed a weapon to kill a demon...." She paused a moment, then continued. "There was magic at work with this, too. The sword sort of forged itself. But I think just starting to work on it was the catalyst for...whatever happened to me. I started forging the sword before I was healed, and by the time I was done...I was better."

She could still remember that first sight of herself in the water of the forge's trough: her skin pale and smooth as alabaster, every blemish of thirty-odd winters purged away, her hair red as a cardinal in the summer sun. She had passed out from the shock.

"Gen?"

"Huh?" She had missed whatever Skarn had said.

"De name? Sword like dis, it has to have de name."

"Lightbringer. D'Lyrian called it Lightbringer."

"Lightbringer. And did ye kill de demon with it?"

Argentia grinned. "Of course."

Skarn laughed. "Dat's me girl. Ye think it can kill dis salamander thing too?"

"If I can get close enough to use it."

"I'll get ye close enough," Skarn said. "Dat's a promise."

32

Argentia slept well that night in a bed that was almost as large and comfortable as her own. She woke late in the morning feeling rested but vaguely concerned about Skarn.

It was wonderful to see him again and to see the happiness he had found, which was precisely why she felt badly about imposing on him. She did need help and she knew he would provide it. The question was at what cost? She had an intuition that his intent to make good on his duty to their friendship was going to cause some problems. *I won't let that happen. I'll just wait to hear what Sanla has to say about the aefryt and then I'll go....*

How she was going to go was a more pressing question. She had no real plan. Battling Erkani and the power of the lamp head-to-head had twice proven hazardous. She needed to take him off his guard if she was to have any hope of ending the conflict without collateral damage.

Her hope was that Sanla would be able to provide more insight into the power of the lamp than Ralak had, but Griegvard had raised a valid concern last night. Time was a luxury they did not have. Once Erkani got to land, the next rubies he stole might be the ones that released the salamander from its prison.

Have to end this quickly.... They had been so close on the ship; maybe she should have risked the *Reaver* for a chance to put Erkani and the lamp on the bottom of the Sea of Schisimer.

Too late to worry about it now.... If she had made a bad decision she would have to find some way to make up for it. *Won't be the first time....*

She bathed and dressed and found the others still around the breakfast table. She was barely halfway through her figs and caf before her worst fears were realized.

"So I think it's about de time de Sultan of Sormoria paid de diplomatic visit to de Raj of Makhara," Skarn said. He took a swallow of white grapefruit juice and looked around the table.

"Skarn...." Argentia started.

"Ye think dat's wise?" Skritlana interrupted.

"Isn't your father always tellin me how important de trade relations wit de neighbors are?"

"Yes, but he is not tellin ye to visit de cities where dere are de monsters running loose. And speakin of me father, ye should make no plans until ye hear what he has learned from de scrolls."

"Dah. Already spoke wit 'im."

"And he condoned dis?"

"Wasn't aware de Sultan's decisions needed de condonin," Skarn said mildly. "But he didn't say no, if dat's what ye mean. And Gen needs de help."

Argentia shook her head. "No, Skarn. It's okay. I'll just take the *Reaver* and go."

"De *Reaver*? Last night was all about how ye didn't want to take de *Reaver* into Khemr-kar. Too recognizable, ye said. Got to be some way t' get dere and surprise dis Erkani, ye said. Right? Well ol' Skarn's got de way."

Despite the warning look Skritlana sent her husband, Argentia's heart lifted. "Aetherwalk?"

Skarn flashed his golden teeth. "Nah. Better den dat."

"How?"

"Remember how we got back from Yth?"

The ghost pegasi stood in the courtyard, their shimmering wings folded, wisps of aether steaming from beneath their hooves like silvery fog. It was early evening. Argentia fervently hoped this gathering would not bring a repeat of the arguments that had dominated the morning....

Skritlana had fought with Skarn against going to Makhara until it became clear that nothing she could say would move him. Then she changed her tactic. "Fine. If ye go, den Demby goes with ye."

Skarn shook his white-maned head. "Dat don make de bit of sense. Ye want me t' take de boy into danger?"

"He went with ye to Yth, didn't he?"

"He stowed away on de boat!"

"Mirk was stowaway once," the meerkat said to Demby, who was staring wide-eyed at Skarn and Skritlana as they bickered.

"Dat is no matter," Skritlana said. "If ye are goin on dis trip, den ye will take Demby."

"Dis could be dangerous, Skrit."

"Ha! Dat's *exactly* why ye are goan take Demby. If de boy's wit ye, den ye won't do nothin foolish." Skritlana folded her arms across her small breasts and stared triumphantly. "Dat's de only way I'll permit dis."

"Skrit, I'm sorry," Argentia said. "I didn't mean for this—"

Skritlana waved dismissively. "Skarangella's been lookin for de excuse to get out almost since he settled his fine rear in de throne."

"I have—" Skarn began.

"Ye have. Not for good, I know dat," Skritlana said. "But ye got de wanderin in de blood and de need for de adventurin. So ye go if dis is what ye need to do—dere's some good in it, at least, if ye can help de Lady Dasani—but ye go wit de memory dat dere's more den just de life of Skarangella Skarn dat's affected if ye die. Dere's de whole of dis realm, never mind Seibu and Skritlana."

Skarn pulled her close. "Skrit, nothin's goan happen t' me," he said, winking at Argentia. "Gen's got de luck of de damned."

"And what does dat mean?"

"Every time she's supposed to be dead, damned if she doesn't survive," Argentia and Skarn said in unison.

So their course was made for Makhara and their number set at six:

125

Argentia, Mirk, Griegvard, Skarn, Demby, and Trokelo, who would not hear of letting Skarn go alone. "Ye think I want de ghost of dat damn Martigan hauntin me for failin in me duty?" he asked, referring to the old soldier who had been chief of Sormoria's sariphs until his death in Yth. "Ye couldn't keep me home if ye staked me to de throne."

"Dah," Skarn shook his head. "E'ry damn one o' ye worries too much. De push comes t' de shove, I'll be de one savin de half o' ye at least."

"Watch it," Argentia said.

"I said half...."

"Ye didn't say *which* half." Griegvard scowled menacingly.

Skarn flashed his gold teeth. "Figured dat was obvious. De boy and de meerkat can take care of demselves."

That brought general laughter and a sense that the matter was settled. Even so, Argentia was troubled. She knew Skarn had made his own choice to help her, but if something did happen to him or to Demby she would never forgive herself. *Just have to make sure nothing does, then....* "We leaving today?" she asked.

"Was thinkin dis evenin. Sanla's goan need some time t' work his magic, but de trip's not more'n most of de night. We should be dere in de mornin. Unless ye think we should leave sooner?"

"No, tonight's good." She turned to Demby. "Since we have time, I need help with something."

"What, de Lady?" Demby asked, clearly pleased by the prospect of assisting Argentia with whatever she might be proposing.

"Shopping."

33

Khan's bazaar was jumbled across a half-dozen giant squares formed by the city's canals. Gondolas swarmed the waters, passing incessantly beneath gracefully arched pedestrian bridges. Argentia hired a gondolier named Bua to ferry them from square to square and wait while they shopped.

Unlike the market squares of Teranor, there were no stores in the bazaar, just hundreds of merchants peddling from stands, tents, or lean-tos. Fruits were piled high on wooden tables or sold directly from crates stacked on the ground. Charcoal and spices from meats being roasted over fire-pits sweetened the thick air.

God, I forgot how loud this place is, Argentia thought as she followed Demby and Mirk, who had already grown bored of Mebulkar, through the clotted squares. Khan was famous for its bartering and the noises of men haggling made it impossible to keep focused. Argentia noticed that the women in the bazaar—their heads scarved and their faces veiled, as was the custom of the Sudenlands—still did not participate in the ritual bargaining, but made their purchase silently and went on their way. Skarn may have made some strides since taking the throne, but he was a long way from breaking ages of tradition that women were subservient creatures.

Because of this cultural bias, Argentia stood out even more than she normally did in a crowd. She was still in her halter and buckskins, her red hair dangling in a ponytail down her back. She was far from the only northerner in Khan, but she was very likely the only woman flouting their conventions. Everywhere Demby led her, eyes were on her. She ignored them. *Nothing I can do about it anyway—nothing I'm* willing *to do, at least....*

Women's fashion in Sormoria was a problem for Argentia. They all wore long gowns and wraps—nothing she would be caught dead in, and certainly not functional for hunting down Erkani. She could live with her halter, but her buckskins were not comfortable in the humidity. She needed working clothes of a sort more suited to the weather.

Demby, who had helped her solve a wardrobe and weapons crisis on her first visit, proved that living in the palace had cost him none of his knack for finding the best vendors in the bazaar: places that catered to outland merchants, shipping exotic fabrics and fashions across the seas to cities of more progressive style. In short order Argentia had several pair of lightweight, flowing silk pants and a couple cap-sleeve blouses in leopard spots and tiger stripes whose thin cotton felt like wearing nothing at all. She bought a lemon-yellow gown for no real reason other than she liked it, and four pairs of shoes in rare tavaris leather that was not readily available in Teranor.

For lunch Demby introduced her to chilled coconut milk, which they drank right out of the shell with sticks of crystallized cane for sweetener. Then it was back to the shopping, first for accessories—a new emerald stud for her navel piercing and a pair of glasses with blue-tinted lenses to block the sun—then for a few new vests and juggling balls for Demby, and finally for the serious things.

Rope was easy, but it took Demby a while to find a vendor who had a lead box for sale, and the shadiest apothecary the urchin knew—a man who worked from his home on the edge of a slum outside the bazaar— was reluctant to make the potion Argentia wanted, though he finally agreed when she tripled his price.

They had an hour to wait for the apothecary to finish his work, and were walking aimlessly through the warren of Khan's cramped streets, trying to figure out how to kill the time, when a voice near Argentia said, "Tattoo."

She stopped and turned, surprised. An old man on the stoop of the open archway of a single-story, white adobe building pointed a bony finger at her. "De Lady needs de new tattoo."

"What?"

"Come on, de Lady," Demby said, tugging at her hand. "Dis oldster's soft in de head." The urchin was clearly nervous. Looking at the old man, who was dressed in robes so threadbare they were almost rags, with hair the color of a dirty mop braided down past his skinny waist, age-spots on his hands and gaunt face, and eyes that glimmered with an almost frightening intensity, Argentia could understand why.

But she said, "Wait." This was too strange to be coincidence. She had been considering getting a new tattoo since she headed south: the Sudenlands boasted the best skin-artists in Acrevast. More than that, she wanted to know how the old man had known to call to her. There had been plenty of other people walking by, yet he had singled her out. She did not know what that meant, but she thought it meant something.

"What do you know about tattoos?" she asked.

He raised a pair of skeletal fingers. "De two things. Dat ye need one and dat I am de artist. Come. Come inside and I will show ye." He shuffled beneath the archway and opened a door on a gloomy chamber.

"No, Lady. Don go in dere," Demby said.

But Argentia was going. It was as if some will other than her own impelled her. She stepped up the stoop and followed the old man across the threshold. Demby and Mirk hurried after her but the door slammed shut in their faces.

"Hey! What—" Argentia reached for her sword.

"Do not fear," the old man said. In the low-lit room, his eyes almost glowed. "Dey will wait. And dere is no need for dat. Dere is no danger here."

Argentia lowered her hand. Demby was pounding on the door and shouting her name. "It's okay!" she shouted back. "Just wait for me there." She turned to the old man. "Who are you?" she asked.

"De artist."

"Doesn't look like you're making a very good living at it," Argentia muttered. The room was filthy and choked with dust. Cloths were draped over the furnishings. It looked like no one had lived there for years.

The old man smiled, showing withered brown teeth. "I am not making de living at it. Sometimes, when dere is need, I lend de talent I have. But de time is short. Come. Follow Mikel."

Though part of her was shouting that she was crazy and should just head for the door, Argentia's deep instinct that warned her of danger was quiet, as was the dragon's tooth token at her throat. Whatever was happening here, it was not quite normal, but it was not threatening. *And I was thinking about getting this done....*

The old man shuffled down a twisting stairwell into a basement. It was dark below as Argentia descended the rickety wooden steps, but by the time she turned the last corner a candelabra was aglow, illuminating a table covered with white linens. A basin of water, an array of needles, and a collection of glass bottles holding colored inks stood ready on what looked to be a serving sideboard. Unlike the furnishings in the room above, everything below appeared as pristine as if it had just been cleaned minutes earlier.

"Lie down dere," the old man said, gesturing at the table.

"You don't even know what I want," Argentia said. "Or where." *Demby was right. This guy's crazier than a caged squirrel....*

She turned to go. The old man caught her arm and looked at her with those ancient and deep-glittering eyes. "Mikel knows. Ye must trust him."

I can't believe I'm doing this.... Argentia unfastened her weapons' belt, sat on the edge of the table, shucked her boots, peeled her buckskins down her long legs, and untied her grass-green thong. She felt strange. She was not shy about her body, and she was not afraid of being assaulted by the old man, but Toskan, who had inked her dragonfly tattoo, had been both her teacher and her lover, the first man privileged to every part of her. Argentia knew that to repeat Toskan's work—at least the positioning of the tattoo—required this exposure, but still, it was a lot. *At least I shaved last night...*

"Lie down dere," the old man repeated, moving beside the table. If he was at all affected by seeing her half-naked, he showed no sign. His hands were already busy with the needles, heating them in the open flame of a candle.

Argentia settled back on the table. "I think at least I should tell you—"

"Dere is no need. All dat is needed is dat ye trust Mikel." He held up a needle and nodded, satisfied. Unscrewed one of the bottles. "Close dem eyes," he said when the needle was ready.

"I don't—"

"*Close.*" Mikel's gaze glimmered. His voice was freighted with magic. Argentia blinked once. The air was heavy and full of sweet incense, though she had not seen any censer. *What's...happening...?*

She tried to rise, but her limbs were stupid. The needle pricked her flesh. A wave of delicious warmth spread through her from that single point, washing away consciousness.

34

Argentia came awake to a shaft of sunlight penetrating the gloom.

The light was entering the basement through a small window she had not noticed before. She shook her head, sitting up, groggy, things coming back—

In a rush she was on her feet, looking wildly around, breathing fast. The basement was empty.

I can't believe I fell asleep! But had she fallen asleep, really? Hadn't it been something else? Some spell that had struck her from her senses?

All right, all right, just take it easy. What the hell happened? She was dressed again, except for her boots. A glance showed her all her weapons and her purse were still on her belts. She had not been robbed or suffered any violation. Only a slight tingling in the flesh to the right of her mons denoted where the needles had done their work.

The tattoo! She quickly peeled down her buckskins and peeked beneath her thong. *Oh! It's so beautiful! Perfect!*

She did not know how Mikel had known what to ink or where to place it, but he had, and the image was better even than she had imagined it.

Where is he? There was no sign of him or any of his artistic implements. She pulled on her boots, gathered her weapons, and headed upstairs. The gloom was no different than it had been when she came in.

The house had the same long-abandoned feel to it. She called for Mikel but no one answered. *Maybe he went out....*

She opened the front door. Stepped outside. The door swung closed behind her.

Demby was sitting on the stoop. Mirk was pacing beside him. When he saw Argentia, the urchin leaped up and hugged her. "De Lady! I was startin to worry."

"How long was I in there?"

"Not long, Lady. But it's almost time to go back for de potion."

Argentia frowned, confused. *That can't be. I feel like I slept for hours, and the tattoo...no one could do that in less than an hour...* "Did the old man leave?"

"No, Lady. No one come out of dere til now."

She turned around and tried the knob. Locked. She pounded on the door. "Mikel! Open up!" No one answered.

"Dere's no one dere," said a soft voice behind them. Argentia turned to see a woman watching them from the archway, suspicion in her dark eyes.

"But I was just in there," Argentia protested. "With Mikel...."

At this, the woman's eyes grew wide. She made a gesture of warding and babbled something in Brajenti, backing away as she spoke.

"What did she say?" Argentia asked Demby.

The urchin's eyes were wide, too. "She says dat's not possible. Dat Mikel de old skin art man died dis winter past. Dere's been nobody in dat house since. She says we should go now, go away and leave de spirits t' rest where dey belong. And Lady, I think she's right."

Numb, Argentia nodded and moved away from the door. The woman's crow eyes watched her: she could feel them on her back until she turned the corner. She was suddenly cold despite the oppressive heat. All the way to the apothecary's she wondered what had happened to her. Had the ghost of a master artisan really just given her a tattoo? And if that *was* what had happened, what did it mean?

"Where's de tattoo, Lady?" Demby asked, unable to contain himself any longer.

Argentia smiled. "Someplace secret."

"I bet inside de boot, right?"

She smiled again. "Something like that."

"De Lady likes it?"

"I love it." That was the truth. Whatever magic or haunts had been at work in that house, the design she had received was splendid. *And face it, Gen, a tattoo from a ghost is hardly the strangest thing that's ever happened to you....*

She opened the door to the apothecary's shop. The potion was ready for her. "You're sure this will work?" she asked Mirk when they were outside again.

"Mirk is sure."

"It had better work."

"Mirk said it will work. And Mirk is tired of shopping and tired of waiting."

"Hey, no one forced you to come." But Argentia was finished with Khan's bazaar anyway. The heat was growing more oppressive as the afternoon deepened and she was hungry. *But not for dog-on-a-stick or whatever they're roasting over there....* She had never taken a great fancy to Sormoria's cuisine, though she did enjoy some of the seafood and many of the fruits. "Demby—are we done shopping?"

"If de Lady says, den we're done."

She ruffled his hair. "It's such a shame you don't have a brother who's just like you but twenty years older."

"Why's dat, Lady?"

Argentia grinned and shook her head. "Never mind. Tell you what: let's drop these things at the boat and get another of those coconuts for the trip back. How's that sound?"

"Dat sounds de plenty good t' me!" Demby clapped his hands and they headed back through the crowds to the waiting gondola.

"One more stop," Argentia told the driver. "Can we bring you a coconut milk?"

Bua looked at her, surprised. Argentia knew it was hardly customary for fares to offer to bring food or drink to their drivers, but they had kept him sitting idle all day, and while she was going to pay him handsomely for his time, it seemed impolite not to offer.

"Well, if it's no trouble, dat'd be good of ye. Damn hot today, even for dis place."

"Sure is. It didn't seem this hot the last time I was here."

"Was it de summer?"

"Um...spring, I think."

"Dat's all de difference. Dis is de teeth of de summer. Dese two moons, de weather don' get no hotter. Know de best place for de coconuts?"

"I didn't know there was a best place."

"Sure dere is. De cane's what makes de difference. Dey got de best cane at Zuill's. Know it, boy?"

Demby pressed his thumb thoughtfully to his teeth for a moment. "Down past de snake charmer?"

"Dat's de one."

"I thought dat wasn't open no more," Demby said.

"It was closed for de while, but it is back open now. When was de last time ye were dere?"

"Not for de few years. I moved into de palace wit de great Sultan."

"Ah. Ye know de great Sultan, do ye?" Bua winked at Argentia.

"I'm de royal jester," Demby said proudly.

"Demby, let's go," Argentia said. She had enough notoriety of her own without Demby announcing that they were Skarn's friends. "We'll be right back."

"Bua will be waiting."

35

Demby led them across bridges and squares until they reached the outskirts of the bazaar. There were more houses than vendors now: two- and three-story structures in white adobe with external steps to the upper levels and flowing drapes in arched windows and doorways.

Sitting in front of one building was an old man playing a flute. In a basket before him, a huge green cobra swayed menacingly to the music. The old man was a lean-looking thing with protruding bones and a wisp of beard. No one but the cobra seemed to be paying much attention to him. The coin plate by his knobby knee was almost empty and the traffic passed him by with barely a glance. He was a fixture, timeless, as much a part of the scenery as a fountain or a bench.

Argentia threw a couple coins on his plate as she passed. The old man inclined his head in a deep bow, still playing, and the cobra mimicked the motion.

Across the street from the charmer was a row of stands. One sold fruits—though there were no coconuts evident—another earthenware and pottery, the next dyed silk scarves and wraps, and the fourth jewelry.

"Dat man's de liar," Demby said. "Dat's where Zuill sold de coconuts." He pointed to the jeweler's stand.

Argentia blew a limp strand of red hair out of her eyes. She was sweaty and tired and annoyed with having hiked all the way over here—though it had been her idea to get another coconut to begin with—only to find out that Demby, as usual, was right about his city. "Well...maybe they sell the coconuts over there. Let's go see."

They waited in line for a few minutes at the fruit stand, other people queuing up behind them. Argentia glanced them over out of habit. Khan was one of those cities where everyone looked a little suspicious, even if they were completely innocent. Three of the men had turbans with lime-green bands. One was a big brute that reminded Argentia of a knight she had known: another brave soul lost to the quest to destroy the Wheels of Avis-fe.

When they reached the counter, the fruit vendor told them, so sorry, he had no frozen coconuts.

And then the trouble happened.

Argentia sensed a shape moving quickly behind her. Felt a hand graze her hip, fingers fumbling at her belt.

"Hey!" She whirled around, reaching reflexively, but the thief was quick, evading her grasp, and the huntress found herself staring at the three men who had been in line behind her, now arrayed side-by-side, the big brute in the center, all three of them with their robes flipped back to clear the hilts of their daggers.

She reached for her handbow. Closed her fingers on emptiness.

A moment later, the pickpocket reappeared beside the other men, pointing her handbow at her. He was short and wiry, with a mean, pockmarked face. His turban was black with a lime-green band. "De money, please," the pickpocket said, giggling.

"Ah, Lady...dis is not good," Demby said, shrinking closer to Argentia. The people shopping the stands and the vendors in the four stalls had all scattered and disappeared; they had seen this type of thing before. The snake charmer's flute was loud in the hot air.

"It's fine." It wasn't fine at all, but Argentia was not about to give these thugs any more advantage than they already had. She was past her surprise and her bitterness at being set up—for this had to be a set up: it was too much of a coincidence to be a coincidence—and was already working on getting them out of this alive.

Four-on-one were hardly the worst odds Argentia had ever faced, even with her katana knotted to its sheath, as was the law in civilized cities. It was the handbow she was concerned with. Though it did not look like a conventional handbow, with a string and a bolt to fire, it wouldn't take a genius to figure out that something had to happen when the trigger was pulled. At this distance, that something was liable to be lethal to her or—worse—Demby. *Come on, think....*

"De money, please," the pickpocket repeated, grinning. "Quick quick quick."

"All right," Argentia said. She shifted Demby behind her; if things went bad, he might at least have a chance to escape. Then she unfastened her purse with exaggerated slowness and flipped it forward. It fell a few feet in front of her. "Oops..."

The pickpocket's face darkened. "Dat was stupid. Urlu, get de purse."

The hulk did not respond. His gaze was fixed on the fruit stand, where Mirk was levitating three pomegranates above his head, spinning them in a circle like a juggler. "Look, Bai," Urlu said, his eyes wide with childish amazement.

"What—" The pickpocket's gaze shifted. The handbow moved with him. Not much, but enough.

Argentia swiveled, grabbed a clay pot full of mangoes off the fruit stand, sprang forward, and crunched the pottery over the pickpocket's head. Mangoes went everywhere. Bai went down hard. Argentia kicked her handbow from his grasp.

Mirk altered his levitation spell and sent a pomegranate flying through the air, drilling Urlu in the face. The big man staggered backwards, roaring. Demby darted in behind him, dropping to the ground and tripping him so he fell flat on his back.

The other two thieves charged Argentia. She freed her whip. Snapped it forward, jabbing one of the thieves in the throat. He went to his knees, gagging.

The last thief lunged for her with his dagger. Sidestepping, Argentia kicked him in his stomach. He doubled over. She drove her knee into the jaw, sending him sprawling.

"Behind de Lady!" Demby shouted as he scrambled to his feet.

Bai, blood running down his forehead between his eyes, had crawled over to recover Argentia's handbow and was bringing the weapon up to fire.

The green cobra was faster.

It glided in and reared up, its hood expanding, jaws gaping as it spit its venom into Bai's pocked face. The pickpocket strangled on his scream and crumpled in agony, his face and throat swelling and going purple. Seconds later, he was dead.

Music lifted in the air. The cobra glided back across the dusty ground and coiled in a patch of afternoon sun beside the charmer.

Argentia retrieved her handbow from the Bai's contorted corpse and crouched over Urlu. "Who set this up?" she demanded, jamming her handbow under his chin. "Talk—or I'll blow whatever passes for brains right out of your head."

Urlu had apparently never heard of honor among thieves. He spilled the name to Argentia without her having to threaten him again. *Makes sense*, she thought blackly.

There was a commotion at the mouth of the street. Several of the city's guards appeared. "What's goin on dere?" the captain shouted. Demby knew him from his days living on the streets. He hurried over to explain the situation. Argentia kept her crossbow under Urlu's chin until the captain approached. He was a tall man, dark skinned and suspicious eyed.

"Ye are de outlander dat helped de Sultan?"

Argentia nodded. The captain motioned to his guards. They took the three thieves into custody and marched them away.

"Sorry 'bout dis rabble. Nobody hurt?" the captain said.

"None of my party."

"Dat's good. Ye got to be careful in Khan. Not de nicest city sometimes. Ye have any idea if dis lot followed ye or if dey were waiting?"

"No," Argentia said. She had a very good idea, but she was not in a sharing mood.

The captain nodded and looked around. "Come here, old man," he called to the charmer. Argentia waited for him to ask about the pickpocket's death, prepared to defend the charmer from any repercussions. "Dat your snake?" the captain asked.

"Kala," the charmer said, nodding.

"And ye warned dis one not to put his hand near it?" The captain gestured at Bai's corpse.

The charmer nodded again. "De many times, saib. Kala, I told him, is de motion hunter."

"Dat's what I thought. He paid de fool's price, den." The captain motioned to another guard. "Get a litter down here and get rid of dis trash. Keep de stands clear until it's done."

"Yes, saib."

"Thank you," Argentia said to the captain, appreciating his discretion. "And thank you," she said to the charmer.

The old man gave that grave nod of his white-bearded head again. "De charity is not always repaid only in de afterlife."

Argentia pointed at Kala. "It's really amazing how you can do that with the music."

The charmer gestured with his pipe. "Stillness is de secret, not de music."

"Do ye need an escort back to de palace?" the captain asked Argentia.

"No. But if you could tell me where to get some frozen coconut...."

Bua was sitting in his gondola with his hands laced behind his head and his eyes closed. He looked up, startled, when Argentia jumped down into the boat. "Here," she said, holding out the coconut she had promised in her right hand.

Bua reached with both hands. Argentia stepped forward, uncorked her left hand from her hip and hit him flush in the jaw, knocking him sprawling. Stepping over him, she poured the coconut milk onto his face until he started choking.

"Stop," he sputtered. "Stop, please. What—"

Her katana touched his throat, silencing him. "Your thief friend Urlu told me everything," she said. "Nice little scam you've got going. Point them at the wealthy people and take a cut of whatever they make." She stepped back, keeping her blade extended. "Get up." Bua did, moving slowly, his eyes never leaving the sword. "Jump," she said.

"But...dis is my boat."

"You can pick it up by the palace docks. I'll leave it with the sariphs. I'm sure they'll be real interested to meet you. Now *jump*."

She feinted forward with her sword. Bua went over the side. He came up gasping and cursing. Demby laughed at him as Argentia changed her blade for the gondola pole and rowed them back to Mebulkar.

36

Skarn was much amused when he heard the story of the deceitful gondolier.

"Ye fell for dat?" He laughed. "Dat's de most common scam in de city! Why do ye think all de women put de baskets on dere heads? Dey carry de purchases wit dem so de boatmen don' know if dey got de rich passenger or de poor. Safer dat way."

"How was I supposed to know?" Argentia protested. "In Argo, the drivers charge so much for the ride that they don't need a bunch of thieves to help them rob you."

Skarn laughed again. "Well, dat's four less thieves we got to worry about now. Ye sure ye don want to stay around after dis is done? Figure about a week of de shoppin and de bazaar'll be de safest place in de Sudenlands."

"I don't know. That guy picked my pocket and he was clumsy as a Norden yak." She thought about the attack outside Aventar, about Erkani escaping in Harrowgate. "I think I'm losing my edge."

"Dah, you're just bitter dat ye got set up, dat's all."

"Damn right."

"Like ye said, how were ye supposed to know?"

"It's not the gondolier that bothers me—there's no way to figure that. But I looked right at those guys in line behind me. I even saw they were wearing the same turbans, but nothing hit me as suspicious."

"Dat's good."

"How is it good?"

"Ye got taken by surprise and ye still beat dem and nobody got hurt 'cept dem deservin t' get hurt. Dat's all de proof ye should need dat ye still got de edge."

Argentia thought about it. Shrugged.

"Dah, ye know I'm right," Skarn said. "Now ye better go and pack all dat stuff Demby told me ye bought or we goan be late for de horses."

Feeling somewhat better, as she usually did after talking to Skarn, Argentia went and packed, grabbed some food, and met the others in the courtyard, where Sanla had just conjured the pegasi.

I forgot how beautiful they are....

The winged horses snorted vapors, their cloudy forms steaming in the humid air. Their bodies were opalescent, rainbow-hued like oil spilled on a wet street. There were four of them: one for her and Mirk, one for Skarn and Demby, one for Trok, and one for Griegvard. "What's the matter?" Argentia asked the dwarf, who was staring steadily at the ground.

"Bah! Ye didn't tell me this was how ye got out o' th' damn wastes! Flyin horses? Are ye bloody cracked, girl?"

"Don't tell me you're afraid to fly?"

"Ain't askairt o' nothin—yer knowin that. But I'm a *dwarf*, Red. Kin t' th' earth, not th' damn clouds."

"It's okay. You can stay here if you want. We'll miss you when we find Erkani, but we'll be sure to avenge your beard."

"Bah!" Griegvard fixed her with a scowl fierce enough to crack stone. "Said I'm bloody goin. Don't mean I'm happy about th' way I'm goin, though. Only a bloody wizard could dream up flyin horses."

"De true pegasi, rare dey are," Sanla said. "Rare like de dragon and de phoenix."

"Ain't that rare, then. Seen a bloody dragon meself."

"Is dis truth?" Sanla asked, intrigued.

"Aye. Ask th' lass."

"It's the truth, but a tale for another day," Argentia said.

Sanla nodded sadly. "Dis is so. De steeds know de way to Khemr-kar.

Through de night and into de morning dey will fly. You will be dere by noon."

Three days travel in less than one.... Argentia knew the pegasi were fast, but that was more than she had hoped for. She wondered if they might not beat Erkani to the city after all. She could imagine his face when he stepped onto the dock—if they even let his wreck of a ship put to port—and found him waiting for her.

"Ready t' go, den?" Skarn asked.

Skritlana laid a hand on Skarn's arm and shook her head. "Tell dem of de scrolls, father," she said.

"Yes, yes. De scrolls." The meja motioned for them to gather nearer. "Dis have I learned of de fire-foe. It must not escape de lamp. If it does, dere is no power to drive it back into its prison. It must be destroyed and to kill de host is not enough to accomplish dat."

"What, den?" Skarn asked.

"To destroy de aefryt forever, ye must find de Jade Monkey."

"What's that?" Argentia asked.

"De scrolls, dey do not say."

Of course they don't.... "Do they at least say where we can find this thing?"

"In de possession of de meja Bartemeus."

"More friggin wizards," Griegvard grumbled.

"Do we know anything about this Bartemeus?" Argentia asked, ignoring the dwarf. "Like maybe where to find *him*?"

"De scrolls say his home in de deserts of Makhara."

Trok said, "Dat's a lot of sand out dere t' be searchin."

"If it is de will of de gods, den de Sultan will find dis monkey," Sanla said.

"What if it's not dere will?" Trok asked.

"Den we'll find it anyway," Skarn said.

Demby tugged on Skarn's hand. "Can we start de flyin' now, saib? Like we did de last time?"

Skarn laughed and tousled Demby's wild hair. "Let's go, den." He kissed Skritlana and Seibu farewell. The company mounted up,

Griegvard muttering about how he must have lost his sanity along with his half his beard.

The pegasi started across the courtyard at a walk, then a trot, and then a gallop that was powerful and fast enough that their smoky hooves barely seemed to touch the stone. The wall loomed before them: fifty yards...forty...

Great wings unfurled and stroked in downbeats that lifted the pegasi smoothly off the ground, up and over the wall, up and over the city, their speed increasing, the land shrinking below them as they climbed to the clouds and chased the setting sun toward Makhara.

37

Flying was a wonder.

The first time Argentia had occasion to ride on the ghost pegasi, she and Skarn and Demby had been nearly dead from exposure and exhaustion in the Wastes of Yth. They had survived the crypt of the Revenant King but the merciless wasteland—it could not even be called a desert, for it was a blasted realm devoid of life and hope that was much worse than any desert—had almost killed them.

Sanla and his rescuing horses had come in time, but Argentia had been so overwhelmed that she could do little more than cling to the pegasus as it bore her into the sky and to eventual safety. This time she was fully able to enjoy the ride—and she was loving every minute of it: the exhilarating speed, the wind streaming against her face, blowing her hair out like a pinion of flame, the pulse of the mighty wings as they rode with the currents, streaking along like eagles. The air was cool with coming night, but she had put on a chasubla so it did not bother her. "Isn't this great?" she shouted to Griegvard.

The dwarf's fists were sunken into the pegasus' silvery mane. His face was contorted, his teeth bared, and his color as green as a seasick ship passenger's. He twisted his head around long enough to snarl something that was lost on the wind, but might have been a curse on Argentia's existence.

Laughing, Argentia looked ahead. The sun clung to the rim of the world. She fancied if they flew fast enough it would never set. A glance back showed the gloaming darkening the land with a growing band of shadow. Argentia was reminded of standing at the edge of the ocean as a child, running from the broken waves as they rushed up the shore. Retreat fast enough and she could evade them time and again, but eventually she would be a little too slow, or the wave a little too powerful in its rush, and she would be caught and splashed.

The shadow-tide that was chasing them now was as inexorable as the ocean. Eventually it caught them. The sun limned a last lingering edge to the far side of the world, but the dark was around them. Argentia could not see the ground anymore. The pegasi shimmered and glowed with ghost-light. There were stars in the southern sky and they seemed close enough to touch.

They flew on through the night. Argentia leaned forward and settled her head against the pegasus' pearlescent neck, which looked as insubstantial as cloud but was as solid and sure as any corporal steed's. She closed her eyes, trusting the magic of the pegasus to hold her fast, and let the rhythm of its wingbeats rock her to sleep.

She woke in time to see the dawn. It came in the same way as the night: a stealthy wash of light that overtook them almost without their being aware it was happening. The stars set. The dark faded. Vague shapes—clouds, Argentia realized—became gradually apparent around them. Below, an expanse of water unfolded, rippling like plated gold in the first glimmerings of the day.

"Drim be damned," Griegvard moaned.

They were flying over Talon Bay and land was nowhere in sight.

The others were awake too. "Dere's no more ground!" Demby shouted. Unlike Griegvard, he seemed delighted by this prospect, as if their flight had taken them into some strange other world.

Argentia grinned back at Demby. She fished around in her pack. Found and drank from her waterskin. Looked out over the waters again. Brilliant as the panorama was, she was heartened even more by what she did not see: Erkani's ghostly ship. *We may actually pull this off...*

The tireless pegasi paced on. Toward the ninth hour of the morning, the horizon changed from blue to brown and green: the coast of Makhara. Another hour, still over the water but with the land clearly delineated now, and Argentia descried something amid the undulating ochre plains that held her eye fast: a great flaring light, winking and glittering like an immense diamond held beneath a lamp. "What's that?" she shouted to Skarn.

"Khemr-kar!" Skarn shouted back. "De dome on de Raj's palace."

A few more minutes of effortless flight and the port city on the estuary of the river Ethalus came into view, its walls and buildings dominated by the titanic crystalline dome. Argentia wished she could say she had never seen its like before, but she had: the ice pyramid in frozen Nord, where Togril Vloth had held Ikabod prisoner was all too similar. She shuddered a little at the memory, wondering if Griegvard had had the same thought.

Still, the dome was impressive: a mighty crown to a sprawling sandstone palace. It was by far the tallest building in the city, and she could imagine it shattering beneath a stroke of lightning in a violent thunderstorm. She guessed it had magic to protect it, the same as the spires of Castle Aventar.

Argentia and Skarn did not want to cause a great stir by setting down at the palace itself, so the pegasi mounted higher, swooping through a low bank of clouds that left their riders soaked as surely as a summer rain, and banked wide of Khemr-kar. Past the city, the grassy cradle of the river gave way quickly to a sea of dunes. Beyond that, desert sand ran flat as far as Argentia could see. A road passed through the dunes, which were hilly as the knolls of the Heaths back in Teranor, and ran off into the desert, leading somewhere, though Argentia could not imagine who would willingly live in a desert.

The pegasi swung around, descended, and touched down beyond a copse of palms shading the side of the road about a mile outside Khemr-kar. Argentia dismounted and stretched, rolling her head from side to side. It was near noon and hot but not as humid as Khan. A steady, warm wind rustled the green grasses growing tall on the distant dunes. She stripped away the damp chasubla, stuffing it in her pouch. She had navy blue silk pants on and a pale yellow, cap-sleeve silk blouse with black tiger stripes. She had knotted it beneath her breasts; the lace cups of her black bra were tantalizing shadows beneath the sheer fabric.

The others were down from the mounts as well. Griegvard knelt and pressed his strong hands to the soft, sandy earth as if in prayer. "N'er again," he said when he rose, shaking his hairy head. "Not even fer ye, Red."

"Planning on walking home, then?"

"I— Bah!" Snorting, the dwarf stomped over to a boulder and sat down, his arms folded across his chest.

Argentia laughed and then yawned. Demby came up and hugged her. "Dat was de fun ride!" he said.

"I know," she answered. "You'd better have something to eat." She dug an orange out of her pack and handed it to Demby.

"Look! De horseys, lady!" Demby said. The pegasi were losing their shapes, evaporating into mist and aethereal smoke.

"You have the bottle to make the others, right?" Argentia asked Skarn. Sanla had conjured another quartet of ghost pegasi and bottled their essences to be released for their return trip.

"Damn it all, I *knew* I forgot something." Skarn flashed his golden grin.

"Forgot?"

"Deh. But it's not de problem."

"Oh really?"

"Pretty sure I've got de ship or two docked here," Skarn said. "And if not...."

"If not, what?" She was sure Skarn had planned this all along.

"Den we'll figure somethin out. We always do, don' we?"

Argentia shook her head and grinned back at him. "Yeah, we always do."

"Good. Dat's settled." Skarn shouldered his pack and patted Demby's small shoulder. "Come on, boy. Let's go meet de king of dis sandbox."

38

Argentia had never been to Makhara. As they followed the road to Khemr-kar she felt the thrill of entering a new place. A great proliferation of tents in bright reds, yellows, and greens stood in rows on either side of the road. At first Argentia thought it was some sort of traveling carnival, but she realized there were far too many tents for that.

"It's de bazaar," Trok told her. Before joining up with Skarn's pirates, he had spent some time in Khemr-kar. "Dey don' like de merchants clutterin up de city, so dey moved all de trade outside de walls."

The bazaar was much the same as any other market Argentia had been to: chaotic with motion, loud with bargaining. She heard Tradespeak, though not so heavily accented as in Sormoria, as well as strains of Brajenti, the native tongue of the Sudenlands. There were many animals—chickens, pigs, goats, sheep, and camels—and children roved in packs of a few or a dozen. They were mostly between five and ten years old, dressed in as many bright colors as the tents. They pointed at the strangers and chattered in Brajenti and went running off again.

The company moved through the bazaar and approached the tall, sandstone wall of Khemr-kar. The gates of the city were flung wide. The half-dozen guards stationed there looked bored and lazy. People were filing in and out unmolested, but as Skarn's group approached one of the guards became suddenly alert. He stared at them for a moment, bent his head in a whispered conversation with the man nearest him, and then hustled away into the city.

So much for a quiet entry, Argentia thought as two guards moved to block their way. They wore brown-and-rust uniforms with a red eye emblazoned on the left breast.

Trok stepped quickly beside Skarn and Argentia and Griegvard slid off to the left and right, making an arc. Argentia was not expecting trouble, but after what had happened in Khan, she was taking no chances.

"State your business," the Gatekeeper said. He was a burly man distinguished from the other guards by a burgundy sash across the tanned leather vest. His breath was so garlicky that Argentia, standing several feet away, winced.

"Visitors to de wondrous city of Khemr-kar," Skarn said pleasantly.

"Did you come on the horses out of the sky?"

"Ye see any horses—de flyin kind or otherwise?"

"We saw them in the sky. If that was not you, where did you come from? It's a long walk up the Sandway from Budun. Are you mejai, then?"

"Dis is de great Sultan of Sormoria!" Demby said indignantly, shoving forward to glower up at the Gatekeeper. "Come to see de king of dis sandbox."

"Demby!" Argentia exclaimed. Demby jumped in surprise and then clapped his hand over his mouth.

The Gatekeeper snickered. "That so, boy?" He turned to the guard beside him. "Gusan, the Sultan of Sormoria honors us with his presence." Gusan laughed as the Gatekeeper folded his hands together and bent at the waist in a mock bow.

Skarn stared at him. Said nothing.

The Gatekeeper straightened up, still smirking. "But this is strange company you keep for a Sultan: an islander, a child, a dwarf, an outland woman, and a rat," he said.

Argentia stepped on Mirk's tail and the meerkat's retort at the Gatekeeper's insult came out as a screech.

"De finest company I can think of," Skarn said. "Dese are my friends. Please don' insult dem again." Skarn's voice remained pleasant, but

Argentia saw his hand tighten into a fist: a sure sign he was reaching the end of his patience. *Oh boy, here we go....*

"That a threat?" the Gatekeeper said. The three remaining guards shifted from the wall, joining the Gatekeeper and Gusan, feeding off their captain's hostility.

"No. If I said 'ye ought t' shut dat mouth while ye still got de teeth,' *dat'd* be de threat," Skarn said, flashing a hard, gilded smile.

"You cocky swine. I've heard enough. The only part of Khemr-kar you'll be seeing is the dungeons." He gestured and the four guards rushed Skarn.

Trok butted one in the stomach and swept his legs in a nifty one-two move with his spear. He rested the weapon's tip against the fallen guard's chest.

Argentia quick-stepped around another, caught an arm around his neck, and shoved her handbow against his ear. "Don't," she said. The guard froze as if petrified.

Griegvard dissuaded the last two from attacking just by stepping toward them and swinging his huge axe off his shoulder.

"Now ye see what I mean about dem bein de finest friends?" Skarn asked.

"Assault!" the Gatekeeper sputtered, pointing a fat finger at Skarn. "That's assault on the city Watch!"

"Nah," Skarn said. "Ye got dis all wrong. Dat's not assault, what dey done. *Dis* is assault."

The hand that had bunched into a fist now swung in a short arc from Skarn's waist to the Gatekeeper's jaw. The Gatekeeper's head snapped sideways, spewing blood and teeth. The strength left his legs and he went heavily to his knees. His head lolled forward, blood drooling from his split lips. "Warned ye about dat mouth, didn't I?" Skarn said.

The scuffle caused people passing through the gate to shout in alarm. Their noise hardly mattered, Argentia saw: a dozen troops were headed for the gates at a fast march.

"What is the meaning of this?" one of the troops shouted over the din. Argentia marked him as a commander more by his demeanor than the barked order or the men assembled behind him, all with the red eye blazoned on their chests. He reminded her of a Watch Captain she had known in Argo. He was tall and dark, with a tight cap of black hair and a thin line of beard on his chin. He gave a cursory glance to Skarn, Demby, and Trok, a surprised squint at Griegvard, but his eyes lay long on Argentia: a stare just short of rude, but more an appraisal than a leer. Still, she was about to ask him what his problem was when he gave a curt nod and turned to Skarn. "Step away from that man." He gestured and his troops fanned out, encircling the companions. They all had hands on the hilts of their scimitars.

Argentia didn't doubt that her friends would carry a battle, but it would be bloody. She placed a hand on Skarn's shoulder. "Diplomacy, remember?"

"Dah." Skarn stepped back. The Gatekeeper toppled face-first onto the ground, sending up a cloud of dust.

The newcomer shook his head in disgust, crouched down, and roughly hauled the Gatekeeper back onto his knees.

"Captain...Farrad," the Gatekeeper groaned. "These men..." His eyes rolled back in his head and he toppled again, this time not to rise.

"Merciful Ab'Dala. What a disgrace." The captain straightened and rounded on one of the other guards. "What happened here?"

"Captain Farrad, they flew in on winged horses," Gusan said. "We... that is, Dolus felt they might be threats. Mejai of some sort."

"I see no winged horses. And even if I did, are mejai not welcome in our city?"

"Yes, Captain, but that one claims to be the Sultan of Sormoria," Gusan said.

"I don't care if he claims to be Araxis Thul!"

Argentia and Skarn exchanged a glance, wondering how Captain Farrad would feel if he knew that he was looking at the two people who had vanquished the nightmarish Revenant King of Yth.

Farrad continued: "Khemr-kar is a city of free trade. We do not harass visitors for their outlandish ways and we do not detain them without cause—especially when the claims they make happen to be true. This is for certain the Sultan of Sormoria."

Skarn looked at him quizzically. "Can't say I've had de pleasure."

"No, no, of course not, Sultan. We have never met, but I was a visitor to Khan and I saw you address the people from the steps of the palace once. You are not easily forgotten." He bowed, low and formal and full of all the respect the Gatekeeper's jape had lacked. "Ramadus Farrad, Captain in the city's Eye, at service. Welcome to Khemr-kar, Sultan of Sormoria and all those in your company." He bowed again to Skarn and then to each of the companions. "Please know that this swine will be well reprimanded for his disgraceful behavior."

"Dah." Skarn shook his head. "Rather ye take him to de healer and fix up his face. Dis was just de misunderstandin, dat's all."

Farrad stared at Skarn for a moment, then nodded. "As you wish, my lord Sultan. Perhaps to ensure there are no other misunderstandings you would permit me to be your escort to the palace?"

39

Khemr-kar was not so different from Khan in its architecture, though its buildings were mostly sandstone, not white adobe, but the mazy streets winding among them were a startling contrast to the rigorous geometry of Khan's canals.

"Dey built de city on de goat paths," Trok muttered.

Argentia smirked. Whatever their origin, the streets were among the cleanest she had ever trod. They were unpaved: just hard earth packed firm by centuries of human passage. She noticed the system of aqueducts running along the buildings. The technology had long since been antiquated in Teranor's major cities, where magical gemstones powered a system of pipes that pulled water from cisterns. While there was as much magic in the Sudenlands as in Teranor, the southern cultures used the aether much more sparingly. They seemed to have an innate fear of it. *Or more respect for its power,* she mused.

The company followed Farrad and two of his men through the city, though there was never any question of getting lost. The palace was by far the tallest of Khemr-kar's buildings. Its glittering dome reflected the light in a blaze, making it as easy to spot as the beacons on Argo's seawall. As they walked, people stared, though whether for their exotic appearance—you did not see many redheads in the Sudenlands, certainly not many dwarves, and Skarn's imposing size and mane of white hair made him stand out wherever he went—or for their escort of guards Argentia could not be sure.

The palace, Kephalo, was segregated from the rest of the city by a tall wall. Once they passed through the gate, the path ran straight across a manicured green lawn, between rows of palm trees and past bright gardens decorated with ornate fountains and statues to the palace doors. *There's a wonder,* Argentia thought. The winding streets annoyed her. She had an infallible sense of direction and an almost magical gift for backtracking, but Khemr-kar's streets were lazy circles and sinuous coils, wandering and arcing and doubling back, as if their goal was to confound. They reminded her of the labyrinths she had known and those were not good memories.

The palace itself was a series of serpentine wings connected to the domed central building. Had they flown close enough to see it on their pass, from above it would have looked to Argentia very like an octopus. Even so, she was able to approximate something of the idea, which was reinforced by the green octopus on an inky background that flew on the banners of the palace.

The palace doors, great onyx slabs, were almost as impressive as Castle Aventar's. Their guards, like the guards at every palace Argentia had ever been to, wore different uniforms from those worn by the guards of the city. This time it was green-and-black as opposed to the Eye's brown-and-rust. They had the green octopus blazoned on their breastplates and shields. Farrad went ahead and spoke quickly to the guards, gesturing back at Argentia and the others. One of the guards went inside. Farrad returned to the company. "I am told it will be a few minutes while they inform the Raj that he has guests."

It was more than a few minutes. Argentia began to pace, matched by Demby and Mirk. Even Skarn looked surprised by the strange delay.

"Hell're they doin in there?" Griegvard said after twenty minutes of waiting.

"They are preparing the hall for you," Farrad said. "It will be worth the wait."

"Yeah? Ye think they could let us wait where there's some bloody shade?" Griegvard muttered, squinting up at the unrelenting sun.

"Pretend you're at your forge," Argentia suggested, sensing the dwarf, his nerves already frayed by the flight, was close to losing his temper.

"If I were at me forge, I'd be doin somethin useful, not standin around waitin fer some fool t' finish polishin th' floors fer company."

"There is plenty of shade in the dungeon," Farrad said. "Which is where you will go if you speak ill of the Raj again."

Griegvard looked Farrad up and down and snorted in derision. The men of the Eye tensed, anticipating their captain's command to seize the dwarf.

"Whoa dere. E'rybody just take it easy," Skarn said, interposing himself between the guards and Griegvard.

"Bah!" Griegvard shook his head, turning away from the confrontation. He pointed at Argentia. "Yer Crown e'er treat guests like this? She'd fer sure find rooms and refreshments fer em, not leave em out in th' yard like a bunch o' bloody peddlers. Somethin ain't right here. Ye mark me."

Argentia frowned at the dwarf's words. She had the same feeling herself. Pulling Skarn aside, she asked: "Do we need to be here? We should be down at the docks checking for the *Leaper*, or searching the city."

"Don' ye start too," Skarn said.

Argentia blew the forever-stray strand of hair out of her eyes. "I think Griegvard's right, that's all. It feels like we're wasting time."

"Won' be de waste, you'll see. Dis is de diplomacy ye were talkin about before. Five minutes wit de Raj and ol' Skarn'll have dese watchmen fellows lookin for Erkani all over de city."

He winked at her and Argentia felt better. If Skarn could manage it—and she did not doubt he could—having the Eye of Khemr-kar to help them hunt Erkani could make all the difference. She knew she would eventually find him herself, but she was not so prideful that she could not admit that having the Watch on her side in a strange city would be a valuable asset.

She heard Demby laughing. Turned to see Mirk riding on the back of a white peacock. The bird squawked and swerved, flapping its brilliant wings in an effort to dislodge its unwanted passenger.

"Mirk! Stop that!" Mirk jumped off the peacock, his ears flat and a guilty look on his fuzzy face. "Get over here!" The meerkat came to her, Demby in tow, still giggling. "Behave, both of you," she said. Skarn was right; they were here diplomatically. It would not do to be perceived as heathen.

Just then the palace door opened and the guard emerged at last. After another brief conversation, Farrad motioned for the company to follow him in.

The space beyond the black doors narrowed swiftly into an antechamber with barely space to go two abreast. A portcullis hung in the archway ahead and doorways in the left- and righthand walls showed guard stations manned by men with crossbows. Argentia marked it as a simple but effective defensive design. Even if the doors were breached, a small group of defenders could hold this throat against many intruders. If the portcullis came down to block the way forward, archers in the alcoves could quickly turn the antechamber into a killing floor.

"Weapons and packs, please," said one of two guards waiting by the archway.

"They will be returned when you leave," Farrad assured them. "It is the custom of the palace. There have been attempts on the Raj's life before."

Argentia, who had seen several assassination attempts on Solsta and the aftermath of the attack that killed Solsta's parents, nodded her reluctant agreement. She unshouldered her pack and her katana and unfastened the belt holding her handbow, daggers, and whip. The others followed suit. The weapons and bags were placed on a wooden trolley and rolled into one of the side rooms. When the guards were satisfied the group was disarmed, they led them across the threshold into the throne hall.

The massive, circular chamber was given the illusion of greater size by the crystal rotunda, which brought the sky to them. The floor was cobbled sandstone, etched and precisely cut. The walls were a blue marble whose beauty Argentia had never seen equaled. Beneath the dome was a pool in the shape of an octopus, a huge fountain spraying up from its center. The pool appeared decorative, but it was really defensive,

Argentia realized, forcing anyone approaching to go either left or right, where a line of guards waited at attention. The spray from the fountain also concealed the throne from view and would skew arrows or other missiles.

The company followed Farrad to the right of the pool. As they cleared the veil of fountain spray, Argentia saw the throne at the far end of the hall, raised up on a golden dais that was flanked on either side by rows of empty black chairs. She saw the Raj hunched on his great seat, short and toadlike in green silks fretted with gold, a golden turban on his head, an emerald-encrusted scepter in his hand.

And she saw the thing standing to the right of the throne, scarlet-and-ebony robes draped about its shape, which was human and not human.

I think we're in trouble....

PART III

The Aefryt Unleashed

40

"Welcome to Makhara," the Raj said.

He lifted a robed arm and before Argentia or any of the others could react, the guards from the right-hand wall converged. The company was surrounded: swords on every side. But no bows, Argentia saw, and the circle was not as tight as it could have been because Farrad was beside them.

"Seems it will be the dungeons after all," the captain said, smiling mockingly.

Argentia hit him in the face.

Her fist struck his nose squarely, snapping his head back. As Farrad instinctively grabbed at his nose, Argentia ducked in and plucked his sword from its sheath. When Farrad shook off the pain from the punch, he found himself staring at the tip of his own weapon.

It had all happened before anyone else could move, but Griegvard and Skarn were quick to take advantage. The dwarf flung himself at the guards as if their swords weren't even there, tackling one of them down. Skarn grabbed the guard nearest to him so suddenly the man dropped his sword even before Skarn landed a blow. "Thanks for de cooperation," Skarn said as he hurled the guard into his fellows, scattering them. Trok came up with the dropped sword.

Then everything was fighting.

Argentia kicked Farrad in the stomach, driving him back. It was not in her to kill an unarmed man—even a treacherous worm like Farrad—but not everyone present had the same scruples.

"Demby! Down!" Argentia shouted. She lunged, parrying a blow meant for the urchin. "He's just a *child*!" Eyes blazing, Argentia struck the guard's sword again, knocking his blade wide, and reversed her stroke, slashing him across the neck, between the collar of his armored vest and the cuff of his helmet. Arterial blood fanned the air and the guard stumbled backwards, splashing into the pool.

Three more men replaced him: reinforcements racing from the other side of the hall to join the fray. Farrad's scimitar felt clumsy compared to her katana, but Argentia was more than capable of handling three guards with it. She was more concerned about bowmen and magical fire, but she heard no dreaded *twangs* of crossbows from the doorway and a glance at the throne as she cut down another guard showed the salamander standing impassively.

Even so, her warrior's nerves tingled at the expectation of some new danger an instant before she felt the splash of water on her from above.

What— Argentia looked up and spun reflexively, but not nearly fast enough to avoid the monstrous tentacle that coiled down and snatched her off her feet into a nightmare. Her mind was hurled back to a tunnel and a river beneath the Black Crags, and the thing that had guarded that dark passage: an abomination of tentacles just like this.

The blue sky above the dome flashed past as the tentacle whipped her through the air, shaking the scimitar from her grasp and the breath from her body. Gasping, she struggled vainly as she hung suspended above the pool. The tentacle held her fast. She could feel the snakish strength of the thing and knew she was only one contraction away from death.

She managed to look down. The thing holding her was a gargantuan octopus. Its corrugated head was visible above the surface of the pool and two of its other limbs were flung out, one holding Skarn, the other holding Trok.

Demby was huddled on the ground, his head clutched in his hands, wailing. Griegvard was still fighting—and winning—against a group of guards, until the Raj's voice rolled over the combat like a wave: "Desist or they die!"

The dwarf, his fist raised to hammer another guard he had pinned to the stone floor, jerked his head around. "Drim be damned!" he exclaimed, seeing the octopus that held his friends aloft. He jumped off the guard and faced the throne, his barrel chest heaving.

"Did you think us so scantily defended?" the Raj asked.

"Don't think much o' yer defenses at all. But I am fer thinkin we got ourselves a stalemate," Griegvard said.

"How is that?" the Raj asked, amused.

"Yer pet's got me friends, but ye don't have enough guards in this whole bloody palace t' beat me."

"Perhaps. But the octopus has eight arms." The Raj pointed his scepter at the pool and as if on cue, one of those arms erupted from the water and slapped the dwarf down, pinning him beneath its thick coil. "Now, you were saying something about a stalemate, little fool?"

Suddenly the drapery behind the thrones parted. A handsome young man rushed across the dais toward the throne. "Father! By all the gods! Are you all right? What has happened here?"

The Raj hesitated, but the salamander bent close to the throne, whispers hissing from the shadows of its hood. When it straightened, the Raj waved dismissively at the young man. "Go back to your mother where you belong, boy. This rabble is no threat to us."

"Rabble? Dat's a fine way t' be greetin de emissaries of de Sultan of Sormoria—to say nothin of de Sultan himself," Skarn shouted.

"What respect should the Raj of Makhara pay to the ragtag usurper of a mongrel land?" The Raj gestured with the scepter again. Argentia saw Skarn flinch in the grasp of the tentacle, the muscles of his jaw clenched against a scream of pain.

"Erkani!" Argentia shouted.

The salamander's hooded head lifted. "Erkani is gone."

"I don't think so."

"He is gone, I tell you!" the salamander raved. "I am Bazu, Prince of the Aefryt! Soon all shall know my name and tremble before my destroying flame!"

Great—an insane elemental. This just keeps getting better.... Argentia remembered what Ralak had said about the salamanders being the least of the aefryt ranks: not necessarily a comforting thought when she considered the power she had seen it display, but clearly proof that Bazu was dangerously deluded.

"Whatever. Erkani—do you hear me? You're going back to the dungeons in Aventar. Back to Tandun. Back to the dark. You weren't good enough to get away last time and you weren't good enough this time, either. I promise you, it's all over except the trip back to your cell."

The salamander wrenched its hood down. The face that stared at them was squashed and reptilian, its humanity reduced to a few tufts of Erkani's black hair. Its eyes were flaming slits, but its voice was Erkani's. "Liar! You'll *never* take me again you bitch whore! Never! *You'll* go to the dark! *You'll* rot and waste in a cell!" He turned to the Raj. "Take them away! All of them! Right now, or I'll burn this place to ashes!" Smoke was furling from the salamander's red robes. A brimstone stench charged the air.

The Raj gestured with his scepter. The octopus dumped its catches on the stone. They lay gasping and were quickly rounded up and hauled to their feet by the remaining guards. "Bring them to the dungeons," the Raj said.

Argentia almost relaxed. Bazu's reaction was further proof of her hunch that the salamander was not fully incarnate yet: much more than it had been on the ship, but not entirely in possession of its host yet. If there was even a little of Erkani left, then they had that much more hope.

"Wait, my lord Raj," Farrad said. His voice was nasal and blood trickled from his nose. "The woman—I beseech you, remember your promise."

The Raj looked at Bazu. The salamander had recovered its composure and slowly raised its hood back into place, so only its red eyes glittered from the darkness of the cowl. Its voice was its own again: deep and sibilant. "It may be as you have promised your servant. As for the others, I have a more fitting prison in mind than your dungeons."

From a fold in its robe, Bazu produced the lamp and raised it high. Light shot forth: ruby red, but not flaming. It blazed over Griegvard and the two guards restraining him. All three were sucked forward into that lurid corridor, shrinking and shrinking and finally vanishing into the mouth of the lamp.

"Griegvard!" Argentia screamed. The Raj's guards fell away from their prisoners.

The lamp began to glow again.

"Don' do it!" Skarn shouted. "If my people don' hear from me by de morrow, dey got orders t' invade dis city. Are ye prepared t' face de armies of Sormoria in war, den?"

"What cares Bazu for your petty forces, human?" the salamander hissed. The lamp glowered more brightly.

"Wait, Father!" the Raj's son shouted, desperation in his voice. "What if it is the truth? We do not want war. What of...what of your plan?"

The Raj looked at his son for a long moment before nodding. "Timor may be right. It would not do to risk de open war yet. We are not at strength."

"We are all the strength you need," the salamander said. "Dare you doubt that?"

"Strength to conquer, yes, but how to occupy?" Timor said boldly. "Our forces are not yet arrayed to hold what your fires gain, mighty one."

"Ashes," the salamander said. "You need no men to govern ashes."

"No, no," the Raj said. "We are firm in this. Our forces must not be risked wantonly. Let them go to the dungeons until we ascertain the truth of this boast of war."

The salamander glared at the Raj, but finally nodded. "Very well." Bazu lowered the lamp. Turned its simmering gaze on Farrad. "Take her. Break her spirit. Use her. Humiliate her. But do not harm her. Bring her before us at dawn or your own life is forfeit. No army stands upon *her* fate. She will burn slow."

Farrad nodded mutely.

"Get them all from our sight." the Raj said, settling back into his throne.

The guards formed up again, herding Skarn, Demby, and Trok to one side while Farrad remained with Argentia.

"Let her go," Skarn said to Farrad.

"No. What do you think of that, sultan?" Farrad asked mockingly.

"I think you're de dead man." Skarn surged forward, dragging guards with him, but Farrad was ready this time. He stepped in with his cudgel before Skarn could get his arms free, belting the Sultan in the stomach. Skarn stumbled, doubling over. The guards laid into him from behind.

"No, no!" Demby shouted, struggling vainly against the guard holding him.

Laughing, Farrad shoved Argentia ahead of him and toward the doors.

"Gen!" Skarn was on his hands and knees, his voice full of pain.

She twisted back. "It's all right! Don't worry about me. I'll be fine. I promise!"

The guards dragged Skarn to his feet. Argentia watched as they marched him and Demby and Trok away down another corridor. They would be safe enough until Skarn's bluff about his army was uncovered. *Safer that Griegvard....*

Aeton only knew what had happened to the dwarf. Argentia did not have time to worry about it now. If Griegvard was dead, she would pay it back in kind. If he was trapped in the lamp she would find a way to free him.

First she had to get out of her own mess—and that was going to take a little work.

42

Outside, Argentia's hands were bound behind her back and she was flanked by the two members of the Eye who had accompanied them from the gate. Farrad was walking a pace or two ahead. Argentia planned to play no part in what he had in mind for her, but her unfamiliarity with Khemr-kar was working against her. Their destination could be minutes away or miles away. She needed to focus, to think of a plan quickly—but she kept seeing Griegvard get sucked into the red light and hearing Demby's cry as she was dragged away.

Come on, Gen. Get it together....

She decided to stall for time. "Wait," she said, and stopped walking. The guards moved closer on either side of her. Farrad turned. "How did you know?" she asked.

Farrad laughed. "We were told to watch for an Outland woman with red hair."

Argentia winced. She remembered the guard who had whispered to the Gatekeeper and left his post before the scuffle at the gates. *How could I have been so stupid? Erkani knew I was after him....* Her anger passed as quickly as it had flashed up. Her plan to enter Khemr-kar and catch Erkani unawares had been predicated on him going to ground in the city. *How the hell was I supposed to know he'd go to the palace and take control of the throne?*

There was no mistaking that the Raj of Makhara was no longer ruler of his lands. Argentia wondered what Erkani had offered him. The salamander's ability to seduce had clearly worked on the Raj. Was it conquest, as his son had alluded? Skarn had never mentioned that Makhara was an enemy of Sormoria, but the lamp, like the Wheels of Avis-fe—like all such tokens of power—drew on latent urges, so it was not impossible the Raj had been harboring such desires in secret.

"Where are you taking me?" Argentia asked Farrad.

"The barrack. I'm a generous man," he said. "After I have my fill of you, I may share you with the men. There are worse ways to spend your last night."

"I doubt it."

Farrad slapped Argentia across the face. She staggered sideways, almost falling into a doorway flanked by two large potted plants. Her head was ringing, but she still felt the bonds at her wrists suddenly loosen.

She hid her surprise—she was not about to question such a stroke of extraordinary Fortune—and quickly surveyed the street. It was labyrinthine, like almost all of Khemr-kar's streets, and it was not greatly trafficked. She smiled at Farrad with bloodied lips. "You'd better hit me until I'm unconscious," she said. "That's the only way you'll get me anywhere near your bed, camel-lover."

"Outland whore!" Farrad swung at her again.

Argentia caught his wrist before his arm was halfway to her face. She stepped in, hesitating a split second to relish the surprise on Farrad's face, and then headbutted him squarely on his already maimed nose.

As Farrad crumpled, Argentia jumped the next guard before he had a chance to react, lashing an elbow across his jaw that sent him sprawling atop Farrad.

She spun for the third guard, but he staggered past her, his head enveloped in a cloud of black shadow. Argentia stared in amazement as he careened headfirst into the doorframe and went down.

"Mirk is here."

The meerkat hopped out from the doorway, his paws still glimmering. In the chaos after the battle in the throne hall, he had slipped from sight.

When he saw Argentia being dragged away, he had followed unseen and used his magic to unlock her manacles.

"Mirk!" Argentia stooped and took the nearest guard's sword. She looked at Farrad. The quick impulse to kill him pulsed through her again. She turned and sprinted away instead: if they crossed paths a third time, she had little doubt it would end in bloodshed. For now, he was beaten. A beaten guard or three she would be able to elude. A dead one would have the Eye hunting her. That was the last thing she needed.

With Mirk scampering beside her, Argentia took the first turn she saw, and the next and the next, running until she was deep in the residential maze of Khemr-kar. Finally, she darted through an open gate into a courtyard. A vegetable garden grew in a neat rectangle beside stone benches and a round stone table in the shade of an olive tree. A line full of clothes hung between the tree and the back of the house. Argentia ducked in amid tall tomato plants tied to wooden stakes and crouched down. She was essentially invisible.

"Mirk, you're amazing!" Catching the meerkat to her, she kissed his fuzzy head.

Mirk squirmed free. "Lady is slobbering on Mirk. Pah!" But his amber eyes were beaming even as he wiped at his sleek head in mock offense.

"Oh, hush." Taking a deep, steadying breath, Argentia assessed her situation. She was free. Skarn and the others were in the dungeon. Griegvard was in the lamp—beyond her aid, for the present. *If he's even still alive....*

She forced that thought away. The executioner's axe loomed for Skarn, Demby, and Trok. She had to get them free before she worried about Erkani and lamp. To do that, she had to get back into the palace.

"Come on, Mirk," she said. "We're going shopping again."

"More shopping? Mirk should have left Lady prisoner."

"Funny."

Argentia crept forth from the tomatoes, checked that there was no activity near the windows of the house, and stole what she needed from the clothesline, leaving a handful of coins in the pockets of a vest to pay for what she had taken. Minutes later, she was swathed from head to toe in layers of desert clothing: a beige robe loose enough to conceal the guard's scimitar, an orange sarong, and a brown sari, its veil covering her from the bridge of her nose past her chin. Her hair was bound up beneath the headcover, which reached down to her brow. Only her blue eyes showed. There was nothing she could do to disguise their color, but she did not plan on talking to anyone; she just wanted to be able to get around without being arrested. She rubbed dirt from the garden on the backs of her hands, sullying their pale color. *That's the best I can do....*

There was an empty wicker clothesbasket near the bench. She took that too, throwing a few more coins on the bench, and told Mirk to hide inside. With the basket propped on her shoulder, she had another screen to protect her from scrutiny.

She headed back onto the street. None of the few people she passed paid her any mind, but the real test came when she entered one of the main thoroughfares and saw a group of guards from the Eye coming toward her.

Heart pounding, she ducked her head, following the pattern of the other women, who stepped respectfully aside to clear the way for the guardsmen. They hurried by, taking no more notice of her than any of the other women. For once Argentia was glad of the schism between the sexes that was common to the cultures of the Sudenlands. Being part of a subservient gender might actually save her life.

She walked on, confident that she could move about in the city in relative safety and obscurity. The question now was: where to go?

43

Argentia wandered through the afternoon.

Her escape had put a death-sentence on Farrad's head. He would certainly be looking for her; much hinged on whether he was searching alone or with the full force of the Eye. *Alone*, Argentia guessed. Even in a misogynistic culture like this, she doubted gang-raping prisoners was sanctioned by the officials of the Eye. Despite his boast, whatever Farrad had planned for her would surely not have involved all his men. It probably would not even have involved the two other guards with him.

Of course, a sanction from his superiors was better than death at the salamander's hands, so Argentia could not be sure Farrad would not alert the whole city guard, but she was willing to gamble he would hunt her on his own for at least a while. After dark, maybe, he would begin to panic and be forced to expand his net, but she guessed she had until sunset with only a small number of men actively seeking her.

She needed to have a way into the palace figured out by then and she didn't have the first clue how she was going to do that. She knew she could beat the guards stationed at the gates and the doors, but not with any guarantee of silence: she was no assassin. Even if she did win those battles without calling attention to herself, there was the problem of getting the doors open. If she managed that, she would be walking squarely into the crosshairs of the bowmen in the alcoves, assuming those posts were manned around the clock. *No good at all...*

So she wandered the winding streets, making her slow way toward Kephalo, certain that the answer would present itself. No place was truly impregnable. There was always a way in: it was just a matter of being inventive or lucky enough to find it.

Staying on the opposite side of the wall that segregated Kephalo from the city, she made a circuit of the grounds. The wall was twenty feet of smooth sandstone. No guards except at the gate, but no way to scale it, either.

Argentia completed her circuit. Not wanting to call attention to herself by loitering too long, she turned back into the city. She was disgusted with her inability to figure a way past the wall. Lost in dark thoughts, her steps led her all the way to the gates of Khemr-kar. She caught up with a group heading out to the bazaar and went past the gate guards unnoticed. Outside, she wandered among the tents until the stench of the camels and other animals annoyed her. She noticed some people heading down a road nearer to the river and followed them, drawn as she was ever drawn to the water.

The Ethalus was not nearly as impressive as Argo's Dimrythil. This near to the sea, it was more of an estuary, its color clouded with salt. The banks were sandy and lined with bright green and gold cattails and beautiful orange lilies. They were upriver from the port, though the path Argentia was walking would lead her there eventually. Plenty of carts bearing goods for trade were going in both directions, but not everyone on the road had business with the ships. There were women and children down by the river washing clothes. Some people were just sitting on the boulders strewn along the banks, resting or eating or reading or talking.

Argentia walked until she was abreast of the palace. Choosing an isolated clutch of boulders, she set down her basket, let Mirk loose, and sat. The sun was high, the heat brutal even by the water. She was sweating beneath the layers of robes and wraps, hoods and veils. Her discomfort did not make it any easier for her to concentrate on solving her problem, but she did not dare dispense with her disguise.

Brooding, she broke a cattail and dropped it into the water. Watched idly as it floated along and suddenly veered hard toward the near bank and was sucked under. *Huh…* Argentia waited. When the reed did not resurface, she smiled. "Mirk," she said.

The meerkat scampered over. "Mirk is hungry," he said.

"We'll eat later. I need you to do something for me now."

"Rescuing Lady was not enough?"

"Watch it, or I might forget that I promised not to tell Solsta and Ralak how the aefryt woke up."

"Mirk thinks this is blackmail."

"Mirk…" Her cobalt eyes flashed at him from between veil and headdress.

The meerkat jumped back. "Do not beat Mirk, cruel Lady!" he implored, folding his tiny paws in supplication.

Argentia laughed despite herself. "You're too much, really."

"Mirk will take that as compliment. What can Mirk do for Lady?"

She told him. It was not well received. "Go in water? Mirk will get wet!"

"Yes. But this may be our only way into the palace. If I'm right, I need to know now, before I waste any more time sitting here."

"Fine," Mirk huffed. "Watch Mirk's sword." He stripped off his bandolier and the letter-opener that served as his weapon.

"I'll guard it with my life. Now be careful, and remember what I told you."

"Mirk remembers." The meerkat touched a foot to the river, found the water not too cold, and stepped off the bank. Argentia watched him swim away and then sink out of sight in the same manner the reed had vanished.

Again she waited: long, hot minutes with many glances along the road to make sure she was not being observed by any unfriendly eyes. She was just beginning to worry when Mirk's head popped up beside the rocks. The little animal scooted out of the river, clambered up on a boulder, and shook himself vigorously, spraying Argentia with water. "Hey!"

"Mirk is sorry." The meerkat looked at her with his big, bright amber eyes and Argentia was sure he was not sorry at all. *I don't know how Solsta puts up with him sometimes....* Although, she mused, the Crown could be quite petulant herself: she wondered if Mirk had learned it from his mistress or the other way around.

"Did you find anything?"

Mirk took a moment to smooth down the fur on his sleek head. "Mirk found hole in wall."

"How big?"

"Big enough for Lady."

"And it goes that way?" She nodded toward the crystal dome of the palace.

"That way."

"How far?"

"Mirk did not measure!"

"All right, all right." It did not matter, anyway. Mirk had not been gone more than a few minutes and she was certain she could hold her breath longer than the meerkat. "Good job." She scratched his wet head.

"Now it is Lady's turn to get wet?"

"No. Now we wait."

"Wait for what?"

"For night."

Mirk thought about this for a moment, paced a circle on the rock, and then poked Argentia's hand. "Mirk is still hungry...."

44

They went back to the bazaar.

It was risky, Argentia knew, but Mirk was right: they had to eat.

Coin was a problem. Argentia only had Teranorian crowns, which would trade, but which would also call attention to her. That was the last thing she wanted. So she surveyed the crowd until she spotted the boy picking pockets and the fat, well-dressed man he reported to. Moving behind an orange tent, she let Mirk out of the basket again and told the meerkat to relieve the thief of his purse.

Argentia settled herself next to the basket in a patch of shade. Pretended to sleep, hoping that would dissuade anyone who happened by from bothering her. But no one passed behind the tent and a few minutes later, Mirk returned, looking quite pleased as he presented Argentia with a pouch full of coins. She dumped the pouch in the nearest trash basket. Stuffed the coins in a pocket.

A few stands over from the tent, Argentia found a vendor selling dried apricots and figs. Making sure her hood was drawn low and her veil was in place, she queued up. Watched the woman in front of her carefully, noting what she ordered and what coins she used to make the purchase. When her turn came, Argentia placed some money on the warped wooden countertop and pointed at both fruits. From what she had seen, Makhara followed the same Sudenland traditions as Sormoria, where the women were not allowed to barter. It worked in her favor now, allowing her to play a mute, merely nodding her head in thanks and taking her paper sack.

Mirk had wandered off, but she knew he would find her again. She wondered if he might meet another meerkat—they were native to the Sudenlands—among the various animals in the bazaar, but apparently he did not, for he appeared by her boots again before she had reached the river, looking hopefully at the sack in her hand.

There were still people out by the river, many of them children freed from chores to enjoy the last hours of the day. Argentia and Mirk found a spot and settled down to eat. The apricots did not do much for Argentia, but the figs were sugar-sweet and delicious. They walked a bit afterwards, evening falling with the sun in the west beyond the dunes, people tramping back from the docks to the city, their work finished, the barking of the vendors in the bazaar rising to greet them, hopeful for one more sale.

Argentia and Mirk returned to the boulders where they had waited earlier. Shadows grew long. The sky grew dim, then dark. Children were shouted in. Traffic along the road slowed and finally died out. The lamps were lit along the walls of Khemr-kar, but their light did not reach the bank of the river.

On the lee of the boulders, Argentia stripped down to her black brassier and thong, shoving her wraps and robes in amid the boulders. It pained her to leave her boots, but she vowed she would return for them when this was all over.

"Ready?" she whispered to Mirk.

"Ready. Mirk will make light."

"But not until we're underwater, remember?"

"Mirk remembers."

"Okay. Let's go."

Argentia slipped her long legs into the river. The water had lost some warmth with nightfall, but was still a far cry from the frigid Sea of Sleet, where she had almost drowned during her quest to save Ikabod from Togril Vloth. She sank in up to her chin. Her hair was still bound up, so it would not be a problem. She took the guard's scimitar off the bank as Mirk jumped in beside her. "Lead the way," she said.

Mirk swam out, waved, and sank into the water. Argentia took several deep breaths. The current dragged her forward. *Here we go…* Sucking in a final lungful of night air, she let herself get pulled under.

The current was strong, yanking her hard toward the bank. The water was dark and for an instant she was afraid she would slam into the rock and break her neck. Then a spot of blue incandescence appeared below her: Mirk's magic lighting her way.

She levered head-down and swam with the current, following the meerkat into the mouth of the tunnel in the riverbank.

Argentia had grown up around water, captained her own ships, and taken more than her share of voyages as a passenger. She was well studied in the ways of rivers and seas. Sitting beside the Ethalus had started her thinking about the pool in the throne hall of the palace and the giant octopus: a creature far too large to inhabit a space like that. It was likely that the pool connected to a large underground body of water where the octopus lived until it was summoned by the Raj's scepter. That water had to feed in from somewhere. She was betting that it was from one or more tunnels like this.

The tunnel was cramped: large enough for her to swim forward, but not for her to turn around. *I'll be coming out the other side—or not at all…*

But the current was with her and she was a strong swimmer, quickly catching and passing Mirk, who grabbed her bra strap and hung on, his blue-glowing paws giving them a little light. Black rock and black water rushed past. Argentia's lungs began to burn. She swam harder. Saw less darkness ahead: the tunnel was ending.

She emerged in an underwater cavern. There was a huge jumble of boulders beneath her. Things that might have been seaweed swayed in the shadows. High above, the water was lighter: the surface was there—and air.

She started to swim hard, but Mirk tugged violently on her bra. She turned her head and saw the boulders shifting beneath her and a monstrous eye sliding open.

With dawning horror, she realized they were not boulders at all, but the body of the gargantuan octopus, which, chameleon-like, could absorb the colors of its surroundings. She froze, letting her body go limp, praying the thing would not wake.

Fortune was with her. The disturbance of her swimming had been near enough to the outflow of water from the tunnel that the octopus did not register her as prey. Its eye slipped closed. Had she kept swimming a few moments longer, the vibration of her strokes would surely have roused the monster.

Argentia floated with painful slowness up and up, closing her eyes, spots dancing behind her vision, fighting every instinct that told her to kick and swim, her lungs on fire...

...until her head broke the surface and she sucked in a great draught of air, the gasp impossibly loud and echoing in the silence of the hall.

Still fighting the urge to rush, she drifted to the edge of the pool. She had intended to have Mirk check the hall for guards while she hid in the pool, but there was no way she was risking the water one instant longer than necessary now.

She bumped against the stone side of the pool. Mirk scrambled onto her shoulder and leaped away. Setting her hands on the cold, smooth floor and praying she did not rouse the octopus with these last motions, Argentia shoved herself out of the water with one hard push. The moment her feet touched stone, she sprinted away from the pool. Glanced back as she ran, anticipating an eruption of tentacles.

The pool remained serene.

Argentia skidded to a halt, crouching on the stone, the water sluicing off her body, drumming on the floor like rain. Steadying her breathing, she rose and looked around. The hall was deserted and mostly dark: a few oil lamps on iron poles, but no Raj, no salamander, and no guards. Through the transparent crystal dome, the stars glittered like diamonds on an endless swath of black velvet.

Argentia moved farther from the pool. She was shivering—not just from the temperature of the throne hall, which was downright cold now that night lay over the land, but still thinking of the octopus and how insidiously stealthy the beast was. Even now its tentacles might be gliding toward the surface to wrench her down to a watery—

Aeton's bolts! Get hold of yourself! With a final glance at the sinister pool, Argentia put her thoughts of the octopus behind her. *Where the hell do I go now?* She had given so much thought to breaching the palace that she had not considered how she would get her friends out once she was inside.

She remembered seeing them dragged off down the corridor to the right. She would start her search there. She hefted the scimitar and frowned. *I really hate this thing....* She looked through the long dark of the hall, toward the entrance where her weapons had been taken. *My pack, too....* She had her spare clothes in there. Going into the dungeon dressed and with her katana and handbow was a much better proposition than going half-naked with a half-assed excuse for a sword.

Can't hurt to check.... She was going to get her things back one way or another. If she could get them now, all the better.

She sent Mirk to scout the alcoves. His stealth was without parallel: he had once gotten the drop on Gideon-gil, the elf acknowledged across Teranor as the master of all assassins. While the meerkat raced through the shadows, Argentia paced toward the dais. The whole palace was quiet, but she had lived in Aventar long enough to know that castles never really slept. There were always guards on patrol or servants doing chores or chefs preparing meals—

Something grabbed the back of her calf.

Yelping, Argentia spun to see Mirk's amber eyes peering up at her. "That's not funny!" she hissed.

"Mirk is sorry."

"You really need to work on your sincerity when you say that."

The meerkat blinked. "Mirk *is* sorry. Mirk is *sorry.* Mirk—"

"I didn't mean to work on it now. Did you find anything?"

"Lady's weapons."

"Guards?"

"No people."

She could hardly believe it. "Any magic?"

"Not that Mirk could smell." Among his many talents, the meerkat was finely attuned to the aether and could detect when magic had been used to ward doorways or set traps.

"Perfect." Argentia headed for the alcove, but she was barely halfway there when she froze.

Someone had entered the throne hall.

45

Argentia caught a gleam of pale clothing and steady movement against the shadows. A solitary figure was hurrying along the wall. Whoever it was had come from one of the adjoining passages and was making for the entrance to the hall.

Of all the damned luck.... Argentia quickened her step, her bare feet quiet on the stones as she closed the distance, but the figure got to the entrance ahead of her. A moment later, dim light emanated from one of the alcoves. *Must be a guard....*

Argentia passed under the portcullis. Peeked around the edge of the alcove's doorway. *You've got to be kidding me...*

It was not a guard. It was a thief, and he was stuffing her weapons into a sack.

Anger rose in her like a quick wind. She stepped forward and touched the tip of the scimitar to the back of the thief's neck just as he reached for Lightbringer. "Don't even think about it."

The man froze, his hand hovering above the hilt of the katana. "Turn around," Argentia said. He did, and she took an involuntary step back.

The thief was the Raj's son.

"What are you about?" she demanded, recovering quickly and keeping the scimitar leveled at his chest.

He put his hands up in a placating gesture. "Please, Lady. Put that away. I was coming to rescue you."

Argentia laughed a low laugh. "How noble. Coming to rescue me after Farrad and his guards had their way with me for the day?" She poked him with the scimitar, not hard enough to draw blood, but enough to get his attention. "Try again."

"It is the truth, I swear. I am Timor, son of Tidor, Raj of Makhara—"

"I know who you are." He was even better looking up close than he had appeared from the dais, with a strong nose and jaw and lips that had a youthful ripeness. His glossy black hair was tied in a ponytail. His clothes were beige silks, elegant. "I saw you this afternoon, when you stood by and did nothing."

Timor colored and his dark eyes sparked. "Did nothing? It was me telling my father to heed the warning about the Sultan's army that put your friends in the dungeon instead of the boneyard. You were lucky I could even do that. You do not know how much power that wizard has over my father."

"It's not a wizard. And I know all about it, believe me. But none of this is helping me see why I should believe you."

"Because your friend the Sultan told me to help you."

"What?"

Timor nodded quickly. "I've seen them in the dungeons."

"You've seen them? Are they all right?" She was especially worried about Demby.

"For the moment. My father has not been able to determine the truth about the Sultan's army yet—I doubt he has even tried. I do not think your friends are very important to the wizard Erkani, and his will is done in this palace now. It is like he has taken my father's mind. Him and that damned lamp of his."

"I told you, he's not a wizard, but you're right about the lamp. That what it does," Argentia said quietly. "Why did you go to my friends?"

"No one in the palace will stand up to the wizard, but you and your friends did. I went to them to see if they could help my father. The Sultan told me if I wanted to do that, I needed to rescue you and help you get the Jade Monkey."

"Really? He said you'd need to rescue me?"

Timor gave her a strange look. "Ah...well, no. Actually he said I would not need to rescue you. He said that you against a bunch of stupid guards was a bet he would stake his sultanate on. I did not believe him, but apparently he was right, since you obviously need no rescuing. The Sultan said I should bring your weapons, too. That is what I was trying to do here."

"And how were you going to find me?" She believed he had talked to Skarn—the crack about betting the sultanate on her was just what he would say—but something was not adding up.

"Ah...I...the truth is, the Sultan told me to wait here. He said you would be coming to get him out of the dungeons and that you would stop for your weapons first."

"Am I that predictable?" Argentia groused.

"The Sultan said it was what he would do if your situations were reversed, and if a pirate like him could manage it then you could with ease. What did he mean, when he said he was a pirate?"

"Never mind. Long story. So the Sultan told you to wait here but you decided to come rescue me?"

"Yes. I did not believe him about you escaping the guards."

"So what were you going to do? Storm the barrack?"

"I...do not know. I was not even sure I would be able to get these weapons and get out of the palace." He looked earnestly at her, embarrassed by his admission but frank enough to face her with it. Argentia thought he sounded vaguely disappointed, as if some chance to do a heroic thing had passed him by.

"All right," she said. "I believe that." She lowered the scimitar, trying to figure out what to do next. After a few moments, she looked back to Timor. "Stop staring at me," she said.

"A thousand apologies!" He flushed and quickly looked away. Then he muttered, "But it is difficult not to."

God damn it! "Well the show's over. Turn around. Mirk, watch him. If he moves...." She let the threat fall into silence.

"Mirk will savage his ugly nose."

"It talks!" Timor exclaimed.

"And bites," Argentia said, although she had never actually seen Mirk bite anyone. She grabbed her pack and hastily pulled on her spare pants and blouse. She strapped on her katana and other weapons. Felt whole again. "Now—tell me why I shouldn't put a blade to your throat, march you to your father's chambers, and demand he release my friends?"

Timor shook his head sadly. "You are welcome to try. He would probably tell you to kill me anyway. My father is not in control here. He is a puppet to that wizard—"

"For the last time, Erkani's not a wizard. He's just a thief who stole a lamp that happened to be the prison of an aefryt."

"An aefryt? I thought they were just children's tales. Like the djinn."

"Nope. And the djinn are probably real, too," Argentia said, remembering how she had scoffed in a similar fashion when Relsthab the Red had tasked her to rescue Solsta from a vampyr. In her experience, most things from children's tales turned out to be all too real—and far worse than the storytellers ever imagined.

"It's not a man that's the enemy here, it's a monster in a man's body," she said. "An aefryt called Bazu. You need to understand that, and you need to tell me what happened with your father." She was conscious of time passing and the how dangerous that was for her, but before she could determine what to do next, she had to decide how far to trust the Raj's son.

"The wiz— I am sorry. *Erkani* arrived at the palace three days ago and gained an audience with my father. I know not what they spoke of, but when it was ended my father disbanded his council and declared Erkani his sole advisor. Then came this talk of mustering our army and conquering the Sudenlands. It is madness! We are not a military kingdom. We would be destroyed! I tried to dissuade my father. Erkani said I was a traitor. It took all my mother's tears to keep my father from throwing me in the dungeons."

"That's good," Argentia said, remembering how the Raj had also let his son reason with him that afternoon. "It means he's not completely under Bazu's control yet. There's still hope for him."

Timor grabbed her arm. "Then you'll help me?"

"If I can. Take me to the dungeons. We have to get my friends out."

"No, we can not do that."

"What do you mean?" Argentia pulled her arm free.

Timor backed up, shaking his head. "The Sultan said not to. He said it was more important that you get the Jade Monkey."

"That's ridiculous! I don't have the first clue how to do that!"

"That is why the Sultan wanted me to find you," Timor said. "I know where the Jade Monkey is."

46

"You *what?*" Argentia shouted, forgetting where she was. Mirk yipped in alarm. Cursing under her breath, Argentia sent the meerkat off to check the throne hall and see if her noise had attracted any attention. Then she cornered Timor. "You know where this monkey is?"

The prince shrank from her intensity. "Well, I do not know exactly, but I know who has it and pretty much where to find them. I can get you that far at least."

"Tell me."

He told her. "And we can be there and back before dawn?" she asked.

"We can get there tonight—it is only a few hours down the Sandway. Getting back depends on what happens while we are there."

I can't believe I'm even considering this, Argentia thought. But if she could get the Jade Monkey, she could end all this. *And Skarn must be confident he'll be okay a while longer....*

"We'll figure that part out later. But I promise you, if you betray me, they'll never find your body." Timor looked at her, surprised. "Believe it," she said. The ice in her cobalt eyes painted an image of his body amid the endless dunes, vultures circling.

"I do," he said, shuddering.

Argentia nodded and took a last look around the alcove. Seeing

Griegvard's axe reminded her of the dwarf's plight and reinforced her decision. "Let's go."

They met up with Mirk in the still-empty throne hall. "We have to be careful," Timor said. "My father issued orders that after dark, no one is allowed out in the palace except the guards on patrol."

"Why?"

"I will show you on the way." Timor led them through the dimly lit palace. Several corridors beyond the throne hall, a lurid light emanated from a stairwell.

"What the hell is going on down there?" Argentia whispered.

"Erkani," Timor said. "Doing whatever devilry he does. That is why my father does not want anyone out. The guards are loyal to him, but the servants have families in the city. If word got out that the new royal advisor was some kind of meja...the people are very superstitious. It would not be well received."

"What's down there?" Argentia asked.

"The treasure vaults."

Of course.... "Do you have a lot of rubies?"

"Yes. They are the most common stone in Makhara. There are mines all over the Kogom Valley. Why?"

"Never mind. But we need to hurry. We're running out of time for your father and my friends." *And maybe all Acrevast....* Now Argentia understood why the salamander had come to the palace. Why waste time stealing rubies from homes and stores when by taking control of the Raj it gained access to a stock that was certainly plentiful enough to break the spells on the lamp and release it completely?

The salamander had outsmarted her again, been a step ahead again. The taste of defeat was bile in her mouth. She despised it, would not stand for it. She had never failed at any hunt. Wasn't about to start now.

They skirted wide of the ugly light. Argentia could feel the heat of it, like passing near a sunstone. The glow faded behind them, leaving gloom. A few minutes later, Timor said, "My room is just ahead."

"Your room?"

"That is how we are getting out. You will see."

They rounded a corner, and what Argentia saw was a quartet of guards.

47

"Betemit!" Timor exclaimed, lifting a hand to a graybeard guard standing nearest the doors to his chambers. "What is the meaning of this?"

The old guard looked down as if in shame, but another of them—a sneering brute with a thick black beard and a wide nose—leaned off the wall where he had been slouching and said: "You're the one with the explaining to do, seeing how you're out of your chamber past dark, my Prince." He tacked on the title with a mocking air.

"And keeping ill company," another added.

"You dare?" Timor stepped forward. "The Prince of Makhara does not answer to you, guardsman!"

"But he answers to his father," the first guard said. He drew his scimitar. Two of the other guards followed suit, pointing the blades at Timor and Argentia. "Let's go see what the Raj thinks about his son consorting with this Outland whore."

"Let's not," Argentia said.

Timor had half-turned when the first silver streak from Argentia's handbow blasted past him. By the time he flinched, two more shots had been fired. To the Prince, the huntress did not even seem to aim: just passed her hand from right to left and the three guards who had drawn weapons were flung down in the corridor, pale gray smoke leaking from holes in their breastplates.

"Ab'dala!" Timor gasped as Argentia lowered her weapon. "You—You killed them!"

"But I didn't kill you, did I?"

"N-no...."

"Which means I'm trusting that you didn't plant those guards here to capture me. Don't make me regret it." Argentia pointed the handbow at the one remaining guard: the one Timor had addressed at the outset and the only one who had kept his weapon sheathed. "What's his story?"

Timor was still too stunned to answer, so the guard spoke for himself. "Thank you for my life," he said. He was a tall man in his mid-fifties, tan and fit in his green-and-black uniform. His beard and hair were gray and trim, and he had crows-feet around his dark eyes.

"Earn it," Argentia replied.

"I am Betemit, my Lady. Guard to the Prince. I fear this is my fault: I should have come for you myself, but the Prince insisted the risk be his. These men somehow knew he was out of his room. They demanded to see him in his chambers. I refused them entry, so they decided to wait. Trying to stop them from doing that would have been as good as raising the alarm myself. So I waited to see what Fortune would bring. Thankfully, She brought a quick shot."

Argentia decided she liked Betemit. He reminded her of Martigan, Skarn's old bodyguard who had fallen in the quest to destroy Araxis Thul. "Thanks."

"That is a wondrous weapon. Meja-craft?" Betemit asked.

"Cyclops," Argentia said, holstering the handbow. Betemit looked at her blankly. "One-eyed giants from the mountains of my homeland. They have crafting magic, so yes I suppose it's sort of meja-craft."

"Wondrous," Betemit repeated.

"I do not understand how they knew," Timor said.

Betemit turned to him. "I would imagine whomever had the duty at the dungeons told them of your visit, my Prince."

"They would not dare!"

"Remember, my Prince, and please excuse my impertinence for so saying, but it may not be only your royal father who is not in the full control of his mind."

"He's right," Argentia said. "You can't trust anyone anymore. Not as long as Erkani and his lamp are here."

Betemit turned to Argentia. "Things are ill in this palace, Lady. If you and your friends can help us, then do so."

"I'm trying to. Open the doors and help me with these, would you?" She motioned to the bodies.

Betemit shook his head. "I will attend to them. You two must go now. Others may be searching for the Prince as we speak." He pulled the door open and took Timor by the shoulder. "Help her, my Prince. Honor your father and your birthright. Remember what I have taught you and walk with Ab'dala grace."

"Betemit, I—"

"Go now, my Prince." Betemit gave Timor a gentle, guiding push. Argentia nodded at Mirk to follow him.

"Hello," the meerkat said as he passed Betemit. The old guard did not bat an eye. "Take care of the Prince," he said quietly to Argentia. "He is a good boy, and brave enough, but he is still young. If you must fight, he will not run, but he will not be a great asset either."

"I understand. Thanks."

Timor's chamber was an impressive circular space split into two concentric levels. The upper level held a desk and several couches, potted palms, three closets, and a doorway leading to a bath. The wall opposite the door was broken by a series of long, arched windows full of moonlight. The lower circle was three steps below the upper, dominated by a circular bed full of purple pillows and rumpled silk sheets. A round Nhapian rug lay at the foot of the bed; it was probably the most expensive thing in the room, Argentia guessed—she had two herself.

Timor seemed dazed as he went to his closet. *He's got more clothes than me,* Argentia thought as the prince reached past a barricade of hanging satins and silks, groping until he found what he was searching for. There was a grinding noise from the floor by the bed. The center of the Nhapian rug sagged. Timor came out of his closet and yanked the rug away. A square hole had appeared in the wooden floor, leading into darkness.

Argentia was hardly surprised. Castle Aventar had many secret passages—she had been in several and Solsta had told her of others. *Gonna need a light....* She swung her bag off her shoulder and rummaged until she found a moonstone. It had been inert too long and lost what light it held, but it was easy to recharge. Holding it to one of the colored-glass lamps by the bed, she waited until it had absorbed enough light to begin to glow. "How long is the tunnel?" she asked.

"I do not know. I have never had to use it," Timor snapped, descending into the hole.

Argentia watched him out of sight, wondering at this sudden change in his demeanor. Whatever it was, she did not have time to worry about it. "Mirk, let's go," she said, picking up her bag. She glanced around. "Mirk!" The meerkat was on the prince's dressing table, poised over a clutter of rings. He jumped as if shocked by Argentia's voice. "You get over here right now!"

Mirk hopped down and scampered to her, his amber eyes wide and innocent.

"What were you doing?"

"Mirk likes shiny stones," he said.

"You better not have taken any."

"Mirk did not."

"Mirk...."

"Mirk took one."

"Put it on the floor." Reluctantly, the meerkat opened the purse on his swordbelt and extracted an emerald-in-gold ring. "Is that all?"

"Yes."

"I'm warning you...."

"Fine!" The meerkat dumped the pouch open, spilling out three more rings.

Argentia shook her head. "I swear I can't take you anywhere."

"Mistress says the same thing," Mirk agreed, dropping down the hole before Argentia could respond. Blowing a stray lock of hair out of her eyes, she started down the the ladder after the meerkat. Paused to grab the hatch and push it back into place above her, sealing the hidden passage. *If Betemit's smart enough to put the rug back once he's finished with the guards, we might just pull this off...*

48

The moonstone had plenty of light for the space of the tunnel, showing Argentia solid stone walls and a floor of hard-packed earth, cold and gritty beneath her bare feet. Timor was waiting. As soon as Argentia was down with the light, he started walking. A few minutes later, they passed another corridor branching off from the one they were in. Argentia asked where it led.

"My father's chamber." Timor's dispassionate tone made it clear no elaboration was forthcoming.

"Something wrong?"

"No."

They kept walking, silence between them. Timor glanced at Argentia, then away, then back to her again and finally stopped and said, "Those guards outside my room, they had families. Wives and children. You killed them like...like they were...." He shook his head and trailed off.

Argentia closed her eyes for a moment. She had always been able to segregate her actions from her conscience: to summon an emotional coldness and do what had to be done. It was not a part of her that she was proud of, but it was necessary in her life. "I've never killed anyone who wasn't trying to kill me," she said. "It isn't something I enjoy, believe me, but sometimes it's the only way."

The prince gave her a doubtful look.

"Listen, I don't care what you think of me, Timor," Argentia said. "I have to wake up and go to sleep with myself every single day and I do that just fine. But believe me when I tell you if I didn't do what I did up there, we'd probably be dead ourselves. Would you have preferred I left them wounded and screaming to bring the rest of the guards down on us? How would that help your father?"

She pointed her finger at him. "Let me tell you something else: more people are going to die before this is over. You'd better get that through your princely little head right now. That aefryt isn't going to go quietly. It wants nothing but to burn and destroy. That's what it lives for. My job's to stop that from happening. I'm the Crown of Teranor's huntress. This is what I do—and yeah, sometimes things get bloody. If you can't handle that, just tell me how to get to these Horsair Guardians and go the hell back to your room. But before you do, think about this: you can bet those weren't the only guards who knew what you were up to. You're as much of a fugitive as I am right now."

"You think I do not know this? That I did not understand the risks when I went into the dungeon to your friends?" Timor snapped.

"Then what are you harping about those guards for?" Argentia snapped back.

"Because I am not sure I could do that!" In the light of the moonstone, Timor's cheeks were flaming. "I am no coward, but I am not sure I can kill like that!"

Ah, God.... Argentia felt something move inside her, quelling her temper. She shook her head and smiled gently. "You don't have to kill someone to prove you have courage, Timor. It can be as simple as trying to do the right thing. You went to Skarn in the dungeon and you were going to come rescue me, right? Those were brave things. Don't let anyone tell you different. Betemit thinks you're brave, too. He told me so before we left. He believes in you. I think he's a good soldier, a good man. I trust his opinion—and my own."

"I am just...afraid I will not be able to help you. Or my father."

Argentia placed a hand on his shoulder and looked him in the eyes. "Just do what you said you'd do. Get me to the Jade Monkey and I will end this."

After their flare of tempers was settled, silence resumed between Timor and Argentia, but it was a more comfortable kind.

Argentia spent the time listening for sounds of pursuit and hearing nothing but their own footsteps. If Betemit hid the guards quickly enough, the bodies might not be discovered until morning, and by morning everything was going to blow up anyway when Farrad did not bring Argentia before the aefryt. If the bodies were found sooner, then everything depended on how quickly the guards put together what had happened and realized where they had gone.

"Where does this tunnel come out, anyway?" Argentia asked.

"The docks," Timor replied.

"Wish I knew about this before," Argentia muttered. "It would have made getting back into the palace a hell of a lot easier."

"How *did* you get in, anyway?" Timor asked.

Argentia smiled. Her comment had been loaded to get just this response out of Timor, to keep him from brooding on what lay behind and what lay ahead. What better way to do that than with a tale?

So she narrated the story of her escape from the guards and her discovery of the underwater passage into the lake beneath the palace. Timor was amazed. "A lake? Really? I had no idea." He thought about it for a minute. "I have never heard of anything like that."

Argentia laughed. "How old are you? Seventeen, eighteen?"

"Seventeen," Timor said somewhat indignantly. "Why?"

"Imagine, seventeen and there are things he hasn't heard of," Argentia said, gently mocking him.

"That was not what I meant. I meant I had never heard of a lake under the palace before."

"I know. Lighten up or I'm sending you home."

"You can not send me home. How will you find the Horsairs?"

"I'll have Mirk torture the information out of you and then I'll send you home."

It took Timor a moment to realize she was joking. *Another failure of deadpan humor,* Argentia despaired.

"I have never seen a talking meerkat," Timor said.

"Never seen a talking meerkat, never heard of an underground lake, and he's—"

"—only seventeen," Timor completed. "Ha-ha."

Argentia grinned. "There's hope for you yet."

"What about the meerkat?"

"Mirk? He belongs to the Crown of Teranor. He's just with me because he likes to travel to different places and hunt down dangerous monsters from other planes."

"Mirk is not so hot about the hunting monsters part," the meerkat said. "Mirk would rather hunt dinner or breakfast. Mirk is very hungry again."

"Maybe you have a tapeworm," Argentia suggested.

"Mirk does not have filthy worm!"

It was about twenty minutes of fast walking to the end of the tunnel, by which time the moonstone was flagging. Shadows encroached, but the stone still gave light enough to show the brick wall blocking their way. "Well?" Argentia asked.

"I think it is this one." Timor pushed on a brick. Nothing happened. Timor looked confused. He tried again to no effect. "But I thought…."

"Mirk thinks it is *that* one."

Timor pushed the brick the meerkat pointed to. There was a click and a grinding noise and the wall swung open. "Yes, of course. It is the eighth brick over, not the eighth brick down. I could never remember that." He moved through the door.

Argentia rolled her eyes at Mirk and followed the prince out of the tunnel. The moonstone's guttering light showed them a storeroom with a few dusty crates stacked against two of the walls. There were stairs ascending to a door. "What's up there?" Argentia asked.

"The warehouse in the royal berth." Timor pushed the correct brick on the warehouse side of the wall on the first try, closing the secret door behind them.

"Any guards?"

"I do not think in the warehouse itself. There will be one at the entrance to the berth to keep people away from the barge."

"Okay. I'll try not to kill him, don't worry."

They went up the steps into the warehouse, which was not greatly different from Argentia's storage spaces at Argo's docks: a wide space with neatly arranged rows of wooden pallets holding stacks of crates. "The side door," Timor suggested.

Outside, the moon was up and full: plenty of light to see by. The silhouette of the royal barge—a five-deck monstrosity—loomed like a floating palace. Impressive, but not what Argentia was here for.

She hustled to the corner of the warehouse. Peeked around. The royal berth was at the farthest upriver end of the docks, isolated from the merchant berths by a tall, iron fence. The gate was on the far side of a loading yard bathed in moonlight. As Timor had feared, it was guarded.

Argentia considered the situation. Made a plan.

50

Argentia and Mirk raced along the fence, keeping low and as much in the shadows as possible. When they were about halfway to the gate, they stopped. Argentia crouched down and they waited.

Everything now depended on Timor.

Argentia watched as the prince staggered across the yard. He wove a drunken path toward the gate, stumbling every few steps. The guard outside the gate finally heard the noise of the prince approaching. He turned, peering between the bars.

Timor fell to his knees, clutching at his chest and gasping for help.

"Prince Timor?" The guard had a hand on the lock, fumbling for a key, his movements frantic as Timor went face down in the yard. He got the door open and rushed over, kneeling beside Timor, rolling him over. "Prince Timor! What hap—"

Argentia's whip lashed around the guard's throat. With an expert snap of her wrist she wrenched the man off his feet. Pouncing forward before he could rise, she shoved his helmet aside and clouted him in the forehead with the butt of the whip's handle. He slumped and went still.

Unwinding her whip, Argentia checked to make sure the guard was still breathing and quickly looked around. The attack had attracted no attention. "That was great," she said, extending a hand and helping Timor to his feet. "Absolutely perfect!"

"Thank you." Timor glanced at the guard.

"Just unconscious," Argentia said.

Timor nodded. There was a light in his eyes that had not been there after the battle outside his room: a pride in having done his part. Argentia thought that from here on out, he would probably be okay.

"Let's get moving," she said. The docks were quiet. They heard voices on a few of the barges and saw a handful of people still moving around in the various yards, but for the most part the work had ended with the setting of the sun. It was different from what Argentia had expected. In Argo, the docks were worked almost around the clock, patrolled by the dockmaster and the Watch. *About time we got some kind of break...*

They made it to the road without any trouble. Argentia crossed it and headed down the bank to the edge of the river.

"What are you doing?" Timor asked.

"Safer down here until we're away from the city." The lights along the walls were bright on the road, but left deep shadows between the shoulder and the moon-silvered river.

"But you are going the wrong way," Timor said as Argentia set off along the bank.

"Relax. There's something I need to get." A few minutes later they stopped beside a certain clutch of boulders, where Argentia retrieved her beloved boots. She also took the Makharanian wraps; the muted colors would help her blend into the shadows and conceal her Outland identity in case they did run into anyone.

"Okay, now I'm ready," Argentia said. "Let's go."

They kept to the riverbank. The course took them wide of the city and the bazaar: a hard mile along the soft shoals, forging through chest-high weeds, cattails, and lilies. Finally, Argentia caught sight of the grove where they had landed the pegasi. Judging that they were far enough now not to attract attention, she climbed the slope, crossed a field to the copse, and led Timor out onto the road.

"Okay, it's your show," she said.

Timor was wiping at the cuffs of his pants, which he had rolled to his knees. His sandaled feet and calves were soaked with mud. "We follow the road," he said.

"How far to these Horsairs?"

"They live about ten miles from the city. A couple hours walking, maybe three, if they do not find us first."

"What's that supposed to mean?"

"The Horsairs are not under my father's governance. Ages ago, they claimed the dune-lands as their own. My ancestors sent battalions against them to try to bring them under control. They failed every time. Eventually they gave up and a peace was reached. The Horsairs raise horses—the finest in the world—and they welcome trade, but the rule is that they come to the city. Many men who have dared to go to the Horsairs seeking to sell or buy have never returned, although...." He trailed off.

"What?" Argentia prompted.

"Although it is said they do not leave because the Horsair women are incredibly beautiful and have the power to bewitch men's minds." Timor glanced at Argentia and then away, color rising in his cheeks.

Argentia laughed. "All women can bewitch men's minds," she said. "That's what we do. You'll find out some day."

"Anyway," Timor said quickly. "Night is an especially bad time to try to find them. They are very wary of horse-thieves so they keep a heavy guard and sometimes a patrol. That is why I said they might find us before we reach the camp. If they do, just follow my lead and everything should be all right."

"I told you, it's your show," Argentia said, humoring the prince. She was closer to actually trusting him, but she had no intention of following his lead with anything.

Nonetheless, his warning about the Horsairs resonated. She scanned the surroundings. Beneath the full moon, the dunes looked like frozen waves on an endless black sea. The Sandway, firm and rutted with years of caravan travel, carved a track through the sand hills. You could see ahead for a long way, but the dunes blocked the approach of anything from the sides. Even in the daylight, Argentia imagined, it would be all too easy to be taken by surprise. *No help for it....* She would just have to be ready if and when something happened.

They walked on. The air was cold and would only get colder. The moonlit land was beautifully bleak. It reminded Argentia of the Ice Reaches of Nord: awesome in its emptiness, but not lifeless and blasted like the Wastes of Yth. She listened to the grass rustling on the sand mounds and the hoots of the desert owls, which prompted Mirk to hitch a ride in Argentia's pack lest he fall victim to one of the raptors. "How far does this road go?" she asked Timor.

"All the way to the Crescent Jewels," Timor said.

"Ah, translation?"

Timor explained that the Crescent Jewels were six mining cities arrayed in an arc in the Kogom Valley a few hundred miles out from Khemr-kar. They were the sources of the precious gems and metals that were Makhara's chief exports.

They spoke for a while about trade. Timor was amazed to learn that Argentia owned ships and was quite knowledgeable about commerce between Teranor and the Sudenlands. Eventually, silence fell between them again. Argentia noticed they were moving more slowly. She was hungry and very thirsty; she had hardly eaten or drank anything all day. "Do you think the Horsairs have any caf," she asked, only half in jest.

"Mirk hopes so," the meerkat piped up from her pack.

And the shadows erupted.

51

"Do not move!" Timor shouted, grabbing Argentia as torches and men and horses converged from the dunes on either side of the road.

Light blazed through the darkness. Bare steel glinted. Riders whooped and hollered, wheeling around, raising a storm of dust and dirt and sand. When the cloud of debris settled, Argentia and Timor were encircled by the shiny curves of eight scimitars in the hands of the eight men in black desert robes and turbans mounted upon beautiful black stallions.

"Trespassers upon the lands of the Horsairs, how will you die?" The leader of the riders was a tall man with keen, dark eyes above a red scarf. "With dignity upon your feet, or begging from your knees like dogs?"

"Please your mercy, we would not die at all," Timor said.

"Well answered." The rider dismounted smoothly, gesturing for his fellows to lower their weapons. "You are come from the city," he said. "On foot, with few provisions, unless that pack has been ensorcelled by some djinn to hold more than it appears. A boy and a woman, out for a tryst beneath the full moon, perhaps? But you have walked far for that purpose and past a lovely grove that has served that purpose well for many years, or so we hear."

"Please your mercy, such a…dalliance was not our intent this night."

"What are you, then? Fugitives? Thieves? Two that have fled city justice expecting shelter from the Children of the Sands?"

"Please your mercy, we are no trespassers, if by trespassers you mean those who enter your lands without intending to be known," Timor replied. "We travel openly upon the road."

"Indeed. Yet the open hand can disguise a dagger up the sleeve," the Horsair captain said. "Speak now your purpose, boy. And do not think to lie."

"Our purpose, please your mercy, is to speak with the Lord of the Horsairs."

At this, the Horsairs burst out laughing. The Captain silenced them with a raised hand, though there was amusement in his voice. "What would you with the Lord of the Horsairs, boy?"

"It is said the Lord prizes beautiful horses and beautiful women," Timor said. "I bring this jewel for his harem."

Argentia started to protest. Timor kicked her sharply in the ankle and she bit her lips hard, fuming beneath her drawn hood.

"A jewel for his Lordship's harem, eh? Show your face, then, woman." The Captain took a torch from the nearest man and let the light fall over Argentia, using the tip of his scimitar to flick her hood back from her face.

"An Outlander!" the Captain exclaimed. "A jewel indeed. A ruby for his Lordship's couch."

"You are soooo dead," Argentia muttered to Timor.

"What do you ask in exchange for this jewel?" the Captain said to Timor.

"That is for the Lord to hear," Timor said.

The Captain considered, looking long at Argentia, who glared bitter ice with her cobalt eyes but held her tongue. Finally, the Captain nodded. "Very well. You shall have your audience, boy. If our Lord likes well your jewel, you shall speak your question to him. If he likes her not, she shall join the women of the camp and you shall be blinded and turned loose into the desert to end your days in darkness and despair." Sheathing his scimitar, he gave a sharp whistle.

From the shadow-mantled dunes another Horsair appeared leading a camel laden with waterskins. *Oh this just keeps getting better,* Argentia thought. She had ridden a camel across the Wastes of Yth; to say the least, they were not her favorite mode of travel. *And those horses are just beautiful. Why can't we ride them?*

She burned to ask, but was mindful of their goal. If the Lord of the Horsairs could deliver the Jade Monkey to her, she would keep silent and play her part. *For now...*

One of the Horsairs touched her back to guide her to the camel. "My Lord Balazar, the woman is armed!" he shouted, feeling her katana beneath her robes.

Immediately the scimitars flashed out again. Balazar moved to Argentia and put her at swordpoint again. "What is the meaning of this?" he asked Timor.

"More gifts for your Lord," Timor said. "Rich weapons from the greatest Outland smiths."

"If they are gifts for our Lord, I will bear them to him myself," Balazar said. "Off with the robe, woman."

Argentia doffed the hood and cloak and wraps, stuffing them into her pack. Silently, she unfastened her weapon belts and handed over the arms, palming a single throwing dagger as she did so. She did not know what these Horsairs intended, but she was not going to be left completely weaponless.

Satisfied, Balazar collected her weapons and the Horsairs moved out, dousing their torches in the sand and riding by moonlight. They veered left away from the road. Very quickly it became impossible for Argentia, even with her uncanny sense of direction, to tell exactly where they were going. She could mark their course relative to the moon—it was west—but the dunes all looked the same. There were no crags or broken trees or boulders to mark the way to memory as there were in the Heaths or even in the Ythian Wastes.

There was nothing to do but ride, so she did. The loping gait of the camel became all too quickly familiar again, as did the wretched stench of the beast. Timor, seated before her, seemed unfazed, but Argentia drew the collar of her blouse across her nose and mouth. *At least it hasn't spit on me. Yet....*

Still, the ride could not end fast enough. Though little more than an hour passed in steady progress across the sands, it seemed much longer to Argentia before the first strains of music floated to her ears on the night wind and alerted her to the fact that they were nearing what she hoped was their destination.

They climbed a tremendous dune. From the crest, Argentia at last looked down upon the camp of the Horsairs.

52

Camp? Argentia stared wide-eyed at the spectacle far below her. *It's practically a city!*

The dunes plunged several thousand feet into an immense crater. The hidden valley was so deep that the light of the torches stationed on the wall ringing the tent city did not rise high enough to betray the camp's location in the dark. As they descended, the horses and camel slow but sure-footed on the shifty sands, Argentia could see why the Horsairs had never been besieged with any success. It would be impossible to make an assault on the camp. No force, whether cavalry or footsoldiers, could make swift enough progress down the hill to avoid being decimated by archers on the wall.

It was a thirty-minute, plodding decent to the floor. At the single gate in the sandstone wall, a pair of sentries met the riders. "What spoils, Balazar?" one asked, giving Argentia an appraising glance.

"One, at least, that may please our Lord greatly," Balazar said.

That's what you think, Argentia fumed. *Once we get out of this, I swear I'm going to slap Timor senseless....*

They were ushered into the camp. A group of chattering boys rushed up to take the horses and camel as the party dismounted. They pointed at Argentia, more in amazement than malice. She heard the word "Outlander" several times. Wondered if she was the first Northerner some of them had seen. The boys led the animals to a roofless stable and began grooming them, and Argentia could not contain a smirk when she noticed them arguing over who would have to tend the camel.

"This way," Balazar said. The camp was loud with music and laughter. People were in every open space, sitting and standing around firepits fragrant with roast mutton and milling between the tents, eating and drinking, singing and dancing in a way that reminded Argentia of the gypsy camps she had encountered in her travels through Teranor, though the muted robes of the Horsairs were nothing like the garish kaleidoscope of garments that gypsies favored. Argentia, with her pale skin and red hair, stood out against the drab palette like a phoenix in a hen house. More than a few of the Horsairs paused in their revelry to point and stare and whisper as she went past.

"A thousand years of health to Lord Kazim!" a man shouted. Balazar smiled and nodded. A great cheer went up from the people gathered nearby. Argentia wondered if the Horsair camp was like this every night, or if they had happened upon some special occasion. From Timor's constant glances all around, she gathered he was wondering the same thing.

Balazar led them on a winding course among the tents, which had no geometric order—a similarity to the streets of Khemr-kar that Argentia found amusingly ironic—until they came to a great pavilion of ruby cloth and gold trim. It was easily twenty feet across, supported by poles as thick as barn rafters. A rearing black stallion wearing a gold crown was blazoned on each of the entrance flaps.

"Is my lord and brother within?" the captain asked the pair of brawny guardsmen flanking the entrance.

"He is, Lord Balazar. But not, I think, in the mood to see prisoners."

"No prisoners here." Balazar gestured to Argentia. "This is my gift for Kazim on this fest of his birth. It is come tardy, but I think it will serve, eh?"

The guards laughed and pushed the tent flaps open. Hanging curtains divided the interior into a series of lamp-lit chambers. Thick rugs lined the floor, their work as brilliant as any Argentia had seen woven by the Nhapian masters. Exotic smoke and languid moans from shadow shapes drifted through air thick with perfumes and sweat. *What a lovely harem*, Argentia thought. She glared at Timor, who wisely looked away.

At the rear of the pavilion was a thick, gold silk barricade, also decorated with crowned stallions, with another guard posted before it. He nodded to Balazar and pushed the curtain-flap open.

Balazar led Argentia and Timor into a chamber cluttered with pillows piled two and three high to form a huge bed. Here and there pedestals thrust up, some holding lamps, others plates of food, others pitchers of drink. A half-dozen women, all possessing that sultry Sudenland beauty of tanned skin, dark hair, and ebony eyes, lounged around a man who could only be Kazim.

Argentia caught her breath at the sight of him. *Aeton's bolts!*

The Lord of the Horsairs was tall and chiseled. His brilliant white shirt was unfastened halfway down, revealing a bronze chest that looked as hard as beaten steel, and his blood-red pants ran tight over the rocklike muscles of his thighs. Gold glittered in his ears and on his large fingers, around his neck, and in a thin band holding his lustrous black hair off his proud brow. His face had a rugged handsomeness dominated by a stern nose and wide mouth.

He set a golden goblet to rest on one of the pedestals and bounded up with the grace of a tiger. "Brother Balazar—home from the night watches!" The brothers exchanged a strong hug. "What is this you bring before me?" Kazim's onyx gaze fell on Argentia like lightning, igniting something deep inside her.

"A birth-fest gift," Balazar said. "Or so this city-born whelp claims."

"Is this so?" Kazim took his eyes from Argentia only for an instant, glancing at Timor, who had moved a protective—or possessive—step closer to Argentia. "A rare treasure indeed. Your beauty shines for the merit of good Outland stock," Kazim said, catching Argentia's hand and kissing it. His lips left a warm tingle on her skin; she could not remember having so visceral a reaction to a man since Skarn's brother. *Look where that got me....*

The thought was like a slap of cold water, reminding her not only of her wretched Fortune with men, but of Skarn's danger and her reason for being here. She withdrew her hand from Kazim's grasp. "The merit of Outland stock? That's a new one," she said.

A murmur went through the guards in the tent. Kazim and Balazar exchanged a glance, their brows raised. The women, who had been spearing Argentia with jealous eyes, now looked surprised.

"Forgive her impertinence, my Lord," Timor said. "She is ignorant of the customs of our land and does not know that a woman's place is silent in the company of men."

He gave Argentia a 'keep quiet' look, but she was not having it. "I'm not ignorant of your customs," she said. "I just don't care for them."

Kazim laughed: a rich, melodic sound, like the bass keys of a piano. "As much fire in her tongue as her hair."

Oh please, Argentia thought. But she saw an opportunity. "I've been told my tongue's quite skilled," she said. Licked her lips.

"I am afraid I could never take another's word for proof on such a matter," Kazim said, shaking his head. From the dazzling glint in his eyes, he was clearly enjoying the repartee. "Perhaps a demonstration is in order?"

"Perhaps, but is there somewhere...private we could go? I'm not much on the group thing. I was an only child. Never really got used to sharing...." She trailed a finger down Kazim's chest.

Kazim flashed his white teeth. "Balazar, see the boy well bestowed. I think I will be a long time unwrapping this gift."

"What of my request, Lord?" Timor asked, stalling for time. He looked pale; he had never expected the bluff to be taken to its extreme. "Horsairs deal in trade. You have taken my gift, and—"

"I have not *taken* your gift yet, boy," Kazim said, drawing laughter from Balazar and the guards. "When I have, then we shall speak. You have my word, never broken."

With that, he led Argentia through another set of drapes into a small space where a single huge pillow served as a bed, surrounded by stone pedestals bearing tiered candle-stands. "Private enough?"

"Perfect."

"Then, my pretty Outland mare, prepare for the Stallion." He reached for her.

Argentia took a step back and revealed the dagger she had palmed. The blade glinted in the candlelight. "Unless you want to be the Gelding of the Desert, I'd stay right there. I hate to disappoint you—*really* hate it—but I'm not a gift."

Kazim looked at the dagger for a moment. "It appears my guards need better instruction." He sounded more amused than concerned. Moving to one of the pedestals, he poured a measure of wine out of a decanter. "Who are you?"

"Argentia Dasani, the Crown of Teranor's huntress. I've come for help only the Lord of the Horsairs can give."

Kazim lifted his goblet and drank. "So, Argentia Dasani, Huntress of Teranor. What help do you believe Kazim can give you?"

"I need to find the Jade Monkey."

"The Jade Monkey?" Kazim laughed. "Who told you to seek that fable here?"

53

As Kazim's words fell to silence, Argentia's fear that she had been a played for a fool rose up. She fought it down, but it went hard, and when she spoke her voice was bitter. "Timor told me. The boy."

Kazim nodded. "What does the son of the Raj want with the Jade Monkey? Oh yes, I recognized him," he added, seeing the surprised look on Argentia's face. "I have been to his city many times, though he and his father and their soldiers are doubtless unaware of that."

"He wants to save his father and all Makhara," Argentia said. The time for deceptions was past. She set the dagger down on one of the pedestals and told Kazim about the threat of the aefryt. "You won't escape it if it comes," she said. "That thing will burn this entire kingdom down."

"I am not unfamiliar with the tales of the aefryt," Kazim said.

"Then help me, please."

Kazim shook his head.

"Didn't you hear anything I just said?" Argentia flared. "Or don't you believe me?"

"I both heard and believe you."

"Then why won't you help?"

"There are two reasons. First, as the Rajling said, the Horsairs are a people of trade. Terms of trade are on the table, but unfulfilled...." He looked at her frankly and Argentia felt herself heat up in deep places again. "Second, even if I were satisfied on that count—and I have no doubt I would be—I cannot deliver the Jade Monkey to you or to the Rajling."

"You don't know where it is?" Now she was furious with Timor. *I never, never should have trusted him!*

Kazim raised a big hand. "Ease. Of course I know where it is. The entire purpose of the Horsairs, generation to generation, is to guard the Jade Monkey until the Destined One comes to claim it. The Bearer of the Brand."

"What brand?" Argentia was confused. *Sanla didn't mention anything about any Destined One...*

"A mark by which we will know him. So did the meja Bartemeus write in the scroll he passed to my ancestors binding us to our duty. 'The one destined to claim the Jade Monkey will be a warrior known by the Brand, the mark of the *veldtlord*.' Until such a warrior is come, the Jade Monkey remains hidden in the care of the Horsairs."

"Who's the veldtlord?" Argentia asked, her heart sinking.

"Not who, but what. The veldtlord is a great cat that roams the grasslands beyond the deserts. In the Outland realms, I think, it is called the lion."

I don't believe this. I really just don't.... Argentia looked Kazim in the eyes. "We're going to deal with your second reason before we even think about your first one," she said. "Just so you don't get the wrong idea." Then she loosened the strings of her pants, letting them drop until they hung low on the curve of her hips. Hooking a thumb in her emerald thong, she peeled the silk down just enough. "Does this count?"

Low on her flat abdomen, just to the right of the clean-shaven arch of her mons, was a tattoo of a lion's head, its mane a brilliant red, its eyes frosty blue.

Kazim was speechless—though whether with shock or desire, Argentia wasn't sure. "Hey, can we focus here?" She laced her pants back up. "Is that the brand you're talking about?"

"Perhaps you should show me again."

"Nice try. Maybe another time." Impulsively, Argentia caught her hands behind Kazim's head and kissed him hard. He had full, fleshy lips and was an excellent kisser. *Okay,* definitely *another time,* she thought, imagining what his mouth might do in other places. She broke away before the heat between them could grow more dangerous. Kazim tried to pull her back in, but she swatted his hand and shook her head. "Behave."

"Why?"

"Because I'm the Destined One, or the Branded One, or whatever, and that means you have to do what I tell you, doesn't it?"

Kazim sighed. "Sadly, this is so." He shook his head. "Forgive me. I am amazed. For thousands of years my people have guarded this site and my line has ruled them. To think that now all that ends...."

"So you'll take me to the Jade Monkey."

"It is not that simple."

It never is.... "Tell me."

"The Jade Monkey is in a dungeon beneath this city. Only the Bearer of the Brand can pass the final door, but there waits a terrible monster: a guardian set by Bartemeus that the Bearer must defeat to claim the Monkey."

"That's it?"

"That is not enough?" Kazim's dark eyes sparkled. Argentia had to restrain herself from kissing him again.

"Monsters are my specialty," she said.

Horns ruptured the night.

59

Kazim snapped his head around and Argentia knew immediately something was wrong. "What is it?" she asked, grabbing her dagger off the pedestal.

"Alarm."

Balazar burst in. "Brother! We are under attack. I think this one and her little friend are not what they say."

"Where is the boy?" Kazim asked sharply.

"Guarded without."

"Unharmed?"

Balazar nodded. "Why?"

"Because he's the Raj's son."

"All the gods be damned! So that is why we have the palace guard assembled atop the dune. But what of her?"

"There is no time to explain now." Kazim pushed through the curtain. "Release the Rajling," he ordered the guards flanking Timor. The men immediately stepped aside. "Now, let us see what all this fuss is about."

As Kazim and Balazar and the guards exited the tent, Timor rushed over to Argentia. "What has happened? Are you all right? What are those horns?" he asked.

"I'm fine, but we're out of time. Your father's men are on the dune."

Timor paled. "What do we do?"

"I'm not sure," Argentia admitted. "Things are a little complicated. I'll figure something out. Come on."

The camp was in chaos, but quick orders from Kazim and Balazar got the women and children moving toward the rear of the camp, the men toward the wall. Argentia noticed that where the Lord of the Horsairs went, calm followed. He had that same unflappable nature as Skarn.

At the wall, Horsair archers stood with bows at the ready. High above, on the crest of the dune, moonlight glinted silver off the armor of a line of men on horses. "If that is all they brought, we may return to the feasting," Kazim said loudly. The men cheered. He looked at Argentia. "I assume they are here for you?"

Argentia nodded.

"Why her, brother?" Balazar asked.

Kazim leaned in and whispered to his brother. Balazar's eyes widened. He looked back to Argentia and bowed deeply. "Thousands of years we have waited for this moment. We are at your service."

"Ah...thanks," Argentia said, uncomfortable with her strange new stature among the Horsairs.

"My Lord Kazim!" one of the bowmen shouted. "A rider approaches."

They watched a single horse, its rider holding a torch aloft, descend the slope, crossing the steep incline in a series of switchbacks that demonstrated exactly why the camp had never been taken by enemies. "He bears a flag of parlay," Balazar said.

"So let us parlay." Kazim whistled a powerful note. Moments later, a magnificent ebony stallion with a white starburst on its forehead trotted from the horse stalls. It was by far the most beautiful horse Argentia had ever seen. "Astrali," Kazim said, touching the animal's long, muscular neck. He swung up bareback and with Balazar walking beside him, went through the gate to meet the Raj's rider. They stopped within the light of the torches on the wall and waited.

Argentia watched from the gate as the rider entered the torchlight. He had a bag hanging from his pommel, and a familiar shape was slung behind his saddle.

"Demby!"

The boy raised his head. "Sorry, de Lady. Dis is all my fault."

"Shut up." The rider cuffed Demby across the face and the urchin cried out in pain.

"Leave him alone!" Argentia shouted. "Don't you hurt him!"

In response, the rider dug into the bag tied to his pommel and pulled out a human head. He raised it aloft.

Betemit, Argentia realized. *Poor bastard....*

"My master orders you to surrender, or this will be also be your little friend's fate," the rider said.

"A bold threat to make against a bound and helpless child," Kazim said scornfully. He seemed unmoved by the gristly display. "In any event, you are on Horsair land. Your words are weightless here."

"Horsair land is an illusion, fool. Give up the woman or my master will annihilate you all."

"Interesting bargain," Kazim said. "Sadly, I must refuse, though I thank your master for his most generous terms. The woman is under my protection. You will not have her."

"Mindless slave!" The rider raised a hand to signal the cavalry on the crest.

"Wait!" Argentia rushed forward. She had a sinking feeling she knew exactly what master the guard meant. *Worry about it later. Just get Demby free...."*

But even as she ran she saw that was not going to be a problem.

Kazim nudged Balazar with his elbow. A moment later both Horsairs were laughing.

"You find this amusing, fools?" the rider sneered. "I will say this once more. Give up the Outland woman or I will kill the boy."

"What boy?" Kazim asked.

"This boy, fool." The rider swiped a hand behind him. Struck only the air. "What?" He twisted around. "Give him here, damn you!"

Demby was hovering above the horse, his little body limned with blue light.

Argentia glanced back and saw Mirk perched on the wall, his paws upraised and glowing as he guided the magic that carried Demby away from the rider and deposited him gently on the sand behind the Kazim and Balazar.

Good job, Mirk! Argentia flashed a thumbs-up at the meerkat and hurried to Demby. In the torchlight, she could see his face was badly bruised, one eye swollen shut. *Oh Demby....* She knelt down and hugged him tightly. "You okay?" she asked, gently touching his face.

"Dis is my fault, Lady," he said again.

"No it's not. Don't you worry. Timor! Come here!"

The Raj's son rushed to join them. "Go with Timor," Argentia told Demby. "Wait by the gate. I'll be right there." She helped Demby to his feet, kissed his forehead and watched him walk back toward the others. His legs were wobbly and he leaned on Timor for support.

"Well, my friend. It appears you have lost your leverage," Kazim said to the rider.

"You will all die!" The rider drew his sword.

"I take it that's the end of the parlay," Argentia said.

"So it would seem," Kazim replied.

"Good." She rose, stepped past the Horsairs, and with a sudden motion whipped her throwing dagger through the air.

From her earliest days, Argentia had an easy way with knives; the silverware set with their dinner in the Dasani manor held a special fascination for her: the steel in her hand had felt so...right. She had earned her place in her first adventuring party by winning a knife-throwing contest when she was just a fourteen-year-old runaway. She had been unskilled in combat, unfamiliar with swords or handbows, but knives had always been intuitive for her. She had proved it that night and many times thereafter. Her mastery with them surpassed even her considerable skills with her other weapons.

Her throw took the rider in the back of his upraised sword-hand. The rider screamed in pain and surprise, dropping the weapon. Argentia sprang forward, tackling him out of his saddle. He landed on his back. Argentia dropped atop him, pinning his arms with her knees, and wrenched his helmet off.

"You—shouldn't—hit—children." She punctuated each word with a punch to his face, leaving him bloodied. "I should kill you for what you did to my friend, but I won't. Go back and tell your master I'm coming for him and he isn't going to be happy when I get there." She rubbed a handful of sand in the guard's face. "That's for Demby."

Rising, she walked away. The guard scrambled up and grabbed his sword, charging after her. She never turned to meet him; she never had to. Kazim gestured and arrows sped past Argentia. She felt the air ruffle in their passage. Heard them slam the guard to the ground again, this time not to rise. "Thanks," she said.

"The sand will drink more blood ere dawn," Balazar observed. As if in answer, horns sounded on the crest.

"Brother, govern the wall," Kazim said. "It is time we bring an end to our Guardianship."

55

The Lord of the Horsairs led Argentia back into the camp. Demby and Timor were waiting just inside the gate. The urchin was holding Mirk. "Wait here," Kazim said to Argentia. "There is something you will need if you are to fulfill your destiny."

Before Argentia could reply that she hardly thought her destiny was wrapped up in an ancient desert prophecy, Kazim was gone. She knelt beside Demby. "What happened?" she asked. "Are you okay?" Demby nodded, but she could see he was fighting back tears. "Is Skarn okay?"

"Oh, Lady. Dey come in de night...de bad man Farrad dat took ye from de hall and de guards. Dey wanted to know where ye'd gone. De great Sultan, he laughed at dem. Den de guards, dey started hittin de Sultan, but he just kept laughin until de Farrad, he told dem to stop and to hit on me until I told dem where ye gone.

"De great Sultan he got angry den and he told dem if dey hurt me he'd kill dem all. Dey hit me some, but I didn't tell. I'd die before I told dem, Lady."

"Oh, Demby...." Argentia hugged him again. She had no doubt that he would have gone silently to his grave and her heart broke at his pure, fierce loyalty. "But what happened?"

"De great Sultan, he told dem so dey wouldn't hit me no more. 'She's goin t' get de Jade Monkey,' he said. "Dey laughed at him an said he was

220

de liar, but den de robed one appeared like de meja do, and he don't laugh. He looked at de bad man Farrad and den dere was de fire and de burnin. I can still smell it...." The urchin shuddered. "De robed one, he made de great Sultan tell him again about de monkey and den he said to de palace guards to ride and find ye wit de Horsairs, and to bring me to make de Lady give up, since dey all care about Demby more den demselves." He looked at her with tears in his good eye. "Dat's why dis is all my fault. De great Sultan told so I wouldn't be hurt."

"Of course he did. What kind of great Sultan would Skarn be if he let his jester get tortured?"

Demby giggled a little. "Not de very good one."

"That's right." She ruffled his cornshock hair gently. "Don't you worry. Everything's going to be fine."

Kazim returned. He was holding a large ring with a tarnished bronze key attached to it and all of Argentia's weapons. "Come," he said.

"Where we goin?" Demby asked.

"Yes," Timor added—somewhat tartly, Argentia thought. "Where *are* we going?"

"You two are going to find a safe place to wait until the battle is over and I get back," Argentia said, buckling on her weapons. "I'm going to do what I came here to do and get the Jade Monkey."

"Alone, de Lady?" Demby's good eye widened.

"I think—" Timor began.

Kazim cut him off. "It does not matter what you think, Rajling. The prophecy is clear: only the one with the Brand can recover the Jade Monkey. She is the one and she must go alone. There is no more time to argue."

While Timor fumbled for some response, Argentia crouched beside Demby. "Listen, I need you to take care of Timor," she whispered. "You can do that, can't you?" Demby looked suspiciously at the prince and then nodded. "Good. I promise I'll be back for you. Kazim won't let anything happen to you while I'm gone."

"Den we goin t' go back to help de great Sultan?"

"Absolutely." She kissed him and stood and faced Timor. "I know you want to help your father, but right now all you can do is wait. Remember what I said," she told him. "Find a place that's out of the way and stay there until I get back. And thank you for bringing me this far."

Cries of battle and death echoed over the tents. "Let's go," Argentia said.

Kazim led her into the rear of the camp, where a black tent was set apart from the rest. A single guard stood beside a solitary torch in an iron stand. "My Lord," he said, bowing. "I hear combat."

"So you do. The Raj's Dragoons were kind enough to offer our warriors a little exercise. It may be that you will be able to meet them. Your watch ends this night."

"Truly? But where is the warrior of the Brand?"

"Here." Kazim nodded to Argentia. The guard looked surprised, but recovered well. "I am honored to have held this place safe until your arrival," he said.

"Thanks," Argentia said. *Why does this prophecy nonsense happen to me all the time?*

Kazim took the torch. The guard held the tent flap open. Inside was nothing but sand and a circular stone platform with a low, crenellated wall that resembled the parapet of a tower. In the center of the platform was an iron hatch. Kazim climbed over the wall, inserted the key, and heaved the hatch open. The hinges grated in protest, but they were no match for his strength. "What's down there?" Argentia asked, moving beside him. She saw the rungs of an iron ladder descending into darkness.

"I can tell you nothing of it. None in my lifetime have ventured to open this door until now."

"Then how do you know there's still a guardian?" *Or the Monkey,* Argentia thought, but kept that silent.

"Did not a warrior marked with the veldtlord arrive to claim the Jade Monkey? It is just as certain the guardian you must conquer is still there." He handed her the key.

Great.... "And this is for?"

"It unlocks the first door and also the last."

She hooked it to her belt. Then she set her boot on the ladder, turned around so she was facing the wall, and descended three rungs. The iron felt secure against the wall. Kazim handed her the torch. "Take care of Demby and Timor," she said.

"Assuredly. I will await your return."

"So the prophecy guarantees my return?"

"Hardly. But a Horsair never fails to collect on a bargain. There is unfinished business between you and I, Lady Dasani. That is my guarantee of your return."

She grinned. "Then I'll see you later."

56

Holding the torch wide and low, Argentia made a one-handed descent of the ladder. Counted the rungs as she went. By the time she reached twenty, the difference in temperature was palpable. Clenching her teeth against the cold, she kept going. Twenty rungs later, her boots hit stone instead of iron.

The flickering torchlight showed an antechamber of some sort, utterly devoid of furnishings: just sandstone walls encircling her. There was no door, but there was another hole in the floor and a helix of iron steps descending into blackness. She was about to step toward it when she heard a soft scurrying.

Something touched her boot.

She jumped, sweeping the torch down.

"Do not burn Mirk!" the meerkat yelped.

"Mirk!"

"Mirk is here."

"You scared me half to death! What are you doing here?"

"Mirk is here to help."

"But you can't. I'm the one with the Brand. I'm the one who has to do this." Even as she spoke the words, Argentia realized she was buying into Kazim's prophecy. *Fine, as long as it gets me the Jade Monkey....*

"Mirk will help," the meerkat insisted. "Mirk let stupid monster out of stupid lamp. Mirk will help put it back in."

Argentia sighed and swiped a stray strand of red hair out of her eyes. "Alright," she said. She did not know what it would mean for the prophecy, but Mirk had a knack for proving useful in situations where he had no business being. *And I trust him more than any prophecy, tattoo or no tattoo....* "But stay close to me and don't touch anything."

"Mirk does not see anything to touch."

"You know what I mean."

"Fine," Mirk huffed.

"Good," Argentia shot back. They stared at each other for a moment.

"We can go now?" Mirk said.

"You go first." Argentia pointed to the spiral staircase. The twisting, open steps were a cunning defense. She could not see what was below and would be vulnerable as she descended: the torch made her an easy target. But with Mirk scouting ahead, she would not have to worry. He was small and quick enough to evade detection. "Be careful."

Mirk nodded, scurried to the edge of the hole, and was quickly gone down the iron steps. Moments later, Argentia heard him peep, "Safe." Torch held before her, she made a careful descent, going faster once she determined the steps were structurally sound.

The next room was a full of shelves. The air was musty with the good smell of old parchment and leather. Books, remarkably preserved, were crammed along the walls, dominating the space except where there had been damage to the walls. Sand had ruptured them, pouring through rectangular spaces to pile on the floor. On a second glance, the rectangles looked as if they had been carved by design, almost like windows. *What sort of nut was this Bartemeus?* Argentia wondered. *Who puts windows in a dungeon? Then again, who puts books in a dungeon?*

It was all very strange, but the answer did not seem to have any bearing on finding the Jade Monkey, so Argentia motioned to Mirk to go down the next twist of stairs. The chamber below was much the same as the one above: walls full of books, no furnishings, and a hole in the floor with another descending stairwell. The same for the next, and the one after that. When the fifth loop of their descent also yielded another level of the circular library, Argentia went over to the shelves and ran her finger along the books' dusty spines. They were real. *If it's not a trick, what's the point?*

She still had no answer, so she followed Mirk down another, much longer coil of steps. Finally the scenery changed. The room was much larger and not circular. There was a burgundy carpet on the stone floor. In the torchlight, it looked like a spill of blood. *All right. Now we're getting somewhere....*

"Stay close to me," Argentia said to Mirk. She started walking, coughing a little at the dust her boots puffed up from the ancient rug. The torchlight showed thick drapes in burgundy that matched the carpet hung around more of the window-like rectangles. Piles of sand had poured in and pooled between the drapes. Large urns held the dirt of ages and the desiccated skeletons of plants. Staring at them, Argentia finally understood where she was. *Windows. Those really are windows....* "It's his *house*, Mirk," she said. "It's not a dungeon at all. Bet you anything."

She was sure of it even before they traced the perimeter of the chamber and found the double doors at the end opposite the staircase. The wizard's home had been swallowed by the desert. *Why didn't Kazim tell me? Didn't he know? If his people have been guarding this place for centuries, some of them must have been around before this place sank or whatever happened to it. Didn't anyone pass that little tidbit on?*

It obviously was not the work of an earthquake: the library in the tower would never have survived such a disaster intact. Had it happened so slowly that it had simply passed from generation to generation as an accepted thing, an incremental sinking that accumulated over the years, until one day all that was left was the rooftop of the tower where she had entered? Perhaps, or perhaps the old generations of Horsairs had known, but the knowledge had been skewed over time, until what came down to Kazim and his people was a story of the wizard's dungeon. She knew the way of legend, how truth became distorted into something strange, especially in the Sudenlands. The last time she had been here, she had nearly died because of just such a thing. *I'll be more careful this time....*

She tugged the gilded handle of a red door. It swung open on darkness. The carpet continued, marching through a narrow hallway. There were no windows, but doors lined both walls. All of them were closed. The torch could not resolve the far end of the hall.

"This isn't good, Mirk," Argentia said. "Searching this place could take hours." She thought of the Horsairs fighting above. Of Skarn in the dungeon. Of Griegvard in the lamp. "We've got to hurry."

"Mirk will help." The meerkat ranged out ahead of Argentia, zigzagging along the hallway, his whiskers and nose twitching as he probed at each door, seeking that special tingle that meant something of great magical power was nearby.

He chose none of the doors, continuing instead down the hallway, and Argentia followed.

57

They went quickly from dusty corridor to dusty corridor.

Argentia was grateful for the torch. It provided not only light, but also a little warmth in the underground, which was cold and getting colder. When Mirk finally stopped at a door, Argentia opened it to find a stairwell—not spiral this time, but a straight flight of stone steps marching down to a landing, where they turned and descended further. Argentia wondered what had been in all those closed rooms on the level they were leaving behind. Reminded herself she was not here to explore, just to find the Jade Monkey and stop Erkani.

At the bottom of the stairwell, she pushed open a door. The torch resolved an island counter with a copper rack of pots and pans hanging from the ceiling above it. Argentia swept the torch from side to side, revealing a perimeter of stone countertops over wooden cabinetry. They were in a kitchen. The counters on the left- and righthand walls ran the length of the room, punctuated by ceramic sinks. Racks of knives were arrayed on either side of a hearth in the far wall.

As Mirk hopped up on the island, the door slammed shut behind Argentia. Before she could spin around, the hearth blazed to life, its roaring green fire flooding the room with emerald aetherlight.

Argentia reached behind her. The doorknob would not turn. *Damn....* "Mirk, how do we get out of here?" The aura of magical power gathering in the chamber was palpable, like the air before a summer storm. Argentia cursed under her breath. *Never trust a wizard...* She should have known there would be more to the defenses than just the single guardian mentioned in Bartemeus' instructions to the Horsairs. "Mirk?"

"Mirk is working on it."

"Well work fas—"

Argentia shoved Mirk off the counter and dove behind the island as a knife shot off the rack, tumbling through the air and sticking in the wall behind her. She scrambled around, back up against the counter.

The knife was wriggling furiously in the wall. It pulled free, making a metallic buzzing as it hovered, and then shot back at Argentia.

The huntress ducked fast to one side. The knife slammed into the cabinet where her head had been a moment earlier. It started to pull free again, but Argentia grabbed it, forcing it deeper into the wood. It thrummed in her hand like a bow after a shot. "Mirk!"

The meerkat scrambled around the corner, head low, ears flat. "Mirk sees way out. Follow Mirk."

Before they could move, the air was filled with a droning louder than a host of bees.

Argentia peeked above the counter. Every knife on the racks was vibrating and about to break loose. She dropped the torch. Jumped up and grabbed a copper skillet just as two more blades came flying for her.

CLANG! WHANG! Argentia swatted the knives with the skillet, sending them careening away. Mirk was up on the counter, racing toward the hearth. A dagger speared at him, but the adroit meerkat veered and the knife crashed into a sink.

Four knives flew at Argentia. She went into a defensive posture, working the skillet like a shield, her deft reflexes countering the flying blades. But even as she dashed them aside, the ones she had already struck away twitched and rose back into the air, and a fresh brace was loosening from the racks.

Mirk fired spears of blue aether at a pair of knives, shooting them down. Argentia battered down another trio with the skillet. She could not keep this up forever. The skillet was heavier than a sword; even her well-trained arms were tiring. Soon there would be too many knives in the air coming from too many directions for her and Mirk to possibly block them all. *Got to get out....*

As if reading her mind, Mirk jumped on her shoulder. "Door in wall," he cheeped, pointing past the counter. Argentia saw a square panel beside a lever. *Dumbwaiter....* It was their only chance. "Get the door!"

Mirk thrust his paws at the panel. The dumbwaiter door shot open, revealing a space that looked horribly small to Argentia. *Screw it....* She sprinted forward, twisting and ducking, the skillet working furiously against a point-blank spate of knives.

Fire in her thigh as a blade slashed her open. She stumbled. Kept going. Dove into the dumbwaiter. Mirk screeched as he was thrown free and slammed into the back of the dumbwaiter. Argentia tucked her knees up and twisted around, grabbing the rope for the door. The top and bottom portions slammed together, sealing her in.

The dumbwaiter did not move. *The lever....*

"Mirk!" Argentia shouted. There was no response from the stunned meerkat.

A squadron of knives wheeled about in the air, homing in on the target trapped in a square of space behind a panel of wood with a circular glass window that would never withstand their assault. They launched forward like steel sleet in a hurricane wind.

Oh holy hell.... Argentia flung the door up and lunged out, swiping the lever with the skillet. There was a sickening moment when nothing happened, and then the dumbwaiter lurched down. As the doors snapped closed again, Argentia threw herself backwards—fast, but not fast enough.

One of the knives sliced through the vanishing space and buried itself in Argentia's left shoulder. Her scream was lost to the rattle of the plunging dumbwaiter.

58

Hitting the floor jarred Argentia back to consciousness. *Owwww....*

She remembered nothing of the breakneck descent or the violent stop that shook the doors open and jounced her out into the darkness of an unknown space. *Must've blacked out....*

She was all twisted up: face and torso on the cold floor, one of her legs still half in the dumbwaiter, the other folded awkwardly beneath her. She pulled her leg free of the dumbwaiter, flopping over onto her stomach.

That woke the pain in her shoulder, which hit her like a crossbow bolt and almost put her down again. Gasping, she rolled gingerly onto her back. She could feel the knife in her, and the warm stickiness of her own blood. For a moment she thought she was going to throw up. Biting her lip, she got herself under control and forced herself to touch the steel. The knife had lodged deep. The slightest movement of her arm was agony. "Mirk?" she groaned.

"Mirk is here." Amber eyes glimmered above her.

Argentia exhaled. "Okay. I'm gonna need some help." Fighting the pain, she shuffled around slowly until she was sitting with her back against the wall. "Can you make some light?"

The meerkat cast white globes of light, like frozen lantern bugs, into the air. Not much, but enough for Argentia to see that they had traded the kitchen for the dining room, which made sense. She turned her attention to her wound. She had to get the knife out, but she was going to bleed a lot when she did. Mirk was not much of a healer, so she would have to field dress the wound herself. She unfastened the buttons of her blouse and shrugged her right arm free. "Mirk, I'm going to pull the knife out now. If I black out you've got to make sure I wake up. Shock me or whatever you have to do, but make sure I wake up."

The meerkat nodded and patted her knee. He could smell the pain on her, but also something else. A frosty scent like a winter morning, bleak and bone cold: her will rising. He did not think she would pass out or that he would need to do anything to help her, but he would be ready.

Argentia pulled her dagger from its sheath. Clenched the hilt between her teeth. Taking hold of the knife in her shoulder, she closed her eyes, took three quick deep breaths, and pulled. "Mrrraaaaahh!" The knife came cleanly out of her shoulder. She spat the dagger onto the rug and gasped, tears tumbling down her cheeks. "Oh Aeton that hurts," she moaned, bowing her head.

"Lady?" Mirk peeped after a few moments.

Argentia sighed. "I'm all right, Mirk." She raised her head. Her eyes sparkled with tears but she managed a tight smile. She looked at her blood on the blade for a moment, then cast the knife aside and ran her fingers along the wound, which throbbed wildly. It was a deep cut, bleeding freely, but not spurting. The knife had missed her major vessels. She had been lucky again. *Story of my life....* She closed her fist around the dragon's tooth token in thanks.

"Help me with this," she said, gesturing to her blouse. When Mirk had tugged the garment free of her wounded arm, she had him lay it across her lap and used the dagger to cut it into strips. "Shove as much in the wound as you can and then we'll bind it. I think as long as I can keep it packed, I'll be okay."

Mirk took part of the silk blouse, scrunched it up, and pressed it into the wound. Argentia hissed in pain and he froze. "Keep going," she managed through gritted teeth.

"Mirk is sorry." He scrunched and pushed again.

"Okay," Argentia gasped. "Bind it. Tight."

Working quickly, Mirk wrapped the strips of blouse around the packing, his clever little fingers creating a secure knot. Argentia raised her arm until her elbow was akimbo. It hurt, but the bandage did not slip. "Now make a sling," she said.

Mirk tied a long piece of the blouse into a loop and slipped it over Argentia's head. She slipped her wrist into the lower portion of the loop, giving her arm as much stability as she could. "Thanks. Mirk," she said, rubbing his head with her good hand, "You're a lifesaver."

"Mirk is getting many new names on this trip."

Argentia laughed and forced herself to her feet. She turned her head from side to side to relieve the crick in her neck. Then she checked her thigh. That cut was superficial, and though it was still weeping, it was not going to hamper her ability to walk or bleed her out. "Can you find the trail again?"

"Mirk can try."

With the will-o-wisp balls of aether replacing the torch, they went out of the ornate dining room and into another hallway.

Mirk paused to get his bearings, chose left over right, and they were off again.

In the aetherlight, Argentia marveled at how well preserved everything in the wizard's house was. Gilt mirrors on the walls still gleamed. Tables holding statues and crystal ornaments looked freshly polished.

Mirk led her through a study crammed with leather chairs, two desks, and still more shelves overflowing with books and scrolled parchment. A door opened into a narrow stone corridor that became a flight of steps twisting downward in the same fashion as the stairs in the tower. Argentia shivered, not entirely with cold, although she was freezing; the blouse had not been much protection, but it was better than just her bra. Rather, it was a sense of impending arrival. She had hunted enough people and treasures to have an almost unerring instinct for when a chase was coming to a close.

That was the feeling she had now.

Mirk seemed to sense it as well. He was going more cautiously than before, keeping close to the arc of the wall, and not letting the light wander so far ahead of them as he had been.

Argentia touched the hilt of her katana. She was not in great shape to fight, but she was pretty sure she was going to have to anyway.

A final turn and the stairwell ended. They stepped through a doorway. The light-spheres fanned out to reveal a circular chamber, its ceiling invisible somewhere far above. Two stone columns, each about Argentia's height, were spaced halfway across the chamber, flanking a circular hole some fifteen feet across that gaped in the center of the floor. The far wall had a trio of doors beneath wide lintels. "Mirk, which one?" Argentia asked.

The meerkat closed his eyes. His whiskers trembled. Then he shook his head. "All magic," he said. "Mirk cannot tell."

Great.... "Okay. We'll try them all." Argentia stepped out into the room. The moment her boot touched the stones, green flames burst to life atop the columns. Argentia flinched backwards against the glare. Mirk screeched in surprise.

There was a great sliding noise, like an endless drapery being pulled open, coming from the pit in the center of the chamber. Before Argentia could draw her katana, the thing erupted like a stream of black lava from a volcano, rising and rising in a gargantuan tower of scales.

Dragon!

59

Even as the thought formed, Argentia saw she was wrong. This was no dragon. Though it had the same sinuous neck as the mighty wyrms, it was wingless and limbless. *You've got to be kidding me—a giant snake?*

Hissing filled the air from on high. Argentia looked up—scores of feet at least (and part, if not most of the thing was still down in the pit)—and saw a hood expanding around a huge, angular head. The slitted eyes glinted with green light like that of the braziers. The mouth gaped, revealing two curving fangs, each longer than Argentia was tall.

With the sound of a thousand fires suddenly extinguishing, the cobra's venom hurled down like a liquid meteor.

Argentia was already diving sideways. She tumbled to her feet, cursing the pain shooting through her injured arm, sprinting toward one of the columns, hearing the deadly spittle spraying the ground behind her. She spun around. The snake's head was diving like a fanged thunderbolt. She had no time to think, just to react, diving clear again.

The cobra's jaws snapped closed on air. Its head whipped up even as Argentia rolled to her knees, clutching her shoulder. Soulless green eyes fixed on her. She tried to focus through the pain for one more dodge.

The head plunged—

—and veered away as Mirk darted across the cobra's field of vision.

The gaping mouth closed over the meerkat. "MIRK!" Argentia screamed.

The meerkat popped into sight on the far side of the snake's head, leaping onto one of the stone columns. "Stupid worm is not faster than Mirk!" As if to demonstrate this truth, the meerkat sprang onto the cobra's back.

Hissing furiously, the serpent looped around on itself, its head slashing. Again Mirk was too quick, springing straight up, tapping down for an instant on the very snout of the snake, then springing clear. The cobra gave chase, its sinuous length a glittering ribbon of black death as it rushed past Argentia's crouched form, whipping around one of the stone columns in its pursuit, Mirk running full out, ever a few skittering paces ahead of the gaping mouth.

In the dance of meerkat and serpent, Argentia saw her chance. Wincing, she unfastened the key Kazim had given her from her belt and gathered herself to make a run at the door. *But which one?* All three were identical constructions of wood and iron. She would only have one chance, and that was presuming Mirk could keep the cobra's attention long enough for her to even get to the door.

She closed her fist around the dragon's tooth token. Made her choice. "Mirk! Go left!"

The meerkat zigzagged past her, ears flat, running as if the Archamagus himself was on his tail. The instant the cobra's head shot by, Argentia sprang, dodging around the stone column and bolting to the right-hand door. She had picked it because the lion's head tattoo branding her as the Destined One was on the right side of her body. As she jammed the key into the burnished lock, she prayed she was true in her guess.

A spark of green aether jumped from within the lock as the metal scraped home. The cobra instantly broke from its pursuit of the meerkat, skidding around and launching itself at Argentia.

She turned the key. The lock tumbled.

She twisted the knob. Slammed her shoulder into the door. It banged open and she fell through into a narrow corridor, scrambling on her hands and knees, crying out in pain, glancing back as the cobra slammed its great head into the stone doorframe. It reared back and fired forward again, but the space was too tight even with its hood retracted. After a protracted hiss that Argentia was certain was a curse in whatever language snakes used, it retreated.

Argentia rose, shuddering out a half-triumphant, half-shocked laugh. Her shoulder was bleeding; she could feel blood dripping down her arm more than see it in the broken light of the corridor, which was lit only by the hectic glow from the green braziers in the antechamber. Ahead, all was shadow.

"Mirk!" she shouted. "You out there?"

"Mirk is here!" came the reply.

"Can you get in here?"

As she spoke, the cobra coiled in front of the door, blocking out most of the light. It dipped its head, baleful eyes blazing at Argentia.

"Mirk does not think that is good idea," the meerkat called.

Why is nothing ever easy? "Are you safe?"

"Mirk is safe."

"Okay. Stay there. I'll get you on the way out."

"Mirk thinks Lady should probably hurry."

"Yeah, yeah. It'd help if I could see where I was going."

A moment later a small globe of bluish aetherlight floated in and hovered beside Argentia. "Best Mirk can do," the meerkat cheeped. "Mirk is very tired."

"I'll be fast. Sit tight."

"Mirk wonders what else Lady thinks Mirk *can* do," the meerkat huffed.

Shaking her head, Argentia started off. She had no idea how she was going to get back out to Mirk, but she would worry about that later.

The light floated along with her, giving small illumination. The stone passage was tight on both sides and sloped downward. The stonework ended not long after the doorway, yielding to uneven rock beneath her boots. The tunnel leveled out after a few hundred yards. Mirk's spell was flickering weakly, no more effectual than a candle, but as Argentia came around a turn, she saw that would not matter.

Up ahead, the roughhewn walls were painted with a flickering green light that was all too familiar: Bartemeus' signature aetherfire. Argentia quickened her pace. Rounded a last bend.

Froze in astonishment at the sight before her.

60

It was a world of gold.

Two gigantic golden statues of horses fronted two parallel rows of gilded columns that framed a thoroughfare into incalculable wealth. The space between the columns was the only unoccupied space. The rest was gold. Stacks of bars, many more than five times Argentia's height, filled the cavern: a treasure vault the likes of which she had only seen matched by the dragon's hoard. *If Mirk could see this....*

The thought reminded Argentia of the meerkat's plight. She hurried forward, passing the horses and following the columned avenue between the rows of gold. Along the way she saw urns, picture frames, gold chests open to reveal hundreds of gold pieces in a currency she did not recognize, swords and daggers and axes, all ornate beyond measure, all aglow with the awful green wizardlight that turned their glimmering into something sinister. She did not touch anything: did not even want to.

The golden alley marched on, winding this way and that, bringing Argentia into the center of the vault. A circular space opened before her.

The Jade Monkey waited up ahead.

Argentia recognized it instantly, though it was not at all what she had imagined. *All this way, stabbed by a flying knife, almost killed by a giant snake, for this thing?*

The Jade Monkey was raised up on a golden chair upon a golden dais. It was a statue, about a foot tall and perhaps half that wide, carved from a single block of jade. It was exquisitely crafted, Argentia saw as she mounted the dais and stood on the small golden rug that lay before the throne. The detail in the simian face revealed a pacific quality in the half-lidded eyes, but there was something in the enigmatic smile on the fat lips that hinted at power restrained. Its chin was propped on one hand; the other arm was draped lazily across its knees. The limpid green of the stone seemed to shift, like seawater, swirling and eddying and moving with the tide. This trick of the light was so effective that Argentia wondered if the statue was not in fact filled with water.

She had no bag, so she just picked up the Jade Monkey, cradled it in her good arm, and turned to go.

The green light flared violently. There was a rending CRACK from high above. A huge stalactite plunged down, impaling the golden chair. *Aeton's bolts!* The impact knocked Argentia sprawling. She fell awkwardly, trying to protect the statue, and ended up in a painful heap on the golden carpet, her injured arm howling.

The entire floor of the cavern was shaking.

Just my luck—an earthquake!

Another stalactite dropped from the ceiling, shattering on the dais, peppering Argentia with stone shrapnel. The shaking was getting worse, but it was not like any earthquake she had ever felt. It was a steady tremble, almost a throbbing—and it was coming from the carpet.

What? She knelt up, feeling the humming through her legs. It was as if the carpet was alive. Before she could much ponder the strange sensation, a third stalactite crashed down, and a fourth. *Time to go....*

Argentia scrambled to her feet, but the rug rolled like a wave beneath her, clipping her heels and spilling her down. She cried out in surprise, bracing for the pain when she hit the stone, but it never came.

Instead, it was as if she had fallen onto a couch of pillows. She sank down somewhat and then was buoyed back up.

The carpet was hovering several feet above the dais.

No way! A flying carpet? She had read of such things in the faerie stories of her youth, but had never seen one or even heard of anyone using one, and she numbered several wizards and people wealthy enough to afford such luxuries among her friends.

She had little time to ponder it. As another stalactite fell nearby with a thunderous crash, the carpet leaped into motion, shooting away from the dais, gaining elevation until it was riding almost as high as the stacks of gold. It was remarkably stable beneath Argentia; she felt almost as if she was on a lowering boat upon the sea instead of a rug flying through the air. *But how do you steer it?* The carpet had bolted away from the falling stone like a frightened deer. If she could not control it, if she was at its whim, or if it remained under the control of some spell cast ages ago by Bartemeus, it could well be carrying her into even greater danger.

"Down!" she shouted. To her relief, the carpet immediately swooped closer to the ground. Argentia grinned. *Okay, now let's get out of—*

A shockwave rolled through the passageway. The carpet tumbled over. Argentia felt herself falling for an instant, and then shoved by some invisible force as the magic of the carpet held her steady while it righted itself. It happened so fast that she really was not sure it had happened at all—but she was absolutely sure things were going to hell in Bartemeus' treasure cavern.

The stacks of gold on either side were shaking violently, spitting gold bricks into the air. The carpet wove past these missiles, but Argentia saw more trouble ahead: entire stacks were moving in unison, hurling a wave of gold into the air. *Climb,* she thought as they closed on the impending disaster. She started to shout the command, but the carpet was already speeding up and rising; apparently its magic extended some sort of telepathic sympathy to the rider.

The carpet mounted above the bullion wave's crest. As the gold tumbled to earth with a metallic roar, Argentia saw a new problem ahead: the promenade of columns was collapsing. "Look out!" she shouted. The carpet dropped with sickening speed, shooting forward. Argentia ducked instinctively as they blasted beneath the crashing horse statues, so low they almost scraped the stone floor, and out into the tunnel, which was also shaking apart.

Argentia shouted for Mirk as the carpet dodged chunks of stone dislodged from the ceiling, but she could barely hear herself above the collapse. *Why does this always happen to me when I come down here?* The last time she was in the Sudenlands, a temple and a crypt had both collapsed, nearly killing her and her friends.

Up ahead, the doorway appeared, lit by the green light from the antechamber. It was unblocked. *Thank God. Now if I can just get Mirk....*

The carpet burst into the antechamber. Argentia yanked a hand back as if pulling the reins on a horse and shouted for Mirk. The meerkat appeared atop the stone column on her right. "Worm!" he shouted, pointing behind her.

Argentia craned her head around. The wickedly subtle cobra had stretched itself against the near wall, arching its body so it rested on the three lintels, invisible to anyone coming through the door. It slammed down behind Argentia, its huge head hooking in from the left, jaws wide, deadly venom spraying.

Acting on instinct, Argentia took the carpet straight up. Only as she saw the toxic spew pass beneath her did she realize she had left Mirk directly in the path of the attack.

61

The cobra's venom struck the column and the green fire, sending up sparks like angry flying lanterns, but the meerkat was not there. Hovering on the carpet, Argentia looked for him to dart out from behind the column, but he did not.

He was simply gone.

Mirk...

A flash beside Argentia startled her so badly she pulled a dagger. Mirk tumbled out of the aether and collapsed on the carpet. The cobra coiled around, striking at them. Argentia tilted the carpet out of the way, feeling the turbulence as the snake's head rushed past, and thought: *Get us out of here!*

The carpet swung around and flashed through the door into the stairwell. There was a deafening noise of gnashing stone all around them, but nothing was falling. *Not yet, at least...* How long they had before the whole place came down, Argentia did not want to think about.

Mirk sat up, shaking his head groggily. "Flying rug?" he asked.

"When did you learn to aetherwalk?" Argentia demanded. "Is that how you get into Ralak's chamber?"

"Um...worm is behind us," Mirk said.

Unlike the door to the treasure cavern, the door to the stairwell was wide enough to admit the cobra. A glance back showed the thing's lambent green eyes blazing in the dark—and gaining.

"Faster!" Argentia leaned forward, urging the carpet on to greater speeds. They flew up the stairwell out into the hall. Everything was shaking around them. The entire house was lit with the green wizard light. The carpet turned down a corridor Argentia and Mirk had not used in their descent, avoiding the dining room altogether.

The cobra was still coming hard behind, its wild passage obliterating tables and chairs and striking pictures from walls. *I hope you know where you're going,* Argentia thought at the carpet.

As if in answer, the carpet turned sharply through a doorway into another hallway, this one lined with windows. Outside, Argentia could see sand sliding past, giving the sensation that they were rising through the earth.

At the end of the hall, a flight of steps mounted to the upper levels of the house. The switchbacks slowed them, and the supple cobra gained ground, at one point closing near enough to lunge at them. The carpet jigged at the last instant and the snake smashed its head into the wall. Shaking off the blow, it surged forward, but the carpet had gained enough distance to make it out of the stairwell. In a straight run down the next hallway it put on speed, opening a lead. It cut a hard turn through a doorway into a chamber Argentia recognized.

The library! They had approached it from the opposite way Mirk had led them on their initial run. She felt her heart leap. *We're almost out!*

The carpet's nose lifted and it launched itself on an almost vertical run up the spiral staircase. The cobra, single-minded in its pursuit, came racing after, winding its length up the metal steps.

"Go, go!" Argentia shouted, clinging to the Jade Monkey with her wounded arm and the carpet with her other hand. Mirk hung on beside her, his ears plastered back, tiny teeth bared.

They shot through the last level of the library and up into the empty room at the top of the tower. The cobra, sensing its prey was about to escape, closed with desperate speed, but Argentia could see daylight through the circle in the ceiling above them. Something struck her as odd about that, but before she could consider it, they blasted out of the tower—

—into midair.

62

"Whoa!" Argentia shouted.

They were hundreds of feet above the ground, flying past the parapets as Bartemeus' castle rose from the earth that had swallowed it, shedding sand in streams like water down a cloak in a storm.

The cobra reared to strike at them from the tower roof. But as suddenly as it had arisen, the castle, its task of housing the Jade Monkey complete, gave a great shudder and imploded. Massive stones cascaded into the middle of the Horsair encampment. The cobra was torn down, its final hiss lost in the earthquake roar. Tents were crushed and scattered by the force of the crash. Smoke and dust erupted skyward in a billowing cloud that forced Argentia to swing the carpet out wide, looping away from the disaster.

Aeton's bolts! Argentia hoped none of the Horsairs had been anywhere near the wizard's castle when it collapsed. When the buffeting from the shockwave subsided, she scanned the encampment. She expected to see a chaos of indistinct forms running amok in the scree of dust, but there was nothing. No sign or sound of anyone. In the wake of the castle's fall, that silence was frightening. *Where is everyone?*

A flash of sun off the sand beyond the wall caught her eye. At first she thought it was a glance off the armor of the Raj's troops, whose corpses littered the slope of the dune, but as she flew over to investigate, she realized it was not made by any metal: it was coming off the sand itself, which had been fused into great streaks of glass that ran all the way up to the crest of the dune. "That's impossible," she said, more to herself than Mirk. "Do you know how much heat that would take?"

Even as she voiced the question, a horrible realization roiled through her. *The salamander....* The Raj's Dragoons might have been no match for the Horsairs, but if Bazu had come....

Heart sinking, Argentia looked back to the camp. Parts of the stone wall had been melted into slag. Tents were just char. As the dust dissipated, she caught the unmistakably foul waft of roasted flesh.

Swooping down, she brought the carpet to rest among the few tents that were still standing and unburned. She dismounted, stepping down to the ground, leaving the carpet hovering a foot or so off the sand. "Um... stay?" she said.

The carpet made a movement almost like a bow or the nod of a head, and settled to the sand. Mirk scampered off and fussed with his windblown fur. Argentia surveyed the ruins. Crystalline streaks of superheated sand marked the ravages of the salamander's attack, but there were no bodies anywhere that she could see. Horses, Horsairs—men and women alike—Timor, Demby, they all were gone.

What happened to them? Were they all burned? Sucked into the lamp like Griegvard? If it's powerful enough to do that, how in hell is this thing supposed to stop it? Argentia almost smashed the Jade Monkey to the ground in frustration, but caught herself at the last moment. Whatever magic was in the statue was her only chance against the salamander. However slim it was, she intended to take it.

She stood there, dazed by the atrocity. She was no stranger to the Harvester's reap, but she had not seen so many die in one place since the Battle of Hidden Vale. *And those were soldiers. Trained fighters. This was families, children....* It sickened her. *And Demby. Oh, Demby....* She thought of Skarn's promise to keep him safe and her heart broke. *How can I tell him? He'll go mad—if he's still alive...*

Mirk tugged on Argentia's pants. "What?" she snapped, wiping tears from her eyes.

"People," Mirk said.

At the far end of the camp, a few women were cautiously emerging from one of the intact tents. At first it appeared to be a ragtag bunch, but the number kept growing: dozens of women, intermingled with children.

Argentia smiled in relief; there had been some survivors of the massacre, at least. *Thank God....*

She hurried to meet them, recognizing a few of the women from the harem, but not many of the others. "What happened?" she called. "Is everyone all right?"

The women stared at her, silent, accusatory. There was a rippling in their ranks. A crone stepped forth. Ancient and bent, her scrawny frame wrapped in patchwork shawls in green and yellow, her dress sackcloth, her thin wrists and ankles barely more than tendons binding her claw hands and crooked feet. Argentia had seen less wrinkles on mummies than on her face, which bobbed like a withered apple on her stick neck, a few wisps of white hair poking from beneath a black babushka. But her eyes were keen.

"Fire," she croaked, waving at the crest of the dune. "Living fire. Pit-spawn. Walking death. And now the Master's house rises and falls. The time of the Horsairs here is ended. The long watching is done." She reached a trembling hand toward the Jade Monkey, but did not touch it.

"How did you survive?"

"Hid. Hid from the fire and hid again from the earth-breaking."

"What happened to your men? They can't all be dead," Argentia said. She was looking among the gathered Horsairs for Demby and Timor, but they were not there.

"Not dead, no." The hag cackled. "Not yet."

Not yet? "Where did they go?"

The crone waved her arm toward the top of the dune again.

Oh those fools, Argentia thought. "Come on, Mirk." She whistled sharply, as if she was calling Shadow. The golden carpet floated to her side. The women gasped and backed away, many forking gestures of warding, but the children ooohed and clapped when Argentia mounted up.

Mirk sprang beside her and the carpet lifted off. They crested the dune. Argentia dipped them low, so they were barely a foot off the ground. There was a riot of hoofprints, many belonging to the Raj's cavalry, but intermingled with those were other prints bespeaking unarmored steeds at a canter, then a gallop, all headed away from the dune.

Some of the Horsairs, at least, had survived. Even as Argentia hoped Demby and Timor might be among them the old woman's cryptic words echoed in her head, knelling like the bells of doom.

The Horsairs were riding full out for Khemr-kar to avenge themselves on the salamander.

They were riding to their deaths.

PART IV

Desert Storm

63

"What are we going to do about *that*, brother?" Riding at the head of a force of Horsairs two hundred strong, Balazar pointed at an imposing barrier to their purpose: the gates of Khemr-kar.

Kazim's fighters had routed the Raj's cavalry with expected ease, but the Lord of the Horsairs would never forget standing on the bloodied sands outside the walls of the encampment, victory in hand, when upon the crest of the dune there billowed a light such as he imagined might be seen in the furnaces of the Everlasting Hells.

The lurid glow bloomed like sunrise over the crest. A silhouetted figure appeared. Everyone on the battlefield froze, looking up at the looming shadow. The figure raised its arms like some giant desert owl spreading its wings.

Fire exploded from its mouth, streaking down the slope so quickly that it was upon its first victims before they were aware of more than a great flash above them. They were vaporized where they stood, nothing left of body, bone, weapons, or armor.

A second, third, and fourth barrage were launched: firespears that struck like lightning from a demonic storm. The last one was headed for Kazim.

"Ware!" Balazar shouted, rushing for his brother. Before he could get there, another Horsair hit Kazim in the back, knocking him sprawling into Balazar. The firespear seared past both brothers. They disentangled themselves quickly, rolling to their knees. There was nothing left of the man who had saved Kazim but a slick of superheated sand as a glassy memorial.

"Where is the Outland whore?" an inhuman voice bellowed down at them.

Kazim stood. "Dead!" he shouted back.

"You lie!"

"I do not lie! She is dead by your hand." He swept his scimitar down, pointing at the smear of glassy earth. "There! She stood beside me in battle and died saving my life from your fire!"

"That looked to be a man."

"She was so guised. That is how she escaped your city."

There was an ominous pause on the crest of the dune. "If we find you lie, we shall return and scorch you, burn you to cinders all, to ash. Worthless rabble! Now comes a taste of what your defiance has earned!"

"Run, brother!" Kazim shouted. "Horsairs, retreat! Retreat for your lives!"

The Horsairs scattered, fleeing back into their camp, diving over the low wall, dodging amid the tents. They were not all fast enough or lucky enough to escape the apocalypse hurled upon them. Fire rode over the ground as if the sand were made of oil, churning into the wall and devouring the stone, passing through to raze the tents. The air was terrified with the screams of men, women, children, and horses, throbbing with heat, stinking with smoke and char.

Then, suddenly, as if a light had been snuffed out, there was a sense of absence. Of aethereal power in abeyance.

Kazim, crouched behind a part of the wall that still stood, realized he could feel the wind again. He twisted and raised his head enough to see over the wall.

On the dune's high crest, the robed figure had lowered its arms and was turning away. Just before it passed beyond Kazim's sight, he saw a tail thrashing behind it.

"Brother!" Balazar embraced Kazim fiercely. Both men were

spattered with blood and ash. "By Ab'Dala, Kazim, what have you wrought by not giving over that woman?"

Kazim shook his head. "I do not know. I did what my heart told me was right. She warned me of this thing. I did not believe."

"What are we to do now? Wait for her—if she is even still alive?"

Kazim stood and helped his brother to his feet. "Hardly. We are Horsairs. The Raj brought this scourge to our kingdom. I think it is time to pay our respects to the throne."

"You cannot attack my father!" Timor shouted. He and Demby were hurrying toward the brothers.

"So the Rajling lives, with not a hair on him singed," Balazar scoffed.

"Peace, brother. This one is not our enemy—are you, boy?" Kazim said.

"Not unless you mean harm to my father. This is not his doing. He is bewitched by the magic of the lamp that monster on the hill uses." Timor stepped away from Demby, who grabbed at his wrist. The prince of Makhara faced the Lord of the Horsairs, a noble light in his eyes. "If you would ride to Khemr-kar, then ride to save my father. That is what Lady Dasani was trying to do. She came to stop that thing. To save us all."

"Dat's de truth, saib," Demby added.

Kazim looked from the prince to the boy and shook his head, a bemused smile breaking across his features. "Balazar, gather the camp. And round up the horses. We will have need of them if we are to save the Rajling's kingdom."

Balazar nodded and left them. Timor looked at Kazim. "What will happen here?" he asked. "Your home is all but destroyed."

"Homes can be rebuilt," Kazim said, sitting down on the wall. "But if your Lady Dasani succeeds at her task, we may have no more need to call this place home. The generations of our obligation to Bartemeus end tonight, I think. Where we go from here, only Ab'Dala can tell."

"So you do not know what you will do?" Timor asked.

"Being the ruler of a people does not mean having every answer, Rajling. Sometimes, the wisest course is to wait and see what the sunrise brings."

The Lord of the Horsairs turned away and silence held there until Balazar returned. "How is it, brother?" Kazim asked.

"I do not think any women or children were killed. They were all in the rear of the camp when the battle started. The fires did not reach that far. Of men, we have taken worse losses than ever before, but even with that, most of us are still alive and unhurt. All save those I sent after the horses are awaiting you."

"Well, then." Kazim dropped down from the wall. "Let us not leave them waiting any longer."

He led the others to where the Horsairs were assembled. His people cheered when they saw he was alive, but he quieted them quickly and issued terse orders. The women and children and any men too hurt to ride were to remain behind and tend to the wounded and the dead. The rest were to follow him to Khemr-kar.

They rode out within the hour, Timor and Demby on a horse beside Kazim and Balazar. Darkness lay over the land, but the Horsairs used no torches, knowing the terrain of the desert by heart. They went fast, and faster still once they reached the Sandway. The steeds were worth their stock. Powerful and nearly tireless, they galloped away the miles between the encampment and the city as if trotting through an oasis.

Dawn touched the eastern horizon, tingeing it with a fire that made Kazim flinch. He wondered what had befallen Argentia in the wizard's dungeon. He was certain of her right to seek the Jade Monkey—the brand proved it unequivocally—but her right did not guarantee that she would claim the prize, only that she would be given the chance to.

If she succeeded, she would return to the city far too late to aid him and his Horsairs. But he could not wait. To wait was to admit that this foe was beyond him, something his bloodline forbade. He heard the voices of his ancestors, father before father, urging him to punish this assault, to remember the honor of the Horsairs, even unto death. He owed that to his men, who defined themselves by this virtue of fearlessness.

He also owed them an attack that was not a suicide charge.

Whether they could defeat the salamander only Ab'Dala would decide. Getting to that battle itself was something more under Kazim's control.

All he needed was a plan.

He pondered it as the leagues kicked away beneath Astrali's hooves. He knew the city well, even the grounds of the palace, though he had never actually entered the Raj's buildings. It was the gate that was the problem. It would be shut until daybreak, so they would lose the cover of night in approaching. Even with their magnificent steeds running full out, they could never make the charge in time to stop the guards from dropping the portcullis and sealing them out of the city.

He was still pondering when the towers and minarets of Khemr-kar loomed into view: shadowy walls and blazing watchfires against the gloam of dawn. Kazim ordered his riders to slow to a walk and to leave the road, moving forward along the river until they came to the same copse of trees where Argentia and Skarn had landed their pegasi.

Balazar asked what they were going to do about the gate.

Kazim looked at Balazar. At the Horsairs assembled behind him on gently panting steeds. At the little foreign urchin boy who stared back with huge, hopeful eyes. Finally he looked at the prince of Makhara, who returned his gaze with guarded expectation.

"What indeed," the Lord of the Horsairs said.

64

Timor tried not to flinch at the cold edge of steel pressed against his throat.

He was seated in front of Kazim on Astrali. His hands were bound before him. Kazim's kukri rested beneath his chin. Balazar and a half-dozen other Horsairs flanked them as they approached the open gates of Khemr-kar at a slow walk. The sun was not long up; Kazim wanted to take advantage of the city's sleepiness. The fewer people who were about, the less chance for any unnecessary casualties.

Traffic entering and leaving the city at this hour was light—the bazaar did not open for trade until seven bells— and the guards, fresh from the shift change, were typically sluggish. The Horsairs actually reached the gates before the soldiers loafed out of the gatehouse doorway to stop them.

There was a moment of complete surprise, and then the guards scrambled for their weapons.

"Hold!" Kazim shouted. The weight of command in his voice froze the soldiers. "Stand down or the Rajling dies!"

The Gatekeeper—fortunately a different man than the one who had greeted Argentia and her company—stepped forward and tossed down his sword, motioning for his men to do likewise. "I will be accountable for your actions," he said when some hesitated. Rumor that all was not well in the palace had reached them, but this was the Raj's son. If he were killed, no matter if they avenged his death instantly, the Raj would have them executed.

Kazim nodded to Balazar, who blew a blast on his horn.

Moments later there was an answering call from the copse. Then the morning was full of thunder as two hundred stallions hurtled into the road and charged the gates of Khemr-kar.

From the walls, alarm horns howled and men shouted to drop the portcullis. The soldiers at the gate remained motionless. The guards on the walls got off a few shots with bows and hurled their spears, but they were woefully prepared to meet the charge. The horses hardly slowed.

"You will never sack this city," the Gatekeeper said.

Kazim shook his head. "We have not come to sack it, but to save it. If you will not join us, at least do not be fools enough to hinder us. Your lives are spared by the Rajling's order, but there are limits to my generosity."

With that, he took the kukri from Timor's throat and spurred Astrali, leaping into the lead as the tide of his cavalry poured through the gates like a river bursting a dike, roaring on toward the palace.

<hr>

As they thundered down the almost empty streets of his city, Timor was torn between exhilaration and fear. The exhilaration was caught from the rush of impending battle. Though he was no fighter, the dream of riding to his father's aid, freeing him from the cursed clutches of the red-cloaked creature and setting all between them back as it once had been, pounded his heart.

The fear—at first—was for the people. If they should fail, the salamander would surely destroy Khemr-kar in retribution. He had seen its power at the Horsair camp and knew it was callous to human life.

Then the cavalry hurtled around the last bend and the walls of the Kephalo loomed before them, and the fear turned inward, to his own life.

He saw the burnished gates, the half-dozen guards before them with their pikes set against the charge. Beyond, there would be soldiers in formation to bring support. And that did not even begin to consider what waited at the palace itself. Archers in every window. Impregnable doors with that deathtrap corridor beyond. The octopus in the pool. He saw his home now not with custom-fettered eyes but from the perspective of an outsider and for the first time realized how formidable the palace was against an assault.

"This is madness," he whispered. "The defenses are too strong."

By then, of course, it was far too late to turn back.

The horses bore down upon the pikemen at the gates. Timor was sure they were doomed. But Kazim never flinched, never broke Astrali's stride. None of the lead riders of the Horsairs did, though steely death was but moments ahead.

Balazar raised a hand. At his signal, the Horsairs in the second rank stood in their stirrups and loosed a volley of flaming arrows. Some struck the pikemen, others the gates. Whatever they hit exploded in a roaring blast of light and heat.

Smoke enveloped the Horsairs. Timor choked, ducking his head, waiting for the spear or the slamming impact of the gate to unhorse and kill him...

...but nothing happened.

He felt the air clear. Dared to open his eyes. They were beyond the gates, which hung in twisted wrecks, mostly blown off their hinges by the Horsairs' thundersticks. Timor stared in amazement. Just like that, the first of the palace's gauntlets had been hurdled. Then he turned his eyes ahead and his quick hope withered.

There was an entire force of soldiers awaiting them in the gardens.

"Get to safety!" Kazim shouted, veering Astrali to the wing of the Horsair ranks.

"What?"

"Your part in this is ended. Rajling. Get to safety!" Kazim cut the bonds at Timor's wrists, grabbed the prince's shirt, and wrenched him off of Astrali. Timor landed in a heap before he fully realized what had happened. By the time he rolled up to his knees, the cavalry was charging past.

Demby—similarly deposited by Balazar—took Timor by the wrist and led the stunned prince behind the cover of a stone sculpture. They crouched there, listening to the battle. The noise was incredible: clashes of steel, screams of men and horses wounded or dying. Timor wished the fall had struck him deaf so he would hear no more.

What's happening out there, he wondered. Part of him, sickened by the violence, did not want to learn. But his father and his mother were at risk if the Horsairs failed. *I have to know....*

He peered around the statue. Demby peeked out beside him. They watched as the soldiers in the gardens met the age-old fate of infantry matched against cavalry, their forces scattered and smashed by the rampaging steeds. For a few minutes it again seemed to Timor that he had been wrong and that the mad assault would succeed after all.

But the flaming arrows the Horsairs sped against the doors of the palace were rebuffed by the magic of those portals. The volley ricocheted to blast great holes in the stone paths and chew huge divots from the lawns, leaving the doors not so much as scorched.

Then the palace windows opened and the palace archers turned loose their heavy crossbows, raining death from above, breaking the Horsair lines. Footsoldier reinforcements poured around the sides of the palace, turning the odds overwhelmingly to the defenders' favor.

"They cannot get through," Timor muttered. So long as the palace doors remained barred against them, the Horsairs would be stalled in the gardens. Eventually the sheer number of the defenders would be their end, and all hope for his father and his family and the people of Khemr-kar would be lost. "We have to get those doors open."

"But how, saib?" Demby asked. "Dey de magic doors."

A shadow loomed over them.

The boys started in terror, wheeling around. But the shape that appeared was not a scimitar-wielding guardsman come to make an end of them. It was just a horse whose rider had fallen in the battle.

Timor looked at the horse for a moment, then stood and grabbed its reins. "Yes," he said to Demby. "But they are not magic from the inside. Come on!"

65

In the dungeon of Kephalo, Skarangella Skarn raised his head.

He was chained to the wall, as he had been for all of his internment except when they had tortured him: then he had been chained to a stone block while guards beat him with cane sticks. He was kneeling—the chains would not stretch far enough to allow him to sit—and half asleep when a commotion outside roused him.

He listened. There was a small, barred window high up on the wall admitting the first pale light of day, shading the shadows in the dungeon from black to gray. It was through this aperture that the noise was coming: urgent shouts mingled with running steps. The clash of weapons. The cries of the dying.

"Dat's about enough of dis pris'ner bit, den," Skarn said, standing up. He was stiff and tired, his body sore from the caning, but the noises of battle outside were what he had been waiting to hear. He had not been sure exactly when or how Argentia would return to the palace, but he had been confident that she would. *Sounds like she brought de whole damn army wit her....*

"Skarn?" Trok asked. He was chained farther down in the dungeon. "Not dat I'm questionin ye after all dese years, but what in de Hells're ye doin?"

"Leavin." Skarn wrapped the chains about his hands and closed his eyes. He took several deep breaths, his chest moving like a bellows. Then, with a cry, he surged backwards with all his might.

The chains held, but the old, rusted eyebolts fastening them to the wall burst from the stone. Skarn fell on his back, tumbled over, lay there for a moment, and then picked himself up. Trok was staring at him in amazement. "What?" Skarn laughed. "Ye thought all dat sittin on de throne made me soft?"

The noise had not brought the guard from outside the dungeon. Skarn crept over to the door. It was locked. He thought for a minute, then went back to the wall, kicked aside the broken bolts, took the chain in his fists.

"Now what're ye doin?" Trok asked.

"Gettin de door open. Start yellin, loud as ye can."

Pressing his hands to the wall so it looked as if he were chained still, Skarn bellowed, "Help! Let us out! Down in de dungeon here!"

Trok joined him. The litany went on for several minutes before Skarn got the response he was looking for. "Shuddup in there!" the guard roared.

"Make me," Skarn shouted back. "Help! Help!"

When he heard the key grind in the lock, he had to bow his head to keep from grinning. "Shuddup," the guard repeated. He was a dark, solid man with piggish little eyes. Skarn recognized him as one of the ones who had caned him. Fittingly, he had the stick in his hand again, and he raised it as he crossed the dungeon to where Skarn was standing. "Want another twenty? I said—"

Skarn turned from the wall and caught the descending cane. "I heard ye de first time." He wrenched the stick from the astonished guard's grasp and crunched it viciously across the man's face, shattering his nose. The guard fell in a heap. Skarn kicked him in the head, not quite hard enough to kill, but enough to ensure he would not be waking anytime soon.

Crouching, Skarn rifled the guard's key ring. "Just hang on dere," he said to Trok.

"Oh dat's real funny," Trok muttered, shaking his chains.

Skarn found the key that unlocked his chains. He freed Trok, took the fallen guard's sword, and headed out into the corridor.

Skarn had little idea of the layout of the palace, but knew they had to go up first to get anywhere. He was mostly intent on finding out what had happened to Demby. He had done what he could to save the boy from punishment in the dungeons, but when they took him hostage on their way to capture Argentia, he had passed into Fortune's whim.

They mounted the first flight of steps they came to. Skarn was not sure how they were going to battle the salamander, but he knew how they could take the palace guards out of the fight.

The corridor was long pools of torchlight and shadow. An intersecting passage appeared up ahead. The right-hand way led down to ornate double-doors. There were no guards outside the doors, but they may have been drawn to battle elsewhere in the palace. Skarn had no idea if what he was looking for would be behind those doors, but they looked like as good a place as any to check.

He reached for the handle and the door swung open from within.

66

Demby and Timor galloped along the riverbank.

They had raced out of the royal gardens, Timor's gorge rising as they passed through the smoking gates, the horse's hooves squelching in the strewn guts of obliterated bodies that had been the wardens of that entrance. Khemr-kar was deserted—the people had locked themselves in their homes, fearing an invasion—but they had a tense moment at the city gates. The guards were assembled again, holding their positions against the possibility of a second wave of intruders, and the portcullis was down.

Timor ran the horse straight up to the Gatekeeper. "My Prince!" the man exclaimed. "What has happened? We feared—"

"Open the gate, quickly, quickly! It is madness. All madness! The palace is fallen! The Raj flees by secret ways to the water. We were separated. I barely escaped. Please, hurry!"

He looked so harried and sounded so convincing that the Gatekeeper signaled for the portcullis to be raised. "I will send an escort, my Prince, to ensure your safe arrival at the docks."

"No! Stand fast with all your men. There may be more of these barbarians coming. Close the gate behind me. Do your duty, in the name of my father! The city must not fall!" Timor said. Kicking his heels into the stallion, he bolted beneath the rising portcullis spikes, wheeled a hard right, and followed the track of the river to the docks, the Horsair steed flying full out.

⊹

The guard at the Raj's berth lowered his speaking shell and frowned. He had just received a confusing message from the sentries at the city wall about the Raj's son coming toward the berth "wild and half-witless" and the Raj fleeing the palace to escape a siege.

He had heard the alarm horns, so he knew something was amiss in the city, but if the Royal Family was fleeing to the barge, he would have received orders from the palace to make the ship ready to sail. He had received no such communication.

Of course, if the palace guards were all dead, that could explain the silence.

He looked up at the sound of hoofs. A single steed hove over a crest in the road, bearing down upon him at all speed.

It was the prince, with some other who looked like a child riding behind him. "My Prince! Halt there!" the guard shouted. He was aware of sweat trickling down his back. Raiders had attacked one of his fellows at this post yesterday and the man had claimed that the young prince had been party to the assault. With that rattling in his mind, as well as the words of the Gatekeeper, the guard did not know what to expect.

The prince brought the horse to a halt. "Quickly, open the gate!" Timor said. "The Raj flees to the barge. We were separated in the battle. Make ready to sail. Haste, haste!"

"But my Prince, I've had no word from the palace."

"The palace is overrun!" Timor put some authority into his voice, trying his best to sound as he had heard his father sound when issuing important orders. "Do not waste time. Do you want my father to arrive to a boat unprepared to sail?"

The guard hesitated for a moment, weighing the consequences. If he detained the prince here and the Raj really was coming, he would be lucky to escape with his life. If he listened and the prince was mad or about some mischief...well, how could he be blamed for obeying a royal order?

"As you command," he said, unlocking the gate. "Follow me, my Prince."

Timor clipped the stallion and they passed through the gate. "Give me the keys to the warehouse," he ordered the guard.

"The warehouse, my Prince?"

"My parents are fleeing by tunnel from the palace. If they are pursued do you want them trapped in there? I will open the warehouse. You prepare the barge."

"But my Prince—"

Leaning down, Timor held a single finger before the guard's the face. "That was a *command*, guardsman," he said, putting every ounce of haughtiness he could muster into his voice. "The keys. Now."

Wide-eyed and red-cheeked, the guard bowed his head and handed a keyring to Timor. "Your royal father will hear of this," he said.

"Pray he is alive to hear it," Timor replied. Then he yanked on the reins to turn the horse and galloped across the yard to the warehouse. "The door, quickly," he said to Demby. He was shaking and his voice quavered.

Demby hopped down from the horse and ran to the door. The lock was a simple thing but there were five keys on the guard's ring and it took him a minute to find the correct one. The door itself proved too heavy for him, however. Timor had to dismount and help the urchin push the big portal open.

"Well done," Timor said. He glanced back at the guard, who was watching them fixedly and showed no sign of attending to the barge. For a moment Timor thought to close the door behind them to buy more time, but that would run counter to his story about opening the place for the fleeing Raj. "Come on." He took the horse's bridle and led it toward the back of the warehouse.

"We're ridin de horsey inside, saib?"

"Yes." At the back of the warehouse they descended the steps into the storeroom. There was barely any light diffusing from the warehouse down into this space, and Timor fumbled about for a minute before finding the correct stone and triggering the doorway hidden in the wall to open.

"De secret door!" Demby exclaimed, charmed by the storybook trope come to life.

"Yes. Quickly now, before that guard decides to investigate." Timor and Demby climbed back onto the stallion, the horse shying only a little upon entering the closed tunnel. They could not run the horse in the dark, but they still went faster than they would have on foot, shortening their journey to the end of the tunnel.

Timor groped in the dark until he found the iron ladder. "Wait here." He climbed the ladder and opened the hatch.

Demby, his heart lightened by the ability to see again—though he had not complained, the tunnel had filled him with bad memories of that nightmare journey he had made with Skarn and Argentia beneath the Black Crags into the Wasteland of Yth—quickly followed Timor up the ladder. "Where's dis?" he asked.

"My bedchamber. We will go to the entrance hall. I will distract the guards. You will have to get the main doors open. Can you do that?"

"I'll try, saib. But what about de horsey down dere?"

"The horse? We will come back for it, or it will return the way we came of its own accord. I am sure it will be fine."

"Okay, saib. Cause I don' think de horsey likes it down dere in de dark."

They crossed the chamber. Timor paused at the doors, the full weight of what they were about to undertake settling on him. He diverted and opened a chest, taking out a scimitar. He hoped he would not have to use it, but he feared he might. Reminding himself that his father's life—and all their lives—likely hung in the balance, he rejoined Demby at the door. Motioning the urchin to stay behind him until he could determine whether the halls were safe, he pulled the door open.

He barely had time to register that a figure was standing there before a tremendously strong hand seized him, yanked him forward, and slammed him into the wall. His sword was batted from his grasp and cold steel touched his throat.

67

"Not de big fish, but maybe de little fish'll do instead," the man holding Timor said.

"Yaaaa!" Demby leaped out from the doorway, plowing head-down into Timor's assailant, striking at the man with ineffectual fists.

"Is dat any way to treat de Sultan?" Skarangella Skarn asked mildly.

Demby raised his head, his eyes huge with astonishment. "De great Sultan!" He hugged Skarn fiercely. "But ye were in de dungeon, saib!"

Skarn flashed his golden grin. "Deh. I got bored down dere." He ruffed Demby's hair. "What're ye doin sneakin round wit dis one?" he asked, removing his sword from the prince's throat.

"We are here to help my father," Timor said. "Why were you going into my chambers?"

"Thought dey might be your father's."

The prince stared at him. "You were going to kill my father?"

"Nah. Was goan take 'im hostage until de guards surrendered. What's goan on out in de yard? Where's de Lady Dasani?" he asked Demby.

"De Lady's not here. She went after de monkey and den de fire monster attacked. Don' know what happened to de Lady after dat, saib."

Skarn frowned. "What—"

"Listen, there is no time," Timor said. "The Horsairs are trapped in the yard. If we do not get the palace doors open, they are all going to be killed out there, and my father and all the rest of us are doomed."

"Den let's go open dem doors," Skarn said.

"Wretched traitors!" The guard from the berth rushed from the prince's chambers stabbing his sword at Skarn's back.

"Look out, saib!" Demby jumped between Skarn and the guard. "Aiiii—"

"Demby!" Skarn roared.

As the urchin fell, Skarn slammed an elbow into the guard's face, leveling him. He dropped to his knees, grabbed the guard's head and wrenched it around, snapping his neck. Then he scrambled over to where the urchin lay. "Demby! Boy, ye hear me?"

Blood ran down Demby's arm in a bright red stream. "Hurts, saib," Demby said, struggling to sit up. He was very pale and his eyes had a shocked glaze.

"Dat's all right. Ain't nothin but de scratch. Goan be just fine." The cut was deep but clean. It would need stitches or a cleric, but Demby would live. Skarn felt a great weight lift from his heart.

"Promise, saib?"

"Deh. Goan promote ye when we get back home. Ye done better at guardin de sultan den dis slow fool here." He pointed a finger at Trok. Demby giggled. "Get some clean cloths and water t' wash and bind dis wit," Skarn said to Timor.

"But my father," the prince protested. "The Horsairs. I told you—"

Skarn rose, towering above the prince of Makhara. "Get into dat room dere, lock de doors, and tend de hurt t' my friend. If anything happens t' him, ye won't have t' worry bout dat salamander destroyin de city. I'll tear dis whole kingdom down stone by stone until won't nobody know dere was anything here but de desert."

Timor shrank back from Skarn's menacing glare. "I did not think the guard would follow. I never meant for him to get hurt," he said, helping Demby to his feet.

"I know," Skarn replied, his voice softening. "But dis is best now t' do what I tell ye. Don' come out for nothin lest ye hear me or de Lady Dasani."

"Where ye goin, saib?" Demby asked.

"T' answer de door."

"Got some sort of plan?" Trok asked.

"Don' I always?" Skarn said.

68

The throne hall of Kephalo was ready for war.

Tidor Uffiti, Raj of Makhara, sat on his throne, head bowed, statue-still, taking no notice of the clamor of battle and the screams of the dying beyond the walls. Taking no notice, in truth, of anything except the lamp in the hands of the red-robed meja.

Except they were claws, not hands, the small part of his mind that was still his own noted. And the thing in the red robes—which were more tatters now than robes—whatever it was, was no meja. It was not even human, not with that tail that slithered behind it, snipping this way and that like a restless snake. And not at the height it owned, towering nearly a dozen feet tall, all thick muscle and sinew beneath mottled amphibian skin.

Devil-spawn, the Raj thought wearily. *And I let it in....*

All of this was his fault, the small, true part of him knew. He had granted audience to the strange meja and he had been fascinated by the lamp the conjurer held. That simple, tarnished, battered vessel whispered to him of things he had held secret in the vaults of his soul. Dreams of power and conquest, scarce even realized by his waking mind, yet there, deep in his subconscious, waiting like rubies to be mined. Dark desires, all of which would be his if he helped the meja.

So he offered residence in the palace, a place beside his throne, a voice in the affairs of the kingdom. It seemed to him that it was another person who drove his son and his wife aside, but he knew it had been him. His ears had been too full of the whisperings of the lamp to hear clearly the protests of those he loved best.

Now it was too late. Timor was gone, turned traitor, they said. His palace was besieged by the upstart Horsairs, his soldiers fighting and dying, and it meant nothing because the Raj understood at last that the lamp and its promises would never be his. The thing possessing it was impossibly powerful. It would destroy him when his usefulness was ended.

The Raj suspected that would not be long after this battle. It would not pain him to die. He deserved it. He had failed his people greatly here. This monster would do them worse, but at least he would not be alive to suffer their cries of slavery and torment.

If only I could see my son once more, he thought. A tear tracked its solitary way down his weathered cheek.

Beside the broken Raj, the salamander called Bazu also waited. It was almost completely in possession of this mortal shell, almost come unto the fullness of its power. It had glutted itself on all the rubies of the Raj's treasury, and still they had not been enough to wholly free it from the imprisonment of the lamp. It was not sure how many more of the stones it needed to break the binding enchantment, but it would strike forth into the desert and wrest them from the earth until the task was complete.

First it would dispense with its enemies here. It would have gone out to meet them in the yard, but its powers were not totally recovered from the exertions of the morning, when it had laid waste to the camp hidden in the dunes, so it preferred to wait until its intervention was needed.

"All is well prepared," it said, nodding in satisfaction at the array of defenses in the throne hall. "We retire. If they break the doors, you will retrieve us and we will burn them all." It turned its hooded head to the Raj, the fires of its eyes blazing at him with a light of magical command.

The Raj looked up under the heat of that gaze, nodded once, and bowed his head again. The salamander swept off for the vaults, tail thwacking behind it. The Raj had little doubt that if he were to make the descent to the vaults, it would be a trip from which there was no returning.

Worse, he knew that if the time came, he would go. There was no questioning. It was the will of the salamander. The will of the lamp. It could not be denied.

Contemplating the doom he had wrought upon himself and his kingdom, the Raj did not notice the sudden commotion as the ring of steel on steel echoed from the hallway leading to the royal residences.

The captain of the throne guards, however, did notice.

"You four check that corridor. The rest of you stand fast," the captain ordered. He and dozens of his best soldiers were there to defend the throne against the unlikely event that the doors should be breached and the gauntlet of the alcoves passed. The captain hardly expected an enemy within the palace, but the clash of arms was unmistakable.

The quartet of guards hustled down the hall and around the corner. There was a crash of battle, screams of pain and death, and then an ominous silence.

"What the devil is going on over there?" the captain muttered. He was about to send another detachment when two palace guards staggered into sight. The larger of them had a shield in each hand and was leaning heavily on his comrade. They approached the throne hall slowly, blood-spattered, clearly wounded.

"What happened?" the captain demanded.

"Dey got away down de hall," the slender guard said. His head was bowed with the effort of supporting his larger companion. "Two of dem."

"What?" Something about the man's voice struck the captain as odd. "Who are you? Come to order. Remove your helm. You are not of my command."

The larger guard took his arm from around the other's shoulders. Stood under his own power. Raised his head and flashed golden teeth. "We're here about de problem with de doors."

Confusion displaced the captain's suspicion for a moment. "What problem with the doors?"

"Dey're not open," Skarangella Skarn said.

Before anyone could react, Skarn sprang away from Trok, slammed

the captain aside, bowled another guard over, and raced past the pool
into the narrow throat separating the throne hall from the palace doors.
"Shoot him!" the captain shouted.

The crossbowmen were quick in their response, triggering their
shots the instant they saw Skarn's shape. But Skarn was ready for them,
presenting the shields to either side, catching the deadly quarrels with
the steel buffers.

Roaring like a tiger, Skarn shed the shields and hurtled shoulder-first
into the palace doors.

69

"We're getting killed out here!" Balazar shouted. He was back-to-back with Kazim behind a statue. Dead bodies were strewn all about them. The battle still raged, but the Horsairs were scattered and trapped in pockets behind boulders and fountains and statues and topiary. To venture into the open yard with no way to get into the palace was to become target practice for the archers on the upper floors. "We need more help!"

Kazim drove his scimitar through another guard. The man fell and died and was immediately replaced by another. The Raj's Dragoons were trained fighters but nothing special. Their only advantage lay in their numbers—but that was going to be enough to defeat the Horsairs. Kazim was beginning to wonder how many more of his subjects he could allow to die before he sounded a retreat.

For what had to be the hundredth time since the futility of their position became apparent, he thought: *What we need is a way to get those damned—*

The doors to the palace burst open.

A huge guard tumbled into the daylight, spun to his feet, drew a sword, and bounded back inside the palace.

For an instant, Kazim could only stare in disbelief. It might have cost him his life, but luckily the Dragoon he was battling was just as surprised and Kazim was quicker to recover, cutting the man down. "There is your help, Balazar!" he shouted, laughing at this incredible turn of fortune. "Sound the charge!"

As Skarn smashed the doors open, staggering to his knees, half-blinded by the daylight, he heard from behind him the captain of the Raj's guard cry: "Drop the portcullis!"

If that barrier came down in the hallway, their effort to breach the doors was for naught.

Skarn spun around as the archers rushed out of their alcoves. The lever controlling the gate was in the hallway, much nearer to the archers than to Skarn: he would never get there in time. *Damn it all!* He pulled out his sword and charged anyway.

Then a spear skewered one of the archers like a fish and Trok vaulted past the man as he fell, tackling the other archer. But the archer was bigger and stronger and Trok had no weapon. The man shrugged him aside and grabbed the lever.

Skarn swung his scimitar and severed the archer's arms at the elbows.

The archer staggered back, screaming, hot blood spraying from his stumps. Trok scrambled up and freed his spear from the other archer. Stood beside Skarn in the narrow hall and faced off against the captain and his guards.

"Fools," the captain said. More of his men were rushing from the rear of the throne hall. "You are hopelessly outnumbered."

The Horsairs thundered through the palace doors.

"Ye were sayin'?" Skarn flashed his golden grin and nudged Trok into the alcove as the Horsairs surged past, whelming the captain's lines like a wave wiping out a wall of sand.

"Dat worked just about like ye planned it," Trok said.

"Don' it always?" With Trok on his heels, Skarn raced in behind the Horsairs to join the battle in the throne hall.

70

Upon the dais at the rear of the hall, where no enemy had yet reached, the Raj rose slowly from his throne. He waved away the guards who looked to attend him. Walked alone into a side corridor that led to the treasure vaults.

The clamor of battle faded. All was quiet here, deep in the halls of this palace that would not much longer be his. The Raj paused in his death march. He touched the stone of the wall, smooth marble threaded with lapis lazuli, beautiful yet taken for granted after so many years.

Turn back, a voice in him urged. *Stop this madness!*

But the voice of the lamp was stronger and more insistent. After a moment the old Raj started walking again. His steps were heavy and slow. He leaned on the wall from time to time, but inexorably he came to the top of the steps leading down to the vaults.

A rutilant light glowed up from those depths, making it look like a descent into the Everlasting Hells. The Raj gripped the iron railing, lifted a foot to begin this last stage of his last journey—

A hand grabbed his shoulder, yanking him backwards.

"Father! Do not go down there!" Timor shouted.

The Prince had seen to Demby's bandages, but the urchin refused to remain in the room. "Got to help de great Sultan," he insisted. Timor did not know how they could do that, but he thought of his father and he burned to do *something*, anything that might help him. He would be in the throne hall awaiting the outcome of the battle. If they could get to him and Erkani was not nearby, perhaps they could draw him away to safety and reason with him.

So they had started out down the passage leading to the rear of throne hall, and Fortune smiled, for as they rounded a corner, they saw the Raj ahead and intercepted him at the top of the steps.

"Father," Timor shouted again.

The Raj struggled, his eyes blank. "Unhand me! I have a message for my master. The battle is come to the palace. The doors are broken! The battle is come!" he cried.

"Stop it!" Timor shook the Raj hard, trying to snap his father out of his deadly trance. "Can you not see this thing is going to kill us all?"

The Raj shoved him, breaking his grip, but stumbled to his knees. "The doors are broken!" he cried again. "Master! They are—"

Demby slapped the Raj across the face. "Dat's de monster down dere, saib," the urchin said. "Stop de shoutin or dis goan be very bad for all of us."

The Raj put a hand to his face, stunned. His eyes focused, first on Demby, and then on the figure that knelt beside him. "Ti...mor? Timor, my son! Alive!" They embraced. "Timor, what have I done?" the Raj whispered. He rose suddenly, pulling his son with him. "Where is your mother? We must flee. We must flee now!"

But it was too late.

The salamander had heard.

Lurid light blazed up the steps. "Run, Timor!" The Raj shoved his son ahead. It was only when they had rounded several turns that the Raj realized he had pushed his son in entirely the wrong direction.

The throne hall was ahead.

The salamander was behind them.

"Swiftly," the Raj urged as a wave of heat as from a great furnace rolled over them. Timor risked a glance back. The corridor was flooded with red light. The stones of the floor were on fire. *That's not possible,* he thought.

Possible or not, it was happening. Timor saw a shape then, just the silhouette in the firelight at the far end of the corridor. Something horribly hunched but still bipedal, with red eyes that might have been lanterns in the deepest Hell.

He cried out in terror and tripped. "Saib!" Demby grabbed his arm and hauled frantically until Timor staggered to his feet. "De monster's comin! Run, run!"

They ran, breathless in the baking heat, the salamander closing the distance but not really hurrying, as if it had no need of urgency. *It doesn't,* Timor realized. *Nothing can stand against it. We're all going to die....*

They were so focused on the nightmare behind them that they were hardly aware of the battle raging in the throne hall until they were amid it. On either side of the pool, horsemen from the desert were fighting the palace guards. The defenders had finally managed to drop the portcullis, but the force of Horsairs that had made it inside before the gate fell were waging a furious offensive.

The Raj pulled away from Timor. "Father! What are you doing?" Timor shouted.

Ignoring his son, the Raj clambered onto the dais and stood before his throne. "Men of Makhara!" he shouted. "Men of Makhara, flee this place! Doom is upon us!"

The Raj's voice went unheeded or unheard in the din and chaos. He fell to his knees beside his golden chair as the doorway filled with fire.

The salamander entered the throne hall.

It had changed even in the short time since descending to the vaults, losing even more of Erkani's humanity. It was almost wholly reptilian now: a giant, bipedal lizard, its skin mottled red and black and yellow, its mouth a snout that opened to spray fire like a dragon. Men burned and died. The stench of char gagged the air.

In the aftermath of that first blast, all combat in the hall ceased. Horsairs and guardsmen whirled to see the salamander stalking forward. Fire etched the stones beneath its clawed feet. It sent a second gout of flame into another concentration of stunned combatants. When the smoke cleared, there was nothing but traces of ash on the floor.

Men of both parties fled in terror, but others stood, some out of bravery, others simply petrified. Then one of the guardsmen looked to the throne. "The Raj!" he cried, pointing. "Rally to the Raj! Dragoons, do your duty! Protect the throne! On your lives now!"

He charged, but no one followed his lead. The salamander's fire took him from the world in a searing flash.

"Father!" Timor shouted, vaulting onto the dais. "Your scepter!"

"Yes!" The Raj grabbed the scepter from his throne. An instant later a massive tentacle shot from the deeps, winding around the salamander like a choke-creeper vine.

A cry lifted from the men: triumph—

—and dismay.

The salamander fixed its claws upon the tentacle. The rubbery flesh turned purple, then red, then black. The pool was a roiling cauldron, boiling, steaming as the aefryt poured its fire into the giant octopus. Eight tentacles thrashed, some striking men in blind agony, others smashing the stone floor. The octopus tried to release the salamander, but now it was the aefryt who held the death grip, burning and burning until the last charred tentacle twitched and was still.

The salamander let the dead limb fall from its hands and swiveled its ugly head, pinning the Raj with angry red eyes.

The Raj dropped his scepter. Timor pulled him behind the golden throne, covering him with his body.

The salamander waved a claw in a mocking farewell. Opened its mouth to loose its killing fire.

A spear slammed into its back.

The salamander staggered, spraying its fire into the floor, burning a hole like a meteor striking the earth. Grunting, it turned, clawing for the spear as if it were a mere nuisance, unable to quite catch it, seeking the source of the attack.

"I think that was a bad idea, brother," Balazar said.

"You might be right," Kazim answered, grabbing another spear and flinging it at the salamander. This one never reached its target, burning up in flight as the monster sent a wave of heat forth like a shield.

"Death," it promised, pointing a claw at the lord of the Horsairs.

Fire speared from its maw.

Skarangella Skarn barreled into both brothers, driving them down as the fire seared the air above them.

Skarn scrambled up. "Hey!" he shouted. "Dat's enough with de dragon bit, ye ugly lizard."

The salamander leaned its head slowly down, bringing its gaze level with Skarn. "You dare?"

Behind Skarn, Kazim and Balazar rose. "Wait on de fire," Skarn muttered. "One of ye go left and de other right. I'm goan straight up de middle. It can't hit us all at once. Maybe somebody'll get lucky and get dere."

"That's your plan?" Kazim said.

Skarn shrugged. "Don' got none better right now." He had remembered a trick Argentia had used once. If he could time the fire right and tumble underneath the blast he might have a clear shot at the salamander. *Risky, deh, but it just might work….*

Kazim laughed. "Spoken like a true Horsair."

"I'll take it dat's de complement?"

"The highest."

They spread themselves apart, forming a triangle with Skarn at the point.

The salamander opened its arms wide and roared in challenge.

Skarn raised his head to take a last look at the sky through the glass dome and send a final wish to Skritlana and Seibu before he died facing this enemy. As he did, a strange flash of green against the blue vault caught his eye. *What in de hells? Is dat—*

Skarn's golden smile appeared like the sun breaking through clouds.

"So eager to meet death?" the salamander sneered.

"Was hopin t' put off de audience for de while, actually," Skarn replied.

"Then why do you smile, fool?"

"Ye goan find out." Skarn glanced back up to the sky. "Right… about…*now!*"

71

Argentia had flown as fast as she could from the Horsair camp, pushing the carpet to its limits to make up the lost time. Mirk clung beside her, his fur matted by the wind. The Jade Monkey was cradled in her injured arm. She did not understand what power it could have over the aefryt. *It's just a stupid statue....*

But was it? It had a strange gravity about it, a quiescent strength. Clearly great measures had been taken to ensure its safety over the passage of the centuries until the time of its need was at hand. *But what do I do with it?*

Argentia thought about it, about the qualities of the statue and the nature of the aefryt, as they flew onward through the twilight before dawn and the sunrise that followed. The dome of Kephalo winked like a diamond on the horizon. *Almost there....*

Would she be in time?

The city rose out of the desert, gaining shape and definition. Argentia took the carpet higher to avoid the chance of being shot at by the guards on the walls. Once she was over the city, however, she swooped low again, gliding above the rooftops of Khemr-kar. The streets were strangely empty, even for the early hour. As she swept over the wall and into the palace gardens, she saw why.

Horsairs and guardsmen warred amid the fountains and flowerbeds.

Arrows flew from the palace windows, plucking away at attackers shielded by statues. She did not see Kazim or Balazar. *Or Demby....*

The palace doors were open. Argentia blasted past the battling men and flew inside.

"Gate!" Mirk screeched.

Shit! Argentia yanked on the carpet, bringing it to a halt so hard and fast it almost bucked her off. Beyond the portcullis, men were fighting furiously—and there in the thick of it were Skarn and Trok and Kazim and Balazar—but what held Argentia's eyes was the growing red light from a corridor at the rear of the hall.

Light like fire.

The salamander appeared, spitting flames.

"God damn it all!" Argentia wheeled the carpet around. "Ride's over, Mirk," she said, shoving him off. Before the astonished meerkat had even hit the ground, Argentia was out the door and mounting to the sky.

She climbed fast, at an almost vertical angle. *I can't believe I'm trying this....* But she had to get into the throne hall and there was no other way she could think of.

Up and up and up and up. Gasping for breath. Was she high enough? She did not know, but she sensed there was no more time.

Dive, Argentia commanded.

The carpet leveled out. Hung for a moment.

Stooped to earth like an eagle.

Fast and faster: plummeting through the blue. The wind whipped painfully, snapping Argentia's hair back like a red war banner, biting at her face, striking the breath from her.

As she fell, trusting the magic of the carpet to keep her alive, the Jade Monkey clutched in her wounded arm began to glow with an emerald light.

The sun blazed off the dome, blinding her. Argentia clenched the carpet, ducked as low as she could, screaming a battle cry as she flew headlong into that light.

The carpet blasted through the dome like a mailed fist through a windowpane.

The salamander turned toward the noise of shattering glass. Surprise and fear flashed in its reptilian eyes. It reared to its full height, bursting into flames from head to tail, but it had no time to attack.

Awash in the eldritch green glow of the Jade Monkey and screaming all the way, Argentia plowed the carpet full-tilt into the salamander. The instant before the collision, she hurled the statue at Bazu's fiery feet.

The Jade Monkey exploded.

The blast of aether—too strong for the carpet's magic—catapulted Argentia into the air. She flipped head over heels, plunging into the throne hall's pool just as a great aqueous ape rose from the shards of its crystalline containment to crush the aefryt in its watery embrace.

The salamander thrashed madly, forcing the ape back with a pulse of fire. They came together again, immortal enemies pitted against each other in an onslaught of flaming claws and foaming fists. The salamander bristled with fire, but the magic of the Jade Monkey was strong and ancient as well—it sole purpose to extinguish, as the aefryt's was to burn. It caught the salamander by the throat, throttling it relentlessly. The green glow grew against the fire of the salamander until a cloud of searing steam enveloped the two struggling elementals.

There was a wail of unearthly anguish—

—and Al'Atin Erkani's body crumpled to the floor.

Silence in the throne hall. Then the survivors, Horsairs and palace Dragoons alike, raised a great cheer.

As the steam dissipated, Skarn, Kazim, and Balazar walked forward to where Erkani lay beside the charred remains of Argentia's carpet and the shattered remnants of the Jade Monkey. Skarn crouched beside the thief. "Still alive," he said.

Kazim raised his kukri. "Not for long."

"Don't!" Argentia shouted.

Kazim stopped his blow and stared as Argentia boosted herself out of the pool. She limped over to the men; the crash into the water had done something bad to her hip. "Erkani's mine," she said.

"The blood of my people is on his hands," Kazim said.

Argentia faced him, soaking wet, bloodied, beautiful. "Not his. The thing that killed your people is gone." She poked Erkani with her boot and he groaned. "This is just some fool who got in over his head." She fixed her cobalt eyes on Kazim, defying him.

"Best heed," Skarn said to Kazim. "Seen dat look before. Dere's no arguin."

Kazim took measure of Argentia, shook his head, and nodded, sheathing his knife. He had seen that look before as well, in horses that would not be broken.

"What do you intend to do with him?" Balazar demanded. "He cannot be permitted to go without punishment."

"I'm taking him back with me," Argentia said. "I give you my word that once we reach Aventar he will end his days without ever seeing the sun again."

Balazar looked at his brother. Kazim nodded, satisfied.

"Ye sure know how to make de entrance," Skarn said to Argentia. "But ye could work on de timin a bit."

"Why, were you worried?"

"See, dese stories dey always get back t' Skritlana and den I got t' hear about how I'm dis second or dat second away from de dyin...."

Argentia laughed. "Sorry. Next time I'll try to be more considerate."

"Dat's much appreciated."

"Where's Demby?"

"Here, de Lady!" the urchin jumped up from behind the dais and ran to them. Argentia held him close.

Trok walked up, Mirk trotting beside him. "Very cruel to throw Mirk off flying rug," the meerkat huffed.

"It was for your own good."

"You're de damn craziest lady I ever met, ye know dat?" Trok said, looking at the shattered portion of the dome. "Flyin through de damn roof."

"Lady made hole in roof?" Mirk asked, lifting his amber eyes to assess the damage and the distance to the ground.

"Uh-huh."

"Mirk thanks wise and kind Lady for throwing him off flying rug."

They all laughed. It was a good sound, delivering some of the weight of death from the hall. "That statue you smashed...that was the Jade Monkey?" Kazim asked.

Argentia nodded. "Not what you expected, either?"

"Not at all. How did you know what to do with it?"

"Lucky guess." It had been, in part, but not completely. Argentia had reasoned that if the lamp was a prison for the aefryt, the statue might serve a similar function, though for what manner of creature she had no idea. "What happened, anyway?"

Skarn told her how the Jade Monkey had doused the salamander.

"I always miss all the good stuff," Argentia complained.

"Deh. It was elementary."

"Skarn...." She rolled her eyes and shook her head.

Timor and his father approached. "The Raj would speak," Timor said. A wave of uncertainty went through the palace guards. The Horsairs shifted, looking to Kazim. Their common enemy defeated, they seemed to remember that they had only minutes earlier been at mortal odds.

"Strange days," the Raj said. "Strange days indeed when the siege of a palace by lawless men restores order and peace. All those of my inclining, lower your arms. There will be no more fighting here today," he commanded. Then he turned to Kazim. "My thanks to you for delivering my people." He gestured with his scepter at Erkani. "That one is not the only fool here. Though his actions caused the deaths of many, I must pity him as well. The lure of the lamp is—"

"The lamp!" Argentia exclaimed. She knelt on the ruins of the flying carpet, wincing at the flare of pain in her hip, and shoved Erkani over. The lamp lay amid jade fragments in a green puddle. *Griegvard....*

Argentia had some experience with magical prisons. Her instinct had been true for the Jade Monkey. She trusted it again. "I need to borrow your chair," she said to the Raj. She mounted the dais and placed the lamp on the throne. "Stand back," she ordered, drawing her katana.

"Gen?" Skarn asked, but he backed up with the rest of them. "Ye sure about dis?"

Argentia shrugged her arm out of the sling, set her feet and raised her katana two-handed before her. She closed her eyes and settling her breathing, shutting away all the hurt in her hip, her shoulder, her leg. Opening her eyes, she focused only on the lamp. Its magic was strong, but her sword had sundered magic tokens before.

With a sudden cry, she swept Lightbringer high over her head and chopped it down upon the aefryt's lamp.

An explosion of ruby light blew her off the dais. She landed in a heap. *Owwwww....* She sat up slowly, rubbing her hip. Something was seriously wrong there, and her shoulder was bleeding again.

But none of that mattered, because struggling up from the ruin of the Raj's shattered throne was Griegvard Gynt.

The dwarf glared fiercely around, saw no apparent enemies, and stomped forward, kicking aside half of the cleanly severed lamp. When he reached the edge of the dais, he set his hands on his sturdy hips and glowered down at Argentia. "Took ye long enough, Red," he said.

"If one more person tells me that...."

72

The day was given to the dead.

The portcullis was raised and the Raj and Kazim went out of the palace together. Their presence quickly put an end to the last pockets of fighting in the gardens. Wearied, bloodied men of both sides looked on cautiously as the two leaders reached an accord. The Raj extended his thanks to Kazim's riders for their bravery and sacrifice, as well as to his Dragoons for their loyal defense of his person.

The combined losses numbered more than a hundred, though of the victims of the salamander there was nothing left but memories. Bodies were taken from the throne hall and the gardens and prepared for their passing to the afterworld: fire for the Horsairs, mausoleums of stone for the palace guardsmen.

Long hours later, the Horsairs were placed on litters behind their steeds and paraded through the city. Chanting and incense filled the air. People watched the funeral procession from their doorways, their faces somber. They did not know what had happened in the palace, but there were rumors that the Red Devil was gone, its curse lifted from their city and land, and that these men had paid the price for that deliverance.

At the gates, the Raj and Kazim stood side by side. "They go with honor to the Gardens of Ab'Dala," the Raj said. "Let it be known that henceforth we recognize and embrace the sovereignty of the Horsairs in the deserts of Makhara. Let peace prosper between us," he said, extending his hand to Kazim.

The lord of the Horsairs took it. "You do us honor, lord of Khemr-kar. Let peace prosper between us indeed."

Kazim and the Raj bowed to each other. Then the Horsairs rode out of Khemr-kar with their dead to hold their own ceremony and let their women and children share in their mourning.

The Raj and his retinue then returned to the palace. The throne hall had been scrubbed clean and turned into a wake chamber. The dead would lie in state, as was the custom, and would be given burial with full honors at the next dawn. The Raj, Rajina, and Timor sat upon the dais as the people entered to pay their respects.

Skarn and Demby stood by the dais to represent Sormoria. Trok was down at the docks preparing one of Skarn's ships—as predicted, he had several in port—for its unexpected passengers.

Griegvard was none the worse for his time in the lamp. The magic space was hewn of red stone and hotter than the Wastes of Yth, but the stoic dwarf, accustomed to the forge, was unfazed. He killed the two guards who had the misfortune of being sucked in with him and started walking, determined to reach one of the walls and find a way free. He never did, of course, for the lamp bounded a plane of infinite space in its shape, but he was indefatigable. "Would've reached th' bloody end eventually," he maintained in the aftermath of the battle. Once everything was sorted out, he took a tun of rum down to the dungeons, where he sat guard over the unconscious Al'Atin Erkani.

Argentia missed the ceremonies entirely.

Battered by the successive explosions of the Jade Monkey and the aefryt's lamp, she had swooned shortly after freeing Griegvard. Skarn had carried her to a chamber in the palace and the Raj had sent his viziers to see to her.

It was evening when she woke. The wound in her shoulder was healed, but her hip still hurt; they had not known about it, so they had expended no magic on it. "No big deal," she told Skarn when he came to see her and noticed her limping about the room. She was more interested in making sure Griegvard was all right and Erkani was safely in their custody. Skarn assured her that all was well and that they were prepared to leave in the morning. "Should probably stay for de funeral ceremonies," he explained. "Dat's de diplomatic thing t' do, right?"

"I would think so."

"Course, we can stay longer. Ye seem t' have de fair amount of admirers here."

"What are you talking about?"

"De Rajling and de Horsair lord, dey both got de keen interest in whether ye recovered. Before de Horsair left, he said t' tell ye he hasn't forgotten de unfinished business between ye. Whatever dat means." There was an amused gleam in Skarn's eyes.

"He left?" Argentia said, surprised.

"Went back for de funerals of his men. So dere *was* somethin, den." Skarn laughed.

"No, there wasn't, actually," Argentia said tartly. She was disappointed Kazim had gone without saying good-bye, but she understood his responsibilities. *Besides, I wasn't even awake....*

"Ye can always take de Rajling's suit instead," Skarn needled.

"Oh shut up." She threw a pillow at him.

Later that night, Argentia awoke to a noise.

She sat up, disoriented in a strange bed in a strange room, and fumbled the sheet around her. The noise came again: from the window. She had opened it to let the night breeze in before she went to sleep. The curtains were moving, but not from the wind.

Someone was coming in.

Can't be Erkani—unless he escaped the dungeons....

Argentia snatched her handbow from beneath the pillow—a habit from many nights passed in unsafe places—as the form pushed through the drapes. She aimed the weapon at the hulking figure's chest. "That's far enough."

"Are you *ever* unarmed?" the intruder asked.

"Kazim!" Argentia set the handbow on the nightstand and sprang to her feet. Pain flared in her hip at the sudden movement. She staggered.

Kazim caught her in his arms. "I told Balazar it was inevitable you would fall for me."

Argentia laughed and leaned against him for a moment, feeling the warmth of his strong body through the thin sheet. He smelled of horse and sand and night. "I'm all right. I can stand." She placed her hand against his chest. His heartbeat was a primal drum. "Kazim...." Silver light from the half-moon bathed them through the window. The Horsair lord's glossy black hair and eyes shone almost to take Argentia's breath away. She wanted him so badly she could taste it. "What are you doing here? I thought you were gone. Skarn said you left."

"That is true."

"And...."

"The Sormorian told me you sail in the morning. We do have the matter of our bargain. Alas...."

"Alas what?"

Kazim flashed a sly smile. "Alas you are injured. I fear concluding our terms will be too strenuous an engagement."

"Oh really?" Argentia let the sheet fall to the floor between them. "Prove it."

In the dark hours of the morning, Argentia felt an emptiness beside her and woke again.

Kazim's place was warm but unoccupied. Argentia sat up. The moon was down and the room was darker than before, but her eyes adjusted quickly and she made out the shape of the Horsair across the room.

"You sleep like a cat," Kazim said, seeing or sensing that she was awake.

"What are you doing?" Argentia asked. When Kazim didn't answer, she turned on the lamp. Kazim was dressed, fastening his shirt. "You're sneaking out?" She threw the sheets aside and got out of bed, folding her arms across her breasts: annoyed, not self-conscious. "You've got a real problem with good-bye, don't you?"

Kazim stared at her for a moment. "I am the Lord of the Horsairs. I am not accustomed to saying good-bye when I do not wish to."

"You son of a—"

Kazim lifted a hand. "You misunderstand. Would you come back with me?"

"Would I what?"

"Would you return with me if I asked?"

"To be part of your harem?" Argentia laughed. "Not for all the sand in your desert."

"No. To be my wife." Kazim reached out and moved aside a loose tendril of hair from Argentia's face. "You are all the harem any man could need."

"I...ah..."

"Would you?" Kazim repeated.

"You're serious?"

"I am the Lord of the Horsairs."

Argentia thought about it. Bit her lip. Stared at the floor. *I can't do it....* To be bound to any place was not in her. She needed variety. Adventure. The freedom to pursue her own way whenever she wanted.

She looked back at Kazim; her smile was shy. "I'm flattered," she said. "But no."

Kazim forced a smile of his own. "As I knew you would say."

"So that's why you were leaving?"

"I told you, I am not accustomed to being denied."

"Well you still could have said good-bye."

"You were sleeping."

"That's what people do in the middle of the night!"

"A technicality."

"I think you should apologize."

"I am—"

She put her hand over his mouth. "Not like that." Taking his other hand, she pulled him toward the bed.

"You Outlanders have a strange way of apologizing," he said.

"Give it a try. You might enjoy it."

"I thought I was leaving," Kazim said. Argentia still had his hand, but he had not moved to follow her. Though his tone was light, she heard the tension in his voice and realized he was genuinely uncomfortable.

"Listen to me, Kazim." She reached up, caressed his cheek. "I do care for you. You know that, right? You're brave, honorable, and true—everything so many women would want, but…."

"But not you," he said.

"Yes. No. Sort of." She sighed. "It's not that I don't want those things. I do. But a throne? That's just not for me. I'm honored, believe me—it's not everyday a girl gets a kingdom thrown at her feet—but that's not what I'm about. I'm sorry."

Kazim stared at her for a moment. Then he nodded. "It is I who am sorry," he said. "You would have made a fine queen."

"Thank you." She knelt on the bed, pulling him down with her. "Now, about that apology…."

73

Dawn came and went and so did Kazim.

He left by the window. This time he said good-bye. "You have passed through my life like rain over the desert," he told Argentia. "I am richer for it."

"Sweet," Argentia whispered. They kissed tenderly. "Good journey," she said: the traditional farewell between warriors.

"Until we meet again."

"We just might," she said. "I kind of get around."

"I will reserve a pillow in my tent," Kazim said. His swagger was back, brimming with the bright confidence that had so charmed her when they first met.

So they parted laughing, but Argentia was still thinking about him later, as she walked to the docks with her companions. She wondered how much she had hurt him by rejecting his offer. *What else could I have done? Argentia, Queen of the Horsairs—I think not!* She did not regret her choice, but she hoped Kazim truly did understand.

"You're quiet dis morning," Skarn said, catching her heavy mood.

"Just tired."

"Deh. I'll bet."

"What's *that* supposed to mean?"

"De walls in dat palace, dey're pretty thin," Skarn said.

"What?"

"Ha-ha! So ye admit it!"

"You rat! You didn't hear a thing, did you? Not that there was anything to hear."

Skarn laughed off the belated attempt at demurral. "Too late for dat. So was it de Horse Lord or de Rajling?"

"Timor's just a boy! Give me *some* credit." She punched him in the arm.

"Dah. He's not *dat* young."

"Stow it," Argentia hissed. Timor, the Raj, and the Rajina were up ahead by the ship, waiting to see them off.

The Raj thanked Skarn for his aid and promised to favor Sormoria with his ships to increase the prosperity of both their nations. To Argentia he said, "On behalf of my people and especially my family, I have not words enough of gratitude. You are a credit to all warriors."

"It wasn't just me, your Highness. Your son played no small role. Without him, I'd still be looking for the Jade Monkey." She turned to Timor. "If not for your bravery, many more lives would have been lost. You will honor the throne some day." She kissed him on each cheek. "Take care of yourself."

"You also, my Lady," Timor said, bowing.

"I always do. And don't call me Lady."

"As you wish, Argentia."

"Much better." She smiled and looked at Skarn, who nodded. Trok and Griegvard had already loaded the comatose Erkani into the ship's brig. It was time to go.

They filed toward the gangplank. "Hold!" came a call from down the dock. They turned to see a Horsair riding toward them, leading another horse on a tether.

Astrali... Argentia recognized the white starburst on the stallion's forehead.

The rider stopped a respectful distance from the Raj and dismounted, bowing.

"Come forward," the Raj said. "What business have you here?"

"I bring a message from my Lord and a gift for the Lady." The rider handed Argentia a note. She unfolded the parchment and read:

So you will not forget your Stallion. Ride well.

K

"You're blushin," Skarn said.
"Am not...."

79

The return to Khan was uneventful.

Skarn took command of the ship, reveling in having the ocean beneath him again. "What say we troll for de pirates?" he asked Argentia one afternoon as they stood together at the wheel. "Like de old times."

"In the old times, *you* were the pirate," Argentia reminded him.

"Dah! But I was pretty good at huntin dem down, too. I hear dese waters are plenty stocked."

"Tempting, but I think we've pushed our luck with Skritlana far enough, don't you? If we take the long way back to hunt pirates she's liable to kill me first and then you."

"Dah. I guess we don't want dat, do we?"

They saw no any pirates anyway, so the question of Skarn resuming his privateer mantle for a few days was moot. By the time they sailed into Talon Bay, with the spires and minarets of Khan rising to greet them, Demby was bouncing all over with excitement to get home and tell the tale of their adventures and Skarn was already talking about Seibu and how Skrit had probably redecorated the whole palace while they were away.

Argentia could tell that he was settled in his life. He might venture forth at need or when the mood took him, but he had grown into the palace and the throne and the roles of father and husband.

She wondered what that must be like, to not have the urge to be on the move, headed somewhere, anywhere, on the chase, on the hunt, or just on the road to the unknown. Someday she might come to the point Skarn was at in his life, or she might not. There was so much to see, so much to do, and she intended to take as much as she could out of the time allotted her.

All of that reaffirmed her decision to reject Kazim's suit. He might have exchanged his whole harem for her, but he did not understand her at all if he thought that would have made her stay. Only Carfax had recognized that she could not be broken or bound—it was why she had loved him so much, and why the rest of the men in her life were just passing fancies. *Like rain over the desert,* she thought, and smiled.

"Hell of an adventure, deh?" Skarn said, drawing Argentia out of her reverie.

"Yeah, well, I try to keep things interesting."

Skarn laughed. "Dat's de good way t' describe it." He draped his big arm across Argentia's shoulders. "We done good, Gen."

Argentia nodded. They had stood and been true against terrible odds and returned to tell the tale. Even Griegvard showed no lingering effects from his entrapment in the lamp, though he was still angry about his burned beard.

The only blemish was Erkani, who was still unconscious. Skarn assured her that Sanla would be able to do something when they got back to the palace, but Argentia had begun to fear the thief would never awaken. *He'd better. He has answers I need....*

As the afternoon waned, the company slipped into the docks of Khan, one among dozens of other merchant ships arriving, and made their way to the palace with little fanfare. At dinner that night, Skarn explained the trip as "de successful negotiation for de return of de fugitive."

"And de lamp?" Sanla asked.

"Destroyed," Argentia said.

"Dis is well," the meja replied.

"Dat easy?" Skritlana asked, suspicious. "How'd ye hurt dat hip, den?" Argentia's slight limp had not escaped the Sultana's quick eye.

"Um—"

"Dat was when de Lady flew through de glass ceiling to put out de fire lizard wit de water monkey before it could make de kebob of de Great Sultan," Demby said.

Argentia clapped a hand to her mouth. Skritlana turned slowly to her husband. "Dis is what ye call de 'successful negotiation'?"

"Deh. Maybe I left out de detail or two."

"Maybe ye should remember dem details den."

Skarn looked at Argentia, who looked at Griegvard. "Don't bloody ask me," the dwarf snorted. "I was trapped in th' damn lamp half th' damn time."

"Trapped in de lamp?" Skrit echoed.

"Better tell de tale, Gen," Skarn said. "Ye never seen de Sultana angry—makes de salamander seem as dangerous as de candle in de rainstorm. Besides, ye haven't told me where ye got dat flyin carpet yet."

"And now de flyin carpet?" Skrit pointed an exquisitely polished nail at Argentia. "Sistah, start talkin…"

The next morning, after a lazy rising and late breakfast, Argentia, Griegvard, and Mirk headed for the docks. They had locked Erkani in the *Reef Reaver's* brig when they arrived at Khan and converted part of the hold into a makeshift stall for Astrali. They were ready to go.

Skarn, Trok, Demby, Skrit, and Seibu saw them off. "Dat was de most fun I've had since de hike cross Yth," Skarn said. "Come by again if ye got de dragon or somethin dat wants de huntin."

"The next time I'm down, it's just to visit, I promise," Argentia said.

"I will believe dat when I see it," Skritlana said, embracing the huntress. "But do not be de stranger. Ye may bring my husband into danger, but at de least ye always return him alive and well."

"Deh, ye got dat all backwards, woman," Skarn protested. "I'm de one bringin de rest back safe and sound."

"Indeed? Apologies, my Sultan," Skrit said, making a mock curtsy. "I must have misheard de tale last night." She rolled her eyes and they all burst out laughing.

"Anytime, anywhere," Skarn said to Argentia, hugging her tightly.

"You know it." Argentia gave Seibu a last kiss and then she was gone, following Griegvard and Mirk up the gangplank onto the *Reaver* to bring her hard-won bounty home.

75

Three days later, Erkani woke up.

He screamed incessantly, banging on the walls and the door of his cell, begging to be freed. The crew got annoyed. Dorn got Argentia. Argentia got Griegvard and Mirk. They all went down to the brig together.

Dorn unlocked and opened the door. Erkani charged out.

Griegvard stepped into his path. Bounced the thief right off his feet and back into the cell.

Erkani scrambled up, dazed and trying to figure out what he had run into: it had felt like a stone wall.

Argentia moved past Griegvard.

"You!" Erkani screeched. "No! Not again!"

"Me," Argentia said. "Again." Then she hit him: a quick left to the jaw that dropped the small man in a heap. "I told you I'd catch you. You've got a lot to answer for this time."

Erkani wiped his bloodied lips. "I don't know anything. I can't remember. Where am I? Where's my lamp?" he moaned.

"Gone. I broke it. Destroyed its magic. It's over."

"Bitch!" Erkani hissed. "You're lying! You took it for yourself. Like last time."

"Bah," Griegvard said. "He's madder'n a cornered badger. Ain't gonna learn a bloody thing from 'im."

"He'll talk," Argentia said confidently.

"Talk? No, no. I don't remember anything." Erkani shook his head. "Rubies. I need rubies. Where's my lamp?"

Argentia frowned. Sanla had prepared her for the possibility that Erkani might not remember anything that happened while the salamander possessed him, especially the later stages, when the aefryt had almost been in its true shape. That was an annoyance because she wanted Erkani to suffer pangs of conscience for all the hurt and death he had caused, but it had nothing to do with what she intended to ask him.

"My lamp," Erkani shouted. "I want my lamp! What are you going to do with me? Where is it? Why don't you just kill me and be done with it?"

"If yer wantin," Griegvard said, reaching for the axe on his shoulder.

Argentia stayed him with a gesture. "I'm not going to kill you," she told Erkani. "That would be too easy. You're going back to Aventar to rot in the dungeons for the rest of your miserable life, which I hope will be very long."

Erkani paled. "No. Not back there. Won't go." He clasped his arms about his knees and started rocking incessantly. "Not going, not going, not—"

"You're going," Argentia said. "But first I'm going to ask you a question and you're going to tell me what I want to know, got it?"

"Won't talk. Don't remember. Nothing. Where's my lamp?"

"Whyn't ye just let me beat it out of him?" Griegvard said, cracking his knuckles.

"Because he might say anything to get you to stop. We need to make sure he's telling the truth."

"No truth. No talking. Shhhhh." Erkani stopped rocking and looked up, raising a finger to his lips. "Lovely lamp. Lovely fire. No answers. Not telling. Where's my lamp? Shhhhh!"

"Enough of this horseshit," Argentia said. "Mirk?"

"Mirk is here."

"Do your thing."

The meerkat came forward, holding a glass vial. His amber eyes glimmered. The potion Argentia had purchased from the apothecary in Khan glowed in response.

301

"Get away!" Erkani screamed. Then he clamped his hand over his mouth. Argentia motioned to Griegvard. The dwarf bent down and poked the thief in the stomach.

Erkani's hand dropped reflexively. He gasped.

Mirk poured the potion down the thief's throat.

Erkani choked, his throat working reflexively, but he could not keep himself from swallowing. When he had stopped gagging, he stared at Argentia.

"Do you know me?" she asked.

"I hate you," he whispered. "You took it from me. Twice. My lamp."

"I'll take that as a yes," Argentia said.

She asked him her question.

Found his answer very interesting indeed.

76

"Welcome home," Argentia said, shoving Erkani into his old cell in Aventar's dungeon.

After the thief's confession, Argentia had left him locked in the brig to rave. She remembered the first time she had captured him and knew the withdrawal symptoms from his association with the aefryt's lamp would end eventually.

But Erkani was still gibbering three weeks later when they put to port at Argo. Argentia told Dorn to give the crew a bonus for their endurance and patience. She stayed in Argo just long enough to turn Astrali over to Ikabod's care and grab a bite to eat and a change of clothes. Then she, Griegvard, Mirk, and the unwilling Al'Atin Erkani were off to Wavegard Cathedral, where they took the aethergate back to Duralyn.

The thief had struggled every minute of the carriage ride from the *Reef Reaver* to the cathedral. Griegvard had to haul him bodily into the aethergate. Once they rematerialized in the Monastery of the Grey Tree, however, the thief had gone entirely slack. He was silent, stumbling listlessly along, as if he finally knew it was over.

Argentia brought him straight into the dungeon, locked the cell door behind him, and turned to go.

Tandun appeared from a chamber deeper in the dungeons. "What you do here?" he demanded, as mean and menacing as when Argentia had last seen him. He looked past her. Saw Erkani. His eyes narrowed. "So! Why you no kill?" he asked, staring hard at Argentia.

"I did my job, like I told you I would."

"How he escape?" Tandun asked.

"Magic," Argentia said.

Tandun shook his head. "Magic not work in Aventar dungeons."

"Some magic does."

In the middle of the night, Erkani's cell door opened.

A figure entered, its tread quiet but confident. As it approached the sleeping thief, it stretched a twisted length of bedsheet between his hands. Suicides were rare in Aventar's dungeons, but not unheard of. After Erkani had been throttled, the killer would drag him across the cell and tie the rope to the crossbar of the cell door, making sure the length was short enough to make the strangulation look convincing. The sheet on the bed he would destroy.

"Good-bye, little thief," the killer whispered.

Some atavistic survival instinct woke Erkani. He saw the killer looming over him with the twisted sheet and screamed, shrinking up against the wall.

Light blazed in the cell.

77

Ralak the Red and Argentia Dasani sprang forth from the aethergate. The Archamagus held the glimmering Staff of Dimrythain before him. "Please," he said to Tandun. "Give me an excuse."

Snarling, the dungeonmaster dropped the makeshift noose and drew a dagger from his belt to make a quick kill of Erkani.

Argentia fired her handbow from her hip. The dagger flew out of Tandun's grasp, clattered off the wall, and fell on Erkani's bed. Tandun clutched his blasted hand to his chest, glaring hatefully.

There were lights in the dungeon and sounds of other people approaching. Moments later, Solsta appeared, hurrying toward the cell with Seb Karal, Griegvard, Mirk, and a troop of Sentinels in her wake.

"Tandun!" The Crown's eyes were blazing with a fury even those closest to her had rarely seen. Solsta was tolerant of much, but she would not brook treachery. "Surrender yourself."

Since his shaming at the hands of Ralak and Relsthab, Tandun had desired nothing more than he desired the wizards' deaths. The elven assassin Gideon-gil had done for Relsthab in the same attack that had killed Solsta Ly'Ancoeur's parents; all that remained to satisfy Tandun's vengeance was ending Ralak.

The dungeonmaster was patient. He nursed his grudge, biding his time, waiting in for Fortune to turn in his favor.

The aefryt, keen to all wishes, had sensed this during Tandun's interactions with Erkani. In the dungeonmaster's dark dreams it saw the key to its own escape. It whispered to Erkani to promise the murder of the Archamagus in exchange for his freedom.

Tandun—as the aefryt had anticipated—could not resist the opportunity. He procured the glyphstone for Erkani to access Ralak's tower and released the thief. He planned to deliver the transmogrification potion only after Erkani had upheld his end of the bargain. Instead, the thief had immediately overpowered the dungeonmaster, who had never imagined the wiry little wretch could have such insane strength: it was as if he was possessed.

When Tandun had awakened bound to the rack, he had nearly gone mad. After he discovered the Archamagus still lived, he realized how badly he had been duped and that he was in great danger if Ralak ever learned of the plot against him. To ensure his safety, the thief could not live. He had to be found and silenced.

But Tandun's bid to join the hunt for Erkani had been blocked. There was nothing he could do but wait and hope the huntress killed the thief. That had not happened, but neither had Erkani betrayed him.

"Magic," the huntress had told him when he asked Erkani's account of his escape. That was ridiculous, of course. Only the magic of the Staff of Dimrythain permitted aethereal travel into or within Castle Aventar. To say magic was involved implicated Ralak in Erkani's escape. Had the thief been so bold as to do so? Was it possible that such a story would even be believed? Tandun was not sure, but he intended to make certain the thief never had a chance to change his account.

Now it was the dungeonmaster who had no chance.

"Well played," Ralak said to Argentia.

"Thanks."

"You bitch! You used me as bait!" Erkani shouted.

"Brilliant observation," Argentia said.

When she had arrived back at Castle Aventar, Argentia left Erkani in Griegvard's custody and went to give Ralak and Solsta the thief's account of his escape. Ralak wanted to take Tandun then and there. Solsta was not convinced.

"Erkani hated Tandun," she reminded them. "While this story is certainly plausible, you have lived in the castle with Tandun for years and he has made no move against you. Why now?"

"A question of convenience, Majesty," Ralak said. "Erkani presented an opportunity. Tandun took advantage of it. It is very simple, really."

"If Erkani is telling the truth."

"I am sure the potion your meerkat delivered was effective."

"Did you not once tell me that truth spells are imperfect in that they cannot distinguish between actual truth and what a person believes to be true?" Solsta said. "If Erkani's mind was damaged by the aefryt, we cannot be certain he truly knows what he did once the aefryt started working its will on him—so we do not know if what he says is what truly happened or merely what he believes happened, perhaps even what he *wishes* were the truth in order to bring blame on a guiltless person."

She is good, Argentia thought, seeing that Ralak looked quite annoyed. "Maybe you shouldn't have taught her so well," she said.

"I do not find this amusing," Ralak said.

"Nor do any of us," Solsta replied. "Please understand I am not seeking to exculpate Tandun. If he is guilty, I will see the full weight of my judgment set upon him. But as I told you, he served my father and he has served me...loyally—until we have definitive proof otherwise."

"What proof would you require, Majesty?" Ralak said. He believed Erkani's account, but he could not wholly argue with Solsta's reasoning and a small part of him wondered if he was not letting his own feelings about Tandun cloud his judgment.

"I think I can help with that," Argentia said. "If Tandun is guilty, he can't allow Erkani to live with this secret. He'll move against him quickly. Let's give him enough rope to hang himself."

So they had returned Erkani to the dungeon and waited, Ralak scrying into the cell with his oculyr. They had watched until there was no doubt of Tandun's intent—Argentia shuddered a little to think how apt her comment about hanging had nearly been—and then they had intervened.

"Majesty," Ralak said after Tandun was brought to bay. "You have the evidence before you. There can be no doubt now the thief's tale is true."

"None," Solsta said coldly. "None at all. Tandun, your service is no longer required. You have released a prisoner from our dungeons, plotted against our Archamagus' life, and failed utterly in your duties to our throne. You hereby sentenced to be imprisoned here for the rest of your days. Lord Commander—get this dog from our sight."

Seb and the Sentinels moved in and surrounded Tandun. The dungeonmaster lanced a viperous glare at Ralak. As he drew abreast of the Crown, he bent his head and spat at her boots. "I curse your mercy," he said.

"I pity your folly," Solsta replied.

"Come on, move it," one of the Sentinels said, shoving Tandun ahead. The dungeonmaster stumbled. As the guards reached for him, he burst forward with manic strength, bulling through them.

Ralak swung his staff but neither he nor Argentia could get a clear shot with the guards and the Crown in the way. Tandun was out of the cell ahead of the scramble of Sentinels when something landed on his head. He saw a brown blur across his eyes, and then pain ripped his world open as Mirkholmes' jaws snapped closed on his nose.

Screaming, Tandun crashed to his knees, clutching at the meerkat. Mirk sprang clear as the Sentinels piled in, pinning the dungeonmaster beneath them.

And Al'Atin Erkani, all but forgotten in the chaos, leaped off his bunk and stabbed Tandun's dagger at Argentia's back.

Argentia heard the bedsprings squawk and glanced over her shoulder. Caught the slashing motion in the periphery of her vision and dropped fast. Erkani's vicious strike cut the air just above her.

Argentia rolled onto her back. Tried to get her handbow into play. Erkani kicked the weapon out of her grasp. Dove on her. She got a boot up just in time. Shoved him backwards.

"I'm fer ye, ye bastard!" Griegvard roared, stepping between Erkani and Argentia.

Ferret-quick despite his emaciated frame, Erkani dodged past the dwarf and lunged for the Crown. He would have traded the satisfaction of killing Argentia for his own death, which would surely have followed, but now that possibility was gone. There was no way he could fight past the numbers in the dungeon. He had only one chance. If he could take the Crown hostage they would have to let him go free.

But even as the thief changed direction, Seb Karal spun Solsta aside with such force that she lost her balance and fell to the floor.

Blue lightning from Ralak's staff cracked the air. The blast of magic lifted Erkani off the ground. Slammed him into the cell wall above the bed. He crashed bonelessly down. Did not rise.

"Majesty, are you all right?" Seb asked, helping Solsta up.

"Yes, thank you," Solsta said. "Ralak, thank you." The Archamagus leaned on his staff and nodded. "Argentia?"

"Yeah. I'm fine," Argentia said. She stood up. Looked at the body on the bed. The smoking hole in Al'Atin Erkani's torso left no doubt that she had hunted down the thief for the last time.

78

Argentia sank up to her neck in the steaming tub. *Ahhhhh, bliss....* She smiled as she recalled Solsta's comment in the baths at Aventar before the hunt for Erkani and the lamp had begun in earnest.

This time she was in her tub. Her bath chamber. Her manor. She was tired to the bone and glad to be home. *I don't think I'm moving for at least a week....*

It was the night after Erkani's death and Tandun's suicide. They had found the dungeonmaster dead in his cell in the morning. He had broken his own neck at sunrise. The other prisoners attested to hearing him chanting in Nhapian, the cadence building to a frenzy loud enough that the newly assigned guard on duty had come in. As he approached the cell, he saw Tandun take his head and chin in his hands and twist violently.

After the snap, there was silence.

Solsta was aghast when she was told, but Argentia and Ralak had both heard of sects of Nhapian warrior monks whose discipline extended to such ritual suicides, which were viewed as an honorable alternative to a life of disgrace.

"Weren't no great loss from where I'm standin," Griegvard said, and that pretty much closed the matter.

After breakfast came another round of partings. Griegvard was headed back to Stromness to make his periodic report to King Durn.

"See if you can make me a lamp—" Argentia said.

"No more bloody lamps!"

"For my library," she completed.

"Yer a riot, Red. Ye call me if yer huntin goblins or ogres or some normal scum. None o' these damn magic trinkets." The dwarf stomped off, shaking his abbreviated beard and muttering under his breath. Argentia's laughter followed him.

The huntress herself was bound for Harrowgate, where she would pick up Shadow from Colla and then head back to Argo. Her love for the road was undiminished, but since rebuilding her ancestral estate, she had been away more than she had been there. She was looking forward to spending time with Ikabod and her few friends in Argo and to making the manor a home.

"You'll be back for Yule, won't you?" Solsta asked as they made their good-byes.

"Absolutely. Maybe sooner." Summer was a good time to be in Argo, but winter in Duralyn, with the snow on the mountains and the forests, was spectacular. "If you need me...."

"I hope I will not. We all could use some peace and quiet."

"It's been a busy year. You should come down and visit. See the new place."

Solsta smiled such a genuinely frank and almost childishly pleased smile that it almost hurt Argentia to see. It made her realize how very much the Crown of Teranor, who was constantly surrounded by people, was alone. She hugged her. "I'm serious. Come down and stay, even for a few days. We'll do the city."

"I would love to," Solsta said.

"Open invitation. Think of the stir *that* would cause. The Crown of Teranor staying with the Outcast Noblewoman." She laughed and Solsta did as well, knowing that it would indeed ruffle the feathers of the staid aristocrats of Argo if she visited their city and showed such favor to Argentia, whom they viewed as a rogue.

"I could not ask for a better host. Or a better friend. Thank you again for your help."

"It was nothing."

"Mirk helped," the meerkat peeped from his place beside Solsta's boots.

"You always do," Argentia said, tipping the meerkat a wink.

So the Crown and her huntress parted ways for a time. In Harrowgate, Argentia found Shadow fully recovered and full of his usual vigor. He leaped at her so hard when she entered Coastlight Cathedral that he nearly knocked her to the ground.

One aetherwalk later, the lady and her dog emerged in Wavegard Cathedral and walked home through the humid summer evening, hoping to beat the storm brewing over the White Sea.

⚜

Argentia closed her eyes. Steam rolled in the bath's perfumed air. Outside the manor, thunder rumbled. From the sound of it, the storm was going to be a big one.

She dozed for a while. When she finally rose from the bath, the tension had ebbed out of her limbs and her mind. She felt good. Tired and hungry, but good.

She had just wrapped a towel around her when she heard the knocking on the front door. *Wonder who that is....* For a fleeting moment, she thought that Solsta had spontaneously taken her up on her invitation.

"Lady Dasani, come quickly," Ikabod called.

"What is it?" Argentia hurried out of the bath, through her rooms, and into the hall. When she reached the balcony overlooking the foyer, she froze.

Below was a group of cloaked men, each wearing a full-faced steel helmet beneath his hood. One of them had a dagger to Ikabod's throat. Another was blocking the door. The others were fanned out at the bottom of the steps. "I am sorry, Lady," Ikabod said.

"It's all right," Argentia said. Then she addressed the cloaked men. "If it's coin you're looking for, take whatever you want. Just let him go."

"It's not coin we want. It's *you*, bitch." The reply from the man in the doorway was muffled by the steel faceplate.

"Fine. Just let him go," Argentia repeated. "Whatever this is about, he has nothing to do with it." Her voice was level, but she burned against this invasion of her home: the assault on her privacy and threat to Ikabod.

She weighed her options. Seven against one and they were all armed. *I'm not even dressed....* She had a just-in-case dagger in her night-table drawer, but the rest of her weapons were in the training room. There was a stairwell down from her bedroom into her study. She would come out on the far side of the foyer and could sprint to the training room. She was confident she could get there ahead of any of the intruders.

But Ikabod....

"You do anything but come down those steps, he dies," the man in the doorway promised, as if reading her thoughts.

No choice.... "All right. I'm coming down." Argentia descended slowly, still assessing. There was something familiar about the men, the way they stood in relation to each other. "Let him go," she said for the third time when she reached the foyer.

"No." The man in the doorway said. "Grab her."

One of the men seized Argentia and pinned her arms roughly behind her back.

"At last." The man in the doorway stepped forward, pulled down his hood, and lifted his helmet off.

I should have known, Argentia thought.

79

Temrun Raventyr's eyes were lamps of insanity. He slapped Argentia across the face so hard her knees buckled. She would have fallen, but the Gryphon holding her—Bogden, she thought—kept her upright. "You're making a mistake," she said, shaking her head to clear it. Blood trickled down her chin from a split lip. "I told you in Duralyn, I didn't kill Vartan."

Two of the hooded and helmed Gryphons glanced at each other, but Temrun just laughed. "Right. His head fell off by itself. How stupid do you think I am, you lying bitch? Deny it all you want. Deny it to the grave. Cause that's where you're going. Get her out of here," he ordered.

"What'ee do with old man?" Cree asked; he was the one with the knife to Ikabod's throat.

"Kill him," Temrun said.

Argentia's blood ran cold. *Do something!* "Don't be a fool!" she blurted. "If you kill me, he inherits everything. If he's dead, there's no inheritor. My entire fortune passes to the Noble Council to distribute among the other estates. Leave him alive and you can make him change the will, sign it all over to you. Easy money for a little mercy."

"You didn't show any mercy to Vartan," Temrun spat. But she'd gotten the attention of the others.

"Lotee money?" Cree asked.

"More than you can imagine. More than you could ever need," Argentia said. "Look around you. This house alone is worth more than you've earned in your lives."

Temrun sensed the indecision among the others. It was a distraction and he did not want any distractions. He had waited too long for this. "Fine." He spun and struck Ikabod a savage blow to the head. The butler folded like a chair with a broken leg.

"Ikabod!" Argentia screamed. "You bastard! I'll—"

Temrun wheeled back and slapped Argentia again, backhanded this time. "Shut up, bitch. Cree, tie that old fool up so he can't go anywhere. We'll be back for him when we're done with her."

Argentia's head was ringing and she tasted blood, but mainly what she felt was relief. Ikabod was still alive. She doubted it was a permanent reprieve—the Gryphons would kill him for sure once the will was signed over—but she had bought him a little time, at least. *All I can do for now...*

Outside, the night was charged with summer heat and coming storm. The moon was up and full in the east, but the wind was blowing and to the south the sky was black where a seething mass of clouds rolled over the water. Thunder growled, lightning flickered. Argentia wondered if she would live to see the storm break.

Then she saw the carriage parked in her turnabout, a huge figure that could only be Wojek standing beside it, and figured she might.

Wojek bundled Argentia into the back of the carriage. Five Gryphons piled in with her. One of them mounted the driving board and was joined by Cree a minute later.

A snap of a whip and the carriage started rolling, crunching white gravel beneath its wheels. Argentia could hear Shadow barking wildly, but he was in his run behind the stables and could not get to her.

She huddled in the corner, her legs drawn up close, her arms wrapped about her, her head bowed, wet hair hanging past her face. It was a defeated posture, one designed to minimize the amount of her body that was exposed. Five-on-one in the back of a carriage: if they decided they wanted to rape her before they killed her, she didn't have a lot of options to avoid it.

Okay, okay, she told herself. *Calm down. Think. You've been in worse situations....*

Then she remembered the blazing insanity in Temrun's eyes and wondered if she had.

80

The Gryphons had been waiting for Argentia for weeks.

After their near miss in Duralyn they had been forced to flee the Crown City. With no idea whether Argentia had survived, they decided that their only sure course was to stake out the one place to which they knew she would eventually return if she still lived. So they journeyed south to Argo. Waited. Watched.

Tonight, their patience had been rewarded.

Thunder cracked and lightning opened the skies. The storm swallowed the moon. The first fat drops of rain began to fall. Argentia pressed her face against the glass. She did not know how she was going to get out of this, but she was going to die trying. *And if I can take a few of them with me, I will...*

She wondered where they were going. They could not leave the city after dark; the gates were locked down. The docks might make sense if they wanted to sink her body in the harbor—she knew for a fact there were other bodies in those watery depths—but they were heading into the city, not toward the port.

Lightning flashed again. She saw the stone wall and the wrought iron gate through the window and she knew exactly where they were going.

And why.

The carriage turned and rolled through the gates of Argo's necropolis.

The lanterns on the posts at the intersection of the paths among the graves were diffuse and ghostly in the rain. Lightning showed the city of the dead in jagged flashes, the marble white as bone, cold as eternity. The necropolis was a place of great beauty, peace, and solemnity, but the storm turned it into something out of a nightmare. Statues of divae, their wings spread wide atop ornate mausoleums became leering gargoyles or laughing demons. The few trees interspersed among the rows of headstones were twisted, tortured silhouettes.

The carriage followed the path cut between the graves and finally came to a halt deep in the cemetery. The drivers jumped down and threw the doors open. Wojek shoved Argentia out. Before she could try to run, Bogden grabbed her.

They started walking, following Temrun among the marble headstones. Argentia, wearing nothing but her towel, was soaked in moments. Temrun led them without hesitation, confirming Argentia's suspicion that tonight's attack had been planned in advance. *Probably they knew the moment I got home....* She cursed herself for underestimating their persistence. She could forgive herself for not expecting their first attack—she'd had no idea they were hunting her—but thereafter she should have been more vigilant.

Too late to worry about that now.... If she did not figure a way out of this soon, her days of worrying about anything at all would be over.

They slogged on through the storm-torn night until they came to the place Temrun wanted. Lightning illumed the open pit of a freshly dug grave. A spade leaned against the headstone. The pile of dirt was mounded nearby, covered by a sailcloth tarpaulin, ready to be returned to the earth.

"Paid a gravedigger to keep me in the know on new holes for when you finally showed, bitch," Temrun said. "Dump you in, cover you up. Coffin goes on top tomorrow, nobody's the wiser. You should've thought of that with Vartan instead of leaving him in that tub, whore."

Argentia shook her head. "I didn't kill your brother."

"You did, you filthy, lying slut. I told you—"

"Wait," Troyen Kressid said. He stepped forward: the oldest of the group, probably the sanest. "There's a way to settle this once and for all." He produced a stone from a pouch.

"Hell's that?" Temrun demanded.

"It's an oathstone," Delk said, moving beside Troyen. "If she swears on it and lies, it glows red. We'll know for certain then."

"I already know for certain!" Temrun roared, louder than the thunder.

"I don't," Delk answered through the pouring rain. "Neither does Troyen. If you're right, then she dies. But I'm not going to let you murder her if she's innocent. That doesn't honor Vartan's memory."

For a long moment there was only the torrential drumming of the storm. They were in the very teeth of it now, lightning flashes coming every few seconds, the thunder an almost constant percussion. *Come on,* Argentia willed. She doubted there would be any way to reason with Temrun, but the oathstone could only support her innocence and that demonstration of the truth might turn some of the others.

Temrun's face was as black and dangerous as the skies above. But he said nothing, so Troyen stepped forward. "Let her go," he told Bogden. "She needs to hold the stone."

Bogden looked to Temrun.

"You're being ridiculous," Troyen said. "She's unarmed, outnumbered, and there's nowhere for her to run."

Temrun gave the older sellsword a hard glare. "Just her hands," he said. "I don't trust this bitch."

Bogden released Argentia's wrists from behind her back and shifted his grip to her biceps. Argentia wiped her palms instinctively on her towel, even though it was soaked through, the thick cotton hanging heavy on her breasts.

Troyen placed the stone in her hands. "Thank you," she said. Now she had a weapon.

Troyen looked old and grizzled and tired. "Did you kill Vartan Raventyr?" he asked.

"No," Argentia said.

The oathstone remained dark.

Something like relief passed over Troyen's face. "You see?" He turned to Temrun. "She's inno—"

Temrun's dagger slashed his throat.

Troyen fell to his knees, gagging on his own blood. Argentia and the other Gryphons stared in shock as Temrun kicked Troyen over to thrash out his last in the muddy puddles like a spastic worm. "Liar!" Temrun screamed. "Traitor! Stone's a fake! She killed him!"

"You're insane!" Delk shouted. He lunged for Temrun but Cree grabbed him from behind. They slid on the wet ground and went down, clipping Bogden's legs.

Argentia felt Bogden's hold on her loosen as he fought for balance. She moved without hesitation, twisting hard, her rain-slick arms slipping free from his hands as she spun, crunched the oathstone into his nose, and drove a knee into his groin. He dropped in a heap beside Troyen's body.

Argentia whirled and fired the oathstone at Temrun, but her wet fingers slipped and the throw missed Temrun's head by inches. *Shit....*

She backed up as Temrun closed on her, menacing the air with his big knife. She could not take him hand-to-hand: he was too big and strong. *Need another weapon....*

She saw one in a flash of lightning. It was beside the headstone. Five good strides on the wrong side of Temrun.

She stopped retreating. Dug her feet into the mud for traction. Flexed her knees slightly for balance. *This better work....*

She let Temrun charge.

He came in hard and fast, the knife slashing.

Argentia grabbed the top of her towel, ripping it away from her body as she pivoted like a Cyprytalyr bullfighter, dodging the knife and flinging the towel into Temrun's face.

Temrun, overbalanced by the miss and pawing at the sodden towel, stumbled past on the slick ground.

Argentia ran for the headstone.

"Stop her!" Temrun roared skidding to a knee as he tried to turn around. But Wojek and Lucianos were trying to separate Delk and Cree.

"Bitch! You're not getting away again!" Temrun scrambled up, charging through the storm, closing fast on Argentia. "Come here and die, bit—"

Argentia spun around, swinging the spade like a stickball bat.

She connected with Temrun's head as cleanly as Griegvard had connected with Croftian's pitch on that sunny morning in Duralyn that seemed so long ago. The spade pulverized flesh and muscle and bone, shattering Temrun's face. Blood and mucous and teeth sprayed in the rain. The blow stopped Temrun's momentum completely, but he did not fall.

Argentia swung the spade again, this time overhand, like an axe.

Buried the sharp edge in Temrun's forehead.

For a lightning-stroke they were frozen in a grotesque tableaux. Then Argentia jerked the spade free. Temrun toppled into the open grave. Thunder drowned the splash of his impact.

Argentia turned toward Wojek and Lucianos, the shovel held before her, ready for a fight. But before the other Gryphons could attack, the sudden flare of aethergates popping open lit the storm-black and a dozen of Argo's Watchmen raced out of the magical portals, moonstones held high and weapons drawn as they converged on the gravesite.

Wojek and Lucianos bolted into the storm. Argentia let them go, staring in amazement at the Watchmen. One group gave chase to the fleeing Gryphons, the rest were coming toward her. Argentia dropped the shovel and plucked her towel out of a puddle, wrapping it around her again. It was cold and dripping and gross, but meeting the Watch stark naked was beyond even her.

She heard a gasp of pain. *Delk....* She knelt beside him. Cree was dead, the hilt of Delk's dagger jutting from his chest, but he had done for the youngest Raventyr brother as well. Argentia saw the Nhapian's dagger buried high in Delk's ribs. "Be still," she said, though she knew it was hopeless. "The Watch is here. They'll get you to a cleric."

Delk shook his head weakly; a veteran warrior despite his youth, he knew a mortal wound as well as Argentia. "Too late. But listen...listen. Temrun...was mad. Troy and I...never...never really believed...it was you. That's why...oathstone...."

"It's all right," Argentia said, smoothing Delk's wet hair off his forehead. "I believe you," she said. And she did. "It's okay. I'm so sorry about Vartan, but I avenged him. I promise, he's at peace."

"Thank you," Delk said. He died with a smile on his bloodied lips. Argentia closed a fist around her dragon's tooth and then closed Delk's eyes with her palm—

A hand clamped in her hair, yanking her backwards.

81

Argentia was slammed down into a puddle. The splashing impact knocked the breath from her. She scrambled madly but her bare feet found no purchase in the mud.

Bogden lurched above her, a dagger glinting.

No! Argentia threw her arms up in a cross that caught Bogden's forearm as he stabbed at her. The blade pricked the towel above her breasts, pressing inexorably down as Bogden brought his weight and leverage to bear.

Something hummed above Argentia like a bee in the rain. Bogden's head snapped back. He toppled over, an arrow jutting from his eye.

Argentia gasped, rolled away, and came to her knees, shuddering. The Watch moonstones were everywhere around her. "Are you all right?" a Watchman asked her.

Argentia shoved herself to her feet and nodded, adjusting her towel, looking past the Watchman at two approaching figures: one short and clad in wizard's robes, the other a tall man carrying a bow. "Good shot," she called.

"Thanks," Kest Eregrin replied, reaching to accept Argentia's offered hand. He was a handsome, bespectacled Nhapian and the best archer Argentia had ever met. "Rain made it interesting."

"What, you can't control the weather?" Argentia asked, looking at the halfling beside the Watch Captain.

"Hey, nobody can control the weather," Augustus Falkyn protested. "And you should be glad I'm here or half this lot'd still be at the barracks... warm and dry," he added. The rain had matted his mop of curly hair to his head. He looked thoroughly miserable.

"What *are* you doing here, anyway?" Argentia asked. "Not that I'm not glad to see you, but I was never a big believer in coincidence."

Kest unfastened his cloak and draped it around Argentia. She nodded her thanks. The cloak was wet too, but at least it covered her entire body.

"We've been watching this bunch for a while," Kest said. "They've been in Argo almost a month now, just hanging around in the Undercity. Our informants down there said they kept asking about you. We figured they probably weren't friends of yours, so we kept an eye on them."

"You used me as *bait*?" Argentia exclaimed. She'd had no problem with doing exactly that to Erkani, but the thief had been in no real danger and he was hardly her friend. The risk to her and Ikabod tonight had been all too real.

Kest shook his head. "No, no. Calm down. We didn't even know you were back in the city until we heard this lot had headed for your place in a big hurry. My men were too late to intervene at the house, but they followed the carriage and called in the location. We got here as soon as we could."

Argentia grinned. *Finally, my turn....* "You think you could have cut it a little closer?"

"Yeah, yeah. You looked like you had it all under control," Kest said.

"Nice," she said, laughing. It felt good to laugh. Good to be alive.

A Watchman came up. "Sir, we've got the other two."

Kest nodded. "Good work. Get them to the dungeons. Secure this area. Get the bodies to the morgue." He turned to Argentia. "Now, what's this all about?"

"It's a long story."

"It always is with you."

"Can we talk in a carriage? The one they brought me in should be that way." She pointed through the dark and realized that the rain had slackened noticeably. The skies were quieter. The worst of the storm had passed. "I have to get home. Ikabod's hurt."

"Why didn't you say something before?" Kest looked to Augustus. The wizard already had his wand out.

Moments later, Argentia and her friends stepped out of the rain into the aether and vanished in a flash brighter than the lightning.

82

Augustus teleported them right into Argentia's foyer, which he knew well enough from several visits. Ikabod lay where he had fallen, his hands and feet bound with strips cut from the cloth of the dining room table. Argentia untied him and, after checking to make sure he was unhurt, she and Kest carried him into his bedroom and let him sleep.

That done, Argentia told Kest and Augustus to make themselves comfortable. She went upstairs and jumped in the shower, turning the water on as hot as she could stand, soaking the cold out of her bones. Her hip twinged a little, but otherwise she was all right. Ikabod was all right. No harm had come of Temrun's insanity, although she regretted the deaths of Delk and Troyen, who had been good men.

She let the water beat down on her from the three lion-head spouts, leaning forward and pressing her palms against the marble wall. Would her past ever stop chasing her? *First Vloth, now Temrun....* And the one person she wished with all her heart would come back was gone forever.

She shook her head, straightening up. No use brooding about it. She could not change anything that had happened and in truth there were very few things she would change. *But I'm definitely changing the locks on this place....*

It was not herself she worried for, but Ikabod. If anything had happened to him, there would have been no Gryphons left for the Watch

326

to arrest. First thing in the morning, she would talk to Ralak about getting some serious wards on the property.

She cut the shower, dried off, pulled on a long emerald silk robe with a black-and-gold dragonfly embroidered across the back, ponytailed her wet hair, and went downstairs. Kest and Augustus were in the kitchen, sipping caf from stoneware mugs.

"You know me too well," Argentia said as she poured herself a mug and sat down opposite Kest. She took a long pull on her drink; it went down hot and strong and good. "Thanks. I needed that."

"So," Kest said. "I have two men in the dungeons and five in the morgue, and you've got some explaining to do."

Argentia nodded. "This all started right before Mouradian captured me," she said. "I'd hooked up with a group of sell-swords called the Harvester's Gryphons."

"What kind of stupid name is that?" Augustus asked.

Argentia laughed; she had thought the very same thing when she met them. "One they took *really* seriously. We went on a raid: goblins in the Heaths...."

She told the tale of her fortnight with the Gryphons, their return to Harrowgate, and her ill-fated night with Vartan that ended with his death and her capture by Mouradian. "They thought I killed him—one of his brothers did, at least. Apparently they've been hunting me ever since."

She could not really blame them, given the circumstances, but it was clear that Temrun had passed beyond sanity in his hatred of her. He had never liked her, she recalled, even when they worked together, and she had never entirely trusted him. He had always seemed just a little off. *Turns out he was a lot off....* "They almost got me in Duralyn a couple months ago, but—"

"Wait a minute," Kest said. "They attacked you in Duralyn? And you didn't think they might come after you again?"

"It's been a busy couple months," Argentia said. "And I wasn't even in Teranor, so no, I really wasn't thinking about them at all."

"Where were you?" Augustus asked.

"Makhara, mostly."

"Makhara! What in Aeton's name were you doing down there?"
"That's another story entirely...."

They talked for a while longer. Kest asked what Argentia wanted to do about the two imprisoned Gryphons. She told him to prosecute them however he felt fit. With Temrun gone, the impetus for her death was probably gone, too. She was not particularly concerned about Wojek and Lucianos coming after her, but she would not mind seeing them locked up for a few decades, either.

"Either way, I'm not going to worry about it," she said.

Kest frowned, though he had expected no other answer. "Well, fine, but you should really get some wards on this place. You have a lot of enemies."

"Really? I hadn't noticed."

"I'm serious."

"I know. I'm way ahead of you. Calling Ralak as soon as it's light."

He nodded. "Good. That's it, then. We're done here."

"Thanks again."

"Don't mention it."

Kest and Augustus disappeared into the aether. Argentia checked on Ikabod. Went up to bed. Before she drifted off she reflected on how lucky she'd been tonight.

The luck of the damned... A smile played over her lips as she remembered Skarangella Skarn's words.

Maybe there was something to it after all.

Epilogue

Ikabod woke.

He was in his bed, covered with his blankets, which made almost no sense, since the last thing he remembered was a hooded man with a knife to his throat. So it was strange that he should awaken at all, much less in his own bed.

Argentia....

He recalled the men taking her prisoner in the foyer. *Dear Aeton, what happened to her?*

Early light was beaming through the seam in his drapes. If it had been the intent of the men to kill Argentia, Ikabod doubted they would have wasted the night. *But if they are holding her for ransom or some other purpose, there might still be time....*

Ikabod shoved the covers aside and rose from the bed. He stumbled in his haste. Almost fell. His heart was hammering against the thin wall of his chest. He barely noticed he was still in the white shirt and gray pants of his livery. His shoes and jacket had been removed; the jacket had been hung neatly on his chair, and his shoes were arranged beside the table.

All his thought was on Argentia. He held himself fully responsible for her fate, for he had opened the door to her enemies. *Please, let me be in time to help her....*

He crossed the foyer. There was no blood on the marble, at least. He headed for Argentia's study. He would use the oculyr there to contact the Watch and then—

There was a strange sizzling noise. *That smell....*

Ikabod changed course, making for the kitchen. He stopped cold in the doorway. His breath caught in his throat, tears welling in his single eye.

Argentia stood at the stove, agitating bacon in a frying pan over the open flame.

She turned when she felt Ikabod's gaze upon her. "What?" she asked.

"Argentia...." Ikabod came a pace into the kitchen, as if he did not quite believe what he was seeing.

"In the flesh. How are you feeling?"

"Fine," he said. "I am fine, Lady. But you... Those men... What happened?"

"Nothing. They made a mistake. They were looking for someone else. We got it all straightened out. Don't worry, you'll never see them again."

Ikabod nodded slowly. He was certain Argentia was sparing him the awful details of whatever the truth was, but he trusted her when she said the matter was put to rest. "I feared I would never see *you* again."

She put down the skillet and came over to him, the hem of her robe swishing on the floor. "You should know better than that," she said, hugging him tightly and flashing her insouciant grin. "I always turn up."

Ikabod nodded and smiled. "I will fetch some flour," he said.

"No way." Argentia shook her head, red ponytail snapping. "You're not fetching anything. I'm cooking breakfast today. You just sit down and— What? Flour?"

"Flour." Ikabod pointed over Argentia's shoulder. "The bacon is on fire...."

Printed in the United States
by Baker & Taylor Publisher Services